FORGET ME NOT

FORGET ME NOT

SUSAN BOWDEN

BEELER LARGE PRINT
Hampton Falls, New Hampshire, 2000

Library of Congress Cataloging-in-Publication Data

Bowden, Susan, 1936-.
    Forget me not / Susan Bowden.
    p.   cm
    ISBN 1-57490-267-9 (alk .paper)
    1.Large type books. I. Title.

PR9199.3.B628 F67 2000
813'.54—dc21   00-024537

This is a work of fiction. Names, characters, places, and
incidents either are the product of the author's imagination or
are used fictitiously. Any resemblance to actual events, locales,
organizations, or persons living or dead, is entirely coincidental
and beyond the intent of either the author or the publisher.
Published in Large Print by arrangement with
Signet, an imprint of New American Library, a division of
Penguin Putnam Inc.

BEELER LARGE PRINT
is published by
Thomas T. Beeler, *Publisher*
Post Office Box 659
Hampton Falls, New Hampshire 03844

Typeset in 16 point Times New Roman type.
Sewn and bound by
Sheridan Books in Chelsea, Michigan

For Shannon and Annie

This book is lovingly dedicated to my son, Iain, who shares my love of Exmoor, Somerset, and the rugged coast of North Devon, and to Nicole and Chelsea, who one day, I hope, will be able to see this beautiful area of England for themselves.

FORGET ME NOT

PROLOGUE

The river lay dormant in its stony bed, its waters lapping against the banks of rust-red soil. As old as time itself, its memories lurked in the earth and the stones embedded in it. Patiently, it bided its time, waiting, waiting . . . .

CHAPTER ONE

LISA COOPER HAD BEEN PAINTING FEVERISHLY ALL night, the brush slapping and slashing, attacking the canvas with a driving frenzy. Only when the birds began their predawn twittering, gradually building to a crescendo, did her pace slacken.

When the first pale light of dawn slid into the room, she let the brush fall from her hands. For a moment she stood in the center of the studio staring blankly out the large uncurtained window at the rose-streaked sky, to avoid looking at the canvas. Then she switched off the spotlights and sank into a chair, arms and legs trembling with exhaustion.

The oily smell of paint filled her nostrils, making her feel nauseated. Her eyes stung from the paint fumes and lack of sleep. She knew she should eat something, drink lots of liquid, but she was too weary to get up.

She was aware of time passing, of dozing and waking. Opening her eyes, she glanced at the clock on the wall and was shocked to see that it was a few minutes after seven-thirty. She had to shower and dress, eat something and feed Paloma, and get to the meeting with the officials from the insurance company by nine. Definitely not enough time to tidy the place.

But she couldn't come back to it the way it was. Even if she locked the studio door—as she did most of the time nowadays—the thought of that freshly painted canvas lurking behind the locked door would haunt her all day. She wouldn't be able to concentrate on anything, never mind land an extremely important—and lucrative commission.

Heart pounding, she forced herself to rise from the chair, walk to the easel, and confront the painting. It was yet another variation on the old theme. A torrent of tumbling water filled the canvas, flowing downward to the very edge, making her feel that the massive force of water was about to pour off the canvas and engulf her as she stood there.

The paint was thick, all the possible shades of gray and white and black, swirling and cascading together to create an immense deluge of water.

She stepped back, eyes closed, trying to shut out the nightmare image she herself had created, but the wave of water remained there behind her eyelids.

"Enough!" she yelled. She grabbed the canvas with both hands and was about to carry it down to the basement, to join the other paintings she'd stacked there during the past few months, when she noticed something different in this picture. Frowning, she stepped back to get it into focus. Yes, there definitely was something new there. From the usual foaming torrent of water rose the faint outline of a small tree branch. She couldn't even remember painting it.

"Well," she said, almost shouting to reassure herself, "at least I'm not making them *exactly* the same as each other."

Resolutely, she hoisted the large canvas from the easel. But as she carried it downstairs, holding it away from her to avoid smearing herself with wet paint, she was aware that the new addition to the painting made her feel even more, not less, uneasy.

It was almost twenty minutes past nine when Lisa swung her car into her space in the small parking lot in Winnipeg's Exchange District. Grabbing the briefcase containing all her lists and figures, she scrambled from the Honda and ran to the art gallery's rear entrance.

As soon as she opened the door she could smell the welcome aroma of fresh coffee, which meant Jerry was there. "Thank God," she breathed. She dragged off her black wool cloak and hung it on a coat hook on the wall.

Jerry came into the back room. "I thought I heard someone come in," he said in a low voice. "What the heck kept you? They've been waiting since before nine."

Lisa helped herself to a mug of coffee. "You could have started without me."

"We agreed we'd do the presentation together." He bent to peer more closely at her. "You look like hell."

"Thanks." Lisa grabbed her hairbrush from her bag and dragged it through her long windswept hair, then hurriedly formed it into a neat French braid. "I was up all night."

"Doing what?"

Her gaze slid sideways, avoiding his light gray, too perceptive eyes. "Painting."

"Painting? Oh God! You poor darling." He gave her a quick hug against his chest, then jerked his head in the direction of the door into the gallery. "You want me to say you're not well?"

"No way. We need this commission. Just think what it could lead to."

"Okay. I'll tell them you'll be with them in a few minutes."

"Have they had coffee?"

"Yep."

"You're an angel." Lisa drew in a deep breath. "Okay. Give me a couple more minutes to finish my hair."

"Sure you're okay?" Jerry asked, his hand on the doorknob.

5a

"I'll be fine."

She got through the meeting on adrenaline, driven by the excitement of sharing the art plan for three floors of the newest and largest corporate building in the city with three moguls from Norville Insurance Company. As she showed them the examples she and Jerry had set up on the walls of the gallery and the portfolio they had been working on for weeks, with photographs of Inuit soapstone sculptures and the newest set of Baker Lake prints, Lisa felt like a human dynamo, her face glowing with enthusiasm—and probably red as a boiled lobster, she thought, but who cared?

More than an hour later, when they'd ushered the executives out the front door and into their chauffeured limousine, Lisa and Jerry went back into the gallery, locked the door, and gave each other a high five.

"Yes!" said Lisa. "I think we've got it."

"They certainly *seemed* to be happy with it. But don't forget they said they were considering proposals from a couple of Toronto galleries as well."

"God, Jerry, you're such a Jonah."

"I don't mean to be, but we have to face reality. We're a small gallery compared with some of the biggies in Toronto. But they certainly did like your presentation."

"*Our* presentation. God, I feel dead on my feet." Lisa looked up at him. "I couldn't do any of this without you and your terrific sense of what works together and what doesn't."

"Maybe so, but you're so great at the selling part. You get so revved up it's contagious. You even had those starched shirts excited."

"I only get revved up when I'm selling good stuff."

"That's why we make such a great team, you and I." Jerry's smile lit up the beautiful bone structure of his angular face. "You did really well." He kissed her cheek. "You look absolutely wiped. Sit down. I'll get you more coffee and a muffin."

He was right. Now that the presentation was over, the pressure off, Lisa felt as if all her energy had drained away, leaving her limp. "Thanks, you're a pal."

Jerry dragged up one of their asymmetrical chrome chairs. "Sit," he ordered.

Lisa sat, her eyes dwelling on the simple lines of the charcoal sketch of an aboriginal head on the opposite wall, but not really seeing it.

Jerry returned with her mug filled with coffee. He drew up another chair and sat down in front of her, tucking his long legs underneath the chair. "Okay. Let's get back to important matters. You were up all night again painting. The usual subject?"

She held the mug of coffee in both hands, breathing in its aroma, relishing its warmth. Her gaze slid sideways. "I don't really want to talk about it."

"But you know you must. That's the fourth night this month."

"Fifth," Lisa whispered.

"Okay, fifth. Five times you've spent all night painting and then you get sick for several days afterward."

"Not sick."

"Exhausted, then. Worn-out. You're losing weight."

"That won't do me any harm." She gave him a faint smile, but he didn't respond.

"Were you okay getting over the bridge this morning?"

Again she looked away. "Fine."

He leaned forward. "Are you sure?"

Lisa shrugged. "Just a bit of panic. Heart pounding, sweaty palms, that's all. But I was worried sick about being late for the meeting. That's probably all it was." She could see he didn't believe her. "I got here, didn't I?" she said belligerently.

"I think you should go back to Dr. Olson before this water phobia gets worse again."

"It's not a phobia, and I don't need a doctor." She glared at him, slamming her mug down on the nearby table. "I just wish this frigging flood would go away."

Jerry took her hands in his, squeezing them. "Lisa, my lovely, it's not going away yet. The Red River won't reach its peak in Winnipeg until the first or second of May. That's six days away. I wish you'd quit worrying about it. We've got the floodway to protect the city. I keep telling you that, over and over again."

"Then why have they already moved some people out of their homes in the city? And why are they sandbagging along the riverbanks?"

Jerry sighed. "Just to be sure the water doesn't go any higher than the bank and breach the sandbag dike. Some of those older houses were built on land that was too low."

She drew her hands away from his. "I'm sorry. I hate being like this. It's so bloody illogical, I know. It's just that . . . every time I read the papers I get this sense of doom."

"Then don't read 'em."

"But you can't escape it. It's everywhere." She jumped up, feeling as if she had insects crawling under her skin. "I just can't get those terrible pictures of downtown Grand Forks out of my mind, the buildings that were burned and flooded at the same time. Then all of southern Manitoba turning into one gigantic lake, with only flimsy walls of sandbags to stop whole towns from being swamped, and—"

"Stop watching television."

"Even if I avoid the papers and TV, all anyone talks about is the flood. I feel as if—" She sought for words to make him understand. "As if it's coming for me, rushing toward me, and I'm rooted to the spot and I can't escape it."

"People are escaping from it every day. The troops are getting them out with boats. So far no one's even been hurt. And houses and barns can be rebuilt."

"I know, I know." She ran her hand frantically down her neat plait of dark hair. "Reason keeps telling me that, but when I get this tired I find it hard to believe that everything will work out okay."

"That's the real problem: the lack of sleep. Try a sleeping pill again tonight."

Lisa shook her head. "They make me dream," she whispered. Her eyes met his and glanced away.

"Want me to come and stay with you for a few days? If you wake up and start painting again, I can talk you down."

"Thanks, Jerry, but I have to deal with this myself."

"You were okay when someone was there with you."

Lisa gave him a wry smile. "You mean I've started all this—this water painting stuff only since Greg and I split up?"

"It does seem to have some connection. You'd been together a couple of years and hadn't had any problems."

"Any problems?" She raised her eyebrows at him.

"You know what I mean; painting and dreaming problems. It's not as if you have them all the time. They

9

only seem to come when you're stressed."

"Exactly. It wasn't just being alone again, it was Mum's death coming so soon after Greg and I broke up." She brushed her hand across her eyes. "A double whammy in the one year."

"That's probably all it is. After all, it's only three months since your mom died. Give it time."

Lisa nodded. "Dr. Olson said it would take a while."

"Yeah, but she also said you should go back and see her if those all-night painting sessions started up again. Why don't you make an appointment with her right now?"

Lisa flung her hands up in the air. "Because I don't need a shrink. I want to beat this stupid bloody thing by myself."

"Okay, okay. No need to yell at me." Jerry unwound himself from the chair and stood up.

"Sorry. What I need most is a good night's sleep."

"Go home now and take a rest. I can manage fine on my own." Jerry hesitated. "What did you do with the painting, the one you did last night?"

"Shoved it in the basement with the others."

"Good. Want me to come back with you?"

"No, thanks. But I'm going to accept your offer and take a few hours off. Besides, I think I shut poor Paloma down in the basement before I left. She hates it down*9++

there. I'd better go home and let her out."

"You do that. And don't bother coming back. I'll hold down the fort. You did a good day's work today."

Lisa smiled. "They really liked our ideas, didn't they? I still don't understand why they wanted to come here, to the gallery, rather than have us come to their hotel."

"Oh, they told me why before you arrived. They

wanted to see what kind of gallery we had."

"Yikes!" Lisa glanced around, taking in the lack of space, the prints crammed together on the walls. "Were they disappointed when they saw it?"

"George Lister said he was surprised how small it was, but when they looked around they seemed genuinely interested in what we had." Jerry grinned. "I told Lister that we preferred to invest our money in our artwork rather than our showroom."

"Good thinking." Lisa closed her eyes, suddenly so tired she could barely stay awake.

"Go on home," Jerry said, "and get some sleep. I'll give you a call later this afternoon."

As she drove home, Lisa tuned into CBC Radio, forcing herself to concentrate on the music and Shelagh Rogers's warm-molasses voice, trying not to think about having to drive across the bridge that spanned the river.

But as soon as she turned into the approach to the bridge her heart started pounding. If she hadn't been trapped by traffic on both sides, she would have made a quick U-turn to get away from it.

Breathing fast, she rolled down the window to gulp in the fresh spring air. When the traffic lights turned to green she gripped the steering wheel with sweating palms, trying to sing along with Loreena McKennitt on the radio.

Then the rise of the bridge was ahead of her. As she drove onto it, praying that the lights would stay green, her gaze fixed on the road ahead of her to avoid catching even a glimpse of the dark waters beneath.

Almost there, she thought. Then the lights changed to red, and the traffic in front of her came to a halt. Immediately, her heart began to race.

"I am safe in the car," she told herself, forcing herself to take long slow breaths through her nose. "I am safe in the car," she repeated, the words like a mantra. But another part of her told her: *there is water below me; water on both sides of me.* The rising Red. The swollen Assiniboine. Fast-flowing water. In just a couple of weeks the slow, muddy Red River had become a massive lake in southern Manitoba. This water, too, could rise up now, flow over the bridge, sweep her up, carry her and the car away forever . . .

The car ahead of her was moving, but Lisa was frozen, her mind spinning, incapable of thinking coherently. From behind her came the impatient blare of a horn. Hands trembling, she changed gear and inched forward, peering through the windshield with the blurred vision that always accompanied one of these panic attacks.

Once she'd cleared the bridge she turned right at the first intersection and parked the car on a side street. Her entire body shook, as if she'd been through some major trauma, instead of just driving across a simple, everyday bridge.

Jerry was right. Much as she hated to admit it, she would have to see the psychologist again. She wasn't about to let this *thing*—whatever it was—ruin her life, especially now that the gallery was all coming together so well.

When she got home and opened the back door, she could hear Paloma's plaintive mewing from behind the closed basement door. She ran to open it, and the cat hurtled out, complaining raucously now, rubbing herself against Lisa's legs in an ecstasy of gratitude.

Lisa stroked her from her soft furry head to the tip of her bushy tail. "I'm sorry, Pal. How about some Kitty

Chow to make up for it 'eh?"

She poured some of the cat food into the plastic dish and then went to close the basement door, but something stilled her hand. The darkness below seemed to beckon her. She heard Dr. Olson's voice in her head. "When you get these feelings, don't fight them. Experience them, drift though them."

Easy for her to say, Lisa thought. *Not so easy to drift when your heart's pounding like you're going to have a heart attack.* She switched on the basement light and went downstairs.

The paintings were stacked up against the far wall of the basement, opposite the washer and dryer. The newest one, last night's, was facing her, its paint gleaming in the artificial light. She bent to peer more closely at it, examining the violent brushstrokes, the thick layers of paint. No wonder her shoulders were still aching.

When she stepped back to get a better view of the painting, the one object in the rush of water sprang into relief.

But it no longer looked like a tree branch. Now it was more like an arm rising from the turbulent water.

CHAPTER TWO

JUDITH OLSON LEANED BACK IN HER CHAIR AS THEIR session drew to a close. "I'd like you to keep on practicing the desensitization exercises we worked out last time you were here." Frowning, she looked down at her notes. "I can't remember if we tried flooding therapy."

"Flooding?" Lisa repeated incredulously.

Judith struck her forehead. "Oh God, that wasn't the right thing to say, was it?"

They both laughed. That was the great thing about Judith. A woman of thirty—five, only four years older than Lisa, she was down—to—earth, not full of her own selfimportance like the psychiatrist Lisa had seen after her mother's death.

Lisa found herself relaxing for the first time since she'd arrived at the clinic. "I know what flooding is. I've read about it in all those damned books. I don't think there's one phobia book in the library I haven't read," she added. Not that they seemed to be doing her any good. But she didn't tell Judith that. She'd probably say that Lisa must try to be more positive. "So . . . you think I should immerse myself for hours in a swimming pool, that sort of thing?"

"You sound rather skeptical."

"Sorry, but I am. I've told you, water itself doesn't seem to affect me. I've read about those people who can't bear to wash their hair or get into a bath because of their water phobia. That doesn't bother me at all. It's—it's moving water I can't stand. Fast-flowing rivers, waves . . . that sort of thing."

"Water that appears threatening to you?"

Lisa nodded. "I guess so." She shivered. "That's why this flood is really getting to me. I know it's creeping up here, slowly, inexorably, and there's nothing we can do to stop it."

"There are some things we just cannot control," Judith said, flashing one of her quirky smiles. "Have you considered going away? Maybe taking a couple of weeks off until the worst of this flood is over?"

"I must admit I have. But then I tell myself it will have won. You know what I mean? The flood will have

14

defeated me."

"How does that make you feel?"

"That question sounds a bit like Psych 101."

Judith shrugged. "Perhaps." She waited for an answer.

Lisa thought for a moment. "It makes me feel . . . weak, incapable, like a coward . . . . All those negative things. You don't see other people running away from the flood, do you? Everyone's pitching in, sandbagging or working in centers for the homeless." She swallowed hard, clenching her jaw to stop tears from coming.

"Any other feelings?"

Lisa straightened up. "Yes. It makes me bloody angry."

"And where do you direct that anger?"

"At myself, of course. I'm mad at me because I can't control myself better. Can't control my mind, I mean."

"As we've discussed before, the more you fight this, the less likely you are to conquer it."

"I know, I know. But I don't want to have these feelings. I don't *want* to accept them. I want to know why I'm getting them so I can make them go away."

Judith sat back in her chair and leaned her chin on the tips of her long, pointed fingers. "We discussed your going back to Dr. Sherrett for analysis last time you were here, didn't we? I think I told you then that even if it's possible to discover what has caused a phobia in any given case, it doesn't necessarily mean the fear will automatically disappear. Sometimes the mind and body have become so used to reacting in a certain way that it takes a long time for them to unlearn those reactions."

"I know that, but I still need to find out what's causing this."

"I could refer you to someone who specializes in

15

hypnotherapy, but it's a long process." Judith glanced over her glasses at Lisa. "And you've told me you're not a very patient person."

"You can say that again."

"Last time you were here, you were still in the early days of grieving after your mother's death. You told me then that your mother adopted you at the age of—five, was it?—and you knew very little about your original parents, except that they had died in a car accident in Switzerland." Judith leaned forward. "I asked you this question before, but I want you to think about it again. Did you never feel the need to know more about your birth parents?"

Lisa hesitated. "Oh, I went through that usual teenage thing when I thought I'd have been much happier with my other parents," she said, trying to keep her voice light and easy. "But that didn't last. Besides, I knew they were dead and that I had no brothers or sisters, so what was the point?"

Judith sat very still, looking at her.

"You think that was strange?" Lisa said, annoyed by her silence. "That I should have wanted to know more about my parents?"

"Some people in the same situation do get curious."

"And go searching for their birth parents, sometimes for years. I know that. But mine were dead. End of story."

Judith said nothing, but her mild stare unsettled Lisa.

"You think this fear of water, these painting fits, could be related to something that happened in my early childhood, is that it?" she demanded.

"It's possible," Judith said. "Some childhood trauma that comes back to haunt you when you're under stress. Have you spoken to your father about it?"

16

"My father can't think of anything that might have caused this, but then he knows nothing about the first four years of my life. Apparently my mother—my adoptive mother, I mean—was my nanny. She began looking after me long before she met Dad."

"That doesn't mean he doesn't know anything. Your mother might have told him something that he doesn't want to tell you, unless you press him on it." Judith glanced at her watch, trying not to make it too obvious that she was checking on the time.

"Time's up," Lisa said, springing to her feet. "Thanks for fitting me in so quickly."

"I'm glad you contacted me. Ask Jenny for another appointment next week. Meanwhile, I suggest you go down to the Forks and spend an hour there."

"The Forks?" Lisa shuddered. "We're talking not one but *two* rivers there. And both of them are flowing fast. CBC Television did a national news broadcast from the Forks last night."

"Ask a good friend to go with you for support. Take one of the beta—blockers beforehand. And remember the breathing and relaxation exercises."

"I will." Lisa busied herself with pulling on her light jacket to avoid looking at Judith. The tension was back in earnest now, knotting her neck and shoulders.

"And when you've done that," Judith said, sitting at her desk to complete her notes, "you might drive to the floodway to check it out. There shouldn't be much water in it yet. It's a massive project, you know; some have compared it to the Panama Canal."

"Sounds as if you know more about it than I do."

"You should read about it. Go and see it. It may not actually help you with your fear of flowing water, but seeing that massive ditch might reassure you that the

17

city won't be flooded."

"Good idea." Lisa turned away to walk to the door. "Thanks again. See you next week."

"And, Lisa . . ."

Lisa turned. "Yes?"

"Speak to your father."

Two days passed before Lisa could summon up the courage to visit her father. The truth was she felt extremely guilty about him. She knew how desperately lonely he was, and he'd been giving her none too subtle hints that he wished she would move back home with him. "This house is far too big for me on my own," he'd say dolefully. He hadn't actually asked her to move in, but the question was there, hanging in the air each time she visited him.

Whenever she saw him she evaded the issue, unable to tell him flatly that the idea of giving up her own little house—small though it was—her independence, and her privacy was unthinkable. Yet the feelings of guilt remained, so that she dreaded going to see him.

A couple of weeks ago, she'd read an article headed "Are You a Nineties Spinster?" in some trendy British women's magazine. The following night, she'd taken it with her to the monthly meeting she and three women friends had.

Three out of the four were single.

Their meetings often became informal therapy sessions, frequently disintegrating into a binge of laughing—or crying—depending on how many glasses of wine they'd had.

That night they'd met in Bridget's apartment in a block overlooking the river. Lisa had thought very seriously of canceling, but her friends would have known why. When she started hedging about it on the phone to Bridget, saying she was too busy preparing the big presentation, she was told that if she didn't turn up, they'd come and bodily wrestle her into the car to get her there.

She had gone, but all evening she'd been aware of the river lapping against the stretch of green lawn at the rear of the building. She'd taken the article, which had a questionnaire, with her. They'd all done the questionnaire, laughing as they answered the questions.

She wondered, though, how much the hilarity had been forced. When she'd read the article and filled out the questionnaire earlier, her first reaction had been panic, a feeling that time was pressing in on her. She realized how fortunate she was to have achieved success with the gallery and to have so many great friends. It was her closest, most intimate relationships that just weren't working out.

Hell, they weren't not working out. They were nonexistent.

She had her own car and home. Her career was her life, constantly spilling into her private time. She worried about her weight. She had a strong network of friends, including a gay male friend—the fact that Jerry was also her business partner hadn't spoiled their friendship, thank God. Her love life was littered with commitment—phobic mennow *there* was a rampant phobia among the male population that deserved close study. And her relationship with her parent—the only one she had left—was particularly fraught now that he was alone and needy.

There wasn't one question she hadn't marked a "yes" to.

Now, as she was driving west on Portage Avenue to

19

the bungalow in Crestview where she'd grown up, and where her bedroom was still waiting for her, unchanged from her teenage years, she braced herself for the coming ordeal: an entire evening alone with her father.

"Why don't I take you out for dinner?" she'd asked brightly when she'd called him. Meeting on neutral ground would be safer. But he'd been shocked by the idea. "Can't have you spending your hard—earned money on some fancy restaurant meal," he'd told her, "when I can cook you one myself for a quarter of the price."

When she passed first the Supervalu store and then the Safeway, those monolithic temples of the late twentieth century, Lisa's heart grew heavier. As she turned into Cavalier Drive, and knew she was only a couple of minutes away from the house, she decided that she must face up to her father tonight. She'd tell him that she would help him in every way possible, but that she couldn't move back with him.

She didn't want even to think about the other matter she should be discussing with him. She hadn't the heart to bring it up again so soon after her mother's death. To remind him now that she was not his own child seemed unutterably cruel. No father could have been kinder or more generous, giving her not only a good home, but also a university education on an aircraft mechanic's wages.

Her father opened the door before she rang the bell, as if he'd been watching for her . . . as he probably had been. She hugged him, feeling as always in his small frame the struggle between the desire to hug her back and the restraint that being raised a male in prewar England had instilled in him.

"You look thinner," he said, holding her at arm's

length. "You on one of those silly diets again?"

"Of course not. Besides, I don't go on silly diets. You always think I look thinner. It's only a week since I last saw you, you know."

"Seems much longer than that. Come on in."

Lisa followed him into the living room. It was as neat as it had been when her mother was alive. "You keep this place looking great," she told him.

"Can't let things go, can I? Your mother wouldn't like that."

"No, she wouldn't." They exchanged smiles as they remembered Meg Cooper's bustling tidiness. "But . . ." Lisa hesitated. "I don't think she'd expect you to keep it as tidy as she did."

Jim Cooper shrugged. "What else have I got to do with my time?"

Lisa felt a knot of tension form in her stomach. "What about your curling club? You haven't been to the rink since Mum got sick. You could join again."

"Maybe I will, when fall comes." He eased himself into his recliner chair. "Depends on the arthritis in my knees. Takes a lot of bending, curling does." Despite his twenty-five years in Canada, his accent still carried tones of south London.

Lisa curled up in a corner of the overstuffed sofa, which was covered with a slippery, rose—patterned fabric. "Something smells good."

"Fried fish for you and roast beef for me. Can't tempt you to try some, can I? It's a prime bit of beef."

"No, Dad, you can't." Her father had never accepted her decision not to eat red meat. Lisa summoned up a smile. "You could always freeze what's left over and make more meals from it. Save you cooking."

"If I don't cook, what do I do instead?"

"Oh, I don't know," Lisa said, unable to curb her impatience. "Garden, go bowling . . . . You have to make a life for yourself, Dad. You can't just stay at home and be miserable all the time."

When she saw the shadow cloud his face she regretted her hasty words.

"I feel nearer to her here, in the house, than anywhere else," he said, looking out the window, over the ledge lined with houseplants, each standing on its own lace doily.

"I know what you mean," Lisa said softly, glancing at the collection of china figurines in the cabinet on the wall. "It takes time, doesn't it?"

He released a sigh and nodded. "Think I'll go have a cigarette," he said, struggling to his feet.

"You don't have to go outside on my account. This is your home."

He kept going. "Meg wouldn't like me to smoke in the house," he said from the hall.

Lisa had to plow through a heavy meal of fried haddock, fries and mashed potatoes, with peas and carrots, followed by a steamed syrup sponge pudding.

"Well, I certainly won't look thinner after that meal," she told her father when she'd finished.

"Enjoy it?" he asked anxiously.

"It was wonderful."

He beamed a proud smile at her. Suddenly she knew that she must take advantage of this rare feeling of companionship between them.

"Dad," she said quickly, "I've asked you this before, but I'm going to ask you again. I want you to think hard before you answer, because it's very important to me." Her father's expression was wary, but she carried on, determined not to allow anything to stop her now. "Are you quite sure that Mum didn't tell you about anything important happening to me when I was with my—my original family? Perhaps it was something really bad and you feel that you're protecting me by not telling me."

He looked stunned and then his expression changed to one of hurt and resentment. "I told you before when you asked; she didn't tell me anything."

Lisa leaned across the cluttered dining table. "I'm sorry to bring it up again, Dad, but I need to know." She crumbled a piece of bread between her fingers. "I'm having that fear of water again."

"It'll go away," he muttered. "It always did before."

"Yes, I know. But I don't want it to ever come back. The psychologist I'm seeing—"

"What do those people know? Psychology's a load of old rubbish." He pushed back his chair, screwing up his paper napkin and throwing it onto the table.

"Judith Olson's a great help to me, so don't put her down, please. And you could help by telling me everything Mum told you about—about the time before you met her, however small or insignificant it may seem."

He stared at her, stone—faced now. She couldn't tell if he was angry or not. "All she told me was that she was your nanny—"

"—And that my parents were killed in a car crash in Europe when they were on holiday. I know all that. But what about the rest of the family? Surely I had grandparents, aunts, uncles. Why didn't anyone want to keep in touch with me?"

He shook his head, looking extremely uncomfortable.

"I really need to know, Dad." Lisa was breathing

hard. "If you can't tell me anything, I'm going to have to hire someone to do a search."

He picked up his paper napkin and began shredding it into pieces. Suddenly Lisa knew, with a quickening of her heart, that there was something he hadn't told her. "*Please*, Dad. It's not the family I'm interested in, it's what might have happened to me. This water thing is screwing up my life."

"Your mother left a letter."

"For me?"

"She—she said I wasn't to give it to you unless you really needed to know," he said hesitantly. "Maybe for medical reasons or something important like that."

"This *is* a medical reason."

"Not the sort she meant."

"Because it's mental not physical? It affects me physically. It makes my heart beat like I'm having a heart attack. It makes me feel giddy and gives me headaches and causes insomnia. Is that physical enough for you?" Lisa shouted. Then, seeing his distress, she calmed down. "I'm sure Mum would have wanted to help me. Where is this letter?"

"It's in the safety—deposit box at the bank. She said it was better there, in case you went snooping around the house and found it."

Lisa felt a chill run down her spine. "Sounds as if I might have an ax murderer in the family, or something like that," she said lightly, trying to make a joke, but the possibilities made her nervous.

"I don't know what's in it."

"Really?"

He nodded. "Yeah. She would never talk about herher life with you before I met her." His mouth twisted into a wry little smile.

24

"That must have bugged you, considering you'd taken me on as well when you married her."

"You were a package. I knew that. You were a cute kid." He grinned. "To me you still are." He stood up.

"I'll get the key to the deposit box." He left the room before she could stop him.

Lisa was amazed. It had all happened so quickly. She wondered why on earth she hadn't pressed him before now.

He came back in a few minutes and handed her the key and the card with the box number on it, but she shook her head.

"There's no point in giving me the key, Dad. You'll need to sign in at the bank."

"You're right. You keep the key in case I lose it. We'll go to the bank tomorrow. You say what time." He stood there, arms hanging by his sides, and she saw to her dismay that he was struggling to hold back tears.

"It's okay, Dad." She put her arms around him, thinking that this was how it felt to be a parent comforting her child.

Sniffing, he pulled away quickly, rooting around in his pocket for the large checked handkerchief he always carried. "I don't want to lose you."

"You're not going to lose me. I haven't a clue what's in this letter, but it might help me. Just think what it would mean if I could confirm that something traumatic happened to me when I was small."

"Apart from losing your parents, you mean? Isn't that traumatic enough for you?"

"There's something else. I'm sure of it. It's like—" Lisa squeezed her eyes shut and then opened them again. "Like driving along a prairie highway seeing something far away on the horizon, but never quite being able to make out exactly what it is. You know what I mean? It's there, but I can never reach it." She looked down at the key. "I'm hoping that this, literally, right be the key to unlock my memory."

Chapter Three

THE ENVELOPE HAD BEEN HIDDEN AWAY AT THE BACK of the gray steel safety—deposit box. Lisa sat in the little enclosed booth in the bank, staring at the small, pale blue envelope lying before her on the desk, the hum of voices and machines in the background.

This was the last communication she would have with her mother. Her name was written on the envelope in the familiar neat handwriting: *For Lisa*.

After the funeral, her father had given her another note from her mother, written only a few days before she died. In it, she had wished Lisa happiness and love, and the hope that she would find someone as good as her dad for a partner. What she meant, of course, was a husband. Using the word *partner* was just her mother's way of trying to keep up with the rapidly changing world, but it didn't sound like her at all. In Mum's world, it was a husband Lisa needed, and nothing less.

She looked down at the envelope, her lips tilted in a faint smile. Then the smile faded, and her heartbeat escalated. Whatever was inside, she had the feeling that her world would never be quite the same once she opened it. But she also knew that she had no real choice.

She took up the envelope and tore it open. Inside was one small sheet of paper. It was dated 1984, the year of Lisa's eighteenth birthday.

My dear Lisa, she read.

Just in case anything happens to me, I have asked your dad to put this somewhere safe. He is only to give it to you if you need to know about your family for health reasons. Although I know for certain that you had German measles when you were three, I don't know about any of your original family's health, as I was your nanny for only two years. If there is some medical emergency, you or your dad can write to Dr. Trewen in the village of Charnwood, in Somerset, England. He should have the family's medical records.

That was it. No other information. No family name. Of course, she could probably find that quite easily by sending to the records' office in Britain for a copy of her adoption certificate. Come to think of it, hadn't she seen the original when she'd needed it for her passport application years ago?

She scrabbled around in the box, pulling out packets of neatly tied photographs, her parents' marriage certificate . . . There it was, her adoption certificate. Scanning it, she saw, to her disappointment, that there was no mention of her original name. It was as if she hadn't existed before the date of her official, court—sanctioned adoption in 1971.

What was it her mother had said when she'd asked her years ago about her original family? "Now, what is the point, when there's no one there anymore? It would only make you fret to think about it."

Lisa could tell at the time that it made her mother fret, too, that she'd even asked the question. "Haven't you been happy with us?" her mother had asked in a plaintive tone, when Lisa had brought up the subject another time.

Her father had opted to wait outside the bank for her. He said he didn't want to see all that stuff. "But don't forget to take your mother's jewelry from the box," he'd reminded her gruffly. "She wanted you to have it."

Lisa fingered the faded, blue—velvet jewelry roll, feelings the bumps and lumps of her mother's few good pieces of jewelry. She didn't really want to see it either, but since her father wanted her to have it .... Without opening it, she gathered it up and bundled it into her bag.

She picked up the letter and was folding it to put it back in the envelope, when she caught sight of another couple of lines of her mother's writing on the other side. *I suppose you will need the family name.* Just reading those words Lisa could sense her mother's reluctance. *It is KINGSLEY,* she had written bluntly.

"Kingsley," Lisa said softly. "Mr. and Mrs. Kingsley," she whispered, experimenting with the sound. Surely she must have heard those words frequently; the names of her original parents.

"Lisa Kingsley." This time she spoke aloud, but still the name brought no blinding flash of recognition. Yet this must have been her name for at least the first four years of her life. She sat in the little cubicle, frowning hard, concentrating on the name, but it was no use. Why didn't she recognize her own name?

And why on earth had her mother been so reluctant to divulge it?

"It's as if she was trying to hide something," she told Jerry, when she showed him the note on Monday morning.

"You've got too vivid an imagination," Jerry told her, as he bent over a picture frame on the large worktable, adjusting the wire hanger on the back with a small pair

28

of pliers. "Knowing your mother, I'd say she didn't want you to dwell on the fact that your birth parents were dead. She was just trying to protect you. You were very precious to her and your dad, you know."

Lisa blinked rapidly. "You know just the right thing to say."

He straightened up. "Well, you were. She told me once that you'd been their little gift from heaven."

Lisa felt her face grow warm. "Shut up, Jerry."

"It's true. Your dad certainly must have thought so. A confirmed bachelor, older than your mom. He must have thought himself pretty lucky to get a complete family all at once."

She grimaced. "I don't seem to be much use to him at present."

"You're doing your best. He has to learn to adjust."

"I'm not sure he ever will. He's totally lost without Mum. I just hate to see him like that."

"Just be there for him, that's all you can do. I'd offer to go and spend time with him, but dads are definitely not my specialty."

He said it with a wry smile, but Lisa knew that the smile hid a lot of pain.

"Once your dad realized I wasn't son-in-law material, he changed. Now he never knows quite what to do when I'm around," Jerry said. "We have those long, awkward silences when we're both trying to think up what next to say to each other."

Lisa grinned at him. "Well, you do have one thing in common: you're both hockey nuts. You could always go over and watch a hockey game with him. Seems to me there's one on TV every night at the moment."

Jerry's face brightened. "That's an idea. Hadn't thought of that. We wouldn't have to talk much with a game on, would we?"

"True." Lisa fell silent. She started fiddling with the roll of picture wire, twisting it into a knot.

"What's up?"

"I've got a big favor to ask you."

"What?"

"I want to go to England, to see this village for myself." The words came out in a rush.

Jerry frowned. "Couldn't you call this Dr. Trewen, get the name and address of your relatives, then write to them first?"

Lisa felt a surge of disappointment. She had thought Jerry would be more supportive. "I want to see the place where I come from."

"There may not be any of your relatives left in the village," he warned her.

"Even if there were, I'm not one bit interested in meeting any relatives. I just want to fill in that huge gap, those first four years of my life. Can't you understand that?"

"Yes, I can, but I also think you should take it slowly, not rush into anything. After all, it's not as if you've had a burning desire to hunt down your past before, is it? You've been to Britain several times, but I don't remember you showing any interest in searching for your roots."

She lifted her chin, annoyed by his lack of understanding. "Just because I don't talk about it doesn't mean that I don't care about who I was and where I came from. Talking about it always upset Mum terribly, so I gave up asking and pushed it to the back of my mind. Perhaps I'm paying for that now with all this stuff about water."

"Do you really need all this turmoil in your life?"

"I've got turmoil in my life already, haven't I, whether I like it or not? I don't intend to let it get worse and take over my life completely." She ran her hand down her long plait of hair. "I don't know. All I do know is that I want to go to this Charnwood place as soon as possible and try to find out if anything strange happened there when I was a kid."

"What about the Norville commission?"

"You know I wouldn't go until we hear from them," she told him, her tone scathing.

"So you're not just rushing off to get away from the river cresting?"

"Is that what you thought?" Lisa glared at him. "That I was running away from the flood?"

Jerry looked sheepish. "Sorry."

"Idiot! I'm not going to be able to get away immediately, anyway. I've got to find a cheap flight. Can't do that in a couple of days. And, by the way," she added, hands on her hips, "Dr. Olson herself suggested that I think about going away for a couple of weeks. She didn't seem to consider it running away, but I certainly did, and I told her so."

"I'm a jerk. Jerry the Jerk. Sorry."

"Apology accepted. I just hate it when you don't understand what I'm feeling."

"I'm not clairvoyant, you know."

Lisa had to smile. "Oh, no? That's the trouble. Ninety percent of the time you are." Ever since they'd met in first year of university, they'd had this weird thing between them, like ESP, one of them getting a kind of tingling sensation around the back of the neck when something bad was happening to the other. "Anyway, I want to do this. I *need* to do it. I spent most of last night thinking it through."

31

"Well, at least that's better than spending it painting."

Lisa rolled her eyes. "You're right. Anyway, if we get a yes from Norville, they won't be ready to let us in for at least another two months. They haven't even plastered the walls yet. If it's a no, we just go on as before."

"If they give us the go-ahead there will be all the art-work to collect and—"

"I'll be away a week . . . two weeks at the most," Lisa assured him. "That should be quite long enough."

"You're serious about all this, aren't you?" Jerry sounded as if he were starting to understand at last. "You really do think this journey into the past could help with your fear of water."

"I'm not the only one. Judith thinks there may be something there, if I could just find out what it is. I know it won't be easy after all these years, but I intend to try."

"Want me to come with you?"

"Thanks, pal," Lisa said softly, "but this is one I need to do by myself."

But two weeks later, as the plane hurtled down the runway at Winnipeg Airport and then lifted off, passing over the swollen waters of the Red and the Assiniboine, Lisa wished with all her heart that Jerry was in the seat beside her—instead of a young mother with a bawling toddler—so that he could help distract her from thoughts of what she was leaving behind.

The Norville commission was theirs, and Jerry had assured her that he could manage, as long as she didn't stay on any longer than she'd planned.

The flood crest had come and gone, leaving in its wake the devastation of wrecked homes and businesses in southern Manitoba and North Dakota. There were still millions of sandbags to remove, mud dikes to level, and hundreds of people with no homes to live in. Some had been able to get their belongings out in time, but still couldn't return to waterlogged homes until they'd dried out. Others had to throw out everything because the floodwaters had done their worst.

As the plane climbed and then leveled off into its flight eastward to Toronto, Lisa felt like a rat for deserting not only Jerry, but also Manitoba, when everyone else was pulling together in the huge effort to ensure that the homeless were being cared for.

She also felt anxious—*extremely* anxious—about what lay ahead of her.

CHAPTER FOUR

THIS WAS LISA'S THIRD VISIT TO BRITAIN. THE LAST time, two years ago, had been with Greg, and he'd done most of the driving. Fortunately, driving on the M4 motorway to the west of England was far easier than she'd expected. It also avoided the coastal roads, keeping her well away from the sea. Yet still she had to concentrate hard to avoid thinking about the seas that pounded against the cliffs and shores of this densely populated island.

However, once she'd left the motorway at Bridgwater—just seeing that name on the signposts had made her mouth go dry—she was forced to follow the road along the rugged northern coast of Somerset and North Devon.

"The sea cannot hurt me," she kept telling herself, like a mantra, but nothing eased the tension. Driving on the slower, two—lane roads also required far more concentration.

After she left the little holiday town of Minehead, where she'd stopped for a cup of typically English coffee—with hot milk—the road became progressively more narrow and winding. *England's Switzerland* her guidebook told her this part of the picturesque west country used to be called. When she'd read that, she'd felt as if a hand had clutched at her heart. It was in Switzerland that her birth parents had died, in a fiery car crash in the Alps.

She changed into low gear, preparing to embark on the steep gradient and hairpin bends of the road ascending almost vertically from the village of Porlock. She tried very hard not to think about the restless sea hundreds of feet below.

"Not bad for a prairie girl," she said aloud, as she urged her rented Nissan up the hill. A moment later, having rounded a particularly vicious bend, she wished she'd kept her mouth shut. Ahead of her, a small blue car with a loaded roof rack had stalled. The woman driver sat there, frozen, her hands gripping the steering wheel. The man in the seat beside her was yelling instructions at her, but the woman seemed petrified with fear. Despite the distance between them, Lisa could sense her terror.

Lisa's hands grew slick on the steering wheel. What would happen if the woman panicked or the car's brakes started to slip and it came hurtling backward toward her? Her head began to spin at the thought of being precipitated down the hill, falling in a slow spiral from the cliffside road into the foaming sea beneath.

Suddenly the passenger door of the car ahead flew open and the man jumped out. He yanked the driver's door open, and changed places with the woman. As she walked around the front of her car, she kept her head down, obviously too embarrassed even to make a gesture of apology to Lisa. Heart thudding, Lisa inched back as far as she could, but a line of cars had backed up behind her, several of them impatiently blasting their horns.

The stalled car lurched backward and then, with a roar of the engine and a blast of smoke from the exhaust, took off, to Lisa's intense relief.

Before she'd left Canada, her father had warned her about the steep roads and hills around Exmoor, but no amount of warning could have prepared her for this.

Her body trembling from the strain, Lisa followed the small blue car, keeping a safe distance behind it, until they reached the summit.

The sudden panoramic view took her breath away. Far below the towering cliffs on her right stretched the waters of the Bristol Channel, a strong wind frosting the waves with white. A shiver ran over her, but she was relieved to find herself so far above the sea. On the map it looked as if it were almost adjacent to the road, not hundreds of feet down from the clifftops. To her left, the vast ravines and green valleys of Exmoor rolled to the horizon. It was like driving across the top of the world.

She was looking for the left turn onto the road to Charnwood when she came to a viewpoint with a graveled parking place. Only two cars were parked there, so she pulled in and parked. The wind gusting against the car, she sat gazing out at the wild, scarred hills of Exmoor and the gentle, wooded valleys beneath them, her artist's eye delighting in the myriad hues of green, the play of light and shade across the terrain.

This is where I come from, she thought. *My roots are*

here. Yet she felt no stab of recognition, no sense of belonging to this dramatic landscape. Maybe when she got to Charnwood she would remember something from her early childhood.

On the other hand, maybe this journey had been a monumentally stupid mistake.

With a heavy sigh, she switched on the ignition and drove back onto the main road.

A few minutes later she came to the signpost pointing to Charnwood. The narrow road that led to the village was little more than a country lane. It wound through a wooded valley, the sun filtering through the trees, intermittently dappling both road and car with light.

A shallow river ran parallel to the road, its water coursing over the stony riverbed. More like a stream than a river, Lisa felt little threat from it, despite the brisk flow of its clear water. It meandered along for two or three miles—sometimes so close that she could hear the ripple of its waters through the open window, sometimes at a distance, disappearing into the darker region of the woods beside her—before the road took a sharp turn and made its descent into the village of Charnwood.

Checking her rearview mirror to make sure no one was behind her, Lisa came to a halt and peered through the windshield at the village. She saw a broad high street, with several attractive thatched cottages on both sides, most of which appeared to have been converted into gift shops. There were also a few larger stone—built buildings. At the end of the street was an imposing inn, its limestone walls the color of pale honey, with wooden tables and benches outside. From a wooden post hung a painted sign proclaiming it to be THE STAG's HEAD.

Well, at least that should give her somewhere to stay, she thought, although the three stars' sign on the wall suggested it could be fairly expensive.

Her eye was caught by another hand—painted sign, this time above the little bow window of one of the cottage shops. It was illustrated with a pair of crossed knitting needles on one side and paintbrushes on the other above its name: NEEDLE AND BRUSH. To leave no room for doubt about the shop's contents, a sign on the window itself read ARTS AND CRAFTS SUPPLIES.

Lisa was about to park the car outside the shop, to take a closer look, when a young man in a uniform and black-and-yellow cap marched toward her. He was shouting at her, waving his arms, as he bore down on her.

"You can't park here. Can't you see the double yellow lines?"

"Sorry," Lisa replied through her open window. "I didn't see them."

"Must be blind," he muttered. "Car park's up there." He jerked his head in the direction of the inn. "Up the side road. Follow the parking signs."

"Can't I park somewhere nearer than that? I only want to stop for a few minutes."

A woman in a floral smock over jeans appeared on the doorstep of the shop. "Harassing our customers again, Ernie?" she said with a smile, but there was an edge to her voice.

"I'm just enforcing the law, Miss Tallis."

"I'll go and park," Lisa said hastily, not wanting to cause an incident. "I love the name of your shop," she shouted to the woman. "I'll be back later."

The woman smiled and waved a plump hand. "See

you soon."

As Lisa drove up the street, she smiled to herself. Although she'd visited Britain before, she felt as if she'd just had her first encounter with traditional English village life. The officious parking attendant and the pleasant, rotund shopkeeper. They were like stock characters from an Agatha Christie novel.

It wasn't until she'd found the parking lot and stuck her ticket on the windshield that she realized that the doctor's office would probably have its own parking. Somehow, her first sight of the village and its inhabitants had temporarily driven all thoughts of Dr. Trewen from her mind.

A woman carrying a wicker basket was locking her car door.

"Excuse me," Lisa said. "Can you tell me where the medical clinic is?"

"Clinic?" The woman frowned. "Oh, you mean the doctor's surgery." She spoke with the soft country burr of the west. "It's just around the corner, my love." She pointed the way. "There's a bit of parking there, but you might as well leave your car here now, to make sure you've got a space. The village gets busy near lunchtime with visitors coming in to find something to eat."

Lisa thanked her and started walking up the slight incline. In a few minutes she was inside a small brick building attached to a much older house with a beautiful garden, which she supposed was the doctor's home.

Her heart sank when she saw that neither of the two doctors named on the sign on the inside door was Dr. Trewen. *He's probably retired*, she told herself, but when she went into the busy waiting room and asked for him her hopes were further dashed.

"Dr. Trewen's been dead for years," the receptionist told her.

"August 1987, he died," said an elderly man in a grubby, Fair Isle pullover who was sitting on one of the hard wooden chairs.

"I see." Lisa turned back to the receptionist. "I'm trying to trace some family medical records. It's for a friend," she added. She spoke in a low voice, knowing that the man who'd spoken was leaning forward in his eagerness to hear what she was saying.

The telephone rang, and the receptionist answered it. She frowned at Lisa as she spoke on the phone. "Medical records?" she repeated, when she'd finished her call. "What sort of records?"

"This is the name." Lisa wrote the name *Kingsley* on a piece of paper and pushed it across to the woman.

"Kingsley?" said the receptionist. "That's quite a common name. Several Kingsleys hereabouts."

"The family I'm interested in lived here about thirty years ago," Lisa told her.

"All Dr. Trewen's medical records that went back more than twenty years were destroyed when he died. Unless the patients transferred to one of the other doctors, of course."

"Oh." Lisa hesitated. "Then perhaps I could see one of the doctors."

"Have you got an appointment?"

"No, I'm just visiting."

The woman sighed and picked up her pencil. "You'll have to make an appointment to see the doctor. Dr. Ridley is on today."

"There's Bill Kingsley, the vet," the man in the knitted pullover said over the noise of a screaming baby. "And Jessie Kingsley that lives on Edgecombe Farm.

39

'Er's been a widow twenty year or more. And of course there be the Kingsleys up at—"

A buzzer interrupted him. "In you go, Tom," said the receptionist.

"Would it be possible to see Dr. Ridley this morning?" Lisa asked her. "That would save me having to come back. I won't take more than five minutes of his time," she added quickly, sensing that the woman was about to say no. "It's really important. My friend has medical problems."

That seemed to work. "I'll have a word with Dr. Ridley when he's finished with Tom. What's your name?"

"Lisa Cooper." Lisa had the feeling that everyone in the waiting room was straining to hear what she was saying.

Tom was with Dr. Ridley for such a long time that she didn't think she had a hope of speaking to the doctor that morning. But, to her surprise, when Tom left she was told to go in next.

"But don't you take too long now," added the receptionist sternly. "There's several here had appointments before you."

Lisa could sense that she wasn't too popular with the waiting patients. "She's got some nerve!" someone muttered.

"Five minutes, I promise," Lisa told the waiting room in general.

When she went into the cramped little office she thanked the harried—looking doctor for seeing her.

"What's this all about?" he asked. "Something about medical records, Damaris said."

Damaris? Somehow the name didn't match the receptionist's strident voice and thick—lensed spectacles. Lisa explained that she was looking for a certain Kingsley family and had been told to speak to Dr. Trewen.

"Dr. Trewen's dead."

"Yes, that's what your receptionist told me. That's why I asked to see you. In case you took over some of his patients. The Kingsley family I'm looking for lived here about thirty years ago."

"Sorry. I'm fairly new," he said. "I came to Charnwood only two years ago, long after Dr. Trewen died, so I'm not up with the local family sagas." He hesitated. "I suppose I could ask Damaris to give you a list of any patients called Kingsley." He didn't sound over enthusiastic about the idea. "But even then we couldn't divulge anything about their medical history."

"No, I understand that. It was Dr. Trewen I wanted to speak to."

"Well, you could do that if you fancy a walk up to the local cemetery." He looked pointedly at his watch.

Lisa stood up. "Thanks for your help. I think it will be just as easy to look up all the Kingsleys in the local phone book and call them, to see if I can find the right one."

Suddenly he became more friendly, as if he realized how abrupt he'd been. "I take it from your accent you're an American doing research for your family tree."

"I'm Canadian, and a friend asked me to do this for her when she heard I was coming here on holiday. She has a health problem and wants to know about the family medical background."

He nodded. "I see. Good luck with your hunt."

"Thanks. And thank you for seeing me."

He nodded in response, already pressing his buzzer for the next patient.

41

As Lisa left the clinic, she saw Tom hanging around outside. As soon as he saw her, he hailed her, holding up his noxious—smelling pipe. " ' Scuse me, miss. Did you find those Kingsleys you were looking for?"

His accent was so thick she had to concentrate hard to understand what he was saying. "No. But it's not really important. I promised a friend I would see if she had any relatives in the area when I was here."

"American, right?"

"Canadian."

He beamed. "I wur at Dieppe with the Canadians. Great lads, they were. Your friend, be she rich or poor?"

Lisa stared. "Why would you ask that?"

" 'Cuz there's Kingsleys of all kinds around Exmoor, as I said. The vet, and Jessie up at Edgecombe Farm, and Betty Kingsley that lives in Simonsbath. Then there's the main Kingsley family, up at Charnwood Court."

"Charnwood Court. Where's that?"

"Couple of miles back up the road." He gestured with his pipe. "Used to own all this land hereabouts, they did, but that be a long time ago, afore taxes hit them. And now a gurt deal of Exmoor is National Trust land, and them busybodies are banning the stag hunting us 'n our forefathers have worked on for centuries past. Taking away all our livelihood and our traditions, they are."

Lisa wasn't about to get involved in a discussion on the merits of hunting. "You've been very helpful." She rooted in her bag for a couple of pound coins and gave them to him. "Please buy yourself a drink."

He peered down at the coins in his grimy hand and then pocketed them. "I'll do that. Thank'ee, miss." Putting one finger to his shabby tweed cap, he limped away, leaving Lisa wondering if she'd offended him by giving him the money—or by not giving him enough.

"The Kingsleys of Charnwood Court," she murmured, but again there was no resonance from the sound of the words, no feeling of recognition. On the other hand, her mother had been her nanny. Wasn't it more likely that a family living in a place called Charnwood Court would employ a nanny than, say, a farmer's family?

She felt a prickle of excitement. This man Tom had given her a place to start, at least. But she must be extremely careful from now on to make sure that she didn't reveal to anyone her connection with the village or the Kingsley family—if it was the right one. The last thing she wanted was an embarrassing reunion with distant relatives.

All she wanted to find out was whether something traumatic in her childhood had caused her crippling fear of rushing water. The answer could lie at Charnwood Court.

CHAPTER FIVE

LISA WALKED DOWN TO THE CAR PARK AND CHECKED her watch. She still had more than an hour of parking time left. First she'd find somewhere to stay, then she could explore the village. Although there really didn't seem that much to explore.

She went into the Stag's Head, pausing in the doorway to enjoy her first impression of low wooden beams, polished oak furniture, and gleaming brass. A log fire blazed in the old stone fireplace in the hall.

She soon learned that the hotel was definitely too expensive for her, but decided to take a room for a couple of nights, anyway. Apart from having fallen in love with the place at first sight, she had the feeling that the Stag's Head could be the social center of Charnwood, a place where she might pick up information without having to expose herself to suspicion by asking too many questions.

"You were lucky to get a room," the friendly young hotel receptionist said. "Someone canceled."

"I didn't think I'd have a problem at the end of May."

"It's the weekend. We're always packed at weekends, especially if the weather's good."

"It's beautiful today."

"Not going to last, I'm afraid. They're forecasting rain tomorrow. Your room should be ready about two o'clock, okay?" The receptionist, whose name tag read BELINDA BLAKE, turned to attend to the couple waiting behind Lisa.

Having moved her car to the hotel parking lot, Lisa walked back down the high street to the arts and crafts shop. The door was wide—open. As she walked in, the familiar aroma of paints and linseed oil made her feel immediately at home. She could also detect the more fragrant smell of scented oils from what appeared to be an entire counter devoted to making potpourri.

The woman in the smock was crouched in a far corner of the shop, unpacking a box, her broad back to the front door.

"Hello," Lisa said.

The woman spun around, her eyes wide. The small bottle she was holding slipped from her grasp and crashed to the floor. "My goodness, you startled me," she said, with a laugh, bending to pick the bottle up.

"Sorry," Lisa said. "The door was wide—open, so I just walked in. Did it break?" she asked, nodding at the bottle in the woman's hand.

"No, it fell on the rush matting." The woman crossed the floor of the shop to close the door. "So you did come back. I didn't think you were going to."

"I went to the hotel to book a room," Lisa explained.

"The Stag's Head?" Lisa nodded. "It's a good place. Expensive, though."

"It certainly is, but once I was inside I couldn't resist it." Lisa turned to look around. "You have a really interesting place here."

"Take a look. Anything special you're looking for? Space permitting, I try to stock as much as I can and to be as eclectic as possible."

Lisa took in the colorful knitting yarns stacked in the small cubicles of a wall—cabinet, the embroidery silks and tapestry sets, stacks of canvases, and boxes of paints . . . "I can see that."

"What's your particular interest?"

"I have a small gallery in Canada."

The woman's eyes gleamed with interest. "An art gallery? How marvelous. It's always fun to meet another professional." She held out her hand. "I'm Jane Tallis, by the way." Her rich, hearty voice matched her fullbreasted body and smiling face.

Lisa took her hand and found hers clasped tightly in a grip more like a man's than a woman's, and then released. She had taken to Jane Tallis at first sight. "Mind if I look around?"

"Of course not. Take your time."

Lisa began looking through a box of small watercolors of the village of Charnwood. She could take one back to Jerry, as a souvenir. "I like these."

"A local artist does them for pocket money. Pretty, aren't they?"

45

"Very."

"Do you paint?" Jane asked.

Lisa's hand tensed on the edge of the box. "I don't have time anymore."

"What a pity."

The door opened to the tinkle of a musical chime. Jane smiled at Lisa. "That way I can tell when someone comes in," she said, "and avoid dropping bottles. Good morning, Marion. How are you this bright, sunny morning?"

"Much better. My knees prefer this kind of weather. I've come for another ball of that green tweed wool." The small, gray—haired woman looked at Lisa with open curiosity. "Morning," she said.

"This is Miss . . ." Jane looked at Lisa. "Sorry, I don't know your name."

"Lisa. Lisa Cooper. I'm visiting from Canada."

"From Canada, eh?" said the customer. She had small round eyes, like bright brown beads, and a nervous habit of blinking frequently. "I've got a cousin in Toronto. I'm still waiting for an invitation to visit her. Is that where you come from?"

"No, I'm from Winnipeg. That's over a thousand miles away from Toronto."

"Never! Is it, really?" Marion shook her head. "My, Canada's a big country."

"It is. And I live right in the middle of it."

"Lisa's going to stay at the Stag for a couple of days," Jane said.

"Hope you've got lots of money," Marion said.

Lisa felt the scrutiny of the beady eyes. She laughed. "Not really." She turned away to continue her search through the box of paintings.

When she came to one of a large stone house with an

46

impressive entrance, her hand stilled. She turned the small painting over to read the inscription on the back: Charnwood Court, residence of Alec Kingsley, M.P., of Charnwood, Somerset.

Her breath caught for a moment, then she released it slowly. "What a lovely old house," she said, trying to keep her tone casual.

Jane leaned over the counter to glance at the painting. "That's Charnwood Court. Our local stately home," she added, a hint of sarcasm in her voice.

"Is it open to the public?" Lisa asked.

Marion answered. "It's open at weekends. You should go and see it. This could be your last chance."

"Why?"

"They're going to turn it into a hotel," Jane replied. "One of those fancy conference places."

Lisa's heart beat faster. "You mean—" She glanced down at the back of the painting. "You mean the owners are turning it into a hotel?"

"Not the owners. They're going to sell it."

"We don't know yet who's buying it," Marion chimed in.

"Probably some big hotel chain," Jane Tallis said.

Lisa looked at the picture of the house. "What a shame."

"Not at all," Jane said with a laugh. "It will bring Marion and me lots of good, year—round business."

"That's right," Marion said, but she didn't sound entirely convinced.

"Do you have a business here, too?" Lisa asked her.

"I have a little tea shop across the street. But they'll probably run all kinds of meals, not just teas, up at the Court, once it becomes a hotel," Marion said gloomily.

Jane handed Marion a ball of wool. "Make sure it's

47

the same dye number," she told her. "If *they'd* had an ounce of business sense, they'd have had not just meals but all kinds of attractions up at the house a long time ago. Then maybe they wouldn't have had to sell it."

Having completed her transaction with Marion, Jane returned to the far corner of the shop. She lowered herself onto her knees and went back to unpacking her box of bottles.

Lisa set the picture of Chamwood Court down on the counter. "If they're going to turn it into a hotel, I'd better buy this before the place is all changed. Don't get up," she told Jane. "I can just leave the money. The sticker says fifteen pounds."

Jane leaned her hand on a nearby counter and heaved herself up. "I have to ring it in," she said. She grinned at Lisa. "I need the exercise."

"Too many cream teas," said Marion, whose pinched face and angular body made her look as if she never ate anything but pickled onions and salads.

"Too many lagers, more like," Jane said, laughing. She peeled off the price sticker, stuck it on the side of the till, and carefully wrapped the picture in tissue paper. "Make sure you don't leave it in your car in this sunshine," she told Lisa. Then she shook her head. "God, listen to me! Telling an artist what to do with a painting."

"That's okay. I'll take it back to my room." Lisa hesitated. "Can you tell me when Charnwood Court opens?" She wasn't sure she was quite ready to go there yet, but it seemed she'd have to do so by tomorrow, at the latest.

Jane placed the wrapped painting in a plastic bag and handed it to Lisa. "It's open two to five, isn't it?" she said, turning to Marion:

"That's right. Two P.M. to five P.M., Saturday and

48

Sunday. Better to go today. It's not quite so busy on Saturdays. You don't get as many day—trippers. You may even have my lady Kingsley showing you over the place herself."

The comment was definitely waspish. "Lady Kingsley?" Lisa asked.

"That's just Marion being nasty," Jane said. "She's not very keen on our lady of the manor."

"Really?" Lisa sensed that Jane wasn't, either. "Is she really a Lady?"

Marion gave a cackle of laughter that made her sound like a rather spiteful bantam hen. "Not her! Not in any sense. What's more, she's—"

"I don't think Lisa's at all interested in hearing about Rachel Kingsley, Marion," Jane said smoothly.

How wrong she was! "Is she a widow?" Lisa asked.

"She's Alec Kingsley's wife," Marion replied. "He was our local M.P. until he retired before the last election."

"Knew he'd lose, that's why." Bottles chinked as Jane piled them into a large wicker basket. "I have work to do, Marion Heasley, even if you don't."

Lisa got the message. "Thanks." She smiled at the two women. "It was great meeting you. I must come and have one of your cream teas before I leave," she told Marion.

"You do that." Marion tilted her head to look at her with her penetrating eyes. "Staying a while, are you?"

"A few days."

"Are you on your own?"

Jane chuckled. "You've probably gathered by now that Marion likes to know everyone's business."

"I'm just being friendly," Marion said indignantly.

"Of course you are." Jane heaved herself up again

49

and put the empty box into a back room that was divided from the front by a black—velvet curtain.

"Yes, I'm here on my own," Lisa told Marion. "Taking a short holiday from work."

Jane came back. "If you're looking for things for your gallery, I might be able to help put you in touch with one or two good local artists."

"I'd like that, but I'm afraid my clients tend to buy mainly Canadian."

Jane's dark eyebrows rose. "Clients, eh? Sounds impressive. You must be doing well."

Lisa merely smiled and went to the door. "I'll probably be back. I'll need a few souvenirs to take home with me."

"Bob next door sells terrific glazed pixies," Jane said, her eyes twinkling.

Lisa laughed. "Thanks, but I think I'll pass on those." She opened the door. "See you again."

"Probably in the bar at the Stag," Jane said. "I'm usually in there on a Saturday night."

"She's usually in there every night," Marion said.

"Okay. I'll keep an eye out for you there." Lisa held the door for Marion, but she was not ready to go yet. It was obvious that Marion Heasley was another stock village character: the village gossip.

It was also obvious that the Kingsleys of Charnwood Court were not at all popular with the inhabitants of the village. Or, at least, not with these particular two inhabitants.

Lisa wondered why.

CHAPTER SIX

LISA WALKED UP THE HIGH STREET TO THE STAG'S Head, her mind filled with thoughts about Charnwood Court. So engrossed was she that she didn't see the child who was gazing into the bay window of an old—fashioned candy store called Susan's Sweets until it was too late. Her legs collided with the child's small body.

"I'm so sorry," Lisa said, grabbing hold of the little girl to stop her from falling. "Are you okay?" she asked, bending to peer into the child's frightened face.

A man in a leather jacket and jeans came out of the shop, holding two ice—cream cones. He frowned when he saw Lisa holding the child. "Can I help you?" he asked, but his icy tone said, *What the hell are you doing with my child?*

The little girl went to him. "It's all right, Daddy. The lady bumped into me by mistake."

"Oh, I see," the child's father said, but he was still frowning.

"Sorry," Lisa said. "I wasn't looking where I was going."

"That's okay." His flickering smile changed his expression, but it still wasn't exactly friendly.

"I am sorry," Lisa said again. "Are you sure I didn't hurt you?" she asked the child.

"Of course not." The little girl gave Lisa a sunny smile.

"Are you staying in Charnwood?" the child's father asked.

Lisa had the impression that he was asking from mere politeness, not actual interest. "Just for a few days."

51

"I hear an accent. Canadian?"

"Yes. How did you guess? Most people here seem to think I'm American."

"There's also a hint of British background there."

"You sound like Professor Higgins in *My Fair Lady*. How do you do that?"

"Daddy, can I have my ice cream now? It's dripping down your arm."

"So it is. Sorry about that." He handed his daughter her pink ice cream.

Taking it, she turned to back to grin at Lisa, her small tongue darting out to lick the ice cream. "What's your name?"

"Lisa. Lisa Cooper."

Her father hesitated, looking from his child to Lisa. "I'm Richard Barton, by the way, and this is—"

"Emily Barton," said his daughter.

"We'd shake hands all round," he said, "but I don't think you want to be coated with strawberry or pistachio ice cream."

"Oh, I don't know," Lisa said. "I could always lick it off." For some reason, her words sounded slightly salacious, and she felt warmth rise in her cheeks. She caught a glimmer of amusement in the man's eyes.

"Would you like one?" he asked. "What flavor?"

Convinced that he was merely trying to be polite, Lisa was about to say no and walk away, but then she saw the silent appeal on Emily's face. "I'd love one. I've no idea what flavor, though."

"Perhaps you wouldn't mind getting it yourself? I don't think Mrs. Anstey would want us to drip all over her floor." He ran his tongue around the dripping cone. "But it's our treat, remember."

Lisa went into the little shop, halting just inside the

door to breathe in the scents of sugar and licorice and chocolate. The floor—to—ceiling wooden shelves were lined with tall glass jars filled with sweets of every description: licorice allsorts, brightly colored jelly beans, chocolate toffees, orange sticks of barley sugar, dark red aniseed balls . . .

A chill ran over her. As she gazed around, the vivid colors and the rows of glass jars all seemed suddenly to blur and darken, and then began slowly revolving about her. She put a wavering hand to her head, clutching at the wooden countertop to steady herself.

"What would you like, my lovey?" said a woman's voice, but it was muffled and seemed to be coming from a great distance.

"Jelly babies, please. Four ounces of jelly babies."

"A quarter of jelly babies. Right, my lovey."

The shadows receded and the little shop steadied and grew brighter. Lisa blinked. "I'm sorry. No sweets. I'd like the clotted cream ice cream. A single cone, please."

The shopkeeper looked over her steel—rimmed glasses at Lisa. "Yes, I heard you the first time."

"Pardon?"

"I said," the woman snapped, "I heard you the first time. No need to repeat it. I'm not deaf." Muttering to herself, she scooped the ice cream into a cone.

"Sorry," Lisa said. She felt a bit like Alice in Wonderland. Had she really asked for the ice cream twice? She took the cone and gave the woman a pound coin. "Do do you have jelly babies?"

" 'Course we do." This time there was no accusation of Lisa repeating herself. "How many? Hundred grams?"

"No, thank you. Just the ice cream."

The shopkeeper raised her pencil—thin gray

53

eyebrows and shook her head in exasperation.

Obviously, Lisa thought, her request for four ounces of jelly babies had been solely in her imagination. As she took her change, a shiver ran across her shoulders. She was glad to get outside, into the reassuring sunshine.

"That looks really boring," Emily said. "It's just plain old vanilla."

"Actually," Lisa said, "it's made from clotted cream." She flashed a smile at Richard Barton. "Very decadent."

"Quite right, too. You said you were on holiday." He gave her a pound coin, frowning at her as she was about to protest.

She handed him the change Mrs. Anstey had given her. "Thank you both very much. This is a real treat for me."

As they walked along the sidewalk, Emily skipped between them, chatting away. "How old are you, Emily?" Lisa asked.

"I'm four, nearly five."

Four, thought Lisa. The same age she'd been when her parents had died, when she'd left Charnwood. She had probably skipped along this same sidewalk, chattering away to one or both of her parents.

Stopping to buy jelly babies in the sweetshop.

Lisa halted, breathing fast.

"Are you okay?" Richard asked.

She drew in a calming breath. "I'm fine. The ice cream got to one of my teeth, that's all."

"Ouch!" said Emily.

"Ouch is right." Lisa quickly changed the subject. "Are you on holiday, too?"

"No, we live here. At least, near here," Richard said. "We're taking the morning off."

"Daddy works in Taunton."

"That's quite a long way from here, isn't it? I remember seeing it on the map. What made you decide to live so far away from where you work?"

Richard turned his face to look across the street. "I prefer the countryside. It's better for Emily to grow up here."

"Daddy doesn't like Taunton much. It's where Mummy died. She was in the hospital."

Lisa was stricken with guilt. That's what came of asking too many questions. "I'm sorry," she said softly.

"So are we." Lisa felt the sticky warmth of Emily's hand in hers. "We really miss her, don't we, Daddy?"

He nodded, his face still averted from both of them. Then his eyes met Lisa's over Emily's head and he gave her a twisted little smile.

They were both swamped by awkwardness, strangers confronted by unforeseen emotion.

"Well," Lisa said quickly, "I must go and unpack."

"Where are you staying?"

"At the Stag's Head."

"You could have found a bed and breakfast for half the price."

"I know, but I fell in love with the place. Besides, I wanted to get a room right away."

They walked up the street to the hotel. Richard held out his hand. "Have a good holiday."

"Thanks."

Emily's hand was still clutching Lisa's. She looked up at her, disappointment turning down the corners of her mouth. "Aren't we going to see you again?"

"Miss Cooper has things to do," her father told her.

"That's right. I'm going to unpack and—"

"Can we help you unpack?" Emily asked eagerly.

"I'm good at it. I help Daddy unpack his clothes when he comes back from London."

Richard gave Lisa a faint smile. "She doesn't want to let you go." He hesitated, then said, "Tell you what. Have you had lunch?"

"Not yet."

"Why don't we have lunch in the garden at the back of the Stag?"

Lisa hesitated. She felt that the invitation had been forced from him by his daughter. "I was going to get settled in first."

"Fine." He took Emily's hand. "Let's leave Miss—"

"Lisa," Lisa said.

"Okay. Let's leave Lisa to get her case unpacked."

"And then she'll have lunch with us, Daddy?"

"She probably has her own plans for the rest of her day."

"I was going to see Charnwood Court," Lisa told him. "The woman in the art supply shop told me it was open to the public today so I—"

"We're going there, too!" Emily yelled excitedly. "To visit Aunt Rachel."

Lisa stared at her.

"Rachel Kingsley, who lives at the Court, is my aunt," Richard explained.

"We can all go and see her together." Emily jigged up and down with excitement.

Lisa and Richard exchanged wry glances. After another awkward moment, he seemed to come to a decision and, for the first time since they'd met, gave her a genuine, full—blown smile that warmed his tawny eyes, turning them to gold in the sunlight. "Why not meet us for lunch after you've unpacked," he suggested, "and then you can walk up to the house with us?"

"The house?"

"Chamwood Court."

CHAPTER SEVEN

LISA COULDN'T BELIEVE HER LUCK. NOT ONLY WAS SHE going to see Charnwood Court, but she also had in Richard Barton a source of information about the Kingsley family that lived there.

"Why don't we leave the car in the hotel car park and walk?" Richard had suggested after lunch. "It's too nice a day to drive, and it's not that far to the house. About a mile and a half."

As she walked with him and his daughter along the narrow road lined with hedges of hawthorn iced with frothy white blossoms, Lisa marveled at how far she had come since her arrival in Charnwood only a few hours ago.

Had it not been for Emily, the walk might have been a silent one, but her constant chatter made up for her father's lack of conversation. He made no more than a polite effort, giving Lisa brief answers to her questions about Charnwood and the surrounding countryside. It was obvious that his mind was on something far more important than her.

Annoyed, Lisa turned her complete attention to Emily, and found to her surprise that a child's conversation could be an absolute delight. Emily asked constant questions, her mind darting from birds to flowers to snails, with barely a breath in between. Lisa had had very little to do with children. Even as a teenager, when her friends had made money from baby—sitting, she'd preferred to shovel snow or cut grass. Emily was a revelation.

From the fields beyond the hedgerow came the incessant bleating of lambs. "The lambs are getting bigger," Emily said, skipping ahead of them.

"What a shame we can't see them," Lisa said.

"We will," Emily assured her. "As soon as we get to the top of the hill, we'll see them. Lots of them." She grabbed her father's hand. "Come on, Daddy. Lisa wants to see the lambs."

He raised his eyebrows at Lisa, conjuring up a faint smile. "Very bossy, my daughter."

Lisa smiled back, thinking how different this reserved man looked when he smiled. Like the sudden appearance of the sun in a sullen gray sky.

When they reached the top of the steep lane, Lisa saw not only the sloping fields dotted with sheep and lambs, but also a broad tree—lined drive leading to an imposing gabled house. It appeared to be built from the same golden limestone that had been used in the Stag's Head.

"Charnwood Court," Richard announced.

"That's where Aunt Rachel lives," Emily said.

As she gazed at the large house, in its lush green setting of parkland and gardens, Lisa was swamped with doubt. Once again, she had no sense of recognition. In fact, she was convinced that there was no way this mansion could ever have been her home. To someone who'd been raised in a small suburban bungalow in midwest Canada, it was utterly alien.

She was tempted to turn back, but knew that this would disappoint Emily, who was now leading her through the open wroughtiron gates in the high stone wall that surrounded the grounds.

"Afternoon, Mr. Barton," said the man in the little

wooden hut by the gate. "Hi, Emily."

"Hi, Joe. This is Lisa. She's visiting from—" Emily had to stop and think for a second. "From Canada."

"Is she now? Welcome to Charnwood Court, miss."

The notice by the hut announced that the entrance fee for the grounds alone was two pounds, plus another two pounds for a tour of the house. Lisa's hand went to the purse slung across her shoulder, but Richard quickly shook his head.

"No charge for Mr. Barton's guest," Joe said.

Lisa felt embarrassed. "Thanks," she mumbled. She wasn't really Mr. Barton's guest at all. They were strangers, people who'd met by chance a short time ago. And he'd made it perfectly clear that, but for his daughter's insistence, he'd prefer to keep it that way.

"Enjoy your visit to the Court," Joe said.

She thanked him and followed Richard and Emily to the path beside the driveway. She was surprised to see how overgrown with wild grasses and weeds the path was.

"Most people drive in," Richard said, as if he'd read her mind. "Watch for the nettles," he shouted after Emily, as she ran on ahead of them.

As they drew near to the house, disappointment surged through Lisa. At a distance, with its gabled roof and mullioned windows, the house was picture—perfect. Up close, it was scarred and cracked. It was like seeing a beautiful woman from afar and then, when you came close to her, realizing that she was blemished and raddled with age.

An uneasy shiver ran across her shoulders. Was this a sign of recognition, she wondered, or merely the pang of seeing a once—beautiful house that had so obviously fallen on hard times? Whatever it was, she felt

59

instinctively that here was a house that had been sadly neglected. Dark strands of ivy trailed across the upper windows, so that the house appeared half—blind. Its stone walls were crumbling or, in places, clumsily patched in a lighter color, emphasizing the effect of unsightly blemishes on an ancient face.

"It must once have been very beautiful," Lisa said but then, realizing how rude that sounded, added hastily, "I mean, it *is* beautiful. Those lovely mullioned windows and—"

"You were right first time," Richard said. "It needs a lot of work. These old places cost a fortune to maintain properly."

She was tempted to ask what it would cost to cut back ivy and let light and air into the house, but kept quiet.

Richard went to a green door in the garden's brick wall marked PRIVATE, but Lisa hung back. "I'll join the visitors and pay my two pounds," she said, nodding in the direction of a sign pointing to the stone steps leading up to the front door.

Richard came back to her. "If you insist."

"I do."

"Okay. We'll come and find you once I've finished talking business with Alec."

"Business?" Lisa said impulsively, knowing she sounded as nosy as Marion Heasley and hating herself for it.

"I'm the family solicitor."

Lisa couldn't hide her astonishment. "You don't look one bit like an English solicitor."

"How do you think an English solicitor should look?" Richard demanded, amusement lurking in his eyes.

"Oh, a tweed jacket, smoking a pipe . . . that sort of thing."

He laughed outright, and Emily grinned up at him, not quite understanding, but obviously enjoying her father's laughter. "You've been reading too many old—fashioned English mysteries," he told Lisa.

She made a face. "I suppose I have. I love them. The next thing you'll be telling me is that you don't go hunting, either."

"No, I don't. Never have." His expression grew serious. "But it's best to avoid that subject around here. There's a great deal of ill feeling about the banning of stag hunting on Exmoor." He glanced up at the house. "Especially here."

"I won't mention hunting, I promise." Lisa hesitated, and then said, "Just out of interest, as I am going to be looking around, can you tell me exactly who lives here?"

"Alec Kingsley and his wife Rachel."

"Have they any children?"

"One daughter, my cousin Kate."

"I don't like Kate," Emily said, frowning. "She's mean."

"Out of the mouths of babes," Richard said. "Kate's what you might term difficult."

Lisa decided she'd asked quite enough questions for now. The rest she would have to find out later. She had so many more things to learn. For instance, if these Kingsleys were related to her, could her father have grown up in this house? If so, it was possible that Alec Kingsley could be her uncle, her father's brother. Which, she suddenly realized, would make Kate Kingsley *her* cousin as well. The thought of being related, albeit by marriage, to Richard and his daughter made her feel strange.

She also felt a twinge of guilt for keeping her real

interest in seeing the house and meeting the Kingsley family from Richard, but that couldn't be helped.

She waved goodbye to Emily and went up the steps and into the house.

"The next tour starts at two—fifteen," she was told when she bought her ticket at the corner desk. She joined the group of about twenty people who had formed an orderly line and were talking in muted voices while they waited "Lovely, isn't it?" said the woman in front of her.

"Yes, it is." Lisa gazed about her. It was lovely. Somehow the fact that the flagstoned floor was uneven and the red—velvet floor—to—ceiling draperies faded seemed right for this ancient wood—paneled hall.

A large wicker basket filled with massive logs, about three feet long, sat by the open fireplace in the wall. The fireplace seemed to brighten, the rest of the hall fading into shadow, and Lisa saw a vision of a roaring, crackling fire, its leaping orange flames ready to greet you when you came in from the snowy coldness.

A child's shrill voice suddenly rang out, startling Lisa as it echoed in the hall. Her right hand curled involuntarily, her fingers clutching some phantom circular object.

A ball.

On a rainy day this would be a perfect place to bounce a ball, to throw it across the wide expanse of the hall to someone who would catch it and throw it back.

When Lisa's hands came together as if to catch the ball, a child laughed softly in her ear.

"Good afternoon, ladies and gentlemen." A woman's brisk, schoolmarm voice hurtled Lisa back to reality. "If you would like to move into the center of the hall, we can begin our tour of Charnwood Court."

As the group moved forward, Lisa wondered if her vision of the fire and the child had been a figment of her imagination—or an actual memory. She also wondered if this woman was Richard's aunt. With her sensible laced shoes and tweed skirt she didn't quite fit her idea of the woman she'd heard about in the crafts shop.

The guide adjusted her glasses, which covered slightly protuberant eyes, and gave the group a perfunctory smile. "My name is Maud Birkett. I will be your guide for this tour of Charnwood Court. Please do not hesitate to ask any questions as we proceed through the house."

Lisa felt a twinge of disappointment. Thank heavens she'd met Richard, or she might still know absolutely nothing about the Kingsley family. She had the feeling she wouldn't get much out of this woman.

But as she explored the house with the tour group she soon discovered that British people had a passionate interest in the families who lived in these old houses, especially the present members of the family. It was as if these houses were *their* heritage, too, and they had a right to know everything about them.

In the hall, the guide confirmed that the Kingsley family actually lived there—in one wing that was closed to the public—and that they had a daughter, Kate. In the paneled bedroom with the four—poster bed draped in sapphire—blue damask, the group was told that the house had been built in 1650. "Until fairly recently, it had been occupied by members of the Templeton family for three centuries."

"The Templeton family," Lisa exclaimed. "I thought—" She hesitated, aware that people had turned to look at her. "You said that the Kingsley family lived here."

"So it does. Now." The tour guide's lips thinned, so that they almost disappeared. "It became the property of the Kingsley family when Celia Templeton died." She turned away abruptly. "We will now move on to the dressing room. The room is very small, so I will ask you to move into it a few people at a time. That way you will all be able to clearly see the fine collection of Chinese porcelain in the corner."

Lisa hung back. She wasn't particularly interested in Chinese porcelain. What really interested her was this new revelation about the Kingsley family and the house. If it had belonged to someone called Celia Templeton, this probably wasn't the right Kingsley family after all.

Perhaps she had never been inside this house before and the feeling she'd had in the hall was pure imagination on her part. Certainly nothing else she'd seen had triggered any memories.

The group moved on, fanning out in the upper hallway, which was lined with old portraits. "Are these all members of the Kingsley family?" someone asked.

"No, the Templeton family," Maud Birkett said, a hint of impatience in her voice. "They're all from the eighteenth or nineteenth century."

"Aren't there any that are more recent?" Lisa heard herself asking. "None of Celia Templeton, for instance."

Frowning, the guide turned to confront her. "No, there are not." She turned to lead the way into another room. "And here we have the nursery."

To a chorus of "Ah!" and "Isn't it lovely?" the group entered the large, sunlit room. Lisa went to one of the tall windows and saw that they overlooked the garden at the rear of the house. Inside a high brick wall, a swathe of green lawn was lined with beds of roses. A path led through an archway to small flower beds bordered by low hedges of golden—box.

Lisa sat down in the cushioned window seat to survey the nursery.

"Kindly do not sit there," she was told. Lisa jumped up, her face warm. "The fabric is very worn," the guide said.

A woman nearby grimaced at Lisa and gave her a friendly smile. "Makes you feel like a kid again, doesn't she?" she whispered, as the guide moved away.

Lisa nodded. A rocking horse, its glazed paint cracked and peeling, stood in front of the fireplace. The guide set it rocking, its rockers squeaking on the wooden floor. Then she turned away to open the games cupboard, where ancient Meccano sets and old—fashioned board games, like Snakes and Ladders and Ludo, were piled high on shelves, their broken boxes mended with yellowing tape.

A group of people had clustered around a display at the far end of the nursery. Lisa went to see what they were looking at. When a few of them moved away, she saw that it was a large doll's house set on a rectangular table. She had always loved doll's houses. When she was seven she'd asked for one for Christmas, but her parents had bought her a bright plastic Fisher—Price cabin. She hadn't been able to hide her disappointment. "This isn't a real doll's house," she'd wailed.

Now this *was* a real doll's house. There were two floors of rooms filled with exquisitely fashioned furniture. Crystal chandeliers dangled from the ceilings, paintings with perfect detail hung on the walls. There was even a miniature rocking horse in the nursery, almost an exact copy of the one that was still squeaking in the background. Lisa put out one finger to set the tiny horse rocking.

She stiffened as she breathed in a strong spicy—sweet aroma that she couldn't identify.

"How many times do I have to tell you that you must not touch!"

Startled, Lisa sprang back, her right hand stinging from the hard slap that accompanied the reprimand. Wide—eyed, she stared at the people beside her, but they were engaged in admiring the house. And the tour guide was over by the bookshelves, talking about the collection of children's books.

Despite the warmth of the sunshine on the windows, Lisa felt icy cold. The walls seemed to close in on her, threatening to crush her. Fighting for breath, she turned to rush from the nursery out into the upper hall.

As she stood there shivering, hanging on to the stair railing, her heart hammered against her ribs. She forced herself to breathe slowly and evenly.

The guide came out of the nursery. "Are you all right?" she asked in a low voice. "I saw you leave and wondered if you weren't feeling well."

Lisa saw her through blurred vision. "I'm fine, thanks. It was a—a little too crowded in there for me."

Maud Birkett nodded. She hesitated for a moment, then said, "I do hope you didn't mind me asking you not to sit on the cushions." She gave Lisa an apologetic smile. "The fabric is worn so terribly thin that they are almost falling apart."

"Of course I didn't mind. I shouldn't have sat on them."

"I'm sure one person doing so wouldn't hurt. It's just the accumulation of people sitting there that could harm them." The woman peered more closely at Lisa. "Are you sure you're feeling all right? You look very pale."

"I'm fine. Really."

"The tearoom in the stable yard is open. Perhaps you should go and get yourself a cup of tea."

"I think I will." Lisa was about to start down the stairs, and then turned back. "Would you mind telling me something?"

The guide looked wary. "If I can."

"The last member of the Templeton family who lived here—"

A shadow passed over the woman's face. "Do you mean Celia Templeton?"

"Yes." Lisa hesitated, sensing the invisible barrier that had gone up between them as soon as she'd said the name Templeton. "Is she still alive?"

"No, she is not."

"What happened to her?"

The guide frowned. "Why do you ask?"

"I don't know." Lisa gave a little shrug. "I just wondered, that's all."

Maud Birkett hesitated for a moment, an almost imperceptible quivering about her thin mouth. Then she said, "She drowned. Celia Templeton was drowned."

CHAPTER EIGHT

LISA WAS GLAD TO ESCAPE FROM THE HOUSE'S unsettling aura. She sat on a wooden bench by the gravel pathway and stared at the roses, breathing in their subtle fragrance. But, despite the heat of the sun on her back, she felt she would never be truly warm again.

Celia Templeton had drowned. "Was drowned," the tour guide had said. The little change in wording had added a sinister touch to the bald statement.

What connection—if any—did Celia Templeton have

with her? And when had she drowned?

Lisa sensed that she wouldn't get much more from Maud Birkett. As it was, the tour guide's suspicions had obviously been aroused. And she couldn't very well ask the Kingsley family these questions, could she?

Her blood surged, and she kicked at the gravel beneath her feet. *Why the hell not?* she asked herself indignantly. *Why shouldn't I ask as much as I want to? I've nothing to hide.*

That was true. Yet something in Maud Birkett's attitude told her that she had to tread very carefully if she wanted to find out any more about Celia Templeton. And she certainly did want to. Had she drowned while swimming, for instance? Was it while she was on holiday or in the sea near her home? Or in her own bathtub?

The one question that was uppermost in Lisa's mind, she forced down, way down inside her, not wanting to deal with it until she had far, far more knowledge.

She was sitting in the busy tea shop, eating scones covered with a layer of clotted cream and homemade strawberry jam, when Richard found her.

"There you are." He looked at her, a smile flickering on his lips. "I should have known you'd be here."

Lisa wiped her mouth with a paper napkin, sure she must have jam and cream smeared all over her face. "Why?" she demanded.

"You obviously have a thing about cream."

"This sort of cream, I do. I never eat the stuff at home."

Richard sat down opposite her, looking a little incongruous perched on the small, red-gingham cushioned chair. "How did you like the house?"

"It's—it's really lovely." She couldn't help the little

hint of hesitation in her voice. She had found the house intriguing, but also infinitely disturbing.

Richard looked somber. "It needs a great deal of repair and restoration, I'm afraid."

Lisa suddenly remembered what she'd heard earlier from Jane Tallis, but decided she'd rather hear the facts from Richard. "Are they planning to do some work on it?"

"The family's on the brink of selling the place. I believe the plan is to turn it into a hotel."

"Oh, what a shame!" Now that she'd seen the house Lisa really meant it. "It would be terrible to see the place all modernized and changed."

"I don't think the buyers intend to change it that much. They're a bit cagey about their plans—and their identity, for that matter. But I understand the plan is to retain the appearance of a country house and estate. That goes over well with both business conferences and wealthy tourists." There was an element of distaste in his tone.

Lisa eyed him. "Forgive me for asking, but are you advising the family to sell it?"

He leaned back in the chair, one arm flung across the back of the empty chair beside him. "I don't know what else to do. The house is desperately in need of repair. They could give it to the National Trust, but to do that they'd also need to give the Trust sufficient funds for its upkeep. Funds they just don't have." He sighed. "Problem is, Alec loves this house. It's his home."

"He must hate the thought of leaving the house where his ancestors lived," Lisa said lightly.

"Actually, they're not his ancestors."

A waitress approached them. "Hi, Mr. Barton. I didn't see you come in. Where's Emily?"

"She's in the house with my aunt."

"What can I get you?"

"Nothing, thanks, Jean. I'm just waiting for my friend here to finish her tea and scones."

The waitress looked at Lisa with an added gleam of interest in her eye. "I brought you your bill. No hurry." She was about to put it on the table, but Richard took it from her, and drew a five—pound note from his wallet.

"No," Lisa protested, but the waitress had already taken the money. "I'll pay you back," Lisa told Richard.

"Okay. You can buy me a pint at the Stag later on."

"I'll do that."

"Are you going to finish that scone? You've still got half a dish of cream left."

Lisa had no intention of eating a scone oozing jam and cream in front of him. "I've had enough, thanks."

"Sure? Then we'll go and find Emily and you can meet the family."

A chorus of *Hi's* and *Good-bye's* came from the staff as they left. "Bring Emily in next time you come," one of them said. Richard promised that he would.

As they walked across the stable courtyard, Lisa wondered how she could return to the subject of Alec Kingsley. Probably by being direct, she decided. Richard didn't seem the type of person you could be circumspect with.

"You were saying that Mr. Kingsley's ancestors didn't live here. I thought the house had belonged to the Kingsley family for centuries."

"No, it belonged to the family of Alec's wife."

Lisa was puzzled. "You mean it belongs to your aunt's family? Then that makes it your family as well, doesn't it?"

"No, no. I meant Alec's first wife. My aunt is his sec-

70

ond wife." He frowned. "Didn't you see all the Templeton portraits on your tour?"

"Yes, I did. But I hadn't realized who they were. I mean . . . in relation to your aunt's husband." It was all a little too complicated for her to unravel at present. "The tour guide said something about a woman called Celia Temple—"

Richard halted abruptly. "Best not to mention that name around here."

"I'm sorry," Lisa said, taken aback by his curt tone.

"Who was the tour guide today?"

"Maud something."

"Maud Birkett." Richard's mouth tightened into a grim line. "I should have guessed." He became preoccupied, as if he'd forgotten she was there. Then he turned and caught her worried expression. "Sorry. It's just that . . . we try to avoid that subject."

"You mean—" She hesitated, reluctant to say the name again after his warning.

"A family tragedy," Richard said succinctly, as he took a pathway around the back of the house. "I know it sounds rather Gothic, but the family prefers that the subject be avoided entirely."

She was being well and truly warned off. She could hardly ask, "How was Celia Templeton drowned?" now, could she?

She began to think that she had the wrong Kingsley family after all. Their family tragedy was the drowning of a woman called Celia Templeton, not the death of a young married couple in a fiery car crash. Not one person in Charnwood had mentioned her parents' death in relation to this Kingsley family.

Richard led her into a small garden, surrounded by a high stone wall that blocked out most of the sunlight.

71

Emily was playing outside on the terrace, which was really little more than a patio.

"Hi, Lisa," she shouted, springing up when she saw them. "Come and see the kittens."

"Really, Emily," said a woman's voice from inside the house. "Must you screech like that?"

"It's Daddy," Emily replied in a more subdued voice. "He's brought Lisa back with him."

"Hello again," Lisa said to Emily. "What darling kittens." She bent to pick one up, a fluffy tortoiseshell that squealed in protest when she lifted it. "Oh, you're adorable," she told it, rubbing her face against its fur.

"Have you got a cat?" Emily asked her.

"I have."

"What's its name?"

"Paloma."

"That's a weird name. How do you spell it?"

Lisa told her. "She's a girl cat."

"I hope someone's looking after her for you," Emily said, her voice as stern as her father's had been a few minutes ago.

"Of course," Lisa said. "My daddy is looking after her for me."

"Come along, chatterbox," Richard said. "Enough questions. Let's go in and say hello."

Although she'd been eager to meet the Kingsleys, now that the moment had come Lisa felt nervous. After all, despite her reservations, there was a chance that Alec Kingsley could be closely related to her, wasn't there? Not that she cared about that, of course, but still it made her feel anxious about meeting him and his family.

Richard had stepped inside and was already talking about her to the invisible occupants of the room. Lisa

72

put down the kitten and followed him through the open French window.

There were two people in the room, which was fairly small in comparison with the rooms Lisa had seen on the tour. A combination of library and sitting room, it looked as if the occupants had had to fit too much furniture into too small a space, but it was still a charming room. Richard introduced her to his aunt first, who welcomed her with an icy smile and cool greeting.

Mr. Kingsley's greeting was far warmer. "How do you do, Miss Cooper. Richard tells us you are visiting from Canada."

Lisa took his outstretched hand and found hers squeezed in a strong grip. "That's right." She had an impression of muted power, controlled energy. In his late fifties or early sixties, Alec Kingsley was still a remarkably handsome man, with hair the color of burnished steel. He fixed his eyes on her with an inquiring look.

"What made you choose Exmoor—or Charnwood, for that matter—for your holiday?"

The direct question threw her for a moment. Then she rallied. "I was told that this part of the country was very beautiful."

"Is this your first visit to Britain?" asked Mrs. Kingsley. She had a dark—timbred voice, pitched low. Seeing the cigarette in her hand, Lisa wondered if her voice was husky from smoking. She surveyed Lisa with blue eyes that were widely spaced in her heart—shaped face, reminding Lisa of a pedigree Persian cat.

"No, this is my third visit," Lisa told her. "I'd done London and the Cotswolds before, so I thought I should see western England this time."

"Why Charnwood?"

"Oh, that was a last—minute decision. I had coffee in Minehead and someone there suggested I come here. She said it was a little too remote for the regular tourist crowd."

"Thank God for that," Mrs. Kingsley drawled. "We get enough day—trippers as it is." Her skin was pale, almost white, and the delicate, fine—lined complexion of her face suggested that the ash—blond color of her hair was—or had been—genuine. But now darker roots were showing, as if it had been a while since she'd had her hair colored. She had high cheekbones and a curving, lascivious mouth, painted with scarlet lipstick.

Emily danced around the room and halted between them. "This is Lisa," she shouted, excitement making her loud.

"Thank you, Emily. There is no need to yell." Mrs. Kingsley sat down and crossed very slim legs, her skirt fashionably short. "I'm afraid we weren't prepared for visitors. Has Richard asked you to tea?"

"No. No, of course not." Lisa felt her face grow warm with embarrassment. She should never have allowed herself to be forced upon them this way. To Rachel Kingsley, she was nothing but a stranger her nephew had met on the street.

"I must say that's not a very hospitable way to treat you," Alec Kingsley said, an edge to his voice. "You must forgive us, Miss Cooper. We don't seem to be very well organized today." He didn't even try to hide the frown he directed at his wife. "Please sit down," he told Lisa, "and we'll get you a drink."

"Thank you, but I've just had a huge cream tea in your tea shop. I couldn't eat another thing."

"I didn't suggest that you eat, did I?" Alec gave her a smile of great charm. "I said drink. What will it be: a gin and tonic? White wine?"

"Wine would be lovely, thank you."

"Let me get it," Richard said, crossing the room to go to the drinks' cart. He came back with a glass of chilled wine and handed it to Lisa.

"How did you enjoy your tour of the house?" Alec asked her.

"Very much."

"It's a lovely old place, isn't it?" Flashes of color appeared in his cheeks. "I'm biased, of course."

"I don't blame you at all."

Lisa could sense the strain in the air. At first she thought it was because she'd landed on them unexpectedly, but as they chatted with her, answering her questions about the house, she gained the impression that it was something they'd been discussing before she'd arrived that had upset them. Probably the sale of the house.

"Lisa's planning to spend a few days in Charnwood."

"Are you, indeed? Using it as a base to tour the area?"

"That's right," Lisa said. "I planned to do some sketching."

"Sketching?" Alec's voice was warm with enthusiasm. "Are you an artist?"

Lisa lifted her shoulders against the sudden shiver that ran down her spine like a cold gust of wind. "I used to be. Now I concentrate on selling other people's work."

"You have a studio?" He seemed genuinely interested.

"My partner and I have a small gallery." Lisa saw Richard glance at her for a split second.

"Have you a specialty?" Alec asked.

"Mainly native Canadian works of art. Particularly Inuit prints and carvings."

"Fascinating."

"Where are you staying in Charnwood?" Rachel Kingsley's intervention put an end to her husband's questions.

"The Stag's Head."

"They'll rob you blind in that place," Alec said. He paused for a moment, then added in a casual tone, "We do B&B here, you know."

Rachel's mouth compressed into a thin line and she stalked away to stare out the French window.

"Do you really?" Lisa said, her heart pounding.

His gaze flicked to his wife's stiff back. "Helps a little with the expense of keeping this place from falling down completely." He gave Lisa a little smile to hide his obvious embarrassment.

"It must cost an enormous amount to keep it going," Lisa said.

"It does," Alec replied. "I don't want to sound as if I'm touting for business, but why don't you consider moving in here? I know for a fact that our rates are much lower than the Stag's. And our rooms are far larger and infinitely more interesting. You could move in early tomorrow evening, as soon as the last tour has gone around the house."

Lisa couldn't believe her good luck. "Are you sure?" she asked, wondering if they had suggested it because of Richard.

Alec gave her a twisted little smile. "Don't think we're doing this as a special favor to you. We have people staying here most of the time. An Australian couple left on Friday, so there's a room available."

"I must tell you that Alec cooks fabulous breakfasts,"

76

Richard said.

"Does he? That decides it, then. I love English breakfasts." Lisa knew she sounded a little too enthusiastic, but their embarrassment was catching.

"Lisa likes ice cream," Emily said.

"For breakfast?" Lisa asked, rolling her eyes at Emily. Everyone laughed. Lisa was grateful for this lightening of what had been a slightly uncomfortable exchange. She sensed that Alec Kingsley was a proud man. One who found it difficult to accept his straitened circumstances.

His wife's scornful attitude didn't help matters. No wonder the villagers talked about her with such ill—concealed dislike.

"I'd love to stay here," Lisa said. "It's such a beautiful house!"

"Capital! We'll discuss the details later. Now how about some more wine?"

Lisa declined, not wanting to outstay her welcome. She could afford to postpone all her questions until later, once she'd settled in at Charnwood Court.

CHAPTER NINE

WHEN SHE RETURNED TO THE STAG'S HEAD, LISA found a sourfaced older woman, wearing a shiny blouse in an unbecoming color of sage—green, at the reception desk. Lisa told her that she wouldn't need the room for a second night.

"Moving into the Court, are you?" the woman asked.

Lisa stared at her. "How did you know?"

"They're always doing it. No sooner does someone book in here than the high—and—mighty Kingsleys manage to sneak them away from us."

"I thought the hotel was full," Lisa said defensively.

"It is now, but the Kingsleys do it all the time." The woman's small mouth pursed up liked a prune. "I'm sorry, Miss Cooper, but I'll have to ask you to pay for tomorrow night unless someone comes in as a casual and takes it."

Damn! Lisa wasn't prepared to pay for two rooms. She would have to postpone moving into Charnwood Court until Monday, which meant losing a day of snooping. Oh well, she'd just need to keep her eyes and ears open this evening, when she met Richard in the bar.

"Why don't we leave it that I'll move out tomorrow if someone else wants the room?" she suggested. "If not, I'll stay until Monday morning, as originally planned."

The woman shrugged. "Suit yourself."

Richard had suggested meeting at eight o'clock, so Lisa ate early, choosing a light meal of spinach salad in a balsamic vinaigrette dressing and grilled salmon with peas and tiny new potatoes. As she sat in a corner of the dining room drinking coffee, she found herself wishing Jerry was there with her so that she could share her day's adventures with him.

She promised herself that she'd call him later.

When she went into the bar, it was crowded, people spilling out the doors into the garden at the rear of the inn.

She found Richard standing by the door, holding a glass mug filled to the brim with ale, topped with creamy froth. "It's a madhouse in here," he said. "Let me get you a drink, then we'll go outside."

"What you're drinking looks good."

"It's a local bitter. Are you sure? It won't be cold, you know."

"I can get lager at home. I can't get this. But a smaller glass than yours, please."

"A half of bitter. Okay."

"And don't forget I'm paying." Lisa started to look in her bag for her wallet.

"Pay me later."

As Lisa watched him quietly make his way through the crowd, a touch on one person's shoulder, a few words of greeting to another, she reflected that the open animosity the village had for the Kingsleys didn't seem to have extended to Richard Barton. Yet she wasn't sure that he was fully accepted, either. There were no signs of warm friendship, no "Hi there, Rich!" or whatever friends said to each other in an English village pub. Of course, Richard himself was rather aloof. She wondered if he'd always been that way, or whether it was the effect of his wife's death. He hadn't said exactly when his wife had died, of course, but Lisa guessed that it must have been in the last couple of years. Certainly, Emily seemed to remember her mother.

As he made his way back, carefully holding aloft the two glass mugs, he caught her watching him and smiled at her. Once again, the smile created such a change in his habitually grave expression that a couple of people who intercepted it turned to look at her, to see who it was that he was with.

"Let's get out of here," he said to her.

Lisa took her beer from him and followed him through the front door and around the inn, into the back garden. They found a table at the foot of the garden, away from the noise and the bright beam of the spotlights.

"I can't stay long," Richard said. "I left Emily up at the Court. I don't like to keep her up too late."

"I'm sorry. You should have said . . ."

"Not at all. My aunt keeps telling me I should socialize more. She practically pushed me out the door." He shifted uneasily on the wooden bench and quickly changed the subject. "Did you manage to cancel the room for tomorrow?"

Lisa made a face. "Sort of. The woman I spoke to said I'd probably have to pay for it if I canceled. I don't—"

"That's nonsense. Must have been Paula Willand. She's the landlord's wife. Not very obliging."

"You're right, but I can understand. After all, I did reserve the room for two nights. If they can't rent it to someone else, I'll move into your aunt's place on Monday, instead. But whoever she is, she was pretty sour about it."

"I'm afraid there's no love lost between the Willands and my aunt and uncle."

"I noticed." Lisa hesitated, wondering if she should say more. "There seems to be some bad feeling against them in the village."

Richard's face became a tight mask. "Gossip can be truly evil." His tone made the back of Lisa's neck tingle.

"What a shame. Charnwood seems such a pretty village. I suppose that's the disadvantage of living in such a small place. Everyone knows everyone else's business."

"Or they think they do," Richard said through gritted teeth. He took a deep breath, as if making a conscious effort to relax. "Tell me about your art gallery in Canada."

She told him, but soon became aware that he wasn't really concentrating. As before, he was making the right responses, but she could sense that his mind was on something else.

Eventually, growing tired of awkward pauses and abrupt answers to her questions, she drained her glass. "You must be wanting to get back to Emily."

He glanced at his watch. "Yes, I should."

"How much for the drinks?" She was aware of sounding as abrupt as he did, but by now she no longer cared. She'd given this taciturn man a chance to be friendly, and he'd remained brusque and aloof.

"Three pounds will cover it," he told her. She handed him the three coins. "Thanks." Richard swung his legs over the bench and stood up, tall against the darkening, pink—streaked sky. "I'm afraid I've been rotten company tonight."

"Not at all," she answered crisply.

If she had known him better, she would have said, "You sure have." On the other hand, if she had known him better, she might have said, "I understand." But she didn't understand. All she knew was that this man seemed beset by demons. And he wasn't about to let his guard down with a stranger.

He looked down at the worn grass beneath his feet, and then away to the skyline. "It's been fifteen months since Angela died. I thought it would get easier, but it doesn't."

Lisa was so stunned she couldn't think what to say. If he'd been a good friend, like Jerry, she would have put her arms around him and hugged him close. But this man was a stranger, and a reserved one, at that. She was afraid to touch him, but instinct overrode her reticence and she put her hand on his upper arm. His muscles tensed at her touch.

"It takes time," she told him softly. "I know it's not quite the same, but my mother died of cancer a few months ago. My dad's utterly lost without her. They were married for twenty—five years. She died seven weeks before their silver wedding anniversary. She kept praying that she'd be able to make it. They'd planned a party, a trip to Britain . . . the works. Instead, we had her funeral."

He turned his head. In the dusk, their eyes met—and glanced away. Lisa drew her hand from his arm.

"Thank you," he said, after a long silence. Lisa bent to gather up her bag and sweater. As they walked silently across the grass, laughter and the pounding beat of disco music issued from the open doors of the bar.

"Richard Barton's a nice enough chap," Jane Tallis told her later that evening, when they'd met up in the bar, "but he keeps to himself."

"Has he always been like that?"

Jane shrugged. "No idea. He moved here from Barnstaple a couple of months after his wife died."

"And before that?"

"I believe he shared a law practice with his dad, and they all lived over Barnstaple way. You'd have to ask Marion. I've only been here a few years."

Lisa was surprised. "I thought you were born and bred here."

"Not me. I've lived in London most of my adult life. But my father was born in Somerset. So I moved here when I got fed up with the noise and the diesel fumes, and having to fight hordes of tourists whenever I set foot outside the door."

"I like London."

"Bet you do. You're one of those tourists. Try having to fight your way through them in the tube and on the buses, when you're trying to get to work every day."

Jane picked up her packet of cigarettes and took one out of it. Then she pushed the packet toward Lisa.

"No, thanks."

"Mind if I do?" She was already lighting up.

Lisa smiled.

"Yeah, yeah. I know. I should have asked first." Jane made a face. "We could go outside if it bothers you."

"I'm okay."

Jane took a long draw on her cigarette. "I hear you're moving up to Charnwood Court."

Lisa sighed. "Is there anyone who doesn't know that by now?"

"Doubt it. Paula Willand was going on about it earlier. I told her she shouldn't charge so bloody much here. What's a room going to cost you at the Court?"

"Would you believe I never asked? Mr. Kingsley said it would be much less than the Stag, so I took him at his word."

"Charmed you into it, did he? Sounds just like the Honorable Mr. Alec Kingsley."

Lisa felt a little uncomfortable, as if she were letting Richard down by sharing in gossip about his relatives.

"A word of warning," Jane said. "Be careful when you're there."

"Careful? Why?"

"I've heard there's been some weird things happening up at the Court."

"What sort of weird things?" Lisa asked uneasily, recalling the strange sensations she'd felt in the hall and nursery.

"That's the trouble. As soon as you ask anyone, they shut up like clams. That's typical of the people who live here. But Maud Birkett told me that the American couple they had staying there left a week earlier than

83

they'd planned."

Lisa moistened her suddenly dry lips. "Do you think the house could be haunted?"

Jane laughed. "That'd bring in the tourists, wouldn't it?" Her brown eyes met Lisa's, her expression suddenly serious. "Haunted? From what I've heard about those Kingsleys, I wouldn't be at all surprised."

CHAPTER TEN

"HI, JERRY! WHAT ARE YOU DOING AT MY DAD'S place?" Lisa sat on the edge of the bed, smiling down at the receiver in her hand.

"I'm speaking to some weirdo on the phone." It was an old joke between them.

Lisa grinned. "Very funny. When I didn't get you at the gallery, I called Daniel. He said you were at my dad's. Seriously, what are you doing there?"

"Seriously, I'm checking up on your cat and your dad, eating enough to last me for a week, and watching a Stanley Cup game."

"It's almost summer, for heaven's sake. Don't tell me hockey isn't over *yet*? Besides, it's still afternoon there."

"It's a match he taped," Jerry breathed down the phone.

Lisa started to laugh. "You poor shmuck."

"Shut up."

"How on earth did you get roped into that?"

"What else can we do together?"

"You're right. Sorry. How's Paloma?"

"Eating too much. She's going to be enormous by the time you get back."

"She'd better not be. I'll speak to him."

"Not yet. He's out in the kitchen getting us more cheese and crackers. How're you doing?"

"Okay. I'm in Charnwood."

"Already? That's great. What's it like?"

Lisa launched into an abbreviated description of the village and its inhabitants.

"Sounds like something out of a book."

"That's exactly what I thought. *Murder at the Vicarage* . . . something like that. Which reminds me, I haven't seen the local church yet. That's another place to meet people. Maybe I'll go to church tomorrow." She told him about her visit to Charnwood and meeting the Kingsleys.

"You've covered a lot of ground in one day."

Lisa sighed. "I know, but I don't feel I'm any further ahead."

"You'll get there. You've had a great start. Here's your dad. He wants to speak to you."

"Don't go away, Jerry. I've got lots more to tell you."

"I'm not going anywhere. We've only watched one period so far."

Lisa grinned to herself. It was great speaking to Jerry. He always made her feel more grounded, somehow.

Her father was curt on the phone. He considered it an instrument for emergencies only, certainly not for chatting. "When are you coming home?" he asked, after they'd discussed first the weather and then the driving in Britain.

"Probably a week Monday. Why?"

"Just need to make sure I've got enough cat food in. Your moggy eats a lot."

"Please don't overfeed her, Dad."

"Don't blame me," he grumbled. "This animal's

85

wanting food all day. And she sheds all over the place," he added in an accusing tone. "You should see your mother's couch."

"Sorry. It's that time of year." Lisa sought for something else to say. "Are you enjoying your visit with Jerry?"

"He wanted to watch hockey, so I said okay."

Lisa had to bite her lip not to burst out laughing, but she was grateful to Jerry for checking up on her father. Knowing how Jerry felt about fathers in general, especially his own, she knew what a strain it must be for him to spend an afternoon with hers. "That's great. Thanks for looking after Paloma, Dad. I'll bring you back some Devonshire cream, okay?"

"Great. 'Bye." Lisa stared down at the receiver in her hand. Her father hadn't asked her how her search was going. Even on the telephone, thousands of miles away, she could sense his disapproval of what she was doing.

Jerry came back on the line. "Hi."

"Hi. It sounds like you're having a good time. I take it both of you have seen this game before." Jerry grunted in response. "That must be fun."

"It's great."

"You're the one who's great. I wish you were here with me."

"Someone needs to take care of the gallery. Besides, it's easier to find out things on your own. People are more likely to open up to someone on their own."

"That's true." Lisa was about to tell him more about Richard and Emily, but decided not to. Not yet, anyway.

"What about this stately home? Did you get any vibes from it?"

Lisa shivered. Vibes were exactly what she had got, and not pleasant ones, either. "I'm not sure that I've been there before, but . . ." She told him about the strange episodes in the hall and the nursery.

"You poor darling! It sounds ghostly—and ghastly." Jerry was being suitably sympathetic, but she knew he couldn't understand exactly how she'd felt. She didn't understand it herself.

"It wasn't like a haunting, really," she tried to explain. "More like—like something I'd seen in a dream. You know that sort of feeling?"

"Or something you remember from your childhood?"

"Who knows? All I do know is that the house belonged to the family of Alec Kingsley's first wife before she died. Want to know how she died, Jerry?"

"How?"

"She was drowned."

There was a long silence at the other end of the line.

"Are you still there?" Lisa demanded.

"I'm here. Don't read too much into it."

"I'm not. But it is weird, isn't it? I'm looking for some connection with water and the Kingsley family, and this woman—a Mrs. Kingsley—happens to have drowned."

"When?"

"I don't know. That's the next thing I have to find out."

"What about the sea? Is it getting to you?"

"Not yet, thank God. This village is inland, so I don't have to go anywhere near the sea, except when I take the main road that runs along part of the coast. All there is here is a gentle little river. Not much more than a stream, really. Nothing to bother me there."

"That's good. Well, I—must get back to this scintillating game. Happy hunting. Call me when you find anything else, won't you?"

87

"I will."

"However small."

"I will. I miss you."

"You'll be fine."

"Sure I will. See ya." Lisa stared down at the receiver, hearing the dial tone, then set it back into its cradle.

Downstairs, the woman at the desk waited for the connection to break before setting the telephone down. She'd made a few notes during the conversation; otherwise, she'd never have remembered any of it. Most of it was boring chitchat, but she hadn't a clue what some of it meant. That bit about the sea, for instance, what was that all about? Oh well, someone else might know.

She pulled down the metal grille, placed a notice behind it to advise that she'd be back in five minutes, and then walked down the corridor in the direction of the bar.

SATURDAY

She's here! I always had the feeling she'd come back one day. But why did she have to come now, just when things are going my way at last? She could ruin my plans.

How much does she remember? It's too early to tell. She didn't recognize me, I'm sure of that.

If she doesn't remember, then why has she come back to Charnwood? I must find out.

CHAPTER ELEVEN

Next morning, Lisa awoke to the drumming of rain on the window. Although it was past eight o'clock the room was almost dark. She switched on the bedside lamp and swung her legs over the side of the bed. The room was also freezing! She crossed to the fireplace and switched on the electric fire. The fire clicked, spluttered, and then the two coils grew red. Lisa held out her hands to the welcome heat.

She dressed warmly in a long, thick sweater and her heavier black leggings. The church, which was sure to be at least as ancient as this inn, would probably be far more damp and chilly.

When she'd fortified herself with a huge breakfast of fried eggs, baked beans, fried potatoes, tomatoes, and mushrooms—she'd felt like asking for the Cholesterol Special when she'd given her order—she went outside.

Shrouded in rain, the village no longer appeared so postcard—pretty. The golden stone of the cottages had turned to a water—slicked gray. The clouds overhead were dark and heavy, pressing down on the slate roofs. Gazing out from the shelter of the hotel porch, Lisa shivered. It was hard to believe that this was the same village she'd fallen in love with yesterday.

"Morning," someone said from behind her.

Lisa turned quickly. Marion Heasley stood there, holding a large black umbrella. She was dressed to match the day in a shapeless suit of gray tweed. "Terrible day, isn't it?" She stepped under the porch and closed her umbrella.

"It certainly is. I hope this won't last."

89

"Forecast's not good. Bad weather blowing in from the Atlantic. Lot of rain."

"Oh no! I was hoping to drive into Doone Valley this afternoon."

From the hills beyond Charnwood Court came a rumble of thunder. "Won't see much today. Been reading *Lorna Doone*, have you?"

Lisa nodded. "Jane lent it to me. I started it last night. I felt I should read it, considering I'm right here in Exmoor, where it all happened."

"It's just a story, you know." The woman's tone was as dampening as the weather.

"I know, but the notes in the book said it was probably based on fact." Lisa stared out at the dismal scene. "I'd also hoped to do some sketching."

"Oh, that's right, Jane told me you were an artist. Well, I should be going. I've just been to the early church service. Must get ready for morning coffee. Although I shouldn't think there'd be many visitors coming in today," Marion added gloomily.

"If any."

Marion glared at her. "The *Lorna Doone* bus tours will still come. They don't cancel them for a drop of rain." Marion snapped open her umbrella, showering Lisa with raindrops.

"What time is the next church service?" Lisa asked, hoping she hadn't made an enemy of the woman. She needed as many allies as possible.

"Eleven. Full choral and communion service. Lasts well over an hour." Marion eyed Lisa. "Thinking of going?"

"Yes." She didn't really feel like it, but it could prove useful. And by next Sunday she hoped to be on her way back to London.

"Didn't think you young people were interested in church."

Lisa merely smiled and pulled up the hood of her rain jacket.

"Oh well, see you sometime." Marion began to move away.

"I'll be in to sample one of your cream teas before I go home."

Marion came back under the porch. "Why? You can eat your cream teas up at the Court," she said, with a sneering smile, "now that you're moving in there."

Lisa stared at her. "Where did you hear that?"

"Someone at church told me. Probably Hilda Martin. She's a cleaner at the Stag. She also works Fridays at the Court. Isn't it true?"

"As a matter of fact it is, but I was surprised that . . . I only told Mrs. Willand last night. She wasn't too happy about it."

"Oh, she should be used to it by now. That woman is always poaching on her preserve."

It was a strange expression, but it came so easily to Marion's tongue that Lisa guessed she'd used it before. "By 'that woman,' I take it you mean Mrs. Kingsley."

"I do." The brown eyes darted venom. "And that's not all she does." Her voice had dropped to a whisper, although there wasn't anyone nearby.

"What else?" Lisa asked, hating herself for stooping to Marion's level.

But Marion merely shook her head and drew herself up. "Now we don't want to be gossiping about people, do we? Perhaps being sued for slander by that nice Mr. Barton."

Lisa could tell by the gleam in her eyes that Marion was well aware of the time she had spent with Richard and his daughter yesterday.

What was it with this village? She had visions of people sitting at their front windows with telescopes.

"Good—looking man, isn't he?" Marion said.

Lisa gritted her teeth, trying to stop the telltale warmth that she knew was sweeping up her neck and into her cheeks. She turned abruptly. "I must be going. I have to ask about my room again. 'Bye."

Before Marion could say another word, Lisa pushed open the door and went into the Stag.

"You're in luck," said the red—haired receptionist in response to her enquiry. "Someone called a few minutes ago, asking for two rooms. Amazing, considering how awful the weather is. But they're in London, so they probably don't know what it's like down here."

"That's great. I'm sorry," Lisa hastily added. "To be leaving here, I mean. The room's very comfortable."

"No skin off my nose, but Mr. Willand gets pretty miffed when he hears someone's moving from here to the Court. I can just hear him now, 'Bloody woman taking business away from hardworking folk.' "

"Mr. Willand?"

"He's the owner of the Stag. You must have seen him in the bar last night."

"Oh, right." Lisa recalled the tall, gaunt—faced man who'd been serving behind the bar. She remembered Jane commenting in an undertone that he looked more like an undertaker than an innkeeper.

Heart beating fast with both excitement and apprehension at the thought of moving into Charnwood Court, she paid her bill and went upstairs to pack.

When she'd finished packing, she went downstairs again, leaving her bags in the room. She'd bring them down when she got back from church.

92

The church was at the top of a narrow lane leading off the road up to Charnwood Court. Yesterday, the walk she'd taken with Richard and Emily had been delightful. Today, walking up a steep hill with the rain lashing down and the wind blowing in her face, it was decidedly uncomfortable. The thought of spending time in the churchyard, reading inscriptions on tombstones—as she'd intended to do—was not a pleasant one. She'd rather be sitting by the fireplace in the Stag, a pot of hot coffee and the Sunday newspapers at hand. But she couldn't waste time. She was determined to do her best to find out if the Kingsleys of Charnwood Court were related to her before she moved in with them.

When she came to the little stone church, there was no one in sight. The solid weathered oak door was shut tight. She pushed the iron gate, and it swung open, rusted hinges squeaking. Green moss grew in the cracks of the uneven flagstone path. On both sides of the path, tombstones loomed from swathes of tall grass beaten to the ground by the rain's onslaught.

Her heart jumped as she caught a sudden movement by the glistening gray wall of the church. Then she relaxed. *You idiot*, she told herself. It was merely a small group of very wet sheep massed together against the wall for shelter.

As she approached down the path they turned to watch her with long, lugubrious faces, their jaws constantly working. Then they returned to their silent contemplation of the wet grass, occasionally bending their heads to nibble at it.

She was about to try the door when it opened, scraping violently across the stone step. It happened so suddenly that she was almost precipitated down the step. A hand shot out to grab her arm.

"My goodness, I had no idea you were there. I am so dreadfully sorry. Please watch the step. It's very steep."

"You're right, it is. Thank you."

A cherubic face above a black cassock peered at her shortsightedly through metal—rimmed glasses. "A visitor. How delightful! Do come in." The clergyman bustled ahead of her, leading the way into the little church. "Are you staying in Charnwood or just passing through?"

Lisa was surprised he didn't know. Everyone else in the village seemed to know what she was doing. "I'm staying in Charnwood for a few days."

He turned so suddenly that she almost bumped into him. "My name is Peter Milverton. I'm the vicar here. Welcome to Charnwood and to Saint Bartholomew's." He held out his hand and Lisa took it, to find hers being pumped up and down exuberantly.

"Thank you."

He peered at her again. "Weren't you in the bar at the Stag last night? I do believe I saw you there. With Richard Barton?"

"That's right."

From behind them came a sudden wheezing of what sounded like a gigantic pair of bellows and then an ancient organ started to play.

"Miss Birkett," the vicar whispered. "We mustn't disturb her. If you come forward into the nave, it should be warmer. I've plugged in the electric radiator there."

He led the way to one of the front pews and then left her, announcing that he must put on his vestments.

She sat at the far end of the pew, the straight hard back digging into her. No special designs to fit the curve of the spine in the days when these pews were built. Hard, uncompromising wood, designed to keep you awake.

The last time Lisa had been in a church was for her mother's funeral. She placed a hassock with a needlework floral cover on the stone floor and knelt on it, head bent on her clasped hands.

She tried to pray, but nothing came. Just an incoherent muddle of different thoughts. Then, all at once, with the organ wheezing Handel's "Largo" in the background, and the smell of mildew and stale incense in her nostrils, the realization of where she was suddenly hit her. Her mother had been an Anglican. This was probably where she had worshiped when she'd been Lisa's nanny twentysomething years ago.

For that matter, this was probably where her *real* mother—her Kingsley mother—had also worshiped. If, of course, she'd ever attended church.

And it was even possible that this was where she, Lisa, had been baptized.

Her sense of connection with this damp and crumbling little church brought such a rush of emotion that she buried her face in her hands.

She felt a gentle pressure on her shoulder. "Can I be of assistance in any way?"

Lisa looked up into the vicar's kindly face. For a moment she was tempted to pour everything out to him. He was old enough to have been here thirty years ago, and might have known her birth parents—and their daughter's nanny. He might even have baptized her! It would be easy to find out. All she needed to do was ask him how long he'd been the vicar of this parish.

Then she remembered that she wanted to have nothing to do with this Kingsley family—whoever and wherever they were now—who'd given her up, handed her over to a stranger, albeit a loving stranger. Not one grandparent, or aunt, or uncle, or cousin had ever tried to find her.

To hell with them all! She no longer needed them.

"I'm fine," she whispered in response to the vicar's question. "I was remembering, that's all. My mother died recently."

His steady eyes held hers. "I am sorry. They were good memories, I trust."

"Very good."

She felt the touch of his hand, like a blessing, on her head, then he moved away on noiseless feet to mount the steps into the chancel.

Exactly seventeen people attended the service. Lisa counted them when they came up to the chancel steps for communion. And, from the sound of it, the choir for "the full choral service" consisted of about three people.

Neither the Kingsleys nor Richard were there.

She had always loved to sing, but the sound of her own voice echoing back to her from these ancient stone walls carried with it such a sense of melancholy that she let it die away in the final verse of the second hymn. She did not sing again.

After the service, coffee from a large Thermos was served at the back of the church. Maud Birkett spoke a few words to her, but they were interrupted by a tall woman wearing a straw hat with artificial roses and violets on the brim, a defiant challenge to the weather. She asked Lisa where she was from and interposed every sentence with a braying laugh. Maud moved away to speak to an elderly woman in a dark beret.

As the woman in the straw hat plied her with questions, Lisa could sense Maud's gaze upon her. She began to feel uneasy. She excused herself and was about to approach Maud, but Maud walked away to the organ to gather up her music. Then she went through a small door behind the organ and Lisa did not see her again.

Lisa waited until nearly everyone had left. Then she approached the vicar. "Could I look around for a few minutes?" she asked him. "Or do you have to lock up the church?"

"Alas, we must. Vandalism is just as prevalent in the country as the towns nowadays. Also, we have a few treasures, and the only way we can get insurance for them is to keep the church locked. A sad comment on our times, isn't it?"

Lisa nodded.

"Was there something in particular you wanted to see?" he asked.

"I'm an artist. I thought I saw some signs of an old wall painting on the wall across from where I was sitting."

His face lit up. "Indeed you did. Fourteenth century. Particularly remarkable in this part of the world, where there are hardly any examples of wall frescoes left. In fact we have a little pamphlet about it. I'll get you one."

While he was fetching the pamphlet, Lisa began to examine the more recent memorial stones on the lower part of the walls.

Peter Milverton returned and handed her a crumpled, copy of the pamphlet. "There we are. The painter is unknown, but there are still fragments of color left, as you can see. Unfortunately, the dampness of centuries has taken its toll."

Lisa spent a few minutes examining the wall. Normally, she would have been thrilled by this discovery, but today her mind was on other matters. After a few minutes she looked at her watch. "I mustn't keep you. You must be hungry."

"Not at all. My wife is used to me being late for lunch. I love to show visitors around St. Bart's." The vicar laughed delightedly. "That's my familiar name for it. St. Bartholomew is so very *formal* for such a dear little church, isn't it?"

Lisa couldn't help smiling at his enthusiasm.

"You can see here," the vicar said, pointing to a high part of the wall, "part of a face."

Lisa nodded and then said, assuming a casual tone, "When I was at Charnwood Court yesterday Miss Birkett told us about the Templeton family."

"Did she give the tour yesterday? She knows her stuff. She was a close friend of the old family. Yes, the Templetons have been the resident family at Charnwood for centuries. They used to have the living of St. Bart's in their power. But that's all changed now."

"Are they buried here, or is there a chapel in the house? I don't recall seeing one."

"No. No chapel. St. Bart's is—or was—their chapel. It was probably Templetons who built it. Yes, they are buried here. There is a vault in the crypt below us. Nothing to see, alas. It's all very dank and musty. And there are mice. We've tried everything, including a cat, but we can't get rid of them."

Lisa shivered. She loathed mice. They terrified her. Yet another phobia!

"Miss Birkett mentioned Celia Templeton," she said tentatively, her heart beating so hard she was afraid he could hear it. "She said she was drowned."

Frowning, he looked at her over his glasses, the benign expression fading. "That was a little before my time." He offered no further explanation.

"Do you know how she drowned?" She was determined to find out here and now, away from the ears of the village gossips. She was sure that she could trust this man to tell her the truth . . . if he knew it.

"Why do you ask?" His voice was sharp.

"It sounded . . . rather creepy, the way Miss Birkett told me about it."

"It was not creepy, as you call it," he said firmly, his tone a rebuke. "It was a dreadful tragedy. Not only for the Kingsley and Templeton families, but for the entire village. Indeed, it was almost as bad as the terrible flood of 1952 that devastated Lynmouth. What is your particular interest in this?" he asked suddenly.

The question took Lisa by surprise. Again, she was tempted to tell this man the truth. Again, she decided against it. "It was . . . the way Miss Birkett told me that Celia Templeton had drowned. I thought perhaps there was some mystery behind it."

He faced her squarely, his eyes wary. "There was no mystery about it. Celia—and her name was Kingsley by that time, by the way—Mrs. Celia Kingsley was one of seven people drowned on that terrible night when the river flooded its banks."

A rushing sound filled Lisa's ears. "A flood?" she whispered.

"Yes. Many of the small rivers and their tributaries that flow down to the sea at Lynmouth flooded their banks, but ours was the worst disaster."

"I don't understand. Why did people drown? Was there no warning?"

"I am not aware of the exact details. As I told you, I was not here at the time. I am told there was torrential rain for several days beforehand, but no one anticipated any real danger. I believe four of the people who died were trapped in their car when they tried to drive across the ford about a mile from here."

Lisa shuddered, her mind working overtime as she imagined the horror of being trapped in a car, screaming to get out, the water pouring in . . . . She gave a little gasp, to force air into her lungs, and realized she'd been holding her breath.

Then all at once it came to her. A family in a car? Could this have been her parents? With someone else from the family——Celia Kingsley—trapped with them? And was it possible that she, too, had been trapped in the car, but had somehow been saved?

Heart hammering violently, she clutched the vicar's arm. "Do you know when this happened, what year?"

He drew away from her, looking alarmed. "I—I can't recall exactly. But it's easy enough to check. There is a plaque on the chapel wall, a memorial to Celia Kingsley."

He led the way back down the church to the little chapel beside the pulpit. Lisa followed close behind him, feeling disoriented and light—headed.

He halted in front of the stone plaque. "There it is. 1970."

Nineteen seventy. Lisa had been four in 1970, when her parents had been killed. Surely *this* must have been how her parents had died. Not in Switzerland, but here, in their own village. But if that was what had happened, why was there only a memorial stone to Celia Kingsley and not one to her parents?

"Was Celia Kingsley in the car?"

"No, she was not."

His reply startled Lisa. "Are you absolutely sure about that?"

Peter Milverton frowned at her. "Perhaps you should pose your various questions to someone else, someone who lived in the village at the time."

"Who would know?"

"Several people. In particular, Miss Birkett." He looked around, peering down the church aisle. "Unfortunately, she appears to have left. She would know far more than I do on the subject." He looked pointedly at his watch.

"Just one more question, please, Mr. Milverton. Can you tell me how Celia Kingsley was related to Mr. Alec Kingsley, who lives at the Court now?"

"Well, of course I can. She was his first wife."

So that, at least, was true.

"Forgive me for pressing you," he said, "but what is your interest in this matter? Are you a journalist? We've had several down here recently, trying to dig up dirt."

The expression sounded strange coming from this rather pedantic man. Dirt about whom? "No, I'm not a reporter. When you say recently, do you mean this year, this month? And what were they here for?"

The vicar stiffened. "Just snooping, as always. Although Mr. Kingsley has retired from office, he is a former member of parliament. Snooping reporters still like to scratch around for scandal to sell their papers, don't they?" His cold tone implied that he numbered her among them. "Now I really must close up the church and get home for my lunch." He gave her a fleeting smile, but it was not friendly. "Or my wife will be sending out the dogs to search for me."

"I'm sorry, I really have kept you a long time, haven't I? Let me ask you one more question, and then I'll go. If Celia Kingsley was not in that car, can you tell me who was? Was it other members of the Kingsley family?"

"Oh no, definitely not. The family who died in the car was on holiday here. A great tragedy. Two young parents, with a three—year—old and a baby."

"They aren't buried here, then?"

"No. I believe they came from somewhere near London."

"But Celia Kingsley is buried here."

"But of course. Her remains lie in the Templeton vault." He looked down at the floor. "As I told you, it is directly beneath this chapel."

The thought made Lisa squirm.

The whole thing was utterly, totally incompre—hensible. Surely he'd got it all wrong. The people in the car *must* have been her parents. It was too coincidental for them not to be. But why then had her mother, her adoptive mother, told her they'd been killed in a car crash in Switzerland?

SUNDAY AFTERNOON

She was at the church this morning. She spent some time with the vicar. Probably pumping him for information about dear Celia. That was a waste of her time. That man knows nothing about Celia.

BUT THERE IS SOMEONE WHO DOES!

The pen pressed heavily as it printed the last sentence in capital letters, then went back to underline the line with such vigor that it gouged the paper.

Chapter Twelve

Mrs. Willand confronted Lisa as soon as she stepped inside the hotel, stopping her at the foot of the carpeted stairway. "Checking out time is twelve noon," she told her, "and your things are still in your room."

"I've been to church."

"Then you should have checked out before you went.

We shall have to charge you for another day if—"

"Don't worry. I can't wait to get out of this place," Lisa shouted, so that a startled couple coming in the front door turned to look at her.

Seeing Mrs. Willand's expression helped to compensate for the thoroughly miserable day she was having.

Lisa swept up the stairs and flung open her bedroom door. She'd hoped to have a little more time in her room so that she could sit down and work out what she should do before she moved to the Court. She supposed she could sit in the lounge downstairs, but she no longer felt the same way about the hotel. Paula Willand had tainted it for her.

There was a small pub at the other end of the high street, but she was sure to meet the prying eyes of locals there. She could drive to Lynton or Lynmouth for lunch, but to do that she would have to brave the coastal road that ran high above the surging waters of the sea. Unless she went further inland, into the woodland of the Exmoor valleys, the only way out was by that coastal road.

She had the uneasy sensation that she was trapped in this claustrophobic village. She felt as if she were an animal in a cage, eyes peering at her, everyone aware of what she was doing. Breathing fast, she picked up the telephone receiver, to be met with silence. There was no dial tone. She jiggled the cradle up and down, and then the unmistakable, strident voice of Paula Willand issued from the earpiece. "Your telephone has been cut off. You will have to make your call from the public telephone downstairs."

Lisa slammed the receiver down. It occurred to her that Mrs. Willand might have listened in to her call to

Jerry last night. By the time she'd carried her bags down, the urge to call Jerry again had dissipated a little. Besides, it was time she learned not to rely on him so much. There was no doubt that her relationship with Greg had suffered because of her close friendship with Jerry. The two men had never liked each other. One night, after the three of them had gone to see a movie together, she'd accused Greg of being homophobic. Greg had lost his temper and said things she knew he later regretted. That episode had marked the beginning of the end of their relationship.

She carried her bags out to the front entrance. The rain was now a downpour, the water bouncing off the road, spilling from roof gutters and spouts. She could hear it gurgling in the drains.

What in God's name was she doing here? *Go home!* The voice seemed to come from the water, but she knew it was in her mind. It was like a warning. A warning and a temptation. *Go home and leave this village and its memories and mysteries behind.* After all, if she went home without discovering anything more about her background, would she really be any worse off?

Lisa jerked up the hood of her rain jacket. Damned right she would be! She hadn't come all this way to be deterred by a shower of rain or a couple of unfriendly strangers. Nor had she become the owner of a successful art gallery by giving up whenever she had a setback.

But you had Jerry to help you then, that negative voice reminded her. Lisa ignored it. She slung her shoulder bag across her chest, picked up her suitcase, and stepped out into the rain.

By the time she'd reached her car, her jacket was soaked. Damn Paula Willand! But for her, Lisa would have been perfectly happy to have had lunch at the Stag, perhaps curl up on one of those soft—cushioned sofas in the lounge afterward, reading the Sunday newspapers or *Lorna Doone.* The rain would probably stop by midafternoon, and she could then go on to Charnwood Court.

Instead, here she was, sopping wet and cold, *and* hungry. And too proud to march back into the hotel. Proud? Embarrassed. It had been infantile to yell like that. Infantile yet rewarding. With a rueful grin, she threw her case into the trunk and scrambled into the car, turning on the heater to warm her.

What was she going to do all afternoon? Sit in the car, listening to Radio Three, reading? She didn't fancy driving on the steep moorland roads in this heavy rain. And it was too wet and chilly to go roaming around on foot.

She was about to pull away, when a Range Rover drove into the parking lot and stopped beside her. The window opened to reveal Richard.

She rolled down her window, extremely glad to see him. She hoped that the spontaneous warmth of her smile wasn't too much of a giveaway.

"We've been trying to call you," he shouted, "but Mrs. Willand said you'd already left."

"I was at the church service," she yelled back. "And she wouldn't put my calls through after twelve o'clock."

"Hang on a minute." He swept the car into a space across from hers, jumped out, and ran back. "I couldn't hear you properly in this downpour. Can I come in?"

She had already leaned over to open the door for him. The rain blew in on a gust of wind, wetting the interior of the car. He slammed the door and settled himself into the passenger seat, pushing it back to accommodate his long legs. Suddenly the car seemed far too small.

"Sorry about that. What a hellish day!" He turned to look at her, frowning. "Are you okay?"

She nodded. "A bit wet. Is it often like this here?"

"Unfortunately, yes. Especially in the winter and spring." He frowned. "But heavy rain like this is fairly unusual in the early summer. It's a shame, when yesterday was so beautiful. Alec sent me to invite you to lunch. We weren't sure if you were eating at the Stag or not."

"I decided not to."

"Mrs. Willand said you'd left, but someone told me they'd seen you at church, so I thought I'd run down and check to see if you were still here."

"I'm glad you did. I have to admit I was wondering what to do." Lisa grimaced. "I made a fool of myself at the Stag."

He raised his eyebrows. "You did?" She was so close to him she could see the glint of humor in his eyes. "How?"

She told him.

He grinned. "Good for you: Paula Willand needs a few more like you. Everyone in the village is terrified of her, including her husband, Ron. Well, there's no point in sitting here when there's roast lamb waiting for us. How about it?"

"Sounds great . . . except for one small thing. I'm a vegetarian."

"Oh, no. Not another one!"

"What does that mean?"

"Kate's a vegan. Let's hope she'll be willing to share her lentil patties with you."

She wasn't sure if he was serious or not. With Richard, it was hard to tell. "I'm not a vegan. I eat cheese, eggs . . . even fish, but still—"

106

"Don't worry about it. It means !There is more lamb for me."

"Are you sure? I mean, are you sure they really asked me to come for lunch?"

"I wouldn't have driven down in this downpour if I hadn't been sure. Besides, Emily insisted that I come and find you."

Lisa smiled. "She's a terrific kid, isn't she?"

"I think so. She's the light of my life." The words and the tone of his voice touched her heart. "She kept me going when I didn't think it possible that I could. I think of her as Angela's gift to me." He immediately turned to push open the door. "I'll lead the way. The road's a bit tricky in places."

What a man of contrasts he was, Lisa thought, as she rubbed the steam off the front window and turned the fan up high to send a blast of air onto it. Just when you thought he was cold and unfeeling, he'd come out with something that completely negated that impression.

She followed the Range Rover up the narrow lane, past the clinic and the turnoff to the church. In a few minutes they arrived at the open iron gates that marked the entrance to the Court, and Richard turned into the driveway. He halted for a moment at a wooden hut beyond the gates to speak to the man there, who then motioned her through. She lifted her hand in response to his wave, then followed Richard down the broad drive and along a small lane that led to the cobbled courtyard at the back of the house.

"Go on in," he told her, when they'd both parked their cars. "I'll bring your bags."

It was too wet to argue. She went up the three stone steps and was about to open the door when it was opened for her and she was ushered into a hallway by

Alec Kingsley.

"Good, good. Richard was able to find you. Come in, come in. You must be absolutely soaked. This is bloody awful weather, isn't it?" His welcome was warm, inviting. He took her jacket and hung it up.

"This is so kind of you," Lisa began, but he cut her short.

"Nonsense. We were thinking about you being all by yourself at the Stag. It's a nice enough place, but being alone in a hotel is no fun." He led the way down the corridor to the room they'd been in yesterday. "Come on in and get warm. Emily's upstairs with Rachel playing with the doll's house." He glanced at his watch. "She'll be down in a few minutes. We have to clear out of the main rooms at one—thirty to make way for the damned tour."

His mention of the doll's house chilled Lisa, conjuring up the spooky experience she'd had in the nursery yesterday.

"You look cold," Alec said. "Here, sit in my chair by the fire. Ridiculous having to have a fire in early summer, isn't it, but it's bloody cold today." He seemed to feel he must keep talking to her, to make her feel at home, when, in fact, his anxiety was beginning to make her feel nervous.

She wished Richard would come in, but he had disappeared as soon as they'd entered the house. "The doll's house is absolutely exquisite," she said to Alec. "Is it very old?"

A darkness, like a gray shadow, passed over his face.

"I'm not sure," he said, his voice curt. "I believe it was made some time in the Regency era, or even earlier. How about a prelunch sherry, Miss Cooper?"

"Please call me Lisa. I'd love one." She cleared her

throat, about to tell him about her being a vegetarian, when Emily suddenly dashed into the room, pulling up short when she saw her.

"You *did* come. Daddy found you."

"I did. He did." They smiled broadly at each other. Emily's joyful entrance into the room brightened it like a sudden burst of sunlight.

Rachel Kingsley appeared in the doorway. "Are you staying for lunch, Miss Cooper?"

Lisa hurriedly rose from Alec Kingsley's chair. "I'm not sure."

"What do you mean you're not sure?" Alec demanded.

Before she could answer, a young woman of indeterminate age entered. She could have been sixteen or twenty-six. Her hair was the color of new carrots, far too bright to be natural, and her right earlobe bore four gold studs, the left a gold ring. She pushed rudely past her mother and stalked across the room.

"Hi," Lisa said.

She was ignored.

Lisa could hear Alec mutter a curse beneath his breath. "This is our exceptionally rude daughter, Kate," he said.

Mouthing "Eff off," Kate flung herself into the chair Lisa had just vacated, her legs dangling over the arm.

"This is my friend, Lisa," Emily told Kate.

Kate shrugged in Lisa's direction, giving her an insolent stare.

For a long moment the Kingsleys seemed to be struck dumb with embarrassment, then both spoke at once.

"How about that sherry now?"

"Will you be staying for lunch, Miss Cooper?"

Emily's laughter eased the tension. "You said it

together."

Alec said nothing, ignoring Emily.

Lisa knew he wasn't actually related to the child, but it bothered her that he seemed to have no rapport, no interest at all in Emily. It was her great aunt Rachel who smiled and smoothed Emily's hair, as they waited for Lisa's answer.

"I'd love to stay," she said, "but there's one problem. I'm a vegetarian."

"Lord, not another one," Alec said, striking his forehead with his palm in a mock theatrical gesture.

From his chair came a sarcastic laugh.

Richard came in, carrying two dishes of hors d'oeuvres. "I've already told Rachel. She said it would be no problem at all."

"You can have some of Kate's muck," Rachel told Lisa, "or a cheese omelet."

"An omelet would be fine. Thanks very much."

Alec stood surveying her, a slight frown creasing his forehead.

"What about the sherry, Alec?" his wife demanded.

"Coming right up," he said, as if he'd just woken from a trance.

When he'd poured the pale golden sherry into crystal glasses, he passed them around and then, coming to stand with his back to the fireplace, raised his own glass. "Welcome to Charnwood Court, Lisa," he said. "I hope you will enjoy your stay with us."

She raised her eyes to meet his and suddenly realized that she was staring into eyes that were exactly the same gray—blue color as her own.

CHAPTER THIRTEEN

MAUD BIRKETT LIVED IN THE SOLID STONE VICTORIAN house that had been in her father's family for more than a century. For five years, since her father had died at the venerable age of eighty—six, she'd been alone in the house. Although it stood on the edge of Exmoor, remote from other houses, and the winds howled around it in wintertime, living there gave her a feeling of continuity, a sense of order.

Maud liked order in her life. She'd had only two teaching positions since she'd left university. The second position, as the music teacher in a girls' school in Minehead, had lasted fifteen years—until three years ago, when subjects such as music and drama were deemed "frills," and cut from the school's curriculum. Although she'd been offered an excellent retirement package, she hadn't wanted to stop teaching. She felt she still had much to give to young people. But for a single woman on her own the package had been too good an offer to turn down.

For the first few months after her retirement, she'd been utterly lost. She missed the girls, despite their increasing unruliness and bad language. "It's like taming wild animals," she'd once explained to someone who'd asked her what modern teaching was like. "Not until they're tamed can you begin to teach them."

She'd been a good teacher, strict but fair, and although, recently, she'd been frustrated by the girls' lack of appreciation for anything other than the latest pop group, she'd kept them interested enough to ensure the continuation of the school choir, which participated in the Glastonbury Music Festival each year. And very occasionally her own enthusiasm sparked a similar interest in one or two pupils. That, in itself, had made all the hard work worthwhile.

After her retirement, she felt like a fish out of water, until she realized that it was the lack of a routine that was making her feel so unsettled. As soon as she'd set up a regular schedule, she began to adjust to her new life.

Sunday was now her busiest day. She arose at six o'clock, fed her two cats, Tiddles and Sammy, and ate a breakfast of muesli, followed by a four-minute boiled egg with two slices of toast, spread with low-fat margarine and her own homemade gooseberry jam. On other days she had only one slice of toast, but she needed extra nourishment on Sundays, to maintain her energy for playing for the two church services at St. Bart's.

Sunday afternoons, if she wasn't engaged in taking tours through the Court or in piano, voice, or music theory lessons, she liked to go for long rides on her bicycle. She had special cycling wear for all kinds of weather. At this time of the year, she wore sturdy, knee-length shorts and long socks, with an oilskin cape for the rain.

She did some of her best thinking when she cycled, especially when she had to dismount to push the bike up some of Exmoor's almost vertical hills. The self-discipline of forcing her muscles almost beyond endurance point not only kept her body fit, but also, she was convinced, helped to sharpen her brain. *Mens sana in corpore sano* had been the motto of the headmistress in her first school.

There was one particular concern on Maud's mind

that afternoon, something that needed her full attention. Despite the miserable weather, she decided not to stay in and be lazy, like others she knew, but to cycle to Malmsmead, have tea at the farmhouse there. It was a favorite indulgence to which she treated herself every now and then. The farmhouse scones were particularly good, light as air and rich with plump dark raisins, and there was usually a pleasant log fire blazing in the old stone fireplace in bad weather. Moreover, it got her away from Charnwood.

There was something unpleasant going on in the village. It wasn't anything new. It was merely that she hadn't really noticed it until she retired. Even then, it was nebulous, nothing she could really put her finger on. Like a wasps' nest hidden away, with individual wasps issuing forth to attack, and then disappearing to who knew where. Some of the wasps were quite easy to identify, but she suspected that there were others involved, others who were not quite so open in their display of venom. The target of their attacks was undoubtedly the Kingsleys at Charnwood Court.

Maud had no particular love for the Kingsleys. Not anymore. Of course, when she was a young girl she had been hopelessly, heart-wrenchingly in love with Alec Kingsley. Alec was from nearby Dulverton and she had known him since childhood because her father and Alec's had worked together in politics for the Conservative party. Alec had been extremely handsome as a boy and even more so as a young man. But he was barely aware of Maud's existence. Long before he left the west country to go to Oxford University and, later, to become a promising young barrister at the Inner Temple in London, Maud knew that her silent longing for Alec was utterly hopeless. Yet still, when he was due to return for the long summer vacation, she would count the days until his arrival, marking them off in the diary she had always kept.

How strange that she had been the one to bring Alec and her best friend, Celia Templeton, together. Once Alec and Celia saw each other, they had eyes for no one else. But Maud had never really resented it, because Celia had become her closest, her dearest, her *only* friend.

When Celia had drowned, part of Maud—the part that was capable of falling in love and having fun—went with her.

Less than a year after Celia's death, she'd been appalled to learn that Alec—the seemingly inconsolable widower who'd suffered a complete breakdown after his wife's death—was marrying again. His choice of wife was eminently suitable for a rising young man with political ambitions. Rachel Fairfax was the daughter of a member of Parliament. There was a great deal of gossip in the village, whispers that the couple "had to get married," but their daughter, Kate, was born a respectable ten months after their marriage.

As soon as Celia Kingsley had been buried, Maud had set a distance between herself and Charnwood Court, although she missed it dreadfully. The house had been her second home throughout her childhood and during those happier days before Celia died.

But when she retired from teaching, she was happy to accept an offer from the Kingsleys' estate manager, George Barrow, to act as a part-time tour guide at Charnwood Court. Her yearning to see the house that still held so many happy memories for her had overcome her negative feelings about Alec and Rachel. Besides, the job gave her something more to do to fill her days, and the remuneration, although not overgenerous, helped to pay for such treats as new sheet music.

For almost two years—apart from that dreadfully upsetting time when Alec had given her notice, only to take her back again quite unexpectedly three weeks latershe'd taken tours around the house on alternate Saturdays and occasional weekdays in the summer. She had enjoyed her work there immensely. Showing people around Charnwood Court made her feel close to Celia again. Maud felt her presence in every room. And in those two years, apart from that short break, nothing untoward had happened on her tours—at least, nothing more disturbing than a child vomiting on the carpet in the drawing room or an elderly woman falling and breaking her leg on the main staircase . . . until yesterday.

As she rode down the steep lane that led to Charnwood, Maud thought about the young woman who'd been so interested in the Court and its family.

And in Celia's death.

When Maud had told her that Celia had been drowned, the Canadian woman had looked horrified, and then her face had taken on a deathly pallor, as if she were about to faint.

Then, today, the woman had waited after the service at St. Bart's to speak to Peter Milverton. Maud had stayed behind after everyone else had left, her presence hidden by the carved wooden screen. She'd tried to hear what they were saying, but there was such an echo in the church it was impossible. But she did see Peter leading the woman to the little chapel, to show her the memorial to Celia.

Maud was determined to find out more about this

young woman from Canada as soon as possible, but deep down in her heart she knew that what she was looking for was merely confirmation of her own certainty.

Then why, she wondered, was she imbued with a feeling of creeping apprehension rather than elation?

She was cycling down the high street, starting out on her journey to Malmsmead, when she saw Marion Heasley come out from her tea shop. Maud watched as she hurried across the road beneath her bobbing umbrella and then slipped into the crafts shop. On an impulse, Maud pedaled over to the shop, tethered her bicycle to a lamppost with a strong chain and padlock, and went inside.

There was another woman there, besides Jane Tallis and Marion. When Maud put back her dripping hood, she saw that it was Paula Willand from the Stag. The sudden silence when she came in was almost comical. She could tell from their body language, the suspended manner in which their heads and bodies were bent toward each other, that they'd been engaged in earnest conversation the moment before she'd entered.

A few bars of music from Verdi's *Macbeth* ran through Maud's mind. Her lips twitched as she identified the music as being that of the witches.

"Terrible day," was Jane's hearty greeting. "You look half—drowned, Maud. I don't know why you go cycling in this weather."

"Rain doesn't bother me."

"What can I do for you?"

"I wanted to look at cardigan patterns. Cotton cardigans for the summer."

"You can buy one for half the price at Marks," Marion said.

116

"Thanks a lot," Jane said in mock indignation. "Why don't you just park yourself at the door, Marion Heasley, and warn off all my customers?"

They all laughed, but Marion's cheeks flared scarlet. "Sorry," she mumbled, "I wasn't thinking."

"That's okay." Still grinning, Jane set a thick book filled with knitting patterns on the counter.

"I prefer to make my own," Maud said. "Handmade lasts much longer." She started riffling through the patterns. "Has anyone met that Canadian woman who's staying at the Stag?" she asked casually.

"Not anymore, she isn't," Paula Willand said, her thin lips twisting. "She's moved to the Court. Canceled her second night at our place."

"Oh dear," Maud said.

"I'm surprised Alec Kingsley doesn't walk around the village with a sandwich board strapped to his back," Marion said, "advertising bed—and—breakfast at Charnwood Court."

"Or maybe Rachel should do a Lady Godiva and ride out naked on a white horse to entice people there," Paula said.

Marion gave her high—pitched giggle. Maud joined in the laughter, but she felt uncomfortable doing so. Much as she despised Alec and Rachel Kingsley, she knew that matters had gone beyond mere gossip. It was common knowledge that the police were now involved.

"Who is she?" Her question silenced the laughter.

"The Canadian, you mean?" Paula said. "Her name's Lisa Cooper. She's from Winnipeg. That's in western Canada, I think."

Lisa? Maud's heart skipped a beat.

"In the middle of Canada," Jane said. "She told me she owns an art gallery. She's just here for a week's holiday." She turned to Maud. "Why?"

The abrupt question took Maud by surprise. "Oh, I don't know." She frowned. "She was asking me some rather odd questions about Celia when I did the tour at the Court yesterday. And today in church she was questioning Peter. I couldn't hear what they were talking about—"

"But I bet you tried to hear," Marion said.

"I did, but they moved down to the chapel. I could see them through the screen. Peter was showing her Celia's memorial plaque."

"Sounds like she's another reporter," Paula said triumphantly. "Maybe the story's going to break at last and go international."

"It's about time!" Marion said. "You should've let her stay on free at the Stag, Paula."

"No, she wanted to get into the Court. Now that she's wheedled her way in, with the help of Richard Barton, she might even be able to get some concrete evidence against the Kingsleys."

"I say good for her," Marion said. "We could tell her a thing or two, couldn't we?"

Maud felt a little sick. She'd frequently participated in these hen fests herself, happy to pull Alec and Rachel apart. She herself had suspected them of being guilty of the horrible crime that Marion and Paula—and many other members of the village—attributed to them. If they were guilty, she'd be happy to see them rot in jail forever. But she had never felt quite the same certainty of their guilt as other people. She knew things about the past that other villagers did not know.

"You haven't one scrap of evidence, Marion Heasley," Jane said. "You keep your mouth shut, or you'll be had up for slander." She shook her head. "I've never known such a village for gossip."

"I tell you," Marion continued, "the Kingsleys aren't going to last much longer."

Jane slammed a cupboard door shut. "They're leaving the Court anyway. What more do you want?"

"We want justice," Paula said, her face flushed. "However long it takes. You'd have to be part of this place to understand."

It was a definite snub. Maud could see how Jane sucked in her plump cheeks in an effort not to snap back. Paula had a nasty tongue.

"I like this one," Maud told Jane, pushing the open pattern book toward her. When she'd paid for her pattern, she thrust it in its brown paper bag into the deep pocket of her rain cape. Her hand closed over the metal whistle she kept there in case she was ever attacked, although she often wondered how she would get to it if someone pulled her off her bicycle. Still, somehow it gave her a sense of security to keep it there, at the ready. "I think I'll have a word with this Canadian visitor," she said quietly. "I could ask her if she was a reporter, couldn't I?"

"Ah, the voice of reason at last," Jane said. "Sounds like a good idea."

"I'll do it later this afternoon when I get back from my ride. I phoned Alec Kingsley before I left, and told him I'd stop in on my way home and drop off some notes I've written for the new guidebook."

"I don't know why you have anything to do with that lot up at the Court," Marion said. "Besides, they won't need any new guidebooks now they're selling the place off for a hotel. Come to think of it, I suppose you'll be out of a job."

Maud's heart pinched. She looked forward to her

days at the Court with inordinate pleasure. "Probably. Unless the hotel is planning tours. I should especially miss the nursery. Celia and I spent so much time together there when we were children. We particularly enjoyed playing with the doll's house."

"Maybe you could buy it from them?"

Maud gave a wry smile. "You must be joking." The smile faded. "Rachel has had it valued. It's worth thousands of pounds. They're going to sell it to some museum." Tears pricked her eyes. "It means absolutely nothing to them."

"They're monsters."

Abruptly, Maud turned and put up her hood. She walked to the door. "I must be going. I'm riding to Malmsmead for tea."

"In this weather?" Jane said. "You must be mad."

Maud smiled. "A drop of rain doesn't bother me. My cape keeps my back dry; that's all I worry about."

"Better you than me," Jane said. "Well, girls, I've done all the work I'm going to do today. I'm going to shut up shop, draw the curtains, put my feet up, and watch a video."

"Good idea," Marion said. "I don't think I'll have many people coming in for tea today, apart from the bus tour. I'll go home and do some baking for tomorrow. I've asked Pat to take over. She can call me at home if it gets busy."

"I'll be needed at the hotel," Paula, said. "We've got a full house, and most of them will be staying in, I should think." Her small mouth wrinkled. "I suppose we'll be serving tea all afternoon."

"What do you expect?" Jane muttered. "No point in people traipsing about the countryside in this bloody awful weather."

Maud pulled up the hood of her cape. "Have a good afternoon," she said, and opened the door. She was glad to be leaving. She knew it wasn't Christian to dislike people, but there were times when she couldn't abide that Paula Willand. There was something definitely unpleasant about her.

The rain seemed to have grown heavier since she'd been in Jane's shop. As she bent to undo the padlock on her bike, the water lashed down, bouncing off her cape, running into her eyes. For a moment, she considered canceling her afternoon ride, but the thought of missing her Sunday tea was too disappointing. Besides, she thought, straightening up, she didn't give in to the elements that easily.

But an hour later, when she was nearing Malmsmead, she would have been prepared to admit it had been a singularly unpleasant journey. The combination of wind and slanting rain had drenched her, even managing to get inside her protective cape, so that everything felt soggy. Only the thought of the blazing fire at the farmhouse and Mrs. Dunmow's fluffy scones and coffee—walnut cake kept her going.

When, at last, she crossed the bridge over the foaming river, and rode into the muddy forecourt at the farmhouse, Maud was dismayed to see that the front door was tightly closed and no light shone through the windows. Her heart sank at the thought of having to cycle back without any respite from the relentless rain. She knocked the brass knocker on the door and rang the bell, hoping that they might let her in once they knew who she was, give her a cup of hot tea, at least, before she had to turn around for the return journey.

Then she saw the notice attached to the door lintel, flapping in the wind. She wiped her glasses with a sodden tissue and bent to read it. *Due to a sudden death in the family, we regret the tearoom will not be open today.*

Well, that was that. Weary and dispirited, she mopped her face with a large handkerchief. Then she mounted her bicycle again and started pedaling back the way she had come. Now she was riding directly into the driving rain. The wind blew hard against her, sweeping her hood off and dashing biting cold rain into her face, so that she was riding almost blind. It was a truly miserable day.

Why on earth had she gone out? What a fool she was! To think that at this very moment she could be toasty warm by her electric fire, reading *Mansfield Park* for the umpteenth time, with both cats purring on the sofa beside her. And she could have made her own scones for tea. Not as good as those at Malmsmead, perhaps, but still hot and fluffy and spread with fresh golden butter.

Instead, she was wet and cold . . . and deeply concerned. That, of course, was the crux of it, wasn't it? The main reason she'd wanted to get out of the house today. She couldn't have settled at home. There were too many things on her mind. Not the least of them being the woman from Canada, Lisa Cooper.

The sooner she had another meeting with Miss Cooper, the better.

She came to the crossroads and waited, to make sure the way was clear. But there wasn't a soul about. Throughout the journey to Malmsmead, she'd passed not more than four or five cars. She was about to pedal across the intersection when suddenly she heard the unmistakable sound of a revving engine. She hesitated, not sure which direction the sound was coming from.

Then, from the corner of her eye, through the curtain of mist and rain, she saw a car hurtling toward her.

Heart galloping, frantic with fear, she tried to throw herself from the bicycle, but her reflexes were too slow. Although she felt the impact, it was the noise her mind registered. A great clattering sound, like saucepan lids crashing together in her ears. Then she felt herself being precipitated through the air, her legs still somehow entwined with her bicycle. She had time only to cry out once before she landed with an explosion of unbearable pain . . . and then, thanks to God's mercy, felt nothing but velvety blackness.

CHAPTER FOURTEEN

IT WAS NOT THE MOST RELAXED MEAL LISA HAD EVER eaten. They didn't move into the dining room until after two o'clock, so that she was almost past hunger by the time they sat down. Rachel Kingsley presided with icy hauteur at the head of the table, and Kate glowered and snapped at every opportunity. Even Alec's charm and Richard's attempts to engage Lisa in their conversation couldn't make her feel comfortable. Only Emily seemed oblivious to the strain.

On the other hand, the food was delicious. If this was a lunch, what would dinner be like? Lisa had thought when she'd seen the huge oval platter of roast lamb sprinkled with fragrant rosemary, surrounded by crisp roast potatoes. The table was set with green—sprigged white—china tureens filled with vegetables: French beans and brussels sprouts, buttered leeks and roast parsnips, and tiny new potatoes.

Alec had encouraged her to heap vegetables on her

plate to accompany the crisp-edged, fluffy yellow omelette, remarking—with a dark glance at his daughter—that at least it was better than the tofu rubbish Kate chose to eat. Lisa might have been inclined to feel sorry for Kate, but by that time she'd realized that the Kingsley's daughter was actually far older than she appeared, and that her sulky teenager act was either a sign of rank immaturity or designed to annoy her parents. The latter, Lisa suspected. Both sides seemed singularly incapable of dealing sensibly with the other.

When Lisa felt she couldn't eat another morsel, in had come two desserts: an apple—plum crisp and a cream—laden trifle, redolent with sherry.

"I feel as if I've eaten enough food for a week," Lisa said, as she struggled to finish her trifle, having been encouraged to try a little of each dessert. "Everything has been absolutely delicious."

"We'll have our cheese and biscuits in the library," Alec announced, "so Betty can clear the table."

"Not more food," Emily groaned, taking her cue from Lisa.

Kate shoved back her chair. "You're right there, young Em. It's disgusting. There are homeless people on the streets in London who wouldn't eat this amount of food in a week, never mind for one meal. Would you like me to take the leftovers back to London, Mother? Then I could be Lady Muck on your behalf, distributing food to the poor"

Rachel rose from her chair, two spots of color high on her cheeks, and stalked from the room.

Alec exploded. "For God's sake, Kate, can't you be civil for just one hour in your life?"

Lisa wished herself anywhere else but here. There was nothing more embarrassing than a family squabble

124

in front of strangers. Then, with a sudden lurch of her heart, she caught Alec looking directly at her, and she was forcibly reminded that these people were probably not strangers at all, but closely related to her.

She'd tried to avoid looking at him throughout the meal, glancing down at her food whenever he spoke to her, but still she'd felt his gaze upon her. She wondered what she'd say if he asked her outright who she really was.

Alec picked up the wooden tray of cheese and biscuits and went to the door. "I'll take these through and make sure that Betty has set out the coffee. Would you bring Lisa into the library?" he asked Richard.

Emily went to stand in front of Kate, who had slouched lower in her chair, her long legs clad in black tights stretched out, her brief black skirt rucked up to the top of her thighs. "You're rude, Kate," Emily said.

"Am I?" For the first time, Lisa saw Kate smile. A genuine smile, displaying even, white teeth. "Why am I rude?"

"That's enough, Emily," Richard said.

"No, she's right." Kate sat up, pulling Emily to her. She bent to kiss her. When she looked up again, Lisa was surprised to see tears shining in the eyes that were now directed toward her. Kate had the same clear blue eyes as her mother. "I'm sorry if I was rude, as Em puts it. We're none of us very good company nowadays." She jumped up, dragging her skirt down. "Come on, Em. Let's take the dogs for a walk."

"But it's raining."

"So what? After all, if it's raining cats and dogs, the dogs should be out in it, shouldn't they?" Kate flashed another smile at Lisa, demonstrating that she had a good amount of her father's charm, when she chose to use it.

125

"Hope you'll excuse us."

"Of course."

"Can I go, Daddy?" Emily asked her father.

"As long as you put your boots on."

" 'Course I will," she said scornfully. Richard crouched down to hug her, and she flung her arms around his neck to hug him back. "Bye, Daddy. 'Bye, Lisa."

" 'Bye," they said in unison. As the door closed, they turned to exchange smiles.

"I'm afraid that wasn't a very easy introduction to the family," Richard said, after a pause.

"All families have their good and bad moments." Lisa hesitated. "Kate seems to have things on her mind."

Richard sighed. "The family's going through a tough time at the moment. I can tell you that much, because you've probably already heard things in the village. I'm sorry I can't give you any more details than that."

"I wouldn't want you to," Lisa said quickly. "It's none of my business."

The door opened. "Oh, I am sorry," said the elderly woman Lisa had seen earlier when she'd helped to carry in the lunch dishes. "I thought you'd all moved into the other room."

"We're just about to go in. Have you met Betty before?" Richard asked Lisa. She shook her head. "Mrs. Betty Aylward. Betty's been our right—hand woman at Charnwood Court for years."

Betty blushed. "Get away with you, Mr. Barton."

"Hi, Betty," Lisa said. "Did you cook the meal? It was great."

"I just helped. Mrs. Kingsley does most of the cooking."

Lisa was surprised. The willowy Rachel Kingsley

126

hardly looked like the sort of woman to slave over a hot stove.

"I only do the side things like the veggies and the gravy," Betty added, as she gathered up the dessert plates.

"Well, it was all delicious. Can we help you clear the table?"

"No, no. You go away into the other room. Mr. Kingsley's put the cheese through there and I've brung in the coffee."

"Thank you."

"Thanks again, Betty," Richard said. Lisa caught a glimpse of the folded five—pound note he passed to Betty, but it was done with such delicacy that she could quite easily have missed the handoff.

"You don't need to, Mr. Richard," Betty said, sliding the money into the pocket of her blue—and—white—striped apron.

"I do, indeed. As Lisa said, it was a delicious meal. And you're far too modest. I know for a fact that you make the best apple crisp in the county."

"Get away." Betty beamed at him, her face as red and rosy as a polished apple. "By the way, Mrs. Kingsley asked me to give you her apologies, but she's gone to her room with a headache." She gave Richard a warning glance over her glasses. "She'll be down later for tea, I 'spect."

"I am sorry," Lisa said. She really was. She was not looking forward to spending the rest of the afternoon with Alec. She was beginning to wish that she'd never left the Stag. She'd been so determined to discover as much as possible about the Kingsleys that she'd completely discounted the fact that they, in turn, might want to know something about her.

Alec came forward to greet her when she entered the library, which glowed with soft pink light from the various table lamps strategically placed about the room.

Lisa turned to look at the books lining one wall of the room, to avoid eye contact with Alec. She wished she could put on a pair of dark glasses. "I'm sure I've said it before, but this really is a lovely room."

"You have, but I thank you. It has far too much stuff in it, of course, but at least it's warm and reasonably free from damp, unlike some of the larger rooms in the house, which are impossible to heat." Alec indicated a chair. "Come and sit by the fire." He turned to Richard, who had seated himself on the sofa beside Lisa's chair. "Richard, are you sure Emily will be all right going out in this frightful weather? I don't know what Kate was thinking about, taking her out for a walk on a day like this. Not to mention the poor dogs." His glance darted anxiously to the window.

"Don't worry about Emily. She'll be fine. She has her new yellow raincoat and matching wellies." Richard sent a faint smile in Lisa's direction. "She'll grab any excuse to wear them."

"I bet she will. I used to love splashing in the puddles of melted snow in April."

"Do help yourself to cheese, Miss—"

"Lisa, please," Lisa reminded Alec. "I'm sorry, but I couldn't eat another thing."

"You'll take some coffee?"

"Yes, thank you. May I help myself?" She went to the mahogany sideboard and poured the dark, rich coffee from the glass coffeemaker into one of the delicate coffee cups, adding cold milk.

"There's a jug of hot milk there," Alec said, hovering at her elbow.

"I prefer cold, thank you." She sat down again, wondering how she was going to endure an endless afternoon of being plied with food, drink, and stilted conversation.

Plus Alec's constant scrutiny.

"I'm sorry Rachel had to go for a rest," he said. "She has a headache. She tends to get migraines in this kind of weather."

"Betty told us. A rest will probably help her." Lisa found herself wanting to reassure this man, to do anything to ease the tension that was fizzing, like static electricity, between the two of them.

He sat down at last in the chair opposite hers. "Tell us about yourself, about Canada."

Lisa stirred her coffee, watching the brown liquid swirling in the cup. She took a sip, then set the cup down on a small table beside her chair. "What would you like to know?" she asked, shading her eyes with her left hand, as if the heat from the fire was troubling her.

"What made you become an artist?" It was Richard who asked the question.

She turned to him. "We have a vibrant visual arts community in Winnipeg. I was always fascinated by colors, the way they worked together. I was lucky enough to have an excellent art teacher in high school. He encouraged me to go in for competitions. Then I took a Visual Arts degree at the University of Manitoba." She shrugged and gave Alec a wry smile. "Later on, I found out, as many artists do, that there were lots of people who were far more talented than I was."

Alec made a polite noise, as if wanting to refute her statement, but she talked over him. "So I decided I'd rather sell the work of good artists, help them make a

129

living, than keep on wasting my time. It was the best decision I've ever made."

"You said you had a partner," Richard said.

Lisa smiled. "The best. Jerry and I were at university together. We were inseparable. Yin and yang. We make a great team."

"You've never thought about coming to work in Britain?" Alec asked.

"Why would I?" Lisa demanded.

He looked taken aback. "Oh, I don't know. More opportunity, perhaps. A more cosmopolitan environment."

"There couldn't be a more cosmopolitan environment than Winnipeg. We're a mix of just about every ethnic background imaginable. And our arts community reflects that. It's very exciting."

Alec gave her a nervous smile. "So it seems." He thought for a minute, obviously searching for the right words. "If you'll excuse me for being personal, you don't sound very Canadian in your speech. Are your parents Canadian—born?"

"My father emigrated from England." From a corner of her eye she saw Alec's cheeks flush and then the color leached from them. "He was a bus driver," she added, this time looking directly at him, her eyes challenging him.

"In Winnipeg?" Alec asked.

"No, in London, before he came to Canada."

Suddenly she was tired of this whole rigmarole. She was tempted to shout: "You must have guessed I'm a relative. Why don't you tell me who I am?"

"I think we've asked Lisa enough questions," Richard said. "Maybe it's her turn to interrogate us. I'm sure she has more questions to ask about Charnwood Court."

She was grateful for his sensitivity. She wished she could take advantage of his offer. However, her questions would be about the family, not the house. What would the two men think if she blurted out the questions she was burning to ask? *How exactly did your first wife die, Mr. Kingsley? Did my parents die at the same time? Why is there no mention of them anywhere in Charnwood?*

Perhaps it would be worth giving up her anonymity to have her questions answered. But the more she became involved, the more she was determined never to be part of a family that had abandoned her as a small child. She didn't want to hear Alec's sorry excuses for his family having tossed her aside, without giving her anything but their genes as a legacy.

There was always Richard, of course. He would know all the family background. She was tempted to take him into her confidence, but could she trust him not to tell Alec who she was?

She became aware that both men were waiting for her response to Richard's suggestion. "Sorry, I'm almost falling asleep here." She feigned a yawn. "It's that sort of day, isn't it?"

Alec looked at his watch. "Half past three. The tour should soon be over. Only six people today. I'm surprised we even got that many. Once they've gone, we can take you to your room and you can get settled in."

"I'd like that." She sat back in her chair, wishing herself anywhere, even out in the rain with Emily and Kate, but here.

"I promise you we're far more lively when the weather's good," Alec said. "If it had been fine today, I would have challenged you to a game of croquet on the lawn."

"How lively can you get!" Richard said, and they all laughed. Richard leaned over and handed her a newspaper with several sections. "Make yourself at home. Read the Sunday *Times*."

She raised her eyebrows at him. "Wouldn't that seem a bit rude?" she mouthed at him.

"Not at all," he said, smiling. "That's what everyone does on a rainy Sunday afternoon in England."

Lisa glanced at Alec. "Richard's right," he said. "This is your home while you're here. Relax. Read, sleep . . . If there's anything at all you need, you have but to ask." He stood up. "Excuse me, I have to make a call to my estate manager."

To Lisa's great relief, he left the room. She expected Richard to make some sort of conversation, but he picked up his newspaper, the Saturday *Telegraph*, and started reading it. Lowering it for a moment, he smiled and said, "Catching up with old news. Hard to read when Emily's around," and returned to his paper.

At first Lisa felt strange, lolling about in front of a soporific fire in someone else's home, but soon she made herself comfortable, tucked her feet beneath her, and picked up the Sunday *Times*.

She must have dozed off, because she awoke with a start to the sound of the door opening.

"Did I wake you?" Alec asked.

Her face warm, she swung her feet to the floor. "No, no, of course not," she said. Her hands smoothed her hair, checking to make sure it hadn't come out of its coil at the nape of her neck.

Alec smiled. "It's not a sin to fall asleep, you know. I came to tell you that you can go to your room now, if you wish."

"Thank you. I'll just tidy this paper up first." Lisa gathered up the sheets of newspaper, sorting them into some semblance of order. "Did Emily get back yet?"

"No. I think Richard's starting to worry. He went outside to check for them a few minutes ago."

From beyond the closed door came the muffled sound of the doorbell ringing. "That's probably them now." Alec started to cross to the door, and then paused to listen to the voices coming from the hall. Betty's and a louder, male voice.

"That's not Richard," he said, frowning. "I'd better go and see who it is."

But before he reached the door, there was a knock and it opened to reveal Betty and, behind her, a tall man in police uniform.

"Afternoon, sir."

"Sergeant Brewster, what can I do for you?"

"Sorry to trouble you on a Sunday, Mr. Kingsley, sir." The policeman spoke with a strong west—country accent.

Alec cast a glance over his shoulder at Lisa. "I'm sorry, too. We'll go into my study." he said in a cold voice. "Richard!" Richard was already there, coming to stand beside him.

"It's nothing to do with the other thing, sir," the policeman said. "Leastways, I don't think it is. It's Miss Birkett."

"What about Miss Birkett?" Alec snapped.

"She was found on the road near Malmsmead. 'Twas a wonder the driver that found her didn't run right over her again."

"Run over her *again?* What the devil are you talking about?"

133

Richard put a hand on Alec's arm. "Calm down. Bill's trying to tell us."

Lisa rose from her chair, her hand at her throat.

"That's right, Mr. Barton. Miss Birkett were riding her bicycle," he explained.

"I know that," Alec said. "She told me she was going to ride out to—"

"Let the man finish, Alec," Richard said quietly.

"The driver who found her said the rain was that heavy he could barely see. He stopped at the crossroads and was about to start off again, when he heard this whistle blowing."

"What whistle?"

"Miss Birkett always carried a whistle with her wherever she went. Told me so, she did. Well, it came in handy this time, I can tell you."

Although Lisa couldn't see Alec's face, she could sense his impatience from the taut lines of his angular body.

"Had she been knocked from her bicycle?" Richard asked.

"Got it in one, Mr. Barton. Someone had knocked her flying and left her there on the ground for the Lord alone knows how long, all broken and bleeding. If this other man hadn't happened along, she might have died. As it is, she's in serious condition."

"My God, you mean someone—" Alec said.

"A vehicle," the sergeant said.

"Yes, yes, a vehicle," Alec said impatiently. "It collided with her when she was on her bicycle and then left her bleeding in the road, without going to her aid?"

"That's right, sir. There's an outside chance that the driver didn't see her in the mist, but he must have felt the impact. We're treating this as a hit—and—run."

"Where is Miss Birkett now?"

"They've taken her to the hospital in Taunton. Broken leg, skull fracture, and internal injuries."

Lisa came to stand behind them at the door. "That's terrible. I was speaking to her only this morning."

The policeman turned to her, his eyes brightening with interest. "And where was that, miss?"

"At church. St. Bartholomew's. She was playing the organ there this morning. We exchanged just a few words afterwards when we were having coffee at the back of the church."

Sergeant Brewster took a notebook from his pocket. "May I have your name, miss? Just for the record."

"Lisa Cooper."

"And are you staying with Mr. Kingsley?"

"Yes, I am. At least, I have been since lunchtime."

"And before that?"

"I spent last night at the Stag."

"So you're a visitor. I'll need your permanent address as well, miss."

"For heaven's sake, Brewster," Alec protested. "Is this really necessary? Miss Cooper has nothing at all to do with Maud Birkett."

"That remains to be seen, sir. I must get all the information I can about those persons who have seen or spoken to her recently."

"Including me, I suppose." There was no mistaking the acid in Alec's voice.

"Yes, sir. And Mrs. Kingsley. Someone told me that Mrs. Kingsley spoke to Miss Birkett by telephone this morning."

"About the notes for the new guidebook. That's right."

"I'd like to speak to Mrs. Kingsley if I may."

"She's resting at the moment. You'll have to come back later."

"It would be best if I spoke to her now, sir."

Alec opened his mouth to protest, but something in the policeman's expression changed his mind. "Oh, all right. Betty, go and ask Mrs. Kingsley if she'd come down, would you? Apologize for disturbing her, but tell her it's an emergency."

Betty left the room. They could hear her footsteps tapping across the flagstones in the hall and then mounting the uncarpeted staircase. Several minutes later, she returned.

"She's not in her room."

"Did you try the bathroom?" Alec barked.

Betty nodded. "I did. She's not there. I went into the main house and checked with Mrs. Swinton, who took the tour today. She hasn't seen Mrs. Kingsley about the place. And, what's more, her bed's not been slept in."

CHAPTER FIFTEEN

"WHAT THE DEVIL DO YOU MEAN?" ALEC SHOUTED at Betty. "She went up for' a rest. Of course her bed's been—"

"That's enough, Alec. Don't say another word." Richard turned to Sergeant Brewster. "What's this all about? Why are you here?"

"I only came to advise Mr. Kingsley about Miss Birkett's accident," the policeman protested.

"And to ask him and Mrs. Kingsley questions that might have some bearing on your investigation into the accident, right?"

Brewster eyed Richard, then nodded.

136

"Exactly," Richard said. "Then, as their solicitor, I must ask that you give Mr. and Mrs. Kingsley time to confer with me before you interrogate them."

"Do you know where Mrs. Kingsley is, Mr. Barton?"

"No, obviously I do not."

Sergeant Brewster peered around him to Lisa. "Have you seen Mrs. Kingsley since she went for this supposed rest?" he asked.

"This is disgraceful," Alec protested. "How dare you interrogate my guests, Brewster."

Richard stepped back to stand beside Lisa. "Although Miss Cooper is not my client, Sergeant Brewster, I shall be happy to recommend a solicitor to act for her."

The policeman's face grew beet—red. "If she's just a visitor, she doesn't need a lawyer, does she?"

"Do I need a lawyer?" Lisa asked Richard.

"Probably not. But—"

"Then I won't engage one unless it's necessary," she said crisply.

Richard shrugged. "Very well."

"Have you got a car, Miss Cooper?" Brewster asked.

"No more questions," Alec said, "until you call in Detective Inspector Henderson. I take it he knows that you are here?" The question sounded like a veiled threat.

"My car is parked at the back of the house, Sergeant," Lisa said. She saw Richard's impatient move. "It's all right," she told him softly. "I've nothing to hide." She turned back to Brewster. "I've been here since about one-thirty. Both Mr. Barton and Mr. Kingsley will confirm that. When was Miss Birkett found?"

"Sorry, I can't say, miss," the policeman said in an official tone.

"I just hope she wasn't lying there, alone and in pain,

137

for a long time in this terrible weather."

"She was unconscious most of the time, it seems."

"That's a blessing."

Sergeant Brewster was now trying to ask Alec about the other cars parked in the Court's private parking by the stables, but Lisa heard little of what was said. She was recalling how, during the tour yesterday, the starchy Maud had unbent a little, following her to see if she was all right when she'd rushed from the nursery.

Was that really only yesterday? It seemed impossible that she'd arrived in Charnwood little more than twenty-four hours ago. In that short time she'd met Richard and his daughter, a meeting that had led her to the man who was undoubtedly related to her in some way, and she'd become convinced that there was some mystery about the deaths of her parents and Celia Kingsley.

And now she was beginning to wonder if Maud's accident could have anything to do with her arrival in Charnwood.

"Mr. Kingsley, may I make a phone call to Canada?" she asked on a sudden impulse.

"Certainly. You can use the telephone in here. Sergeant Brewster has invited us to go outside in this downpour to look at cars with him." There was no way the policeman could miss the sarcasm in Alec's voice.

"I want to call my partner in Canada to let him know where I am," Lisa explained, "in case he's been trying to contact me at the Stag. I'll use my calling card, of course."

"No need for that," Alec said, but she could tell his mind was not really on her and her phone call at this moment.

Richard gave her a fleeting, speculative look, then followed Alec and the policeman into the hall.

As soon as the door closed behind them, Lisa picked up the telephone on the desk by the window and put through the call to Jerry. If she was lucky, he'd still be at home. He usually played softball with friends in the park on Sunday morning, but it wasn't even ten o'clock his time yet.

His phone rang seven, eight, nine times. She was about to hang up when the ringing stopped and she heard Jerry's voice. "Jerry here."

"Hi! I thought you'd gone already. Why didn't you answer the phone?"

" 'Cause I've had two calls already this morning, wanting to know if I'd like to sponsor things. Whatever happened to sacred Sunday mornings? I don't include you in that, by the way," he added hurriedly. "What the heck happened to you? I've been worried sick. I called the hotel. The woman who answered said you'd left and she didn't know where you'd gone. She was pretty snarly about it, too."

"What time was this?"

"Just after one in the morning, my time."

"Seven my time? I was still asleep."

"But you were still at the hotel?"

"Yep."

"Then why the heck didn't she—"

"I'll explain later."

"Then I tried to find out from Directory Assistance if there were any other hotels there. They said there weren't. I was so worried, I didn't fall asleep until after three. Then I woke with a start around eight—thirty and haven't slept a wink since. I was just getting out of the shower when you called."

"Why were you worried?" she asked, once he'd finished. "I spoke to you just last night."

139

"Haven't a clue," he mumbled.

Lisa felt a chill down her spine, as if someone had opened the door and let in a blast of forty—below air. "You had one of those weird feelings about me, right?"

Jerry didn't reply, but she could hear him breathing. "I'm fine," she said, wishing it were true.

"Then why are you calling again?"

"Because I've moved. I'm in the lions' den," she said in a sepulchral whisper.

"You mean you're actually in the Kingsley mansion?"

"That's right. I moved in after I went to church this morning."

"Did you say a prayer for me?"

"It's too late for that," she joked.

"Why didn't the woman at the Stag tell me where you were?"

Lisa explained. She glanced at the closed door. "As I told you last night," she added in a low voice, "there's no love lost between the Kingsleys and any of the villagers."

"Why?"

"I've yet to find out, but there's definitely something going on. Nothing to do with me, so stop worrying. There's a policeman here now."

"What for?"

"A woman from the village was knocked off her bicycle in a collision with a car. It's a terrible day, thick mist and heavy rain, so I expect it was just an—"

"Had you met this woman?" There was no mistaking the urgency in his voice.

"Yes. She was the one who showed us over the house yesterday, the tour guide."

"The one who spoke to you after that episode in the
140

nursery?"

"That's right. I saw her again this morning. She wasI mean, she *is*—the church organist."

"Did she speak to you?"

"This morning? Yes, just a few words over coffee after the service. Nothing important. But I did learn something from the vicar later, when everyone else had gone." She told Jerry about the flood and Celia Kingsley.

Jerry whistled. "If you were somehow involved in that flood, it could explain your fear of water. But still nothing about your parents?"

"Not a mention. No tombstone, no plaque in the church. It's weird."

"Maybe you've got the wrong village."

"No. This is the place. And this is the family. I know that for sure now."

"How?"

"Alec Kingsley has my eyes."

"What do you mean?"

"We've got exactly the same color eyes."

"So? Lots of people have got the same color eyes."

"No, Jerry, I mean *exactly* the same. He's noticed it, too. I saw him looking really hard at me before lunch. And I think Richard Barton's noticed, as well."

"Lisa, I want you to come home."

"Because my eyes are like Alec Kingsley's? Don't be an idiot. That's why I'm here, isn't it? To find out what happened to me here when I was a kid. Or had you forgotten that fact?"

"No, I haven't, but I thought you had. Why the hell don't you ask this Alec Kingsley straight out about your parents, and the flood, and ask him if he knows why you're so terrified of water?"

"I don't want to get involved."

"Then what's the point of being there?" Jerry's voice rose in exasperation. "Either ask him or come home. Or do both. Ask him and then come home. This thing is getting far too spooky for my liking. Have you ever known me to have these weird feelings about you for no reason?"

"You probably had indigestion from my dad's cooking."

"Don't joke about this." His tone was deadly serious. "Those other times it's happened I was right to be worried, wasn't I?"

"I suppose so, but nothing happened to me last night or today, so quit worrying."

"Maybe I should fly over. I could be there with you tomorrow. Or Tuesday, at the latest."

"Don't you dare. I'm fine. I'll probably end up doing what you said, asking Alec, but for now I'd rather do it my way, okay?"

"If you must."

"Was Dad okay when you left him?" Lisa asked, eager to change the subject.

"He asked me to stay the night."

"Oh, God." Lisa heaved a sigh. "He's so lonely. You got out of it okay?"

"Sure. Actually, I was touched that he'd ask."

Lisa knew what he meant. Her father had never been comfortable with Jerry. It sounded as if some sort of barrier had been broken. "That's nice. You're such a good friend."

"Yeah, yeah. Promise me something."

"What?"

"That you'll call me every day and let me know what's happening. That way I won't worry so much about you."

"I promise."

"If you don't call, I will. Give me the number there."
She gave him the number. As she did so, she could hear
some commotion outside in the hall. Footsteps, raised
voices. "I have to go. They're coming back."

"Okay. Don't forget to call."

"I won't."

"Love you."

"Love you, too."

She put the receiver down and turned to find Richard
standing in the doorway, his face grim.

Chapter Sixteen

LISA STARTED FORWARD WHEN SHE SAW RICHARD'S
expression. "What's happened?"

"Have Kate and Emily come back yet?" His tone was
brusque.

"No. At least, if they have, they haven't come in
here."

Richard turned on his heel, about to leave the room
again.

Lisa went to him. His jacket and hair were drenched
from the rain and she could see that the shirt collar
around his sun—browned neck was also soaking wet.
"Please tell me what's happened."

He drew in a deep breath and released it slowly.
"Sorry. All hell's breaking loose. The police just called
Brewster. They've found Rachel's car."

"Rachel's?"

Richard nodded.

"Was Rachel in it?"

"No, it was in the car park of the Hare and Hounds. Rachel was slumped inside the pub, drunk."

"Oh, God," Lisa whispered.

"Why the hell am I telling you about this?" Richard demanded, his eyes flaring. "I certainly shouldn't be."

"I don't know. Because you're shocked and worried, and there's no one else you can talk to about it?"

"Something like that." He sighed heavily. "God, what a mess!"

"Rachel's car . . ."

"Yes?"

"Is it . . ."

"Yes. As far as they can tell, it's the car that ran down Maud. Alec's demanding that he be taken to the police station to get Rachel. Brewster's trying to keep him here. And I wish to hell I knew where Emily and Kate have got to."

"They'll be fine. You go with Alec. I'll stay here and wait for the girls." Lisa put her hand on his arm. "Don't worry. They've got two big dogs to protect them."

Richard's mouth twitched. "You're right. Thanks, Lisa." He looked into her eyes, and frowned. "When this mess is all settled you and I have to talk. There's something going on here that I can't fathom."

"It can wait."

"Are you sure about that?"

"If you mean, did I have anything to do with Maud Birkett's accident, you *know* I didn't. I've been here all afternoon."

They heard Alec shouting in the hall, "I'm going to fetch my wife, and there's nothing you can do to stop me."

"I have to go," Richard said. "When Kate gets home, don't tell her what's happened."

"I'll have to tell her something. She's not a kid."

Richard made a scoffing noise. "Wanna bet? Tell her as little as possible."

"That won't be hard, considering how little I know."

He gave her a wry grin and went out to the hall. Lisa went to the drinks trolley and poured herself a good—sized cognac into a brandy glass. As she took her first gulp, she heard the slamming of car doors, and then the sound of wheels churning up gravel.

Betty appeared at the door, her face ashen. "More trouble," she said.

"Come on in, Betty. I'm pouring myself a drink. You look as if you could do with one, too."

Betty's gaze flicked to the drinks trolley. "Oh, I couldn't, miss."

"Yes, you could. What will it be? Gin, brandy, sherry?"

The older woman moistened her lips in anticipation. "I'll have a sherry, if you think it's all right."

"I think you deserve one."

"We're all that worried about poor Mrs. Kingsley."

Lisa was surprised to hear the obvious note of compassion in the woman's voice. "I'm sure she'll be fine. The police have found her. Mr. Kingsley is going with them to fetch her." She poured a large measure of sherry into one of the delicate cut—crystal glasses and held it out to Betty. "Sit down."

"I shouldn't. I still have to prepare a cold supper for them."

"You'd better rest first. You look white as a ghost."

"Well, just for a moment." Betty sat down on the edge of the sofa and accepted the glass of sherry with a trembling hand. "Thank you, miss. I hope little Emily's all right. I couldn't bear to think of her being hurt."

145

"Why on earth should she be?"

"Well . . . there's all the other things that have happened, and now poor Miss Birkett . . . who knows where it will all end?"

"What other things, Betty?"

Betty looked scared. "I'm not supposed to talk about them. 'specially not to strangers."

"No, that's right. You shouldn't." Lisa's heart was beating fast. This might be her best opportunity, her only one . . . . A silence ensued, during which Betty gulped down her sherry. Lisa refilled her glass, ignoring Betty's protests, and then sat down in a ladder—backed chair, drawing it close to Betty. "The Kingsleys have been having tough times, haven't they?" she said in a sympathetic tone.

"They most surely have. Since the day they were wed, they seem to have had a curse on them. Some say it's well deserved," Betty added darkly, "but I don't know about that. All I know is that they've been plagued with problems, most especially since the twentieth anniversary of Miss Celia's death. There's been nasty happenings in the house ever since that day. Then there's the letters."

"Letters?" Lisa didn't want to interrupt the flow, but she needed to hear more about these letters.

"Poison—pen letters. I'm not telling tales out of school. Everyone in the village knows there've been letters coming to Mr. and Mrs. Kingsley." Betty leaned forward, eyes gleaming. "I've seen them myself," she whispered.

"Have you really?" Lisa's voice dropped to an appropriately low level. "You mean threatening letters?"

"Well, I haven't actually seen what's inside. Just the envelope and the printed page. From a computer printer,

Sam Martin said they were."

"Who's Sam Martin?"

"Sam's the local police constable. Sam says they can't trace them the same as they used to when they were written on typewriters."

"No, I suppose they can't."

"They started coming more'n a year ago. Nobody can tell where they come from. They've both been getting them."

"Mr. and Mrs. Kingsley?"

"That's right, and now poor Kate's getting them as well. Really evil, they are."

Lisa filled the sherry glass up again, feeling a twinge of guilt, but not enough to want to interrupt Betty midstream. "In what way are they evil?"

"They accuse her mother and father of killing his first wife."

Lisa's heart thumped in her chest. "You mean Celia Kingsley?"

"That's right, miss." Betty peered up at her through the wedge of gray fringe on her forehead. "How did you know her name?"

"Miss Birkett told me."

"She did?" The frown deepened. "When was this?" she asked, her voice edged with suspicion.

"On the tour around the house yesterday. Miss Birkett was the guide."

"Oh, right." Betty looked relieved. "Yes, Celia."

"Did you know her?"

"Indeed I did. A beautiful lady she was. Her and her lovely little girl. Such a tragedy it was . . ."

Lisa could hear Betty's voice droning on, but nothing more made any sense. Only those four words she had spoken repeating in her mind, over and over, like a needle stuck in the groove of an old 78 record.

Her lovely little girl.

She gripped Betty's arm. "You mean . . . Celia Kingsley had a child?"

"She surely did, my lovey." Tears came to Betty's eyes. "The poor little thing."

"What was her name?"

"I told you. Celia. Celia Kingsley."

"No." Lisa's fingers tightened on Betty's arm. "The child's name."

"Oh! Her name was Elizabeth. Little Elizabeth. They would never let anyone shorten her name. I remember my Mary was but a year old when Miss Celia's baby girl was born and then my little Jimmy came along two years later, but . . ."

Lisa heard no more. Her mind was spinning like a child's rainbow—colored top, spinning fast, its high—pitched hum singing out *Elizabeth.*

It would be difficult to change the name of a child of four or five. However much you wanted to give her an entirely new identity, she would have grown accustomed to her own name. How much easier to call her something that was at least part of her original name.

Elizabeth, Lisa. Lisa, Elizabeth.

Lisa released Betty and stepped back, the older woman's face wavering and blurred, as if Lisa, too, was growing groggy with drink. She must get away to think, to work through what seemed totally incredible. But there was one more question to ask Betty before she left her. One vital question.

"Then Elizabeth was Mr. Kingsley . . . Mr. Alec Kingsley's daughter, is that right?"

Betty's eyes widened, as if she was suddenly

148

realizing what she'd said. "You must never let on I told you that, miss. He'd never ever forgive me."

Lisa ran her tongue over her dry lips to moisten them. "I don't understand," she said, genuinely puzzled. "Why wouldn't Mr. Kingsley want people to know he had a daughter?"

"He can't bear to have her name mentioned in this house . . . or anywhere, for that matter."

"Did she die, then?" In a way, Lisa wanted Betty to answer the question in the affirmative.

"Not really," Betty whispered, "but she might as well have done." She put her right index finger on her lips.

"He sent Elizabeth away after his wife died," Lisa said. It was not a question.

Betty's eyes were round and solemn. "However did you know that? That's just what he did. He couldn't bear to see her or even hear her about the house. When she cried for her mother, he would go mad, and yell at the poor child's nanny to keep her quiet. In the end, he sent them both away."

Lisa swallowed hard, unable to speak. Her jaw grew stiff in her effort to hold back scalding tears. "He sent her away with her nanny."

Betty nodded. "Had a complete nervous breakdown, he did. He got rid of everything to do with Miss Celia and her little daughter. Dogs, clothes—even burned all their photos—everything was destroyed. Those were terrible times."

"And now someone is accusing him of killing his first wife."

Betty looked down at her empty glass and then up at Lisa. "Shouldn't have told you that," she murmured.

"It's common knowledge in the village," Lisa said, recalling Richard's words.

"I suppose so."

"Don't worry, Betty: I won't tell anyone what you said." Lisa turned away and walked to the door, feeling as if she were wading in mud down a long, dark tunnel. "Would you mind showing me my room now, please? I need to unpack before Emily gets back."

Betty walked a little unsteadily to the door. She led the way out into the hall. "Do you want me to come up with you?" she asked, anxiously looking up at the staircase that led to the darkened upper hallway.

"No, there's no need. Just tell me where my room is."

"At the top of the stairs, go through the door into the front part of the house. The room's decorated in green and white. Door's open, and your suitcase is in there."

"Thank you, Betty. You go and sit down." The right words came instinctively to Lisa, but she felt as if someone else were speaking for her. "All this has been a great strain for you. Have you someone to help you in the kitchen?"

Betty nodded. "I'll be all right, miss. Don't you fret."

"Please be sure to call me when Emily and Kate get home," Lisa said, recalling her promise to Richard. Whatever the rest of the family were, Emily was an innocent child.

She mounted the stairs, her hand gripping the rail tightly. She was certain now that she had done this as a small child. Certain that Charnwood Court had been her home for the first four years of her life.

Certain now that her mother had been Celia Kingsley and her father Alec Kingsley.

And it was entirely possible that either her father or his second wife, Rachel—or both of them—had somehow been the cause of her mother's death by drowning in the flood of 1970.

150

Chapter Seventeen

AT THE TOP OF THE STAIRS THERE WAS A DOOR IN THE dividing wall. It was covered with green baize to soundproof the private section of the house. Lisa pushed it open and found herself in the upstairs hall she'd seen yesterday on the tour.

At the far end of the dimly lit hallway, the door of the room next to the nursery stood open. She peered inside and saw that it was smaller than the other rooms that had been on view. She switched on the light. The room was dominated by a four—poster bed hung with damask curtains of ivory and spring—green and its walls were covered with a green—sprigged wallpaper. The sight of her bags on the padded bench at the foot of the bed confirmed that this was to be her room.

The rain lashed against the windows, the glass panes shuddering under the onslaught. Lisa shook with them. Her trembling legs gave way, and she sank onto the chair by the glass—topped dressing table, overwhelmed by the significance of what Betty had told her and by the weight of her own suspicions.

The mother who had raised her to adulthood had done everything she could to cover up the past. Only her concern about possible illness had broken down her resolve never to divulge Lisa's background. Now, at last, Lisa understood her mother's reluctance even to write the name of *Kingsley* on the outside of the note she had left for her daughter.

It was obvious that her one desire had been to shield Lisa from her past, but Lisa's own memory had betrayed her.

She was convinced that the truth of what had

happened to her birth mother was still tantalizingly locked away in her own mind, her own sublimated memory. And now she had returned to the village where Celia Kingsley had died under suspicious circumstances. A village where someone else, God alone knew who, was actively seeking to force Alec, perhaps Rachel as well, to acknowledge their guilt.

If only she could find out who was sending the letters, she might get at the truth of her mother's death. But she knew, instinctively, that the truth could also put her in mortal danger.

Was it possible that she could be in danger from her own father? The thought was repugnant to her, but she couldn't force it from her mind. What she couldn't think about now was the fact that the father she'd believed dead all these years was very much alive. Indeed, she had been speaking to him, eating with him . . . this very afternoon.

The enormity of it all was just too much for her mind to take in all at once. Her brain felt as if it would burst.

She sprang up from the chair, a sudden, driving desire to paint surging through her. She looked wildly around the room, but she knew that all she had with her were her pencils and sketchbooks. From experience, she knew that they would do nothing to satisfy the relentless craving. She needed oil paints, canvas, brushes. Of its own volition, her right arm was arcing in the formation of a broad brushstroke on a large, invisible canvas.

"I have to get out. Must get out," she muttered to herself, her head reeling. She knew she was acting irrationally, but there was nothing she could do. If she couldn't find paint, she would work with water, with an invisible brush on that invisible canvas, to create her water image. It was foaming, seething, rushing water she craved. The kind of water that haunted her, goaded her, overwhelmed her, governed her life.

She dragged on her rain jacket. "I must stay for Emily," she told herself, but her promise to Richard was drowned by her desire to paint. She stumbled down the stairs and ran to the main door, wrestling against the pull of the wind to open it.

Down the front steps she ran, into the slanting rain. It was ice—cold against her face and bare hands, cold enough to take her breath away. As she started off down the driveway, the wind blasted against her, and she bent, like the trees, beneath its on slaught.

Halfway down the driveway, the urge to paint left her as suddenly as it had come. There was no longer any need to create water. Water was here, all about her, spilling from the gutters, swirling in the air, splashing from muddy pools onto her legs. She fought against the driving rain, trying to make her way down the drive toward the lodge gates.

Instinctively, she knew that she was seeking her way to the river.

She had almost reached the gates when a car's head-lights raked the stone wall and the gates, then captured her in their full beam. She jumped back, trod on a fallen branch, and felt her ankle give way with a painful wrench. Her leg crumpled beneath her, and she fell in an ungainly heap on the wet gravel.

In the dim light, she could see someone jump from the vehicle, which she saw now was Richard's Range Rover. She could tell, from his height, that the person approaching her was Richard himself, the hood of his green rain jacket pulled down over his eyes.

"Are you okay?" he shouted. He bent to help her up. "Lean on me." She felt his arm strong about her waist.

"I'm fine. My ankle gave way on the gravel." Leaning on him, she scrambled to her feet, feeling very foolish. A bolt of pain shot through her ankle. "Ouch, that hurts," she groaned.

"Don't put your weight on it," he warned her. "Kate!" he yelled.

To Lisa's immense relief, she saw Kate get out of the car, and Emily's face peer from behind her. "You found them," Lisa said. "Thank God."

"Hang on to Lisa, would you?" Richard said to Kate. "I'll move the car nearer. This gravel's not easy to maneuver on one leg."

Lisa wobbled on her left leg as Richard's strength was replaced by Kate's not—so—firm grip. "Thanks. I feel such a fool. Where were you?" she asked Kate. "We were getting really worried about you."

"No need," Kate said curtly. "We were in the Stag having tea by the fire when Richard burst in like a hound from hell."

There was no time for any further exchange. Richard drew the Range Rover in beside Lisa and got out to help her into the front seat. All these maneuvers were punctuated by muffled barking from the dogs in the back.

As they drove to the house, Lisa sat there, head lowered, unable to speak, even to Emily, who wanted to know if she had broken her ankle and was given a sharp, "Of course not," by her father. The dizziness and nausea Lisa always suffered when she'd had one of her "episodes" was compounded by the throbbing in her ankle.

"I think I'll go and lie down for a while," she said, when she'd hopped up the two steps at the rear entrance and hobbled into the house with Richard's help.

"I think we should call in the doctor to take a look at that ankle. Emily might be right. You could have fractured it." Richard looked down at her, concern in his eyes, as she sat on a chair in the back hall.

Lisa shook her head. "I'll be fine." She couldn't stop shivering, and felt as if she were about to throw up.

Beside her father, Emily stood, eyes wide, looking even more concerned. Lisa rallied herself and gave Emily a smile. "It's not broken, Emily," she assured her. "Just a little sprain. I'll be fine tomorrow."

"Does it hurt lots?" Emily asked.

"Just a bit." Lisa had hoped to be able to go directly to her room, but Emily's big, worried eyes prevailed, and she took her hand. "Will you help me, please?"

Richard reached into the section of the old wooden coat stand that held a motley mixture of umbrellas and sticks. "This should help as well," he said, pulling out a strong cane with a sturdy handle.

Giving him a whimsical smile, Lisa took the stick, leaning on it to stand up, but still holding on to Emily with her left hand. They slowly made their way down the back hall and were about to enter the library when the front door crashed open.

Lisa froze when she heard Alec's angry voice. "Leave her alone, Brewster. You can see she's in no fit state to answer your asinine questions."

Now they could see, clustered just inside the front door, the four figures of Sergeant Brewster and a uniformed policeman, with Alec Kingsley and his wife.

Even from this distance it was easy to tell that Rachel was extremely drunk. Alec was having to support her, and she was talking gibberish punctuated by a sudden shriek of hysterical laughter.

"Help Lisa, would you?" Richard murmured to Kate,

155

and strode away to join the group in the hall.

"I think it would be better if I went up to my room," Lisa said to Kate. She was determined not to encounter Alec again today. "I don't think your family's going to want me around at the moment."

"Can I join you?" Kate said, with a bitter smile.

It was obviously a rhetorical question, but as Lisa's gaze went from little Emily, whose grip on her hand had tightened perceptibly, to the shouting group in the hall, she felt it wasn't such a bad idea. "Why don't we all go up to the nursery?" she suggested, with a reassuring smile at Emily. "We could go up the back stairs. And maybe Kate could get some nice hot chocolate and biscuits from the kitchen and we'll have a nice tea together."

"But we already had some tea," Emily said.

"So what?" Kate said, picking up Lisa's cue. "Daddy came in before we could eat most of it, didn't he?" She turned to Lisa. "I'll help you get upstairs first," she said, looking embarrassed, as if helping strangers was not her thing.

"I can manage fine with Emily's help."

Kate nodded and turned down the passage that led to the kitchen. Emily was watching her great—aunt being taken into the library. "Is Auntie Rachel sick?"

"I think she must be," Lisa replied, "but I'm sure she'll be fine by tomorrow."

"Maybe she hurt her ankle, too," Emily suggested.

"Maybe she did. Come on, let's go up to the nursery."

They made their way slowly up the staircase, Lisa trying to hang on to the banister rail, the stick, and Emily's hand at the same time. She longed to be able to go to her room, lie down in darkness, and try to put all that had happened this afternoon into perspective, but

156

for Emily's sake she knew she had to postpone being alone.

She paused for a moment when they reached the nursery, reluctant to go in after what had happened to her there yesterday. Then she switched on the light and the modern lighting fixture beamed warm light over the room. Perhaps, thought Lisa, Emily's presence would banish the ghosts that had haunted her the day before.

"Isn't this a wonderful doll's house?" she said, making her way to the end of the room. The house was closed, its outside wall latched. "Shall we open it?" she asked Emily.

"You just open it at the end. See? You undo the hooks, like this," Emily said, eager to demonstrate her knowledge. "But I don't know how to turn on the lights."

Lisa's fingers felt around behind the house, seeking the switch that she knew was there. In an instant, the house was flooded with light. Light from the tiny bulbs in the chandeliers that hung from the ceilings, light in the little wall lights of the library whose shelves were filled with minuscule books, light in the bare bulb that swung from the ceiling in the attic room in the roof, where the housemaid slept.

"How did you know where the light switch was?" Emily demanded. "I didn't know where it was."

"Oh, I expect I was told when I came on the tour yesterday."

But, of course, she had known where it was since her childhood. Her fingers had reached automatically, with assurance, as they must have done dozens of times when she'd played with the house. In a shadowy corner of her mind that barbed voice was warning her never to touch the light switch, that she must never dare open the house

157

when she was by herself or she would be severely punished, but this time Lisa mentally blocked it out.

From below came the rumble of voices. As Lisa watched Emily setting the oak table in the paneled dining room of the doll's house with little plates and tiny silver knives and forks, she wished she could listen in to what was happening downstairs. She wanted to know whether Rachel had in fact been responsible for Maud's accident, but she was determined to stay out of sight, to avoid seeing the Kingsleys again today.

She wished she could leave right now, drive back to London, and never see them again. Yet she knew that she must stay on, however much she hated doing so.

Now there were *two* questions needing answers. Why was she obsessed with water? And exactly how had Celia Kingsley, the mother who had given birth to her, drowned?

And it didn't take much to surmise that the two were connected.

CHAPTER EIGHTEEN

LISA STAYED IN THE NURSERY WITH KATE AND EMILY for more than an hour, but, despite her efforts, she was unable to engage Kate in any sort of conversation Knowing that she must be affected by what was happening to her parents, Lisa felt sorry for her, but she also felt like taking her by the shoulders and shaking some sense into her. After all, she wasn't a child anymore, although she seemed determined to act like one.

Eventually, Richard came up to tell them that the police had left, and Rachel had been put to bed.

"I'm going to take Emily home," he said. He looked tired, his face drawn. His eyes avoided Lisa's.

Emily looked up from the doll's cradle, where she was tucking an ancient, china—faced doll into bed. "Not yet, Daddy. I'm having fun playing with Kate and Lisa."

"You can come back again another time to play. Come along, now."

Lisa came to his aid. "I'll make sure the dolly gets to sleep," she told Emily. "You go with Daddy." She glanced at Richard. "He needs his sleep, too."

He gave her a faint smile. "You're right there, but I won't be sleeping for quite a while yet. Will you be okay?"

"I'll be fine. I've got Kate."

Kate scrambled up from the floor, where she'd been kneeling beside Emily. "Not for long, you haven't. I'm getting the hell out of here. I plan to leave tonight." She glanced at the large sports watch on her wrist. "I can make Plymouth before midnight."

Lisa was surprised. "I'm sorry, I thought you lived here."

"No way. I live and work in Plymouth. Just came here for the weekend. Big mistake, eh?"

"Kate . . ." Richard hesitated.

"What?"

"Could you take a few days off from work? I think your parents might need your help."

Kate gave a screech of laughter. "You must be joking! What could I do to help them?"

"For one thing, you could quit that phoney adolescent act," Richard snapped. "It's ridiculous at your age."

Eyes narrowed, Kate raised one finger with its long, purple nail and wagged it in Richard's face. "Screw

159

you, Cousin Dick! No one gives me orders."

"That's enough," Lisa found herself saying. "You're scaring Emily."

Kate swung around on her. "Keep out of this. Who do you think you are, interfering in our family's affairs?"

Heat rushed into Lisa's face. For one heart—stopping moment she felt like telling Kate exactly who she was. That would shut her up! Then reason prevailed. "I don't want to interfere," she said, her voice cool, "but I do think you shouldn't be arguing in front of Emily. Shall I take her into my room while you talk to Kate?" she asked Richard.

"There's no point." He turned back to Kate, his face as white and hard as the coastal cliffs. "I just want you to know this. Your mother is going to be charged with drinking and driving, plus leaving the scene of an accident. She could also be charged with causing death by reckless driving, if Maud Birkett doesn't pull through."

Kate's blue eyes, ringed with black like a raccoon's, stared at him. "I didn't realize . . ." Her voice died away.

"What you do is up to you, but I thought you should know the facts. Your father's pretty shattered. I must take Emily home, but I have to spend a lot more time with him. I'll be back first thing in the morning."

"Can I help?" Lisa asked Richard. "If you wanted to stay with Mr. Kingsley, I could look after Emily. Or, if you like, I could go back with her to your place, stay with her until you've got things a little more settled here."

She wondered for a moment if she'd gone too far. He looked surprised, almost shocked, as if she'd trespassed into some forbidden territory. Then the surprise faded. It

160

was followed by one of those rare warm smiles of his. "Would you do that?"

"Of course." It would be a relief to get out of this house. And to be able to avoid Alec for a while longer.

"But what about your ankle?" Richard asked.

"It's fine. Just a bit sore, that's all."

He still looked doubtful. "I'd ask Mrs. Clayton, our usual sitter, but she's away for the weekend, visiting her daughter in Bristol. Of course she could be back by now—"

"I'm happy to do it."

"Is Lisa coming to our house to sleep, Daddy?" Emily shouted, jigging up and down.

They exchanged embarrassed smiles, ignoring Kate's snorting laugh. "No, sweetheart," Richard said to Emily. "But she might stay with you until I get home. Is that okay with you?"

"Yeah!" Emily grabbed Lisa's hand. "And then I can show you my dolls and my new Barbie and you can see the bed where I sleep, and—"

"Maybe you will have to sleep at Richard's place," Kate said with a smirk.

"Why?" Lisa demanded.

"How are you going to get back here?"

"You've got a point there," Richard said.

"I could take my car," Lisa said, "but I'm not quite sure I'd find my way back on these country roads in the dark. Is there a taxi?"

"There is, but he shuts down early on Sundays. I suppose, if I'm still here, I could ride over later and pick Lisa up," Kate said with little enthusiasm.

"Ride?" Lisa asked.

"On my bike."

"Kate has a Harley Davidson," Richard explained.

"Oh!" Lisa hoped that her lackluster response to the idea of riding on the back of a motorcycle driven by Kate wouldn't be taken the wrong way.

"It's okay. I won't kill you. I'm not my mother."

"Not funny, Kate," Richard said. "But thanks for the offer. We may take you up on it. Okay, sweetheart," he said to Emily, "let's get going. You can show all your things to Lisa when we get home." Richard turned back to Kate. "Will you be around when I get back here?"

Kate hesitated for a moment, then nodded. "I'll be with my father."

He put his arm around her shoulders and hugged her to him for a brief moment. "Take it easy on him," he said softly. "He's pretty shaken by all this."

Again, Kate nodded. "If I don't see you later, I'll see you tomorrow," she said to Lisa.

"You'll still be here?"

Kate shrugged. "Looks like it, doesn't it?" She bent to hug Emily, saying, "'Bye, sugarpuss," and left the room.

Lisa and Richard exchanged glances. "It's going to be tough for her," Richard said. "She's not used to acting like a mature adult."

Lisa wanted to ask, "What's her problem?" but decided that this wasn't the time to go into family psychology. Particularly not with *this* family.

"Do you want to take anything with you? We've got television, of course, and plenty of books. I'll try to be as quick as possible, but . . ."

"Take your time. I'm sure you have lots to discuss with Mr. Kingsley." Lisa hesitated, then asked, "Is someone looking after Mrs. Kingsley?"

"Betty stayed on. She'll take good care of her. I'm afraid it won't be the first time."

Lisa glanced at Emily, who had wandered off to make

162

sure the doll's house door was closed. "I know it's none of my business," she said in a low voice, "but has your aunt been like this for a long time?"

"It's grown worse in the last few years. Since—" He halted abruptly. "Come on, Emily. We're going."

Since the letters started coming. Was that what he was going to say? Lisa wondered. "I'll just go get my copy of *Lorna Doone.*"

Richard smiled. "Soaking up local atmosphere, eh?"

"Jane Tallis lent it to me. She thought I'd enjoy reading all about the Doones and Doone country while I was staying so close to it."

Richard's smile faded. "Maud was in Doone country when she was run down this afternoon." He shook his head. "What the hell was Rachel doing driving there in weather like this?"

Emily ran back to join them, putting an end to any further conversation about Rachel. Lisa fetched her rain jacket and the book, then hobbled down the back stairs again, assuring Richard that she'd be fine.

She was hurrying, afraid that Alec would come out and speak to them, but when she reached the hall the door of the library remained firmly closed. If there was any conflict going on between father and daughter, it was being kept at a low level.

Father and daughter, thought Lisa. She closed her eyes momentarily, but the image that arose was that of her blunt—faced father in Winnipeg, bending over his precious roses, clipping off a small pale orange bud and handing it to her. Tears welled at the back of her eyes. She would give anything to be back home with him at this moment.

Richard looked up from buttoning Emily's coat. "Are you sure you're okay?"

Lisa sniffed and nodded. "Must be starting a cold."

"I'm not surprised. This is a bloody awful day . . . in more ways than one."

"Daddy!" Emily said in a shocked voice. "You said bloody!"

"Oops! Sorry."

"That's 10—p for the swear box."

Richard rolled his eyes. "See how henpecked I am?" he said to Lisa. He swept Emily up in a bear hug and kissed her neck.

"Ten—p, Daddy," she yelled between giggles. "You owe ten—p."

"Okay, okay. I'll put it in the box when we get home. Let's go, Jo."

In a few minutes, they were driving away from Charnwood Court and out onto the road. Although it was not yet seven o'clock, it was pitch—dark from the low black clouds and constant rain.

"This isn't good," Richard said, as they drove out of the almost deserted village on the road beside the river.

Lisa glanced around nervously. "What isn't?"

"This heavy rain. This part of the world has a history of flooding."

Lisa's heart began a violent hammering. "At this time of the year?" She moistened dry lips. "I thought floods only happened in the spring."

"It's more usual then, but if we get continuous rain here it can fill the rivers and streams. Some of them are pretty shallow. Then they overflow and the water merges as it flows downstream, creating torrents cascading down the hills. That's what happened in the disastrous Lynmouth flood in 1952."

"What time of the year was that?"

"The summer. August. That flood was caused by

164

heavy rain."

Lisa drew in a shuddering breath. "What about the flood here in 1970?"

"What's a flood?" demanded Emily from the backseat.

Richard gave Lisa a warning glance. "Better change the subject."

"Sorry"

"My fault."

Despite the darkness, Lisa knew that he was frowning. She sensed that he wanted to ask her questions. Was it about her and Alec? Surely, as Rachel's nephew, he must know about Alec's first child . . . even if he'd only been a young boy at the time. After all, Betty knew all about Alec's daughter being sent away with her nanny and banished from Charnwood forever, so Richard must know, too. And surely if, as she suspected, Alec had guessed who she was, wasn't it likely he would have told Richard? Yet neither of them had mentioned a thing to her about it.

What kind of father would ignore the fact that his longlost daughter had returned and was staying beneath his own roof?

Lisa gritted her teeth. Well, two of them could play at that game. As far as she was concerned hell could freeze over before she acknowledged her relationship with Alec Kingsley. On the other hand, she wasn't going to forget her drowned mother.

An image of Millais's painting of the drowned Ophelia, adorned in meadow flowers, swam into her mind. She blinked then rubbed her forehead vigorously, trying to erase the image, but it lingered there, just behind her eyes.

"It's dark, Daddy." Emily's voice from the back of

the car startled Lisa back to reality.

"I know it is," Richard replied, "but that's okay. I'm here, and so is Lisa. We'll be home very soon now."

Lisa turned around and squeezed Emily's knee. "Would you like me to come and sit with you in the back?"

"No, thank you. I'm okay. Put some music on, please, Daddy."

"Certainly, madam." Richard pressed a button and the familiar sounds of Oscar Peterson and his group playing Gershwin filled the car.

"Is that okay?"

"Perfect," Lisa said, pleased to find that Richard shared her love of the great Canadian jazz pianist. She forced herself to relax, allowing the music to take over, but still the image of the painting remained imprinted on her mind. And now, as if there were an epitaph written beneath the painting, Shakespeare's words about Ophelia came into her mind . . . *her garments, heavy with their drink, pulled the poor wretch . . . to muddy death.*

CHAPTER NINETEEN

RICHARD'S HOUSE WAS IN A VILLAGE ABOUT FIVE MILES from Charnwood. It was set back a little way from the village green, which it overlooked. In the dim glow of the sporadic streetlights, it was hard to discern much detail, but Lisa could see that it was an attractive, medium—sized Georgian house built of stone.

Richard drove around to the back of the house and parked the Range Rover in a double garage, beside a lowslung dark green sports car. This was another side to

166

Richard, Lisa thought, with a little smile.

When she got out of the car, the smell of rain—sodden earth and grass came to her and, in the dim light from the coach lamp, she could see a stretch of lawn, bordered by flower beds. "You have a large garden."

"Unfortunately it's too wet to show you around. You'll have to come back again when the rain stops. Down past the garden and then the vegetable garden, there's an orchard, with dozens of fruit trees." Richard hurried her through the rain to the rear entrance. "We get hundreds of pounds of apples and pears—"

"And plums," added Emily. "They get all squishy on the ground and the wasps get inside and eat them. One of them stung me."

"Oh, poor you," Lisa said. "What a nasty wasp!"

"Daddy killed it. He squashed it to pieces with his foot," Emily said with great satisfaction.

"Good for Daddy." Lisa exchanged smiles with Richard in the doorway.

They entered the house through an attractive sunporch that had been added on to the main building. Richard switched on the light and Lisa saw that the conservatory, as Richard called it, was practically empty. To her, it cried out for plants in terra—cotta pots, colorful blinds, and lounge chairs with bright Van Gogh-style floral cushions.

When they'd taken off their rain jackets and boots in the conservatory, Emily grabbed Lisa's hand to pull her down the hallway to the living room. This room, at least, looked as if it was used. Bookshelves laden with books lined the wall beside the stone fireplace, and the sofa and chairs, covered in a burgundy—and—cream—printed fabric, looked comfortable.

But, apart from the rather dark wallpaper that covered

167

them, the other three walls were bare.

"It's a bit stark, I'm afraid," Richard said, gazing about him, as if he were seeing the living room through new eyes. "I haven't got around to hanging the pictures yet." He nodded at a stack of paintings leaning against the wall, their images hidden.

Lisa guessed that he preferred bare walls rather than having those things he'd chosen with his wife constantly reminding him of his loss.

"It takes time to get a house organized," she said. "I've been in mine for more than two years, and it still isn't right."

Richard shrugged. "Mine probably never will be. Right, I mean. It's just a house, really. My sister has offered to come and help me get it all sorted out, but I keep putting her off."

"Am I going to have a bath?" Emily asked, pulling them both back to the important things of life.

"No, you don't need one," her father said. "You had a bath this morning, remember? Up you go and start getting washed. I'll get Lisa a drink, and then I'll come up and put you to bed."

"I could put her to bed," Lisa said. "If that would be okay with her. You'll want to get back to the Court as soon as possible."

"What I want is to get back *from* the Court." Richard sighed heavily. "It's been a very long day. Or so it seems. How about it, Em? Would you like Lisa to put you to bed?"

Emily looked as if she wasn't quite sure. "Daddy always puts me to bed," she said in a whisper, her round eyes suddenly wary.

"I could read you stories," Lisa said in a coaxing tone.

Emily's eyes brightened. "How 'bout Daddy puts me to bed and you read me stories?"

"Sounds good to me," Richard said.

"Great. You go on up with her," Lisa said. "I can look after myself down here, if you don't mind me scouting around."

Richard hoisted Emily onto his shoulders. "Make yourself at home," he told Lisa. "There's white wine in the fridge. Other drinks on the trolley over there."

"Thanks. Don't worry about me, I'll find my way around." Lisa took hold of Emily's foot. "I'll be up as soon as Daddy tells me you're ready for story time."

Emily unexpectedly leaned down and kissed Lisa's upturned face, drawing all three of them close together, as if they were a family. Her face glowing with the warmth of that brief moment, Lisa watched father and daughter climb the stairs.

The kitchen was not large, but it was neat and well organized, everything in its place. Quite unlike Lisa's kitchen, which was always cluttered with containers and jars on the countertops and, in winter, pots of fresh herbs and miscellaneous plants on the window shelf.

She opened the fridge. Another revelation. Well stocked and, again, everything in its place. Carefully, she slid open the vegetable drawers, hoping she wouldn't be heard. There were vegetables in them, but no furry peppers or mushy cucumbers. Grimacing, Lisa slid the drawer shut. Richard either had an excellent housekeeper or he was incredibly well organized.

She found the white wine, poured herself a glassful, and then carried it back into the living room. Stacks of CDs were piled on the top of one of the bookshelves. It was an eclectic collection. Some jazz, including Humphrey Lyttelton—one of Greg's favorites—and more Oscar Peterson. (It was Greg who had sparked her interest in jazz. His best—his only!—legacy to her). Lots of traditional classical stuff: Bach, Mozart, Brahms . . . and some of the more accessible moderns: Benjamin Britten, Arvo Part, Philip Glass . . .

She smiled to herself. Their kitchens might not be compatible, but their taste in music certainly was.

She sat down on the couch and surveyed the room. It was furnished tastefully with a mixture of modern and a few beautiful old pieces that Richard had probably found in antique stores.

Or Richard's wife. Or both of them, shopping together, arm in arm.

Strangely enough, there was not one photograph of his wife anywhere in the room. In fact, there were no photographs at all. It was as if Richard had sought to obliterate his entire past from the room: Recalling her friends with children, and how their shelves and fridges were loaded with pictures of the kids and parents and grandparents, Lisa wondered how this total loss of her mother must have affected Emily.

Tears stung her eyes. Then she mentally shook herself. Emily seemed a perfectly well adjusted child. Besides, what Richard Barton did was absolutely none of her business . . . and never would be.

She picked up the Arts section of the Sunday *Times* and was about to start reading it, when she heard Richard coming down the stairs.

He came into the living room. "All tucked in and ready for her story. Are you sure you don't mind about this?"

Lisa put aside the newspaper and stood up. "I wouldn't be here, if I did."

"No, I suppose not." He surveyed her for a moment

with those perceptive eyes. *Legal Eagle*. The term came, unbidden, into Lisa's mind. Once again, he looked as if he were about to ask her an important question. Then he turned away, to pick up his briefcase. "I'll be back as soon as possible. A list of numbers, including the number of my cell phone, is by the phone. Emily can have half a glass of water, but nothing else." He smiled. "She knows the rules, but she may try it on with you."

Lisa grinned. "I'll make sure she toes the line, boss."

His smile faded. "Do you think I'm too heavy-handed with her?" His anxiety was palpable.

Lisa was appalled at his reaction to what had been nothing but a silly joke. She wanted to reach out and hug him. "No, of course not. I was just being stupid." She swallowed. "I think you're a terrific father."

A slight flush colored his jawline. "Sorry. I get a bit paranoid at times. Sometimes it's hard when you have no one to . . ." He stopped abruptly and walked briskly to the door. "I'll be as fast as possible, I promise."

"Take as much time as you need."

"Thanks. I'll turn the alarm system on when I leave. Just press the EXIT button if you need to get out for some reason."

"I won't. Don't worry about us. I can always call you if I have any questions."

"Do that, please." He turned, and shouted, " 'Bye, sweetie," up to Emily.

"Bye, Daddy," Emily shouted back. Lisa heard the pad of her small, bare feet across the landing. "Is Lisa coming up to read to me?" she called down.

Lisa joined Richard in the hall. "Coming right up," she replied and slowly started up the stairs.

More than two hours later, Lisa was lying in a halfdozing, half—waking state on the couch, a Bach Brandenburg Concerto playing softly in the background, when the harsh roar of a motorcycle's engine penetrated the rural silence. She sat bolt upright, her heart thudding. The engine cut out and she knew it had stopped directly outside the house. Then she remembered that Kate had said she'd probably be riding over on her Harley—Davidson.

A loud rapping came on the front window. Lisa went to the window and pulled back the burgundy—velvet curtains.

It was hard to recognize the figure clad in skintight black leather and a gleaming black helmet as Kate Kingsley, but the voice was unmistakable. "Open up," Kate yelled.

"Sssh!" Lisa hissed through the window. "You'll wake Emily." She made a gesture toward the front door, indicating she'd open it. She went out to the front hall, turned off the alarm system, slid back the bolts, and turned the key to let Kate in. Kate strode into the narrow hallway, dragging off her helmet to reveal her rumpled red hair. She smelled of leather and motor oil.

"Where's Richard?" Lisa asked her.

Kate grinned. "Oh, I passed him way back." She ripped open the fasteners of her jacket. "Phew, I'm hot! I'll have a beer, if there is one."

"Let's wait until Richard comes. He'll know where the beer is."

Kate pushed past her. "I know where it is. Don't worry, he won't mind." Her tone suggested that Lisa was totally pathetic to even consider waiting for Richard to get her a beer.

The sound of Richard's car put an end to the

discussion. He came in the back door, carrying his briefcase, his face drawn. "Is Emily asleep?" was his first question, as soon as he'd shut the door behind him.

"Fast asleep," Lisa confirmed. "We got through the whole of *Slinky Malinki and A Child's Garden of Verses*. That was for me," she added. Emily's room had been stacked with books and toys. There were also several photographs of her mother—a smiling woman with curly brown hair—which Emily had insisted on showing Lisa.

"Thanks so much, Lisa." Richard came into the hall and took off his jacket. He led the way into the living room, but didn't sit down.

"I hope it helped."

Richard rubbed his eyes. "Alec was grateful to you for—"

"I did it for you and Emily, not Alec or Rachel." She didn't want to help someone who'd run down a defenseless woman and left her bleeding on a deserted road in the pouring rain. She knew Rachel had a drinking problem, but why had she been driving in the first place? Those who'd allowed her to drive when they knew she drank should be charged with being accessories to the accident.

If it was an accident.

"Thanks, anyway," Richard said.

If Kate hadn't been there, Lisa might have asked him more about both Rachel and Maud. But Kate or not, the little she'd learned about Richard in the short time she'd known him made her doubt he'd tell her much, anyway.

One thing she could ask, and she did. "What's the latest news about Miss Birkett?"

"Alec called the hospital this evening. She's alive, but still unconscious."

173

Kate had fetched a can of lager from the kitchen. She took a swig from it and raised it in the air. "Hang in there, Maudie! If you die, my mother's in deep shit."

Richard gave her a quelling look. "She is, anyway."

Kate's lip quivered. "Don't you think I know that, you asshole?" Glaring at him and Lisa, she shoved past them both and went outside, slamming the door hard behind her.

"I don't know Kate at all, of course, but I'd say she's really hurting," Lisa said. "She just doesn't seem to know how to deal with it."

Sighing, Richard ran his hand through his hair. "I know. I just wish she wouldn't behave like a fifteen—year—old with an attitude. It only makes a bad situation worse."

Lisa didn't want to talk about the Kingsleys' situation. It only reminded her that this adolescent twenty-five-year old was her half sister, her own flesh and blood. Thank God, Rachel Kingsley wasn't any blood relation to her. Alec and Kate were more than enough.

"I'll just switch the CD player off."

"Bach?" Richard said, with a faint smile.

"Nice and soothing."

"We can do with some soothing. Leave it on."

They stood near the couch, within touching distance of each other, both suddenly falling silent. It was, for once, not an awkward silence, but a reflective one. Lisa sensed that they were experiencing the same longing: to be able to sit down on the couch and listen to Bach together, putting all that had happened today from their minds.

"Kate will be waiting for me," Lisa said, breaking the spell. She frowned. "Has she had anything else to drink

174

this evening, do you know?"

"No. I promised her a beer when she got here, as long as she had nothing to drink beforehand. She was with us all the time, and she drank nothing but Pepsi."

"Good. I hope you don't mind me asking."

"Not at all." He gave her a wry smile. "I should imagine you're worried enough about riding pillion on Kate's bike, without her drinking as well." He shook his head. "With all her faults, I'm glad to say that her mother's example has turned Kate off any kind of substance abuse."

"It must have been tough for her to see her mother—"

Richard's expression hardened. "My aunt never drank to excess until a few years ago, when this terrorist campaign against her and Alec began."

"And the police haven't been able to find out who's responsible?"

"Officially, no. Unofficially, it looks as if the entire bloody village of Charnwood is in on it, as far as I can make out."

"But . . . that's crazy."

"Crazy or not, it's true. The police can't find any one person who appears to be responsible."

"Then . . . is it possible your aunt attacked Maud Birkett deliberately, because Maud was one of those who've been sending those letters?"

He stared at her, his face impassive. Lisa wished she hadn't asked the question. He took a breath, as if was about to answer her, but then Kate hammered on the front door, and shouted. "Lisa, are you coming or not?"

"I'd better go before she wakes Emily." Lisa took her coat from Richard and pulled it on before he could help her.

He accompanied her to the door. "Thank you, again,"

he said in a formal tone. Opening the door, he stepped back. Outside, the rain poured down incessantly.

Lisa turned to face him, not wanting to leave with this distance still between them, but in the light from the overhead porch lamp she saw that his expression was cool, remote. He had set up not only a distance but also an invisible wall between them.

"The Kingsleys probably don't want a stranger around while they're going through such a tough time," she said. "Perhaps I should move back to the Stag."

He frowned for a moment, then said, "Perhaps you should." He put an end to any further discussion by muttering a quick, "Thanks again, Lisa," and closing the door on her.

CHAPTER TWENTY

KATE WAS SEATED ASTRIDE THE MOTORCYCLE, revving the engine. Lisa barely had time to scramble onto the pillion before the bike roared off, so that she had to grab Kate around the waist to avoid being sucked off the machine.

It was a scary ride. Kate could probably drive along the steep, narrow roads blindfolded, but Lisa was used to broad prairie roads and, tonight, her nerves were on edge. The speed coupled with the high—pitched roar of the bike, the constant twists and turns, and being hemmed in by trees on both sides, gave her the disorienting feeling that she was on a nonstop roller—coaster ride.

The pouring rain didn't help, either. The horrific images of Maud's accident still in her mind, Lisa expected the bike to go skidding off the slick road and

176

smashing into the tall hedgerow at any moment.

By the time they turned through the gates of Charnwood Court, however, she had abandoned herself to her fate, whatever it might be. Still she thanked God for the sight of the ancient house, its gabled roof black against the clouds that scudded across a watery moon.

"Enjoy that?" Kate asked, breathing fast. She switched off the engine, kicked down the stand, and jumped off the bike.

"I was just starting to."

"Haven't you ever been on a bike before?"

"Of course I have, but on wide, open roads, not narrow, twisting roads like these."

"That's no fun." Kate's voice was full of scorn. She nodded in the direction of the side door. "Go on in. I'll put the bike away. I have to wipe it down." Before Lisa could say anything, Kate wheeled the heavy bike away in the direction of the garages at the rear of the house.

There was a light above the side door: Lisa tried the handle, and found that it was unlocked. She carefully pushed it open, flinching as tire hinges creaked. The last thing she wanted now was to meet Alec.

"Is that you, Kate?"

Lisa winced. *Damn!* "It's me, Lisa Cooper, Mr. Kingsley," she called out. "Kate's putting away her bike."

He came out of the kitchen, his face impassive, unsmiling, without even a glimmer of welcome. "Ah, Miss Cooper. I was just making myself a sandwich." He was turning away to go back into the kitchen. "Have you eaten?" he threw at her over his shoulder. It came across as a polite afterthought, not actual concern for her wellbeing.

Lisa's chin lifted. "Thank you, but I'm not hungry."

She hadn't wanted to speak to him tonight, but his cold disinterest was getting to her. Her desire to avoid him was now superseded by a wish to confront him, to see again the way his gaze slid away from hers. She went to the kitchen door.

He was standing by a large pine—topped table in the center of the massive kitchen, a bread knife in his hand. Her sudden appearance startled him into looking directly at her. For not much more than a couple of heartbeats their eyes engaged . . . and then he turned away and moved to the sink to run water into a kettle.

"You will have to excuse our lack of hospitality tonight." He spoke not to her, but to the wall ahead of him. "Everything is rather upside down at present."

"I wanted to speak to you about that, but it might be better to leave it till the morning."

"I'm not sure where I'll be tomorrow. You had better speak out now." His tone was that of a man expecting the worst.

He thinks I'm going to confront him right now as his long—lost daughter, Lisa thought. She felt like bursting into bitter laughter. *Think again, you jerk*!

"I realize that you and your family are going through a difficult time." She addressed the taut shoulders, the stiff spine. "I can move back to the Stag tomorrow. I don't think it would be possible tonight. It's getting late and, anyway, I think they were fully booked until tomorrow."

"I see no need for you to move, unless you'd prefer to do so." Now he turned, but remained at a distance from her. Again, their eyes locked. This time it was Lisa, not Alec, who looked away.

"I thought it would be easier for you."

"The room is yours." His words startled Lisa. Did he

178

mean it literally? Her eyes widened . . . but then he added, "For as long as you require it. The only problem might be . . . the meals. Rachel . . ." His voice cracked.

"That's no problem at all," Lisa said quickly. "There are plenty of places in the village where I can eat."

He came forward to the far end of the table. "Feel free to use the kitchen whenever you need anything. Treat this . . ." His voice trailed away again. Lisa guessed he'd been going to say, "Treat this like your own home."

It was the perfect opening. Do it now, her inner voice shouted. Get it over with and get on with your life. Tell him, *I'm your daughter, you rotten scumbag!* But the words wouldn't come. His distress was all too evident. She couldn't pile more problems on him at this moment. Besides, if she confronted him now, there was no way she could stay on in the house, and her access to its secrets would be lost.

"Thank you." She turned away. "Good night."

"There's a kettle and things to make tea and coffee in your room," he called after her. "And a tin of biscuits."

"Thanks again," she replied, and continued on down the hallway.

SUNDAY EVENING

I screwed up. Maud's still alive. But at least she's unconscious. Let's hope she stays that way!

Not a perfect day, but on the whole not a bad one, either. Killed—or maimed—two birds with one stone: Maud and Rachel. Maud's face when she saw the car coming straight at her was a picture!

179

Now I must think of a way of getting E. to leave without hurting her. But if it doesn't work . . . . Well, it will be her fault for coming back to Charnwood.

I think I'll drop in on her tonight, just to see how easy it is.

Damn her! Why couldn't she have stayed in Canada, where she was safe?

CHAPTER TWENTY-ONE

LISA WAS AWARE UPON WAKING THE NEXT MORNING that she'd had vivid, unsettling dreams, but couldn't recall their content. She sat up and immediately became aware of a sweet herbal scent in the room that she couldn't quite identify.

Then she noticed the vase of garden flowers on the small table beside the bed. But when she bent over to inhale their scent, she knew it was not the same as the one she'd smelled when she awoke. She was left with the uneasy feeling that something disturbing had happened to her while she slept.

She swung her legs over the side of the bed and stood up, to test her ankle. It was still a little sore when she put her full weight on it, but she was glad to see that the swelling had gone down.

The white telephone sat on the dressing table, tempting her, as it had done the previous night before she went to sleep. She was dying to call Jerry, even though it was two in the morning his time. He wouldn't mind being woken, she knew, especially once she'd explained why. But something told her not to call from the Court. It was too easy to pick up another receiver and listen in. She'd call him later from a public phone—preferably one in a place that was miles away from the village of Charnwood. She'd been there less than two days, but already she felt she couldn't trust anyone in the place.

As soon as she'd showered and dressed, she went down the front staircase, hoping to avoid meeting any member of the Kingsley family. As she tiptoed across the flagstoned floor of the main hall she could hear sounds from the kitchen, but to her relief, no one appeared.

She was about to go out through the main entrance when Betty suddenly came out of the library.

"Morning, Miss Cooper."

"Hi, Betty." Lisa felt slightly foolish, as if she'd been caught trespassing. "I'm trying to avoid everyone this morning," she admitted. "I don't expect they want to make polite conversation."

"You be right there, Miss Cooper. They're in a fair fix, the family." The strong Somerset accent made her pronounce her *Fs* like *Vs*.

"How is Mrs. Kingsley this morning?"

Betty shrugged. "Not good." She wasn't in an expansive mood. "They're 'specting the police and Mr. Richard again at nine."

"Nine?" It was just after eight-thirty. "I'll get out of here, then."

"Is your car at the back? If 'tis, you'd be quicker to go out the side door."

"I'd rather go this way. I don't want to disturb them by going past the kitchen."

"Right. The rain's eased off a bit, so you won't get too wet."

181

"Good."

Lisa opened the front door and went down the steps. It might have eased off, but the rain was still falling like a fine, gray curtain. There were pools of water in the gravel driveway, as if the earth was incapable of soaking up any more water.

When she drove into the village parking lot, she found it almost empty. Her stomach felt the same way. She hadn't had a proper meal since the previous day's lunch . . . and that seemed like it had happened ages ago. Last night, all she'd had was the mug of hot chocolate she'd made herself and some oatmeal—raisin biscuits. What she really fancied now was another one of those massive English breakfasts.

She started off down the hill to the village, looking for a place to eat. Although the Stag was the one place she knew she'd certainly get a good breakfast, she crossed the road to avoid even passing it, determined never to set foot in the place again.

She tried Marion Heasley's place first, but the blind was down on the door and a sign stated, CLOSED. Glancing across the street, she saw that the door to Jane Tallis's shop was open. Jane was sure to know where she could get a good breakfast. Besides, apart from needing a friendly face, she might hear some valuable village gossip at Jane's.

She was surprised to find that the shop was packed with people. Some of them she'd met on Saturday, but there were others there she'd never seen before. Although she'd heard a loud buzz of conversation when she'd approached the shop, as soon as she stepped inside everyone fell silent.

"Morning, Lisa," Jane, sang out, her voice breaking the silence.

"Morning," Lisa replied, rather daunted by all the faces turned in her direction.

Paula Willand marched to the door. "I must be going." Lisa stood aside to let her pass. "Sleep well?" Paula asked her. Her smile could have corroded iron.

"Very well, thank you. Charnwood Court is *such* a beautiful house," Lisa added, with a sweet smile. Against this woman, at least, she would take a stand solidly on the side of Charnwood Court, if not its inhabitants.

" 'Bye all," Paula said. "Thanks for coming."

"See you later, Paula," someone said.

Nose in the air, Paula pushed past Lisa and went out. Lisa stepped down onto the floor of the shop.

"And how is Mrs. Kingsley today?" That came from Marion Heasley.

"I haven't seen her."

"Likely sleeping it off," said a man with the weathered face of a farmer, and several people laughed.

Lisa didn't know him, but she did catch sight of Tom, the old man who'd been at the doctor's office when she'd first arrived on Saturday morning.

Both men seemed out of place in the setting of an arts and crafts shop. It was obvious that she'd interrupted some kind of village meeting.

"What can I do for you?" Jane asked. Her tone said *Ignore them*.

"I'll come back later," Lisa turned.

"Come on over," Jane said, lifting the counter flap to let her in.

Lisa went to join her behind the counter. "I'm looking for a place for breakfast," she said in a low voice.

Obviously not low enough. She heard another snickering laugh, and then Marion said, "Not feeding you well up at the Court?"

"Leave her alone," Jane said. "It's not her fault. She's a visitor." She turned her back on them. "Everyone's up in arms about what happened to Maud Birkett," she explained to Lisa.

"I can understand that. I wanted to get out of there fast this morning." She gave Jane a rueful smile. "It's not a very pleasant atmosphere."

"I can imagine. I haven't eaten yet, myself. Everyone descended on me at the crack of dawn. Why don't I cook up some breakfast and we can eat together?"

"No, I can't expect you to do that," Lisa protested. "I thought you might know of somewhere, other than the Stag, that served breakfast."

"Today, you eat breakfast here." Jane banged on the counter with a rolled—up newspaper. "Okay, everyone," she shouted. "I'm going to shut up shop for a while. See you all tonight at the Stag."

Still talking and arguing, they slowly filed out.

"That didn't sound like just a drink you were planning," Lisa said, once they'd all gone.

"I'm not planning anything. It was Paula who called a meeting here this morning." Jane rolled her eyes. "She's on the warpath."

"About Miss Birkett?"

"Exactly. Maud's a good friend of all of us. I've dropped a word into Bill Brewster's ear that there's trouble coming. I was trying to calm them all down this morning, but they just tell me I'm a newcomer and don't understand how they feel."

"Betty was telling me yesterday that the Kingsleys have been getting threatening letters."

"God, they've been getting those for ages. It's common knowledge." Jane gave a bark of laughter.

"Bill says he thinks everyone in the village is in on the act."

"That's what Richard said, too."

"You mean Richard Barton?"

"Yes." Lisa grimaced. "I probably shouldn't have told you that, but he says everyone knows about it, so I don't suppose it matters, really."

"You're right."

"Why does everyone in the village hate them?"

Jane frowned. "I don't know all of it, of course. It was going on long before I came. But once I settled here, I soon found out how the village felt about the Kingsleys. For one thing, Alec didn't carry out the promises he'd made before he was elected."

"That's nothing unusual, surely."

"True. He was good at the social side of it, but, apart from hunting, Alec doesn't care much about anything, really. And everything he takes on seems to turn to dross, rather than gold." Jane went to the door and slammed it shut, turning the key in the lock. "Look at that beautiful house. He couldn't even make a go of it. Now he's going to lose it to some international hotel conglomerate, stupid git."

Lisa felt a spasm around her heart. Suddenly, now she knew that it had been her childhood home, the thought of Charnwood Court being turned into a hotel affected her personally, even emotionally. She stood in the small shop, thinking about the nursery and wondering what it would become when the place became a hotel. An upstairs bar, perhaps? A rest room?

"What's wrong?" Jane asked.

"Nothing much." Lisa swallowed. "I was just thinking what a shame it was to turn a wonderful old house like that into a hotel."

"Better than tearing it down. Have they given you a decent room?"

"It's lovely. Not as large as the other room. Next door to the nursery. You've probably seen it."

"Not me. I told you before, stately homes aren't my thing. And the Kingsleys are too hoity—toity to mingle with us lowly shopkeepers." Jane led the way into her kitchen. "Come along in. It's pretty cramped in here, but it suits me fine." She hooked out a stool from under the table with her foot. "Sit."

"Can I help?"

"No, you can't. It's too small for two to work in. But you can talk to me while I cook. What do you want? The works? Bacon, couple of eggs, sausages, fried bread?"

"Sorry. I forgot to tell you. I'm a vegetarian."

"Bloody hell! You can't have a proper English breakfast if you're a vegetarian, can you? What do you want, fried lettuce?"

"I eat eggs."

"Thank God for that, at least. Okay. Eggs, tomatoes, fried bread, mushrooms, baked beans. Sound okay?"

"Sounds great. I usually have cereal and toast at home."

"Well, you're not home now, girl." Jane slapped her ample thighs. "I believe in enjoying life, as you can see." She nodded in the direction of the sink. "Fill the kettle, would you? We're short on electrical outlets in this ancient establishment. You'll find one under the counter where the recipe books are."

Jane's kitchen was far more cluttered than hers was, Lisa realized. She liked it. It was homey and relaxed. Not cold and unused—looking, like Richard's kitchen. There was stuff piled on open shelves in no particular

186

order. A packet of oatmeal next to a bottle of Sambuca. A large glass jar filled with biscuits beside cans of soup. There was a sort of artistic symmetry to it all. It would be fun to paint it: still life of a chaotic kitchen. She plugged in the kettle, then sat down again.

"So, what do you think of the place?" Jane asked.

"Charnwood Court, you mean?"

Jane nodded. She poured oil from a plastic bottle into a large iron skillet.

"It's a lovely house."

Jane took a handful of large, dark mushrooms from the fridge and put them in a dish. Then she sliced four tomatoes in half. "It looks sadly neglected on the outside. What's it like inside?"

"It's really worth seeing. The old hall has a lovely flagstone floor and oak paneling and there's a nursery with a wonderful doll's house—"

"How many eggs for you?"

"Two, thanks." Realizing that Jane was only being polite when she asked about the interior of the house, Lisa changed the subject. "Have you heard how Maud is?"

"I called the hospital last night and again this morning. They were pretty noncommittal, but Bill Brewster tells me she regained consciousness early this morning and she's been moved from intensive care."

Lisa's heart gave a joyous leap. "That's great news. I didn't think there was any hope for her."

"It is and it isn't. Bill's says she doesn't remember anything about being run down. Her mind's a total blank. And she's still in serious condition." Jane opened a packet of pink pork sausages and snipped the links between them, setting them out on the large pan under the gas grill above the stove top. "If Maud dies, Rachel's going to be in for a load of trouble."

187

That was what Kate had said, last night. "I know. I imagine she will be, anyway."

"Did you see her when the police brought her home?"

"No. And I avoided them all this morning, so I know absolutely nothing about what happened."

"I understand Rachel's to appear in court this afternoon. I wonder what explanation she gave the police. Len told me she was pretty well legless when they took her out of the Hare and Hounds."

"Legless?"

"Pissed. Drunk. Len's the publican there. Rachel's a regular."

"Why would she go there to drink?"

"Who knows?" Jane cracked a couple of eggs on the side of the skillet and dropped them into the sizzling fat. The air was filled with the smell of spicy pork from the browning sausages. Not Lisa's favorite aroma, but she didn't like to ask Jane to open the window. "Maybe she likes slumming it," Jane continued. "She certainly wouldn't go into the Stag to drink. Apparently she said she never left the pub, but Len said she did . . . and that she came back later all bedraggled, as if she'd been out in the rain for quite a long time. So, there you go."

"Looks like she hasn't got a hope of getting out of it, doesn't it?"

"Certainly does. She deserves all that's coming to her." Jane smacked knives and forks down on the table. "Poor Maud."

"I'd like to send her some flowers."

"Maud Birkett?" Jane looked surprised. "Why?"

"She was kind to me."

"Was she? I didn't realize you'd met."

"On the tour I took Saturday."

"Oh, right. I'd forgotten the tour. How was she

kind?"

"I felt faint when we were upstairs in the house." Lisa didn't particularly want to tell anyone—other than Jerry—about the strange experience she'd had in the nursery. "Miss Birkett noticed and suggested I get some tea."

"Oh, I see. She's a strange fish, typical old—fashioned schoolmarm, but she's got a good heart behind that rather desiccated exterior."

"Whatever she's like, no one deserves to be run down and left to die in the road, like a dog."

"You're right there." Jane set down a brown—glazed teapot and two blue—ceramic mugs on the table, her round face flushed crimson from the heat. "Help yourself. Food's almost ready."

Lisa poured tea for herself and relaxed, enjoying the cosy ambience of Jane's kitchen.

A few minutes later, Jane put a large stoneware plate piled with food in front of her. "Eat up!"

"That looks fantastic. I certainly won't need anything more to eat today."

Jane set her own brimming plate on the bare wooden table and sat down opposite her. "You're on holiday, or supposed to be. Let's forget about all this misery for a while."

Lisa started in on the food. Once she'd eaten a forkful of mushrooms and one of the bright—yolked eggs, she thought it safe to get back to the topic of Maud again. "Now that I knows she's conscious, I really would like to send Miss Birkett some flowers. Can you tell me where the hospital is?"

"Not much use sending her flowers. I don't expect she'd even notice them. Waste of money, really."

"I suppose so, but I'd still like to send them,

189

anyway."

"She's at the main hospital in Taunton." Jane's forehead creased. "Actually, I've got to drive in there this afternoon to pick up some supplies at the rail station. Why don't you come with me and you can drop off your flowers at the hospital?"

"Thanks, but I'm sure they won't be allowing visitors yet, especially a stranger. I'll just send the flowers."

Jane shrugged. "Suit yourself."

Lisa's heart was beating fast. She hated deceiving Jane, but now that Maud was conscious she was going to do her damnedest to get in to see her. And she would have to do it on her own, without anyone in the village—even Jane—knowing about it.

Something deep inside her told her that Maud knew something about her mother's death. If Maud died, that knowledge would die with her.

CHAPTER TWENTY-TWO

JANE WOULDN'T LET LISA HELP WITH THE WASHING UP. "You go do some sight—seeing before the weather turns bad again," she told her. "One place you have to see is Lynmouth."

"Lynmouth?" Lisa swallowed. "Isn't that where the big flood was?"

"That's right. But they rebuilt it with a new waterway, so that it couldn't happen again. At least, that's what they say. You can't come to this part of the world and not see Lynmouth. It's a beautiful village at the foot of the cliffs. The scenery around it is spectacular."

Lisa gathered some of the plates together and carried

them over to the wooden draining board by the sink. "I thought I'd wait until the weather got better before I started sightseeeing."

"You could be waiting a long time for that. They're forecasting heavy rain again for tonight."

A shiver ran over Lisa. "Richard Barton was saying there could be problems with the river here if it kept raining."

"Could be. We had a lot of rain yesterday. The river's running pretty high. I was checking it out this morning. It must be up a couple of inches, at least."

Panic surged up from the pit of Lisa's stomach. She took a deep breath, trying to fight it off, but her heart began racing, and the sense of warm relaxation was gone.

Jane swatted her with the dish towel. "Get lost. Leave those things for me to do."

"If you insist." Lisa put the cutlery she'd collected into the sink. "You were going to give me the florist's number," she reminded Jane.

"I use the florist in Dunster. You can order them over the phone."

"What's the name of the hospital?" Lisa asked, trying to sound as casual as possible.

"Oh, they'll know at the florist's. It's the Somerset Hospital." Jane scribbled the florist's number on a piece of paper and handed it to her.

Lisa put the damp piece of paper into her wallet. "Thanks. And thanks, too, for the terrific breakfast. I owe you a good dinner out somewhere for that."

"Sounds great."

"Think of somewhere nice."

Jane grinned. "How about the dining room at the Stag?"

Lisa grinned back. "If you must. See you later."

"Need anything in Taunton when I'm there?"

"No, thanks. There'll be stores in Lynmouth, won't there?"

"Lynmouth or Lynton. Lynton's the upper town and has larger shops. Grocery, butcher, chemist . . . that sort of thing, as well as the touristy places."

"Then I'll get anything I need there."

Now I've committed myself to going to Lynmouth, Lisa thought ruefully, as she made her way back to the car. Still, Jane was right, she might as well see some of the beauty spots, even if that wasn't her real reason for being here.

But first she'd go to Taunton and do her best to get in to see Maud.

Sitting in the car, she studied the map, working out a route that avoided the coast. If she took the road to Simonsbath, she could do it, taking minor roads through the valleys of Exmoor. It would take much longer, but it was worth it. Once she reached Taunton, she could call the florist and order the flowers for Maud, to cover her tracks.

And just in case anyone saw her go and wondered why she was heading east instead of west to Lynmouth, she would leave Charnwood by the road that led to the coast.

It was a good decision. As she drove through the village, she saw Marion Heasley and Paula Willand standing outside the Stag with old Tom. All three heads turned to watch her as she passed by.

Once out of Charnwood, the road ran close by the river. Panic surged back again. Jane was right. The water had risen considerably. Even from the road, Lisa could see how fast it flowed, tumbling over the rocks and partly eroded banks. She braked suddenly, paralyzed by the sight of the foaming water, then forced herself on, knowing that she could turn away from the river at the next crossroads.

The journey on the narrow road was a long one. Frequently, she was trapped, unable to pass, behind slowmoving vehicles weighted down with all kinds of agricultural loads: hay, a chained—down tractor and, once, a load of frantically bleating lambs, probably going to the slaughterhouse. She hated the thought of the pretty little creatures being killed and eaten.

She also regretted having to push almost blindly through one of the most beautiful areas in England, unable to take the time to stop and relish the superb views from the heights of Exmoor or the lovely little villages, with their thatched cottages and flower—filled gardens. But she was literally driven by the urge to speak to Maud about Celia, before someone else got to her.

When she joined the main road to Taunton she was able to travel faster, but the traffic was heavier, some of it probably making for the nearby motorway. To save time, she stopped at a gas station on the way into the town. After she'd called the florist and ordered the flowers for Maud, she asked the man at the counter how to get to the hospital.

She was glad she did. The hospital was not in the town itself, but on its outskirts. Armed with the right directions, she was able to avoid the busy town center— and a bridge! The man at the gas station had mentioned that a river ran right through the center of town and that the main street crossed over it.

She was tense enough as it was, without having to undergo the ordeal of driving across a bridge.

When she walked from the hospital parking lot, she looked around, checking to make sure that no one she knew had followed her. *I'm getting totally paranoid*, she thought, as she approached the information desk. After all, if Rachel had run down Maud while she was drunk, surely it had nothing to do with a visitor from Canada.

Unless, of course, Rachel knew who Lisa was and wanted to keep Maud from telling her something about the past.

"Can I help you?" asked the older woman at the desk.

"I wanted to inquire about Maud Birkett," Lisa told her.

The woman's fingers clicked over the keyboard. "From Charnwood?" she asked.

"That's right."

"She's still listed as being in serious condition, but she has been moved out of intensive care."

"That's great." Lisa's heartbeat revved up. "I was wondering if I could visit her for a few minutes?"

"Are you a relative?"

"She has none, I'm afraid." Lisa hadn't a clue whether Maud had relatives or not. "But she was my mother's closest friend." That was a fabrication, as well. "I'm really all she has."

"I'll check with the staff nurse on duty." She left her desk and went to phone from the office behind her, so that Lisa couldn't hear what she said. Then she came back. "Staff Nurse Sanders said you can come up. No guarantees you can see Miss Birkett, though. Check in at the desk on the second floor."

When Lisa reached the elevator, she released her breath, feeling as if she'd been holding it for the entire conversation. At the nursing station on the second floor, she had to deal with the brisk Staff Nurse Sanders, a

194

tall, lean woman with a thin mouth, whose personality seemed as stiff and starched as her blue—and—white uniform.

"There's a police officer with Miss Birkett at present, taking a statement from her. You'll have to wait until she has finished. Then I'll check with Miss Birkett and the police officer to see if you can be allowed a five—minute visit."

As Lisa waited in the tiny waiting room, leafing through a tattered 1995 copy of *Woman's Own*, the time seemed to tick by with agonizing slowness.

She'd just finished scanning an article about getting on with your mother—in—law when she heard the stiff rustle of the staff nurse's skirts. She beckoned to Lisa from the doorway. "Come with me."

A young, sturdily built woman dressed in navy pants and a bottle—green sweater stood in the doorway of a room halfway down the hall. "I'm Detective Constable Logan." She spoke with a strong Scottish accent. "Can you give me your name, please, together with proof of your identity?"

Although the policewoman made Lisa nervous, she was glad to see that Maud had this kind of protection. If someone other than Rachel had run her down . . . But that was ridiculous. It had to have been Rachel. Lisa took her Canadian passport from her bag and showed it to the policewoman.

"And what exactly is your relationship to Miss Birkett?"

Lying to a clerk at an information desk was one thing, lying to the police another. "My mother and Miss Birkett were close friends," Lisa told her.

"I'll see if she can confirm this," DC Logan said.

"And if she wishes to see you," the staff nurse added,

195

her tone suggesting she thought it highly unlikely.

The two women went into the room, but the staff nurse returned almost immediately. *Well, that's it,* thought Lisa, her heart sinking.

"Miss Birkett wants to see you," the nurse announced, to Lisa's surprise. "She seemed very pleased that you were here," she said, her smile melting the starch a little.

"Oh, good," was all Lisa could say.

"Just a few minutes, please. She's still very weak. You'll find she's unable to talk much."

When Lisa went in, the policewoman moved over to the window. "I have to stay here, but I'll give you and Miss Birkett some space."

"Thanks." Lisa sat down on the metal chair. Maud was hooked up to all kinds of gadgets, including an intravenous stand and a heart monitor, and tubes led from her thin body. Her head was swathed in bandages and her right arm was in a cast. Beneath the bandages, her face was swollen and mottled with dark bruises. But her eyes were open and very much alive.

She murmured something and her left hand lifted toward Lisa, trying to clutch at her. Lisa laid her own hand on the bedcover and the thin hand gripped it.

"Do you know who I am?" Lisa asked her softly. If the policewoman was listening in, that would be a natural thing to ask someone who'd been seriously injured.

Maud made a noise in her throat as if she were trying to speak, but couldn't. She tried again. "Celia." The word came from some place deep in her throat.

"I'm Celia's daughter."

The hand gripped even tighter on hers. In the battered face, tears swam in the faded blue eyes. " 'Lizbeth."

Now there were tears in Lisa's eyes as well. Maud had given her the confirmation she needed, the final key to her identity. "That's right. Elizabeth. Were you my mother's friend?"

Maud's eyes closed and a small sound like a sob came from her throat. She nodded.

"Am I like her, like my mother?" Lisa had to ask. There was no one else she could ask.

A rasping in the throat again, then, "Alec's . . . eyes."

"Yes, I know. I saw that yesterday. He doesn't know who I am. Or at least he pretends he doesn't know."

The blue eyes became glacial. " 'shamed."

"He's ashamed? Because he abandoned me, you mean?"

Maud nodded slowly, then winced with pain.

"Maybe I should go," Lisa said quickly. "I don't want to tire you."

Maud's eyes widened. Her hand gripped Lisa's, holding on to keep her there. "Danger," she rasped.

"No, you're not in any danger now. You have someone guarding you." Lisa nodded toward the policewoman who stood at the window, her stocky body turned from them.

Maud shook her head. "No, no," she said vehemently. "You!"

Lisa's heart began pounding again. "I'm in danger?"

Maud muttered something that sounded like "Gem Fur."

Lisa repeated it, but it was obviously not right. Maud screwed her eyes up with frustration and repeated the same sounds.

"I'm sorry," Lisa said. "I just can't get it."

The policewoman stirred. "I had the same problem," she said from the window. "I think it's *Jennifer* she's trying to say. Ask her if that's it."

Lisa turned back to Maud. "Jennifer? Is that what you're saying?"

Maud nodded, relief in her eyes. "Danger . . . to . . . you."

"Jennifer means danger to me? Right?"

Maud nodded again.

"But I'm afraid I don't know who Jennifer is. Does she live in the village?"

Maud shook her head. Then her eyes closed again in frustration. Her mouth tried to get something else out, but it wouldn't come. She tried again, her bruised face growing red with exertion. "Ssss . . . Sister!" she spat out.

"Whose sister?"

Maud's head fell back against the pillow. "Don't try any more," Lisa said. "You're tiring yourself out." But Maud's hand gripped hers, compelling her to stay.

"Ask her who did this to her," the policewoman said quietly.

Lisa turned to face her. "Are you sure that's wise?"

DC Logan shrugged. "Anything she can tell us, however small, could help."

"Okay." Lisa turned back to Maud. "Do you know who knocked you down? Did you see who was driving the car?" Maud shook her head slowly. "Rain . . . too heavy," she whispered. "Waiting . . . for . . . me."

Lisa felt very cold, as if the temperature had suddenly plummeted. "You mean," she said slowly, "that the car was waiting for you?"

Maud nodded. Her eyes met Lisa's; this time Lisa saw fear lurking there. Lisa sensed rather than saw that the policewoman had moved nearer to the bed.

"No . . . noise," Maud said. "Then . . . car."

198

Lisa heard a sigh come from the police officer. They were both thinking the same thing. This had been no accident.

Maud's hand moved to clutch at Lisa's arm. "Go . . . home . . . Canada. Danger." Her breathing was coming fast, her face contorted with pain.

The nurse rustled into the room and checked the monitor. "Miss Birkett needs to rest now. You will have go to.

But Maud's hand was still gripping Lisa's arm. "Ask . . . him," she said. "Ask . . ."

"Ask who?" Lisa asked her urgently.

"Alec."

The reply surprised Lisa. "Ask Alec? Is that safe?"

"Ask . . . Alec," Maud repeated.

"Right, my dear," the nurse told Maud. "She'll do just what you want her to do. Won't you?" she said to Lisa, nodding to the door.

"Key," Maud said, this time quite clearly.

"You want Miss Cooper to have your key?" the nurse asked her.

Maud nodded.

"Which key?" asked the police officer. "Your house key?"

Maud nodded again and, for the first time her thin lips slid into a faint smile. Then the smile faded. "Take . . care," she said. Before Lisa knew what she was doing, Maud had borne her hand to her face. Lisa felt the dry lips pressed to it.

Hot tears scalding her eyes, Lisa bent to press her own lips to the forehead beneath the bandages. "I promise I'll take care," she whispered. She glanced up to see that the police officer and the nurse were standing together, engaged in some sort of conference. "I also

199

promise that I will find out who killed my mother," she whispered to Maud, "and bring him or her to justice."

Maud's weary eyes opened again. "Never . . . forget her."

Lisa wasn't sure whether Maud meant that she had never forgotten Celia, but she responded, "I shall never forget her."

That seemed to satisfy Maud. Her body appeared to go limp, and she released Lisa's hand.

Alarmed, Lisa called to the nurse, "Is she all right?"

The nurse hurried to Maud's side and checked her. "She's very weak, but she's still with us. You really must go now. Do we have your address and telephone number?" she asked.

The question sounded ominous to Lisa.

"I'll get all the details," DC Logan said briskly. "If you can spare a few minutes to stay with Miss Birkett," she said to the nurse, "I'd like to have a few words with Miss Cooper. But don't leave her side for even a moment," she warned.

Lisa was escorted back to the tiny waiting room. The police officer motioned to her to sit down and took out an official—looking notebook, flicking the page back. "Let's see what we have. Set me straight on anything I might have misheard or not understood. You are Miss Lisa Cooper visiting from Canada. Your mother was a close friend of Miss Birkett. Is your mother deceased?"

"Yes."

"And her name was?"

Lisa held her breath for a moment. "She was my birth mother. I was adopted as a young child."

"Yes, but I take it you know the name of your real mother, as you've been in contact with Miss Birkett."

There was no way of escaping this. After all, she'd

been allowed to see Maud on the basis of being the daughter of her closest friend. "My mother's name was Celia. Celia Templeton."

"Right. Now would you confirm that Miss Birkett mentioned the name *Jennifer?*"

"Yes."

"Do you know of anyone by that name? I mean, anyone connected with Miss Birkett?"

"No. No one at all. But I must remind you that I arrived from Canada only two days ago. There could be someone living in Charnwood who—"

"We'll get on to that immediately. But you don't personally know anyone called Jennifer connected to Miss Birkett."

"That's right."

DC Logan made a note in her book. "Miss Birkett also mentioned a sister. Do you know what she meant?"

"I haven't a clue. I couldn't tell whose sister she was talking about."

"We've tried to trace Miss Birkett's relatives. Do you know if she has or had a sister?"

"I'm sorry I don't know. As I told you, I just arrived from Canada."

"To trace your parents, is that right?"

This woman was like a bulldog. She wasn't going to let go until she had the whole picture. "Yes," Lisa said.

"And all you had, perhaps, was the fact that Miss Birkett was your mother's friend?"

Lisa swallowed hard. "Yes."

"So it could be," the policewoman said slowly, obviously thinking as she spoke, "that your quest for your parents might have had something to do with Miss Birkett's accident?"

"I don't see how it could. No one in Charnwood

knows that I'm here for that purpose."

"Except for Miss Birkett."

"Right," Lisa had to agree.

"And Miss Birkett might have told a friend about the real reason for your visit."

"It's possible. I don't know."

"Did you at any time in your conversation with Miss Birkett hear her mention the names Kingsley or Rachel?"

"No."

DC Logan scanned her notebook, then flipped the cover over and slid it into her leather shoulder bag. "Thank you, Miss Cooper. I know that Miss Birkett asked that you be given her house keys. Those keys must be kept by the police investigation team at all times. However, it is likely that you will be permitted to enter the house and examine anything you wish, but you will be under police surveillance while you do so."

"Thank you."

"Detective Inspector Henderson may also want to interview you. I do want to make sure that you understand you cannot leave Charnwood until you have permission to do so."

Panic surged as the sense of being trapped swept over Lisa. "I have to fly back to Canada next Friday. I can't change my ticket."

"I will advise DI Henderson of that. Meanwhile, please do not leave Charnwood without speaking to one of the police officers there first." The policewoman cleared her throat. "I think you must have realized that we have a possible case of attempted murder here."

Their eyes met. "Or murder," Lisa said, thinking of Celia.

"I hope not," Detective Constable Logan said,

obviously thinking she meant Maud Birkett.

Once she was released, with another warning not to leave Charnwood, Lisa walked down the stairs, her legs like jelly. When she reached the ground floor she hesitated, wondering if she should get a cup of tea in the hospital cafeteria, but then decided against it. What she needed most was to find somewhere quiet, somewhere far away from the hospital—and from Charnwood, so that she could try to make some sense of all that she'd learned from Maud.

She was about to walk to the exit when a horribly familiar voice froze her to the floor. She spun around to see the three unmistakable forms of Paula Willand, Jane Tallis, and Marion Heasley standing at the information desk. It was Paula's strident voice Lisa had heard, arguing with the woman there.

She paused, wondering if she could make it to the exit without them seeing her, but before she had time to move Jane had caught sight of her.

"Lisa?" she called, incredulity in her voice. "What are you doing here?"

CHAPTER TWENTY-THREE

THERE WAS NO ESCAPING THEM. SQUARING HER shoulders, Lisa walked to the information desk. "Hi." She gave them a nonchalant smile, her mind frantically searching for some credible explanation for being here.

"What the hell—" Paula started to say, but Jane spoke over her.

"I thought you were going to Lymnouth this morning." Her voice was frosty.

"I was. But then I decided to come to Taunton instead. I thought I'd find the stuff I needed more easily in a larger town."

Jane's dark eyebrows rose. "In a hospital?"

"That was an afterthought. As I was here, I thought I might as well—"

"Did they let you in to see Maud?" demanded Marion Heasley.

"Excuse me," said a man, who was trying to get to the desk.

They moved away, but it was only a brief respite. Once they'd moved a little way from the desk, they turned on Lisa again.

"Did you get to see Maud?" Marion asked again, her sharp voice rising.

Lisa lifted her chin. "I saw her for a few minutes."

"What nerve!" said Marion.

"Bloody cheek!" said Paula. "What right have you got to get to see her, when they won't let us in?"

Jane was silent. When Lisa met her gaze she saw the coldness in her eyes. She could understand why. She'd accepted her hospitality, milked her for information, and then deceived her. Not a very promising start to a friendship.

One day soon, when this was all over, she would explain everything to Jane. But now, in front of the two other women—particularly Paula—was definitely not the time.

"I wanted to thank Maud for her kindness to me on Saturday," Lisa explained. It sounded rather lame.

The women seemed to think so as well.

"When she's seriously injured and in the hospital?" Marion squeaked. "You must be daft."

"I'd like to know what you have to do with Maud,

204

Miss Cooper," said Paula. "And, by the way, where were you yesterday afternoon?"

That seemed to unthaw Jane. "Now you're the one who's daft," she told Paula. She turned back to Lisa. "We're pretty pissed off. We've all known Maud for a very long time, yet they refuse to let us in to see her. But you, a total stranger, are allowed in. Why?"

"Perhaps because I was on my own and there are three of you. She's too sick to see a group of people."

Jane shrugged. "Could be. And, of course," she added, "you were here ahead of us." There was no escaping the note of accusation in her voice. "Anyway, that's all water under the bridge. How is she?"

"Maud?"

"Yes, Maud. Who else are we talking about?"

"She's very weak." Lisa hesitated, not wanting to give away too much with the other women there. "But she's being well looked after."

"Does she say it was Rachel Kingsley who knocked her down?" Paula asked.

"I've no idea. You'd have to ask the police officer who's with her."

"So they're guarding her, are they?" Marion looked over her glasses at Paula. "Maybe they're afraid Alec will come here and get to her."

"You'd be better to keep your big mouth shut, Marion," Jane said. "Or it'll get you into big trouble." She glanced at Lisa and away again. "I'm dying for a cup of tea. Let's go down to the cafeteria. Maybe they'll let us in to see Maud after she's had a break from visitors." She turned to Lisa. "Want to come?" It was a less than lukewarm invitation.

"Thanks, but I've got things to do."

"Are you still going to Lynmouth? You haven't left

much time for it."

"I'll see." Lisa hesitated, then said, "Maybe if only one of you goes in to see Maud, they'd let you in."

She started off down the hall, and then turned back. *Sorry,* she mouthed to Jane. But either she'd caught her by surprise or Jane was not about to forgive her so easily, for her apology met with a glacial look, and then all she could see was Jane's substantial back.

Lisa walked away, cursing fate. If she'd left just five minutes earlier, she probably would have missed them. Paula seemed to suspect her of having something to do with Maud's accident, but that could have been a cover for her own involvement. Lisa did not trust Paula Willand.

Jane was different. She'd try to see Jane this evening and give her a fuller explanation. She owed her that, at least, for her kindness since she'd arrived in Charnwood.

As she walked to the exit, Lisa had an overwhelming desire to get out of that place. Not just the hospital, but the town and the busy roads leading to and from it, and the restless sea that she rarely saw but she knew was lurking nearby, and the bleak moorland and closed—in valleys of Exmoor. She wanted to be home in Winnipeg, where life was uncomplicated and safe.

Yet even as she felt the pangs of longing for the spacious streets and endless blue skies of home, she knew that life would never again be uncomplicated for her. Wherever she went, she could never forget that the mother who'd given birth to her had died under mysterious circumstances and that, twenty—five years later, danger stalked those who had known her. Poor Maud had confirmed that. Lisa knew that only by staying in Charnwood and seeking out the truth would she be able to find peace—both for herself *and* her mother.

She halted at the exit, eyeing the bank of telephones beside it. She must tell Jerry about her visit to Maud. At least, there, she could make a call without fearing someone might be listening in on an extension.

She was about to tuck herself into the small booth at the end when she realized that the three women would be able to see her on their way out to the parking lot. She hesitated, telling herself that they'd said they were going to the cafeteria. But they could change their minds and decide to go into town for lunch, couldn't they? She didn't want to be trapped by them again.

She glanced at her watch. Twenty past one. If she waited another hour or so Jerry would be in the gallery and she could call him there. That was better than calling him at his apartment. Less chance of getting Daniel that way. Jerry and he had been together for more than six months now, and she'd been getting the distinct feeling that Daniel resented Jerry's close relationship with her. Because of that, she tried to avoid contact with him. Part of her wanted Jerry to be happy in his personal life. The other part wanted things to remain the same as before, with Jerry always there for her whenever she needed him.

She pushed the revolving glass door and walked across the parking lot, glad to feel fresh air on her face, riffling the loose tendrils of hair about her face. A father pushing a baby carriage smiled at her as she passed. She felt heartened by this confirmation that there was life beyond what she was going through at present.

Not until she'd left the busy roads converging on Taunton did Lisa start to mull over her rather one-sided conversation with Maud. What she'd learned made her feel even more puzzled than before.

Who was this Jennifer? And why had Maud told Lisa to ask Alec. Ask Alec what? Before she asked Alec anything, Lisa decided, she'd get into Maud's house and see what she could find there. That's what Maud wanted her to do, so there must be some reason for it.

Her heart pumped fast. Why not do it as soon as she got back to Charnwood, while those two gossips were still in Taunton with Jane? That way, she'd have less chance of running up against them.

The thought of making progress in her investigation so exhilarated her that she missed the turnoff to the country road across Exmoor. She'd either have to turn and go back a few miles or carry on and face the coastal road and that horrendous hill at Porlock.

At the next lay-by, she pulled off the road to consult her map and guidebook. No, she was okay. She could take another turning and still avoid the coast. But then she thought of how long it had taken her that morning. She wanted to get back to Charnwood and into Maud's house as quickly as possible. Ignoring her churning stomach, she took the coastal road, telling herself that it didn't really approach the sea until she'd gone through Porlock.

A short time after the turnoff to West Quantoxhead—what quaint names they had in Somerset!—Lisa suddenly realized how hungry she was. It was a long time since she'd eaten Jane's massive breakfast. When she saw the signpost to the little town of Dunster, she took it, turning left off the main road. Within a few minutes, she was pulling into the parking lot of an old inn directly across from the open-air Yarn market, an ancient stone circular building standing in the center of the high street.

She went into the oak-beamed bar and ordered a ploughman's lunch, thinking it might be faster than one of the cooked meals listed on the blackboard. But when she saw the size of the plate and the food piled upon it, she wasn't so sure about that. Several inches of crusty French bread, a hefty wedge of creamy—white Cheddar cheese—"Good Somerset cheese, that be," the barman told her, pronouncing it 'Zummerzet'—with three fat pickled onions, a great scoop of dark pungent chutney, and a large salad. She was persuaded to have a half of the local cider to go with it. Jane had warned her about "scrumpy," the name given to the more potent version of the local cider, but the barman assured her that what he'd given her was quite mild.

"I've my license to think of, m'dear," he told her.

She'd noticed a public telephone outside the inn as she'd come in. Once she'd finished all she could manage of the ploughman's lunch—and warded off advances from a couple of local youths—she finished her cider and went out.

The uniquely British telephone booth was painted scarlet, very attractive from the outside. The interior was a little less so. Cigarette butts littered the cement floor. An empty potato chip packet sat on the shelf above the telephone and the booth reeked of stale cigarette smoke, but still it was a haven to Lisa. No one could overhear her conversation.

She got through to the international operator, gave her the gallery's number and waited for Jerry to answer. He picked up after the fifth ring.

"Danco Gallery."

"Hi, Jerry. It's me. Thought I'd just check in and bring you up-to-date." Lisa tried to sound relaxed, not

209

wanting to worry him.

Jerry wasn't so easily fooled. "What's happened? I tried to get you at the house an hour ago, but they said you'd gone out early in the morning."

"I decided to visit Maud in the hospital."

"The woman who was run down?"

"Yeah."

"How's she doing?"

"Not good." Lisa told him what she'd learned from Maud.

When she finished, there was a long period of silence at the other end. Then Jerry said, "So she was run down by Mrs. Kingsley."

"By her car. Maud didn't mention Rachel's name. But the police still think Rachel did it."

"The police always prefer to go for their first suspect," Jerry said dryly. "Makes it easier for them that way." Another silence. "And she actually said there was danger for you?"

"Well . . ." Lisa drawled, not wanting to make too much of it.

"You'd better take this seriously," Jerry warned. "I told you I had that weird feeling about you, but you didn't want to know. Now will you believe me?"

"I promise to be careful."

"How's the weather?"

"We had pelting rain all day yesterday. It's still raining today." Lisa shivered. "The river's rising."

"God, that's all you need."

"Talking of rivers, how's the Red doing?"

"It's good. Down another inch or so yesterday."

"That's great news."

"Are you okay?" Jerry asked. "I'm worried about you. I wish you'd let me fly over."

210

Lisa felt tempted to say "Come right away," but didn't. "I'll be back on Friday, as planned," she said lightly, "and I intend to have this all sorted out by then. You do understand, Jerry, don't you? It's not only for me now. It's not even just for my birth mother. I've got to find out for Maud's sake."

"Let the police deal with all that. I think you should confront your birth father right away. I tell you, that man's got a lot to answer for. Ask him about what happened, and once you've got all the information you need, come on home."

"Before I ask him anything, I want to see Maud's place. Once I've had a look around, I'll speak to him." Her hand was damp on the black receiver. "It's not going to be easy," she whispered.

"I can imagine. Why not speak to . . . what's his name?"

"Richard. Richard Barton."

"He sounds like a sensible guy. Get him involved."

"He's a relative. Rachel's nephew. If Rachel did this thing—after all, she's still the number one suspect—I'd be putting myself in the enemy's hands by speaking to him, wouldn't I?"

"Okay, okay. Then don't enlist his support. Whatever you do, make sure the police know what you're up to. Whoever's behind all this stuff won't be so likely to do anything to you if they know the police are involved."

"Quit worrying. Nothing's been done to me. No one's after me."

"I hope it stays that way. Where are you going now?"

"Want an hourly report from me on where I am and what I'm doing?"

"No need for sarcasm. Just keep in touch, okay?"

"Okay. I have to go. There's three people lined up

outside, waiting for the phone. The guy in front's got a bull terrier. I think he's about to open the door and set it on me. I'll call you tomorrow."

"Do that. I need to talk to you about those Pangnirtung prints we ordered for Norville."

"Problems?"

"Not really. Just clarification, that's all. It can wait until tomorrow."

Lisa eyed the glowering man outside. "I think it had better, unless you want me torn to pieces. Tell Dad I called, would you?"

"You should call him yourself."

"I know, I know, but I'd have to pretend I'm having a great time here, and he'd guess I was lying."

"I'll lie for you and tell him you're fine."

"I am fine, you idiot. Love you. Have to go." She crashed down the receiver and hurriedly gathered up her wallet. "Sorry," she said, holding the door open for the man with the terrier, which bared its teeth at her.

Murmuring something that was fortunately unintelligible, he dragged the terrier into the booth with him, and pulled the door shut.

CHAPTER TWENTY-FOUR

WHEN SHE WAS HAVING LUNCH IN DUNSTER, LISA HAD asked about the drive through Porlock and discovered, to her great relief, that there was an alternative route, a toll road that was far less steep than the one she'd taken on Saturday. She decided to take it.

She was rewarded with a drive through a densely wooded area—and a surprising break in the weather. Although the rain had ceased and the sun come out, the trees were still dripping water onto the sodden ground. The sun shone through the tracery of branches and leaves, dappling the narrow corkscrew road that wound ahead of her with moving shadows. Through the open window she could hear birdsong punctuated by the rhythmic tapping of a woodpecker.

It was certainly better than being stuck behind nervous drivers on a perilously steep hill.

When she reached the summit, she drove west along the route that ran parallel to the sea, her eyes fixed on the road ahead, not allowing herself even to glance to her right, where the expanse of turbulent water stretched all the way to the coast of south Wales.

She hesitated when she came to the signpost that pointed left to Charnwood, thinking how pleasant it would be to drive on to Lynmouth, to pretend, just for a couple of hours, that she was a tourist exploring the countryside.

But the guidebook had described the descent into Lynmouth down Countisbury Hill as being hair—raising, with a steep, unprotected drop to the sea hundreds of feet below.

Lisa was pretty sure she wasn't in the mood for that kind of ordeal today. She clicked on her turn signal and turned the car down the now familiar road to Charnwood.

When she drove into the village, it was filled with visitors taking advantage of the break in the weather, while it lasted. She managed to find a spot in the parking lot and immediately made her way to the police station. It consisted of a two-story stone cottage with a blue lamp advertising POLICE over the door and a noticeboard pinned with tattered notices on the wall.

She went in and asked the policeman at the counter

213

for Sergeant Brewster.

"He's in Taunton, at the court," she was told. She'd thought Brewster had a pronounced country accent. This man's was even broader.

"Oh, I see." She hesitated. "Is that for Mrs. Kingsley's case?"

"That's right, miss."

So Jane had been right. Rachel was appearing in court today. She felt a pang of pity for the family, especially Kate.

"I doubt he'll be back till evening," said the policeman, who looked as if he must be near retirement age. "Can I help you?"

"I'm not sure. I was speaking to DC Logan, who was with Miss Birkett at the hospital in Taunton and—"

The policeman's ruddy face broke into a smile. "Oh, now you must be Miss Cooper, right?"

Lisa smiled back at him, relieved that she didn't have to explain any further. "Yes, that's right."

"DC Logan called to tell us about you." He held out a hand the size of a small ham. "Police Constable Sam Martin," he said. "I'm to take you to Miss Birkett's place, but you must understand I can't leave you there on your own."

"I know that. When could we—"

He glanced at his watch. "Time for my tea break soon. Tell you what, m'dear, why don't I take my break now and meet you up at Miss Birkett's house in, say, a little more than half an hour?"

"Sounds great. There's only one problem."

"What's that?"

"I don't know where her house is."

He gave her a frowning look. "I thought you told DC Logan you were a friend of Miss Birkett's."

214

"My mother was. I met Miss Birkett for the first time on Saturday at Charnwood Court."

He seemed to accept this. "I see. W—well," he drawled, "that's easy remedied. If you wait a minute, m'dear, I'll lock up here, then I can show you the way before I go home for my tea."

She marveled at the casual way he talked of just leaving the police station for his tea. "What if someone needs you?" she couldn't help asking.

"Oh, everyone hereabouts knows where I live. If I'm needed, someone'll send to my house."

"But you might be at Miss Birkett's with me."

"Then my missus'll tell them where to find me. Want me to drive you up to the house? It's a bit of a walk, uphill all the way to the moor."

"I'll walk. I could do with the exercise."

Having locked up, he led her to the top of the high street and then went a little way up the road with her, to show her a narrow lane. "Keep on going till you get to the top. You can't miss it. It's the only house up there, on the edge of the moor. And there's a sign hanging outside, with the name of the house on it."

"What's it called?"

"Resignation."

"Resignation? That's a strange name for a house!"

"It used to be called Hilltop. Miss Birkett changed it when she stopped working. I asked her why she'd chosen such an outlandish name; 'specially as she hadn't resigned from her school, she'd retired. But she just gave me that funny smile of hers and said something about it applying to all her life, not just to her retiring from teaching."

Resignation. It had a gloomy, melancholy sound to it. Lisa wondered if she would ever learn the true

215

significance of the name.

"I'll be there in half an hour or thereabouts," the constable told her.

Lisa walked on, climbing up the steep, unpaved lane. When her ankle started to throb again, she wished she'd accepted Constable Martin's offer of a drive. Oh well, nothing she could do about it now. Limping slightly, she carried on, carefully avoiding loose stones and water—filled holes. Before long, she reached the pathway that led up to the solitary house.

The tall Victorian house stood at the top of the rise, overlooking the moor. Today it was bathed in sunshine that warmed its gray stone walls, but it must be extremely bleak in the wintertime. She went around to the back and leaned against the garden wall, gazing up at the house. She imagined the biting winter wind blowing across the open moorland, moaning around the Gothic turret on its roof, rattling its windows, whistling down its chimneys. It was not a house that she'd choose to live in, especially on her own.

She said as much to PC Martin, when he arrived in his 4x4. "It's very isolated up here, isn't it? It must be very cold in the winter."

"You be right, there, miss. 'specially when it snows."

Lisa shivered. "I wonder why she chose this house?"

"She didn't. 'Twere her father's home, and his father's before him. Seems the Birkett family were local gentry, but they lost their money when Maud's grandfather was killed before the last war." Sam Martin shrugged. "Folks say John Birkett thought himself too good to work the farm himself. They ended up selling the farm and all the land that went with it. It was in such a sorry state they got next to nothing for it. After that, this house was all the family had left." He gave her a

216

sharp look. "But you know all that, don't you? You being a friend of the family."

"I'm afraid I don't really know that much about them."

He produced a small bunch of keys and proceeded to unlock several locks. "Hard to remember which is which," he said with a grin.

"She must have been nervous, living up here alone."

"Seems so, though I can't see why. We get very little crime here. Leastways, we did." Frowning, he pushed open the door. "Even then, it's been all petty, spiteful stuff . . . until now."

Lisa followed him into the dark hallway. There was a strong smell of beeswax polish, with a faint overlay of pine cleaner. A dark oak coat stand with an oval mirror took up much of the room in the hall. In addition to brass hooks for coats and jackets, it had a boot rack and a compartment filled with a variety of umbrellas and walking sticks.

Constable Martin led her into the front room. "This is the parlor."

Lisa gazed around. The room was filled to capacity with cumbersome dark furniture and an overstuffed sofa and matching chairs covered in worn brown corduroy. The walls were covered with paneling of dark wood, and smoke from wood fires had stained the glossy cream ceiling. "It looks exactly the way I imagined a Victorian parlor would look."

Constable Martin looked around the room. "Too dark for my liking."

"You're right." Then Lisa caught sight of a delicate watercolor of a marsh marigold on the wall beside her. "Except for this lovely thing." The petals of the simple flower were a luminous gold. And now she saw three more watercolors of wildflowers on the walls, their simplicity and subtle coloring a potent contrast to the oppressive darkness of the room. She wondered who the artist was.

"Now what exactly is it you're looking for, Miss Cooper?" The policeman's voice brought her back to earth.

"I'm not quite sure, really. Papers, photographs, newspaper clippings . . . that kind of thing."

"Ah, now then I can help you with that. Young Davey and me were going through the desk in what must have been Mr. Birkett's study in the old days. We found all kinds of albums and things in the desk drawers. Very organized, Miss Birkett was." His face went brick red. "That makes her sound as if she's passed away already, doesn't it? Sorry, I didn't mean to—"

"That's okay. I know what you meant. Would you show me the albums? They might be exactly what I'm looking for."

He led the way down the hall to a smaller room. At the far end of the room was a window with a border of stained glass through which the sun shone, throwing blocks of color onto the papered walls. In front of the window stood a massive mahogany desk with brass handles.

"Here, I'll open it for you," Constable Martin said. "These drawers weigh a ton." He tugged open the top drawer to reveal a stack of albums. "There's dozens of them. Some of them go back to Miss Birkett's grandfather's time. That's the leather—bound ones in the lowest drawer. Everything's labeled and dated."

"That's a help." Lisa laid her hand on the uppermost layer of albums, her heart beating fast.

"Mind if I sit down?" Sam Martin asked, trying to

218

catch his breath. "Those drawers are mighty heavy."

"Please do. I'm sorry, I know I'm taking up your time, but . . ."

He sat down on one of the ladder—backed chairs with worn brown—leather seats. "DC Logan said you might be able to shed some light on the accident." His face darkened. "If it was an accident."

"I doubt it. I don't even know what I'm looking for."

She lifted out an armful of albums and carried them to the table. One slid from beneath the pile. Catching it before it fell to the floor, Lisa opened it. It was labeled *1939* and filled with old black—and—white and sepia photographs and postcards of the area. She recognized the Yarn market at Dunster and the Ship Inn in Porlock, which she'd passed on Saturday.

She set the older albums aside and opened one dated 1958/1959. Several small black-and-white photographs had been stuck onto the first page, pictures of three teenage girls in clinging one—piece bathing suits. *The Three Musketeers* was the heading, written in faded ink on a strip of paper and stuck onto the black page. The photographs were so small that it was hard to see the faces clearly, but the one in the center of the page was slightly larger—and clearer—than the rest.

Exuding the smell of stale tobacco, Constable Martin leaned over her shoulder to take a look. His nicotine-stained finger pointed at the thin girl on the right, who was taller than the other two. "That looks like Maud."

"I think you're right."

"The other one's quite a looker," the policeman said.

He was pointing to the girl in the middle, who stood with her arm around Maud's waist. Her hair was tied back, but although the photo was black-and-white, it was easy to tell that her hair was golden. The clinging bathing suit delineated her swelling breasts, slim waist, and curving hips. Lisa knew instinctively that this was her mother. Nineteen-fifty-eight, she thought. Celia Templeton would have been fourteen then, but she was already a woman, and a beautiful woman, too, with none of the gangling adolescence of the other two girls. She smiled seductively into the camera. Yet the smile was entirely natural, as if she was still unaware of her own sexuality.

"Do you know who she is?" Constable Martin asked.

"I think so," was all Lisa said. She swallowed hard, trying to check the tears forming behind her eyes.

"Who's the third girl?"

"I don't know."

She stood beside the other two, yet she didn't seem to be part of the group. Shorter than both girls—probably younger than them—she was not just lean, as Maud was, but positively skinny, her legs like sticks. The space between her and Celia was made particularly eloquent by the obvious warmth of Celia's feelings for Maud. Her arm around Maud's waist, Celia leaned away from the third girl, her head almost resting on Maud's shoulder.

"I wonder who took the picture." Lisa spoke her thought aloud. When she turned the page the answer was before her, in the form of a photograph in the center of the page. It was a picture of a boy—a young man of about eighteen—taking up a typical male pose on the same beach, chest out, hands on hips, dark hair slicked back, white teeth gleaming in his tanned face as he laughed into the camera.

"Alec Kingsley," Constable Martin said. "Handsome devil, wasn't he? Still is, for that matter." He pointed to the other photograph of Alec with Maud and the younger girl. "No wonder those two girls are drooling over him."

He was right. Although *drooling* was not quite the word Lisa would have used. The expression on the faces of the two girls signified not only infatuation, but also the knowledge that their passion was totally without hope.

As she turned the pages, there were more pictures of this strange quartet. Whatever the occasion, the camera had unwittingly captured the longing in the eyes and bodies of the two girls who stood in the shadow of Celia Templeton's bright beauty.

Had she deliberately chosen two friends whom she could so easily eclipse? Lisa wondered. And did the two beautiful creatures—who were to become her own mother and father—realize how their flagrant attraction to each other affected the other girls? And, come to think of it, how did the two girls—Maud and the unknown third girl—feel about each other?

Not unknown for long. As Lisa leafed through the 1959 section toward the back of the album, she found a photograph of the third girl on her own, glaring at the camera. The face was slightly blurred and turned at an angle, as if she hadn't wanted to have her picture taken.

There was a caption beneath the picture, written in Maud's neat hand. *Jennifer, on her 13th birthday.*

CHAPTER TWENTY-FIVE

JENNIFER! "THAT WAS THE NAME MAUD WAS TRYING to say," Lisa blurted out.

"So DC Logan told me," Constable Martin said. "But I told her there weren't any Jennifers in the village that I know of."

"Maud said I should ask Alec Kingsley about her," Lisa said slowly. "At least, I think that's what she meant."

"Well, he certainly did know her, didn't he? If this is the Jennifer that Miss Birkett was talking about."

"It looks as if Jennifer was Maud's sister."

"Could be. I wouldn't know for sure, being from Winsford myself."

Lisa released a sigh. It was all getting far too complicated. She had wanted to come here as an unknown Canadian tourist, find out what she could, and leave again without anyone knowing that she had any connection with the place. But now everything was closing in on her.

A knocking came at the door, echoing the painful beat of her heart. Startled, she sprang up from the chair.

"I'll go," Sam Martin said.

A rumble of speech and then she heard quite distinctly Richard's voice saying, "She should not be here on her own, Sam. I wish she'd called me." Although she'd been determined not to involve Richard in this and was surprised to see him, just the sound of his voice made her feel better.

When he came into the room, dressed in a formal dark gray suit, his face was grave. "You should not have come here alone," he said to her immediately. "You should have waited until I could arrange for a colleague from another law firm to come with you."

"I didn't see any need," she protested. "All I'm doing is looking through Maud's albums. She wanted me to have her house key, so I assumed she wanted me to go through her pictures and papers."

"But no doubt you've had some sort of interchange

222

with Constable Martin."

"Of course I have. We're not going to sit here together and not speak. Don't worry, I haven't said anything that could incriminate me."

He shook his head, releasing an exasperated sigh. "You never know," he warned her, but the corner of his mouth had already twitched into a smile. He surveyed her with his steady gaze, then said, "What have you been up to?"

"I went to visit Maud."

"So I heard."

"How did you know?"

"The police told me when I was in the courthouse at Taunton."

Lisa's hand went to her throat. "Oh, Richard. I'm so sorry. I forgot to ask how it went today. For your aunt, I mean."

"She's out on bail. They're holding off on more serious charges pending further investigation. It seems your visit to Maud could have helped Rachel a great deal. Even if you shouldn't have gone there alone." He glanced sideways at Constable Martin, who was listening in quite openly. "I'll give you more details later." He turned to look at the open albums on the table. "Anything of interest here?"

"I've only just started looking." Her fingers brushed over the open page of the 1958 album. She stared down at the youthful pictures of her mother and father. Without warning, her eyes filled with tears. A sob rose in her chest, and she turned away blindly.

"Give us a minute alone, Sam, would you?" she heard Richard say.

"He's not supposed to leave me alone with all this stuff," she muttered.

Sam murmured something about having to get some papers from the car and left the room.

With infinite gentleness, Richard put his arms around her and drew her against him. She pressed her face to his crisp white shirt and silk tie, and sobbed against his chest.

"It—it was seeing them. Seeing . . . the pictures of them when they were young. So beautiful. So young. And . . . I never knew them. I—I don't remember them at all." She abandoned herself to an outpouring of grief, aware only of the comfort of his arms and the fragrance of his soap or cologne.

He let her cry against him, not saying anything at all, just holding her. At one point she felt his hand touch her hair.

After what seemed like a very long time, she drew away from him. "I need a tissue." He handed her a folded white handkerchief, and she blew heartily into it. She lifted her tear—stained face to his. "I'm sorry," she said, giving him a wry smile.

"Don't be. All this must have been very difficult for you."

"You know, don't you?" She could see by his face that she didn't even have to say the words.

"Yes, I know."

"Did he—did Alec tell you?"

Richard nodded. "I told him he should talk to you, tell you he knew who you were, but he wouldn't. And he begged me not to say anything to you about it." His expression became grim. "It was hell having to pretend I didn't know."

"It's my fault. I shouldn't have come in the first place. But when I did, I should have been straightforward about who I was."

"Why weren't you?"

"Because I didn't know that my father was alive. I thought both my parents were dead. That's what my adoptive parents had always told me. That both my birth parents had been killed in a car accident."

"You mean that you came here not knowing that your father was alive?"

"Yes. Even when you took me to Charnwood Court on Saturday, and I met Alec, I thought he was a relative, perhaps an uncle on my father's side. It wasn't until Betty told me that Celia and Alec had had a daughter . . . I put two and two together."

"When was that?"

"Sunday. When you and Alec went off to look for Rachel."

"It must have been a terrible shock for you."

"It sure was. Not only that, but I suddenly knew that Alec must have realized who I was. He knew he had a daughter. He saw the resemblance. He *must* have known who I was."

"He did."

Lisa stared at Richard. "He knew I was his daughter, yet still he kept his mouth shut. How could he do that, recognize me and not say anything?"

"He's riddled with guilt for having abandoned you."

Lisa seethed with white—hot anger. "He obviously thought if he said nothing, I'd just go away and never learn the truth, right?"

Richard's jaw tightened. "He thought you knew who he was, and that you were playing some sort of game. Looking for money, perhaps. I told him he was . . . Well, I was pretty heated with him. Then the whole mess with Maud and Rachel blew up in our faces yesterday, and we had to put everything else aside to

225

deal with that."

"I'm not blaming you for this. It's not your fault that my—that Alec didn't want to acknowledge me." Lisa gave him a twisted smile. "After all, he abandoned me before, didn't he? When I was a small child who'd lost her mother and desperately needed her father."

He took her hand, gripping it so tightly she thought her bones would crack. "God! How could he have done that?" She saw, to her surprise, the tears in his eyes.

Only then did she remember.

She drew her hand from his grasp and lifted it to touch his face. "Oh, God, I am sorry, Richard. Here I am, babbling on about myself, totally forgetting that you've been through the same terrible thing yourself. But the difference was that you kept Emily."

"I told you before, she was the one who kept me sane."

"I guess I didn't have that same capacity for my father."

"Alec told me that he wouldn't let you near him after his first wife died. He blocked out not only you, but everyone else who'd been connected with Celia."

She drew away from him and turned to look down at the page of photographs again. "I think she was murdered." Just speaking the words aloud made her go ice cold.

"Apparently that's what a lot of people think, according to these poison-pen letters he and Rachel have been receiving. Alec was sure that it was Maud who was sending them."

"Why?"

"Because she loved Celia so much, and she suspected him or Rachel, or both of them together, of killing Celia. She'd actually accused him to his face of doing so. Alec laughed it off at first, but then the letters got even more vicious, and Rachel started to fall apart."

"Then why on earth would he keep Maud on as a guide at Charnwood Court?"

"He fired her once, but then the letters grew worse, and the villagers started boycotting them, gardeners quitting, shops refusing to deliver stuff to them . . . that sort of thing. Rachel told Alec he was more likely to catch Maud red—handed doing something—the letters were left in the house, not posted—so they reinstated her as a guide, to keep an eye on her."

"Did you know that Maud hasn't mentioned Rachel to the police?"

"You mean in connection with the accident? Yes, that's why they're continuing their investigation."

"It doesn't sound as if it was an accident." Lisa told him what Maud had said to her.

Richard frowned. "The car was waiting for her, but she didn't see who was driving?"

"That's what it sounded like, but we have to remember she is in serious condition. Her mind may be all muddled. But if it isn't . . ." Lisa turned back to the albums. "I think the answer may lie here, hidden somewhere among all these books."

"You could be right."

"That's why Maud wanted me to have the keys. Trouble is, I don't know what I'm looking for or where to find it. There's so much stuff here . . . . It will take me days to go through it all." She went to the desk and drew out another album at random. Carrying it back, she opened it on the table. "Oh, Richard," she breathed.

"What?" He moved to her side to look at the open page.

They were wedding pictures. Alec and Celia, looking

radiant and invincible in their youth and beauty. The same two girls were in the picture, older but still obviously ill at ease in their long dresses with puffed sleeves.

"Who are the two bridesmaids?" Richard asked.

"Maud. She's the taller one. The other one is Jennifer."

"Jennifer who?"

"I don't know. That's what we have to find out. But I suspect she may be Maud's sister. All I know is that Maud warned me of danger, then mentioned the name Jennifer. She said I should ask Alec. But I'm not sure if she meant me to ask Alec about Jennifer or something else."

"It's time you and Alec talked."

Lisa made a face. "I'm dreading it. I wanted to come to Charnwood and find out . . . what I wanted to know, and then just leave."

"I don't understand. If you thought both your parents were dead, what did you come here for?"

Lisa hesitated, reluctant to tell Richard about her fear of water. "Oh, I don't know. The need to see where I came from. Perhaps to discover if I had any relatives. I didn't want to tell them who I was, you understand," she added quickly. "I just wanted to know."

The door opened, and Constable Martin came in. "Sorry, but I can't leave you alone in here any longer. You understand, Mr. Barton. These albums could become important exhibits, if—"

"Of course I do, Sam." Richard looked up at the mantel clock above the fireplace. "I should go. It looks as if you've still got a lot of stuff to go through."

Sam glanced at his watch. "Sorry, Miss Cooper, but I need to get back to the station."

228

"Then I'll drive you back to the Court, if you like," Richard told Lisa.

It was too soon, Lisa thought, in a panic. She couldn't face Alec yet. Besides, she hated to leave all these albums, knowing how much of her own past they could contain. Perhaps even pictures of herself as a child. And she still hadn't found anything about the flood or Celia's drowning. She turned to Sam. "Please could you give me just another few minutes here?"

He frowned. "All right. But no more'n twenty minutes at the most, or I'll be in a gurt deal of trouble."

"Great. Thanks a lot." Lisa turned to Richard. "I'll drive down with Constable Martin. I have to pick up my car. I left it in the village parking lot."

Richard looked from her to the policeman, then indicated he wanted to talk to her. She followed him outside.

"Don't discuss anything connected with Maud's accident or Rachel with Sam Martin," he warned her.

"I won't. I just wish I could go through everything here today, but I know I can't. It's really frustrating."

"You can come back tomorrow. I'll arrange it with Brewster. Then you can have much more time to work on all those books."

"Thanks so much, Richard." She fell silent, unable to put what she wanted to say into words. Then she said, baldly, "About Alec . . . . I need a little more time, to prepare myself. You understand?"

"Of course I do. But postponing it won't make it any easier."

"Are you going home now? I expect Emily's there, waiting for you."

"I was. But I'm going to call Sally Clayton, our sitter, and arrange for her to stay on with Emily. I'm going

229

back to Charnwood Court to wait for you."

She gave him a shaky smile. "You're not going to let me wriggle out of this, are you?"

"It has to be done. The sooner the better."

"You're right." Lisa drew in a deep breath. "I will do it today, but there's no need to call your sitter. I can manage by myself."

"I thought—"

"It's going to be difficult for Alec as well as me. It'll be even more awkward if we have onlookers."

"I thought I might draw off Kate and Rachel for you."

"Oh."

"You'd forgotten about them, hadn't you?"

"Kate, certainly."

He gave her a quizzical smile. "Want to change your mind about my being there?"

She thought, and then said, "You're right. I don't think I could take Kate and Rachel being there when I make that first . . ." She sought for the right word.

"Foray?" suggested Richard.

She nodded. "Good word."

He looked as if he wanted to say more, but he stood there, silently gazing down at her.

"I'll be okay," she assured him. "It's not the way I wanted it to be, but I'll manage."

"I know you will."

Impulsively, she did what she would have done with Jerry, put her arms around Richard and gave him a quick sisterly hug. Only he didn't feel at all like a brother. She released him quickly. "Thanks for everything, Richard."

"My pleasure."

She stepped inside the house again. "I must go, or I'll lose those few precious minutes Constable Martin's giving me."

"See you soon." Richard got into his car, and she closed the door.

"Sorry to keep you," she told the policeman, when she went back into the study.

"I really can't stay much longer, Miss Cooper," he warned her.

"I know you can't. I'm just so grateful for all the time you've given me." She turned to the open desk. "You said you'd been through some of these papers already. What I'm looking for is clippings."

"Clippings?"

"Newspaper clippings."

"Oh, you mean cuttings. Right. There was one scrapbook with some old newspaper cuttings, mostly about Miss Birkett's choir."

"Oh." Lisa was disappointed. "Where is it?"

"In this cupboard." He indicated the cupboard with drawers that stood against the wall, but made no move toward it.

"I'm hoping to find some cuttings about the flood, when Mr. Kingsley's wife was drowned," she explained. "Did you see any?"

"Not that I recall."

"Can I take a quick look? Please," she added in a coaxing tone, when he hesitated. "I promise I won't read them all."

He drew Maud's bunch of keys from his pocket and chose a small, old—fashioned steel key. "This is the key," he muttered.

Lisa seethed with impatience. The clock on the mantelpiece was loudly ticking away the time.

Slowly, he pulled out the drawer and lifted out a faded red scrapbook. "There you go," he said, handing it to her.

The room had grown dark. Outside, the sun had gone, blotted out by heavy clouds. "We'd better turn on a light," Lisa said. She carried the scrapbook to the table and opened it, her pulse quickening. But as she leafed through the book, she saw that the constable was right. The clippings were mainly pictures or accounts of the accomplishments of Maud's choirs and students over the years.

The last few pages were blank. Lisa was about to close the book, but then opened it to the final black page, in case there were any loose papers there.

THE FLOOD. Maud's stark heading jumped out at her. Centered beneath the heading was a yellowed newspaper picture of a river in full spate, its waters spilling over its banks. Lisa recoiled, her heart thumping furiously in her chest.

Breathing fast, she turned the pages backward, but there was nothing else about the flood there. Just that one picture of a raging river.

CHAPTER TWENTY-SIX

"FIND ANYTHING?" CONSTABLE MARTIN ASKED.

"Just this picture from a newspaper." Lisa showed him. "Nothing else. Maybe there's another scrapbook somewhere."

"I've looked. That's it." The policeman patted his ample stomach. "Time for me tea. I'll just call Sergeant Brewster, let him know I'm shutting up shop here. Then we'll go."

While he was making his call, Lisa glanced through the scrapbook again, hoping to find something else about the flood that she might have missed, but apart from the heading and the picture there was nothing there. All she could find in the faded scrapbook were the achievements of Maud's narrow life. Her students' exemplary piano exam results. One of her school choirs winning an award at Glastonbury Festival. A picture of Maud herself, conducting a group of children in the center of the village, for a visit by Princess Alexandria. The souvenirs of a lonely, loveless life lived in the best way possible.

But Celia had loved her, Lisa thought, recalling the picture in the first album. Her death must have been a terrible blow to Maud.

Sam Martin had finished his call. "Bill Brewster's coming up here," he said grumpily. "We're to wait. He's got a few questions to ask you."

"I'd prefer not to answer any questions unless Mr. Barton is here."

"Did he say where he was going?"

"Charnwood Court, I think. I'll call him." Lisa made for the telephone before Sam Martin got there. Then she hesitated, realizing that Alec would probably answer. Too bad. She dialed the number on Maud's black rotary telephone. To her relief, Kate answered.

"It's Lisa. Is Richard there?" Lisa asked.

"I'll get him." Kate crashed the receiver down.

Richard came on the line. "Don't answer any questions until I get there," he said succinctly, when she told him that Sergeant Brewster was on his way to Maud's house.

"Okay."

Sergeant Brewster and Richard arrived at almost the same time. Lisa went outside to find the two men talking, their cars parked behind each other in the narrow lane. Dark clouds hung low over the moor and there were splashes of rain on the cars.

"Okay," Richard said when he saw her. "I've arranged with Bill that you'll meet with him Thursday morning at nine—thirty, if that's okay with you. By that time I'll have found you a lawyer who can also be at the meeting."

"That's fine." She turned to Sergeant Brewster, as he came to join them. "I don't think those albums should be left in the house."

"Mr. Barton and I've been talking about that, Miss Cooper. We're going to take the albums and the scrapbook to the station."

"Thank God for that." She hesitated, then said, "There are things in those books that have great value for me. Great sentimental value."

"So Mr. Barton was telling me. Don't you worry, Miss Cooper. We'll look after them at the station."

"Thank you."

"And we'll do another thorough check to see if Miss Birkett has any more newspaper cuttings about the flood."

"Maybe she destroyed them," Lisa said.

"No problem. We have quite a few copies of the newspaper stories of the flood and Mrs. Kingsley's death on file. I'll let you take a look at them tomorrow."

"Thank you."

"If all the rumors are right, and your mother's death wasn't accidental, we'll do our best to find out who did it."

Lisa felt her face flush. Richard had certainly spilled more than a few beans! "Thank you," she said again.

"I'm going to take Miss Cooper back to Charnwood Court now," Richard said. He and Brewster exchanged glances.

"You'll tell her?" Bill Brewster asked.

Richard nodded. His expression was grave.

"Tell me what?" Lisa demanded, when Richard had turned his Range Rover and started back down the hill.

"It's not good news, I'm afraid."

"I can see that." She waited for him to say more. When he didn't she asked, "It's Maud, isn't it?"

"Yes.

"Is she dead?"

"No. But she's had a severe heart attack. She's on the critical list. They don't think she'll last out the night."

Lisa looked down at her hands, gripped tightly together in her lap. "I thought she was going to get better," she whispered.

"So did everyone, but apparently she had the coronary about an hour after you left."

"Oh God, I hope it wasn't my visit—"

"No. Brewster told me the nurses said she was fine immediately after you left. In fact, her pulse rate improved after your visit. So, stop blaming yourself. These things happen. She had massive injuries."

"Did he say if anyone else had been allowed in to visit her?"

"Why?"

"Because I met Paula Willand by the information desk of the hospital when I came from seeing Maud. She was there with Marion Heasley and Jane Tallis."

"So?"

"They were making a big fuss, at least Paula was, because they couldn't get in to see Maud. They were even more annoyed when they heard that I'd been allowed in."

"Did you tell Bill that?"

"I don't think so."

235

Richard picked up his cellular phone and pressed out a number. When Sergeant Brewster answered, Richard handed the phone to Lisa.

"So that's who it was," Brewster said, when she told him. "The receptionist told us there'd been three women trying to see Miss Birkett and one of them had kicked up a fuss because they wouldn't let them in. She couldn't recall their names."

"I just wondered if they'd allowed one of them to visit Miss Birkett later."

"No. She had no other visitors after you were there. Thank you, anyhow, for letting me know."

Lisa clicked off the phone and gave it back to Richard.

"I take it that was a no."

"That's right. No one else was allowed to visit her after I was there." Lisa sank into her thoughts. "Thank God I was able to see her," she said eventually, as they drove up the driveway to Charnwood Court.

"Did she know who you were?" Richard asked.

Lisa nodded. "She'd guessed. It was as if she'd been . . . waiting for me to come back."

"And you did. Come back, I mean."

A violent shiver ran down Lisa's spine. "I think that's why she was attacked," she said in a low voice. "Someone didn't want Maud to talk to me, because she knew something about my mother's death."

"Don't think about that now. Later on, we'll talk. Put all the pieces together and try to make something of them."

"Maud asked me never to forget her."

"Forget who?"

"Celia. My mother. She was so beautiful, Richard."

"So are you."

236

The words startled her, coming, as they did, as a matter-of-fact statement. "Don't be silly. I'm nothing like my mother."

"Who said you were? You have your own beauty." He glanced across at her, and she saw that he was smiling. "You're not very good at accepting compliments."

"You're right there. I've never wanted to be beautiful." It was one of the reasons she plaited her long hair. Vanity kept her from cutting it, but her distrust of beauty made her hide it away. "For a woman, being beautiful makes people worship you for your beauty or stalk you—or hate you." Talking about this made her feel uneasy. "Thanks, anyway."

"My pleasure."

"I was thinking, when I looked at the photographs of my mother and father together, how tough it must have been for friends who were just ordinary-looking to be with them. People like Maud, for instance."

Or Jennifer.

Richard drew up the car at the back entrance. Lisa sat there, her stomach muscles tightening. "I'm not looking forward to this."

"Remember, you're not the only one who's apprehensive. I'm sure Alec is dreading it, too."

"He's got good cause to."

They went in the back door, one of Alec's golden retrievers bounding up to greet them as soon as they opened the door.

"Here, Sheba," Alec's voice called. Then Alec himself appeared. His eyes widened when he saw Lisa, then he conjured up a smile. "Come on in. You must be wornout after your long day."

He led the way into the sitting room. Kate was there, watching television.

237

"Turn that off, would you, kitten?" Alec said.

Kate opened her mouth to protest, but, seeing Lisa and Richard, she pressed the remote control, and the picture faded away.

"You and I have things to talk about," Richard told her.

"We do?" Kate said. Frowning, she looked from him to Lisa, and then swung her legs down from the couch.

"Is your mother still up in her room?" Richard asked.

"She's sleeping. Dr. McKenzie gave her a sedative."

"Good. She needs lot of rest." Richard put his arm around Kate's shoulders. "So do you, from the look of it. Come on, let me buy you a pint at the Stag."

"I hate the Stag."

"Then we'll go to the Hare and Hounds."

Lisa winced. Too late, Richard realized his mistake, but Kate took it well. "Somehow, I don't think so," she drawled.

"Sorry. I'm an idiot."

"Can I have that in writing?"

"Let's go."

"Okay." Kate looked at Lisa with open curiosity as she passed her, but said nothing.

Richard gave her a small, encouraging smile, then followed Kate from the room, leaving Lisa and Alec standing there, facing each other, in a strained silence.

CHAPTER TWENTY-SEVEN

"CAN I GET YOU A DRINK?" ALEC ASKED, ALWAYS the gracious host. "Wine, sherry . . . ?"

"I'll have a glass of white wine, please." Lisa's mouth felt parched. Her heart was pounding so hard she felt it would choke her.

238

Alec started toward the door. "I'll get a bottle from the cellar."

"Please don't. I'll take whatever's open." *For God's sake*, she wanted to shout, *let's get this over with*.

"It's no trouble." The skin over his cheekbones was flushed.

"What have you got here?" Lisa insisted, her voice rising. "Sherry, gin and tonic . . . anything will do."

His mouth twitched. "All right. You win. I have a red Merlot open. Will that do?"

"That's fine."

A black Persian cat was stretched out on the small couch by the fireplace. It lifted its head when Lisa sat beside it, staring unblinkingly at her with round yellow eyes. "Aren't you a beauty?" she said, stroking the cat's soft fur. "What's her name?" she asked Alec. "Or is it a he?"

"Nero. He's an arrogant male."

The cat began to purr, kneading its claws in and out.

"Yes, you certainly are an extremely handsome gentleman," Lisa murmured as she stroked him.

"You always did like cats better than dogs."

Lisa held her breath for a moment and then lifted her head. Alec was watching her with a faint enigmatic smile, the bottle of wine in his hand.

"Did I?" she said. "I still do. I have a cat at home." A pause, and then, "Was there a reason why I didn't like dogs?"

"Not any particular one that I can remember. You did, however, have a morbid fear of mice. Ancient houses like Charnwood tend to get mice in the wainscoting. You insisted on having the cat sleep with you at night."

Lisa shuddered involuntarily. "I still hate mice. We used to take our cat with us to the lake in the summer.

She'd love to hunt field mice and carry them into the cottage. I'd go berserk. Scream the place down, scramble on tables, chairs . . . that sort of thing."

"Then you'd better take Nero up with you tonight. He loves sleeping on beds, but usually we don't permit him to do so."

Alec came to hand her a glass of wine and then retreated to his chair on the other side of the fireplace. He sat with one hand shading his eyes, but although she was looking down at the cat, Lisa knew he was watching her. The room had grown even darker, the only sounds the cat's purring and the heavy patter of rain on the windows.

Lisa took a gulp of wine and waited for him to say something. She wondered if she should mention Rachel, then decided against it. Eventually, when the silence became unbearable, she said, "Why didn't you tell me you knew who I was?"

He started, as if he hadn't expected her to be quite so blunt. "I was waiting for you to make the first move."

"But I didn't know you were my father."

"What?" He sounded genuinely surprised.

"I was told that both my parents had been killed in a car crash."

"Who told you that?"

"My mother."

He frowned. "Your—"

"My adoptive mother." Lisa lifted her chin. "Margaret Haines was her maiden name. I believe she was my nanny here."

A tide of red surged up from his neck above the crisp white collar and into his face. "That's right," he muttered.

"Did you ask her to tell me that both my parents had

died, to make it easier for you?"

"No, not at all," he said vehemently. "In fact, I kept expecting you to turn up here. I had begun to give up hope when . . . there you were, coming in the door with Richard. You can imagine what a shock it was after all these years."

"Not half such a shock as it was for me," Lisa said, "considering I thought my father was dead. At first I thought you must be an uncle, my father's brother."

"What made you realize that I was your . . . ?" He seemed unable to say the word.

"Nothing remotely sentimental, I can assure you. Betty told me on Sunday, after lunch. Of course she hadn't a clue who I was. Once she'd told me that you and Celia had had a daughter I probably could have guessed the rest, but she filled me in on the whole sordid little story. How you had a breakdown and couldn't bear to have me around."

His face was like gray granite. "It wasn't like that," he said, his lips barely moving.

"Oh, really? You mean you didn't banish me from my home with my nanny?"

He sat without moving, his hands turned to fists on his knees.

Lisa wanted to goad him, to make him react, instead of just sitting there as still and stony as a monument. "I hope you paid her well to keep me away from you."

"Were you . . ." He swallowed visibly. "Did she treat you well?"

"I had the best parents in the world."

"Parents?"

"Oh, yes. If you had tried to find me—which I'm sure you did not—you would have discovered that my nanny married a man named Jim Cooper. They emigrated to

241

Canada when I was six. Maybe you know all this already. Maybe you even set it all up to make sure I didn't come back to get in your way."

"No. I had no idea that Miss Haines had married. And, although I did give her a large sum of money to—"

"So you did pay her to take me."

"No. I wanted to make sure that she had sufficient funds to take care of you properly. It may interest you to know that several months later, after she had adopted you, Miss Haines returned the money to me, intact."

Tears pricked Lisa's eyes. "That sounds like my mother."

"I wouldn't have let anyone else take you. I trusted her implicitly. I also know that Celia . . . that your mother trusted her also. Margaret Haines had been her choice for your nanny. She said she wanted someone who would love you, not just a strict disciplinarian. But I admit I did encourage Miss Haines to leave the country. I gave her enough money to cover all her travel expenses and to help set herself up, wherever she settled with you. When she returned the money, with no explanation, I was worried sick."

"But not worried enough to try to find her—and me?"

Those gray—blue eyes that had given him away locked with hers. "That was the arrangement. She had adopted you. Legally, I was no longer your father."

"How very convenient. A legal document and a court order, and you gave up all your responsibilities as my father."

His mouth set in a grim line. "I missed you like hell. I've always missed you."

Lisa shrugged. "What can I say? Except . . . thanks for choosing such a good substitute mother for me." She drew in a deep breath. "None of this is really important

242

to me. I thought my birth parents were dead. It turns out that they were, really," she said, with a bitter smile.

For the first time, anger flashed in his eyes. "Then why the hell are you here?"

Lisa swallowed hard. How could she betray the basic fear that haunted her to this man who was worse than a stranger to her? Yet he was also one of the few people who could hold the key to her recovery.

"I need to know exactly what happened to my—to Celia when she was drowned twenty—seven years ago."

"I don't want to talk about it." He turned his head away, to stare into the empty hearth. "Is that what you came here for? I thought you said you knew nothing about the Kingsleys."

"I didn't. I have to know what happened to my mother."

"Why?" he demanded. "What good does it do to dig up all those painful memories?"

"Apparently someone else is also digging them up."

"What do you mean?"

"Threatening letters."

His face flushed. "How did you know about those? Did the police tell you? I'll have Brewster's badge, if they did."

"For heaven's sake! Everyone in the village knows about the letters. I wasn't here more than a day when I heard about them. This village is a hotbed of gossip, as you must know."

"Damn Maud Birkett for that."

"How touching, with poor Maud lying in the hospital in critical condition."

"I deplore what's happened to Maud, but it's hard to feel sympathy for someone who has deliberately set out to destroy me and my family. That woman is

243

responsible for all that's happened to us. She's vindictive and unstable. Ever since Celia drowned, she's hated me. Then, when I married Rachel, Maud went to work on her. Over the years, she's turned the entire village against us with her vile rumors."

Lisa was confused by Alec's sincerity, his obvious conviction that Maud was entirely to blame. Could this be another side of Maud that hadn't become evident to her? Could all those scrapbooks and photo albums be indicative of an obsession, a mind warped by envy and grief and solitude?

"But . . . if Maud is responsible, who ran her down yesterday?" Lisa was thinking aloud.

Immediately, with Alec's silence, the answer became clear. Rachel *must* have been the one who tried to kill Maud. She was the obvious suspect, and now Lisa could understand her motivation. Maud had persecuted Rachel for years. So much so that she'd started drinking heavily because of it. No wonder Rachel had snapped.

"If it was Rachel," she said slowly. "I'm sure she had good cause, if what you say about Maud is true."

Alec slumped in his chair. "She even made us doubt each other," he whispered. "I began to wonder if Rachel had something to do with Celia's death."

Lisa leaned forward. "Please tell me what happened to my mother. I need to know." She hesitated, and then said, "I was there, wasn't I?"

She waited for him to deny it, but he did not. "Do you remember anything about that night?" he asked, anxiety sharpening his voice.

"That's the trouble. I don't, but my subconscious does."

"I don't understand."

"I'll explain once you've told me what happened."

"Before I do, I want you to know one thing. I adored your mother. She was the light of my life. When she died, I was devastated. I didn't want to live."

"Until Rachel came along a few months later," Lisa said, not even trying to hide her skepticism.

"I know, I know. You're not the only one to question the sincerity of my feelings for Celia." He gave her a painful smile. "I married Rachel because I was desperately lonely. I'd lost not only the wife I'd loved, but also my beloved daughter."

Spare me, thought Lisa, tempted to roll her eyes.

"Rachel was good to me. Good *for* me. She brought me back to life. But, of course, all the friends who'd known and loved Celia disliked Rachel. They despised me for marrying another woman so soon after Celia died. Maud, in particular, hated to think of Rachel as the mistress of Charnwood Court. When Celia was alive, Maud had free run of the house. She'd turn up at all sorts of inconvenient times. If I complained, Celia would say it had been Maud's second home throughout her childhood, because her own home had been so cold and austere."

"Was she in love with you?"

Alec frowned. "Who?"

"Maud. Was she in love with you?"

"I suppose so, when we were young." Alec sighed. "It wasn't love, of course, mere infatuation. I'd catch her gazing at me with those pale gooseberry eyes of hers. The only good thing Maud did was to bring Celia and me together. This is such a close community that would probably have happened sooner or later without her involvement." He frowned at her. "Why did you ask such a strange question?"

"I was looking at some photograph albums in Maud's

245

house and—"

"You were? How did that come about?"

"Maud asked that I have her house keys. We thought there must be some reason for it."

"We?"

"The police constable in the hospital."

Anxiety creased his face. "Don't tell me you were visiting Maud."

"I was."

"That wasn't wise," he said vehemently. "A big mistake. Was she conscious?"

"Yes."

"What did she say to you?" His frown deepened. "Why would she speak to you? She doesn't know who you are."

"You did."

"I'm your father."

"She was my mother's best friend."

"You mean . . . she recognized you? Or you told her who you were?"

"She knew who I was."

"What did she say to you?"

Lisa wasn't about to divulge Maud's words to him. Not if Rachel was the person responsible for Maud's injuries. She wondered if he knew that Maud had had a heart attack. She'd keep that to herself until later.

"We'll talk about my visit to Maud after you've told me how my mother drowned."

"God." He pressed his long—fingered hands against his face, covering his eyes. "How can I?" he whispered. "I've tried to put that night out of my mind forever."

"I can understand why," Lisa said softly. "If I told you that it was vitally important to me, to my health, would you tell me?"

He looked up at her. "Yes. Yes, of course I would."

Lisa sighed. "Okay. Let me try to explain. Whatever happened that day—or night—I'm still suffering from the trauma. I—I have . . ." Her throat closed up, shutting off the words.

"Take your time," Alec said softly. "It will come." In his eyes she saw, for the first time, compassion and something approaching caring.

Her mouth trembled. "I have a terrifying fear of water. A phobia. It comes and goes. Since my mother's death—my adoptive mother, I mean—it has grown much worse. Then, the Red River floods hit North Dakota and Manitoba—"

"We saw the pictures on the news. Terrible."

"When the flood began creeping northward, I was pretty well paralyzed with fear. It affected my work . . . my entire life. My psychologist suggested I try to find out if something happened in my past, something traumatic, that could be still there, in my memory. But I knew absolutely nothing about my first few years, and my adoptive mother was dead. How could I explore my childhood if I hadn't a clue where I came from?"

"But you found me."

"Not you. The village, Charnwood." Lisa explained about the letter in the safety—deposit box.

"And that was all you had? Charnwood in Somerset and the name Kingsley."

"That was it."

"Then you did well in tracking me down."

"Meeting Richard—well, Emily, really—was the best bit of luck. The day I arrived I bumped into Emily and almost knocked her down . . . and here I am."

"Yes, here you are. Right in the middle of one hell of a mess."

"We're off track again. The flood."

"There's no escaping it, is there?" He got to his feet in one graceful movement. "Forgive me, but I just can't sit still while I tell you about Celia's death."

"That's okay."

He walked to the window and stared out at the rain. It had increased in intensity, spattering the glass and bouncing off the flagstoned terrace. "The river was high, much higher than it is now. And it's bad enough now."

"I'm scared of rivers," Lisa admitted. "Unless they're placid, calm streams."

"The Charn was certainly not placid. All the Exmoor rivers that flow down to Lynmouth and the sea were in full spate, overflowing their banks."

Nero suddenly hissed at Lisa, and she realized that her hand had clenched on his back. "Sorry, old fellow," she murmured to him, smoothing his fur down.

Alec continued. "We were worried about flooding. It wouldn't have been the first time the village was flooded. The last really bad one had been in August '52. We'd been extremely fortunate that time. Charnwood had many buildings damaged, but no loss of life. Unlike Lynmouth, where much of the town was washed away and thirty—four people died. I was only twelve then, but I was home for the summer holidays and will never forget the devastation. Rocks and boulders being tumbled along by raging rivers that had once been mere streams."

Lisa's nails were digging into her palms. *Please make him get on with it,* she prayed, her heart racing at a sickening pace.

"Anyway," Alec continued, "in 1970 when the rain kept falling, we were really concerned that the same thing could happen again. There were safeguards in place at Lynmouth, but our part of the river was in full flood. There was talk of evacuating the entire village."

Alec turned and walked back across the room, to lean against the bookshelves. "We decided that Charnwood Court could accommodate many of the people from the village, temporarily, at least. We had a devil of a job persuading them to move from their homes. Some of them refused, said they'd rather guard their houses themselves. In all the confusion of the move, no one had noticed that you'd disappeared. You were only four—"

"Yes, I know."

"Miss Haines was the first to notice you weren't around. At first we thought you were hiding somewhere. This is such a large house that it took us quite a while to realize that you weren't to be found. We got everyone in the house organized, looking in all the cupboards and wardrobes. Then we realized that—"

He stopped suddenly, as if he'd almost said something he didn't want her to hear, and then went on. "We saw that your favorite stuffed bear, Rupert, was gone as well. You were greatly attached to that bear and would never go anywhere without it." He turned. "Do you remember Rupert?"

Lisa shook her head.

Restlessly, he walked to the window and stood with his back to her, staring out at the rain.

"Celia was afraid you might have walked down the road to the river. We arranged a search party, so that we could make a thorough, methodical search. But your mother was distraught. She rushed out before we could stop her and said she would drive to the river."

"On her own?"

"I wish to God I'd gone with her, but I just told her

not to be so bloody impulsive. Let's do this properly,' I told her, pompous ass that I was. She ignored me."

He stopped and leaned his arm against the window, and laid his head on his arm, as if the memory was too painful to bear. Then he straightened his shoulders and stood erect.

"We searched the wood first, all the places nearest to the house. Then we fanned out. When we reached the river, we found you safe, standing on a high bluff overlooking the water. You were soaked to the skin, shivering, screaming for your mother, but safe. Celia was nowhere to be seen. An hour or so later, they recovered her body. It was caught in the low—lying branches of a willow tree two miles downstream."

Like a slide flashed on and off the screen, Lisa saw the scene. Then it was gone. Hard as she tried to recapture it, her memory was blank again. But she had seen it for long enough to realize one thing he hadn't mentioned. "Someone was with me."

"A lot of us were with you. Must have been at least—"

"No, no. I mean someone was with me before you found me."

He turned to face her. "You mean your aunt?" he said. His voice was light, but there was an intensity thrumming behind it.

"What aunt?"

He hesitated. "Your mother's sister." The information came with evident reluctance.

"I didn't know Celia had a sister." Realization came like a blinding flash. "Jennifer was Celia's sister, not Maud's. It was not a question.

"How did you know her name?"

"Maud's photo albums. There were pictures of three girls. I hadn't a clue who the third one was until this

250

moment."

His expression was grim. "Jennifer was your mother's younger sister."

"I had no idea . . . What happened to her?"

"She was . . ." He halted, unable to continue for a moment. Lisa looked away, not wanting to see the naked emotion in his eyes.

"She was devastated by her sister's death. Once the coroner's verdict of accidental death came in she left Charnwood."

"And never returned?"

Alec shook his head.

"Where did she go?"

"Last time I heard, she was in Australia, running a sheep farm. Celia had left her a fair sum in her will." His mouth twisted into a wry smile. "Although Celia left me Charnwood Court and the entire estate, there was precious little cash available. I had to sell a couple of paintings to raise the money for her sister."

"Sorry, I don't quite understand. Why did Celia own this place? Surely her sister already had a share of it?"

"No. Their father chose to will the estate to Celia only."

"That's odd. Wasn't Jennifer upset about that?"

"I've no idea," Alec said briskly. "Their father died when Celia was eighteen. Their mother had died years before, when Celia was twelve, so her father left Charnwood Court to Celia. Jennifer got a packet of money instead."

"I suppose their father wouldn't want to split up the estate."

"Exactly. Even though he didn't have sons, he was working on the old rule of primogeniture."

"Did Jennifer live with you here after you were

251

married?"

"That's right."

"That must have been a bit awkward, considering she had a thing for you."

"What makes you say that?"

"It was obvious from the photographs that both Maud and this other girl, who I now know was Jennifer, had a crush on you. Did it continue after you were married?"

Alec shrugged. "God knows. She never bothered me, if that's what you mean. We managed."

Lisa had the feeling there was a great deal more he could have said, but chose not to. "Do you have her telephone number or address in Australia?"

"No."

Lisa thought all this information over for a moment. "Do you think my aunt saved me from drowning?"

He didn't answer right away. "Apparently." His face was half—turned from her, in shadow.

"Did she see my mother drown?"

"She told the police that she found you on the muddy bank of the river, fascinated by the raging water. Then your Rupert bear fell into the water. You reached for it . . . and tumbled in. The bulrushes at the side stopped you from being immediately carried off. She was trying to grab you when your mother came on the scene. Celia ran down the slope, but it was slippery with mud. She fell into the river when she was trying to get hold of you. There was nothing Jennifer could do to save her. She tried to grab her skirt, but the waters closed over her and carried her away."

The rain was lashing against the windows now, water pouring through the downspouts. Alec had turned his back on her again. He stood at the window, gazing out, his shoulders hunched, unmoving.

"You must have hated me," Lisa said, after what seemed like an eternity.

"I've never hated you." His voice was muffled.

"I caused your wife's death."

He spun around, eyes blazing. "The flood caused it. The weather caused it. I bloody caused it. You didn't."

"No wonder you couldn't bear the sight of me. No wonder you sent me away."

"That's not why I sent you away."

"You banished me from your sight forever. It was the ultimate punishment."

"That was never my intention."

They stood facing each other, divided by the invisible wall that was the past.

Alec moved toward her, about to speak, when Rachel's querulous voice called from the stairs.

"Are you down there, Alec?"

Mingled emotions crossed his face, relief and disappointment in equal measure, Lisa guessed. At least, that was how she felt. She also felt unsteady, fragile from the stress of the confrontation that had opened—but not closed—old wounds.

Alec started toward the door. "Forgive me, I must go to her."

"Of course. I'll go up to my room. It's been a long day."

"Won't you stay? We have so much to talk about, so much to catch up on."

"Alec!" came Rachel's voice again, this time more peremptory.

"Coming, darling," he called. He gave Lisa a wry smile. "Sorry. You must be hungry. Help yourself to something to eat in the kitchen, won't you? Perhaps we can talk again later." He looked dejected. "I wouldn't want to leave it like this."

Lisa nodded. "I know. Don't worry about me," she hastily added, when she saw how reluctant he was to leave her. She wasn't sure if it was mere chivalry or a genuine desire to spend more time with her. She imagined that Alec Kingsley had become so used to charming people it was hard for others to gauge the sincerity of his feelings.

As the door closed behind him, however, she was sure of one thing. Alec had not told her the entire truth about Celia Kingsley's death.

MONDAY

What a day! I wonder what Maud said to E. before I got to her. She won't be saying any more. It didn't take much. I just waited at the door of her room, until the copper moved to the window. I took one step inside and Maud looked up. At first she smiled when she saw me, silly bitch. I soon wiped the smile off her face when I gave her the secret cross—arm signal we used as girls . . . . She knew then, all right! The monitor went haywire and I managed to slip away in the rush.

Now to get rid of E. She had better take the hint this time . . . or else. Damn her! I'm the one that should be sleeping at the Court, not her. I don't think she'll want to spend another night there after I've paid her another little visit.

All this rain is making me nervous. It reminds me of . . .

254

CHAPTER TWENTY-EIGHT

LISA STOPPED BY THE NURSERY ON THE WAY TO HER room. The door was shut, the light in the hallway outside switched off. She turned the handle and peered in. In the gloom of the rain—darkened evening she could see very little. Her fingers fumbled for the light switch and turned it on.

She hesitated, reluctant to venture in. The light from the solitary bulb in the center of the ceiling was insufficient to brighten the shadowy corners of the nursery.

"There's another light—" The voice coming from behind her set her heart galloping.

"Oh my God, you scared me," she said to Alec, her hand at her throat.

"Sorry. I was just going to say that there's another light switch by the fireplace. It turns on the spotlights."

"I shouldn't be snooping around."

"You're not snooping. This is your home. This was your nursery." Alec glanced at his watch, obviously not comfortable with this turn in the conversation. "Forgive me, but I promised Rachel—"

"How is she?"

"Better. I'm going to make her some tea." He indicated the tea tray he'd set down on the hall table. "I heard you coming up, so thought you might need something." He looked around the nursery. "You spent a lot of time playing in here, especially in the winter."

Her gaze went to the closed doll's house. "Was I allowed to play with the house?"

"Only if someone was with you. That was a source of

great annoyance to you, that you couldn't play with it when you wanted to." He gave her a half smile. "You could be pretty stubborn, even at that young age."

"It must be very valuable."

"It is. And many of the things in it are old and very fragile. Hence the embargo."

"Was it my mother's house?"

"It had been in the Templeton family for generations. Since the end of the eighteenth century."

This is my doll's house, not yours. Never forget that!

Lisa started as the words rang in her mind.

"What's the matter?" Alec asked.

"Nothing. Just ghosts." She glanced behind her nervously.

"No actual ghosts in this place." Alec released a sigh. "Only those that linger in our memory."

"I suppose that's what it is. I remember so little, really. It's as if I've blocked everything out."

"That's understandable. Probably any memory at all would have brought the pain of loss, so it was easier to block everything out. At least, that's what I tried to do, but it was hard for me, trapped, as I was, in this house."

"Trapped?"

"That's how I felt after Celia died. I had always loved Charnwood Court. Coveted it, I suppose. Although I can assure you that wasn't why I married Celia."

"I know that."

"How do you know it?" he demanded aggressively. "That's what a great many people thought. That I'd married Celia for this house and the prestige it brought with it."

"I've seen those early photographs of you and my mother."

"And?"

256

"It's obvious to anyone looking at them how much you loved each other, even then."

He looked at her, half-frowning. Then his eyes closed, and he stood before her, his body absolutely still. Moisture glistened on the dark skin below his closed eyelids.

Lisa wondered what she should do. *This is your father*, a voice in her head yelled. *For God's sake, comfort him*. But she didn't move. It was too soon.

For her and Alec, it might always be too soon.

He turned away from her and blew his nose into a checked handkerchief. "Sorry about that." Typically English, he was embarrassed by a public display of emotion. "Do you want to stay here for a while? If so, we could turn on the electric fire to take the chill off the air."

"Thanks, but I think I prefer it in the daylight."

"Come in here anytime you want to. I give you permission to play with the doll's house whenever you wish," he added with a smile. "Without an adult being present."

"I'm now an adult myself."

"You are, indeed." The grin faded. "How much time we've missed, you and I"

Lisa felt squeamish. "I hope you don't mind," she said hurriedly, "but I'm going to lie down for a while. I'm feeling pretty washed out."

"Will we see you again this evening?"

"That depends."

"On?"

"Kate. What are we going to tell Kate? Rachel and I probably won't see each other, but Kate's bound to notice something . . . I mean that there's something different between us."

257

He reddened above his collar. "You're right. She knows, of course."

Lisa was surprised. "You mean she knows who I am?"

"No, no. She knows that I had a daughter with Celia." The red deepened: "Sometimes she taunts me with it. When she was a teenager and we'd fight, she'd say things like: I suppose you're going to send *me* away now.' "

"She was probably afraid you would, knowing that you'd done it before."

"Touché."

"Sorry, but it's true, isn't it?"

"Regrettably, yes." He turned abruptly. "I'd better get Rachel her tea."

"Are you going to tell Kate, or not?"

"That depends."

"On what?"

"On whether or not you want to pursue our relationship further."

"Do you want me to?"

His face became a mask. "Can I be honest?"

I don't know, Lisa wanted to answer. Can you? She merely shrugged.

"As far as I'm concerned," Alec said, "I'd be delighted if you wanted to get to know me—and my family—better. But not now, not when we're all in this appalling turmoil. I'd rather you weren't involved. It would be better if you went home tomorrow. After all, you've learned what you wanted to know." His attractive mouth twisted into a wry grin. "More than you wanted to know, apparently. You found out that you have a father and a half sister of whom you were totally unaware."

"And an aunt, who's somewhere unknown."

He ignored this. "And you've learned what happened to your mother and the very likely reason for your hydrophobia. I take it that is what it's called?"

"Who knows?" Lisa said impatiently. "Are you telling me I should leave tomorrow?"

"Yes."

"With so much still up in the air? Rachel, Maud, the letters . . . ?"

"None of these things affects you personally, does it? Why should you be drawn into our concerns? Go home. Forget about Charnwood and all its horrors. Once everything has blown over, come back and spend some time with us. Get to know us as we really are, not as we are now."

"By that time, Charnwood Court will be a hotel."

Alec's face paled. "Ah, so you've heard about that, too, have you? Who told you?"

"One of the gossips in Jane Tallis's shop."

"Gossips is the right word. I'd burn the lot of 'em as witches!"

Lisa had to smile. "That's a bit drastic, isn't it? It's only words, after all."

"Don't you believe it. A great deal of harm can be perpetrated through the medium of gossip. Gossip can be evil personified."

His vehemence disturbed Lisa. She found her hands suddenly gripped in his. "Go home to Canada, where you'll be safe."

"Aren't I safe here?"

"None of us is safe here." He released her hands. "It must be your decision, of course. I don't want you to think I'm chasing you away. I just see no point in your remaining here when I cannot give you the time and

259

attention you deserve."

"You're right."

His face lit up. "You'll go home?"

"I'll think about it. Now, you'd better get your poor wife her tea, before she dies of thirst."

His eyes met hers. *Yikes,* she thought. *That was pretty tactless.* Anything connected with dying was unmentionable at the moment.

"You haven't eaten yet, have you?" was all he said. "I'll bring you up a roast beef sandwich."

"Thank you, but I don't eat beef," she reminded him gently.

"Oh, sorry about that. I should have remembered. How about salmon and cucumber?"

"Don't worry about me. I'll come down again when Kate and Richard come back, okay?"

"Right." Alec walked with her to the door of her room and opened it for her. "So, have we agreed that we don't tell Kate who you are?" he said, breaking the silence.

"If that's what you want."

"For now, yes. She has enough to worry her, poor girl."

Not only did Lisa object to being considered an object of distress for Kate, she also wished he'd stop treating his daughter—his second daughter—as if she were still a child. Dr. Olson would suggest he was trying to keep Kate a child to compensate for the loss of his firstborn.

She felt a heaviness around her heart. She seemed to have been unwittingly responsible for a great deal of misery. Not the least being the death of her birth mother.

"Okay," she said, emotionally incapable of continuing the conversation. "I'll see you later." She went into the room and closed the door on him.

260

CHAPTER TWENTY-NINE

LISA WAS EXHAUSTED. LYING DOWN ON THE BED, SHE pulled the gold damask quilt over her and tried to sleep. But, as soon as her eyes closed, all kinds of images sprang up behind them. Maud lying in that narrow hospital bed, clutching at her hand, the monitor beeping in the background. The shrewish face of Paula Willand as she spat out her venom in the hospital hallway. The pictures in the photograph album and the faded newspaper clipping in the scrapbook.

Those images, though they were disturbing, were bearable. What followed was not. They were products of her imagination, not actual memories. At least, not conscious memories. She saw the Court as it must have looked on that evening, years ago, thronged with refugees from the flood. Then came the torrents of water pouring down the ravines, the stuffed toy tumbling into the raging river, and the child following it . . .

She sat bolt upright, her heart pounding. Outside, the rain fell relentlessly, drumming on the roof, spilling over the gutters, churning the ground into mud . . . filling the already too—full river. *Go home, go home, go home,* it said. *Go home, before it's too late.*

Shivering, her hands icy cold, she got up and went to sit in the chair by the fireplace. She could turn on the electric fire, but she knew that no amount of artificial heat could melt the ice that ran in her veins, or erase the knowledge that she was responsible for her mother's death.

What in heaven's name had induced a four-year-old child to leave the haven of her own home and run out into the dark, drowning night? Had the invasion of villagers scared her? Had one of them frightened her in some way? What small—perhaps infinitesimal—occurrence had been the catalyst for such chaos? A mother dead, a child banished, a sister gone into exile, and a father's life—and that of his new family—blighted forever.

Not to mention the lonely friend, haunted by the loss of the one person in her life who had loved her.

Danger. Jennifer. As she sat shivering in the chair beside the unlit fireplace, Maud's words returned to Lisa's mind. She still wasn't sure how they were connected. Alec had seemed noncommittal about his sister—in—law, as if her presence in the house had been more a thorn in the flesh than a major problem.

Who else would know about her aunt? She certainly wasn't about to ask one of the village gossips, and Jane hadn't been in the village long enough. Then she thought of Betty. Of course! Betty would know about Jennifer Templeton. But how on earth could she ask Betty personal questions about the family again without raising suspicion?

"I'll find a way," Lisa said aloud.

She heard the crunch of wheels on the wet gravel and then the noise of car doors slamming. Richard and Kate must be back from the pub. The desire not to be alone with her thoughts anymore forced Lisa to brush her hair and reapply the russet lipstick that added color to her face.

She had to admit she was also longing to tell Richard about her conversation with Alec. It was such a relief to have someone else in on the secret, someone who wasn't quite so emotionally involved. But she wasn't sure that she'd be able to get Richard on his own tonight.

She crossed the upper hall and made her way through the baize door and down the back staircase to the Kingsleys' living room. She hesitated for a moment, then knocked on the door.

The door opened, as if someone had been standing right beside it. "Hi," Richard said. "Come on in."

"Are you sure?" Lisa asked, catching sight of Rachel sitting by the fire.

"Of course. I was about to make some coffee."

"Come in and join us," Alec called out.

"Well . . . thank you, I will. Just for a little while. But first I'll help Richard with the coffee." Before they could stop her, she stepped back into the hall again, and Richard followed her, closing the door behind him. "Is that okay with you?" Lisa whispered to him.

"It's fine." He smiled. "I must admit I'd like to know how things went with you two."

"Let's wait until we're in the kitchen." She jerked her head in the direction of the closed door. "He doesn't want Kate to know who I am. Or Rachel, I suppose."

Richard led the way to the kitchen. The back hallway was lit by only a single bulb high in the ceiling. It was so gloomy that Lisa would have fallen down the two steps leading to the kitchen had Richard not caught her arm.

"Thanks," she said. "They could do with some more lights in this house."

"I know," Richard agreed, "but their electricity bills are enormous as it is." He switched on the two lights in the kitchen ceiling.

"Are things really that bad?"

" 'Fraid so. If they don't sell the place, they'd probably have to give it up, anyway. They certainly can't afford to keep it."

263

He filled the electric kettle, plugged it in, and switched it on. Then he took a large black—topped Bodum coffeemaker from one of the overhead cupboards and scooped coffee into it.

"You seem to know your way around this kitchen," Lisa said, smiling.

"Should by now. My aunt's lived here for more than twenty—five years."

"Of course," Lisa murmured. "My mind's been so much in the past these last couple of days, I tend to forget. How's she bearing up?"

"Remarkably well, really. She's so numb at the moment, utterly bewildered by it all, that it hasn't really sunk in. She hasn't had a drink since she was arrested, so she's pretty jumpy, but she's on medication."

"I know you can't tell me what she says happened yesterday, but—"

"She says she never left the Hare and Hounds, other than to go outside for a while to get some fresh air. She walked around the car park and then down the road a little way. When she found it was too wet, she went inside again."

"So she denies having run Maud Birkett down."

"According to Rachel, she never drove the car from the time she first went into the pub, until the police arrived."

Lisa shook her head. "Amazing. Where are the coffee mugs?"

"Cups and saucers in that cupboard over there." He grinned. "Rachel prefers cups to mugs."

"Sorry."

He reached into a tall cupboard by the oven. "Tray." He handed it to her. "There should be a tray cloth in that deep drawer by the fridge."

She set the tray and sat down at the long pine—topped table again.

Richard poured the boiling water into the coffeemaker and came to sit opposite her. "That should take a few minutes." His eyes engaged hers. "Now, tell me what happened between you and Alec."

Lisa drew in a long breath. "It was pretty ghastly at first. Then all at once it just came. Something to do with cats."

"Cats?"

"How I preferred them to dogs. And how I loathed mice. Then it got pretty heated. I got steamed up at him for abandoning me, a kid of four who'd just lost her mother. I was really mad at him." She glanced up and caught the sympathy in his eyes.

"I don't blame you."

"I felt justified for being mad . . . until I found out that I was to blame for my mother's death."

"How?"

"Alec told me I ran away from the house during the flood, and my mother went searching for me."

"Do you remember this?"

"No, not at all. But it makes sense. Why else would she be out on a night like that? Alec told me that a lot of people from the village had moved up to Charnwood Court for refuge from the flood."

"Yes, I did know about that. But Alec never wanted to talk about the rest of it."

"It must have been hard for him, even now, after all this time." Lisa stared down at a round brown stain on the pine table, probably from a teapot. "Apparently, my stuffed bear fell into the river and I tried to get it, and fell in. My mother drowned while trying to rescue me."

"But you were saved."

265

"Yes." Lisa looked up. "By my mother and my aunt. Did you know that Celia had a sister?"

Richard frowned. "I don't think so. I don't recall anyone ever talking about a sister."

"Her name was Jennifer. She definitely existed. There were lots of pictures of her in Maud's albums."

"What happened to her? Did Alec say?"

"She went to Australia. It sounded as if she just couldn't bear to stay here after Celia died." Lisa avoided meeting Richard's eyes across the table. "So, you see I was instrumental in making a great many people very unhappy."

He reached across the table, but she drew her hands away and locked them together in her lap. She stared down at the stain that Betty had probably tried to scrub and bleach, but still it was there, faded but impossible to eradicate.

Richard stood up and came around to her side of the table. He swung one leg over the bench and sat beside her, but not close enough to touch her. "You were a small child," he said. "Scared of all the noise and people in your home. Who knows why you ran outside? Kids have their own reasons for doing things. I know that, from Emily. Your mother loved you so much she'd have given anything to save you."

She felt the warmth emanating from his body, but still she wouldn't turn to look at him. "She gave her life for me. She shouldn't have had to do that. She was younger than I am now."

"It was her choice. And she knows that you're still living because of what she did."

Lisa looked up at him, and gave him a faint smile. "Do you really believe that?"

"That she knows? Certainly."

266

He spoke with such conviction that she felt he must be right. She breathed in air, releasing it in a deep sigh. Then she turned to him. "Thanks, Richard. You've really helped."

"Good." He slid along the bench a little and stood up. "That coffee smells as if it's ready. Kate said there was a slab of gingerbread in the cake tin." He got down the tin from a shelf and handed it to her. "Would you slice that for me?" He got her a knife and a gilt—edged plate.

Lisa began slicing the sticky gingerbread, which was studded with pieces of ginger. She popped a few crumbs in her mouth. "Mmm, this is good."

"You're supposed to be slicing it, not eating it," Richard said.

"Yes, sir."

He checked the tray. "Cream in the jug, sugar in the basin. Now we're all ready."

"You're very skilful at all this stuff."

"Have to be," he said succinctly, and again she was reminded that he had his own burdens—and painful memories.

"Richard," she said suddenly, as he was about to hoist up the tray.

"Yes?"

"Would you put the tray down for a moment?"

"Certainly." He did so, and stood waiting.

"We—we haven't known each other for very long. Less than three days."

"It seems much longer than that," he said, with warmth.

She felt her own cheeks grow warm in response. "Yes, it does. I want to say how grateful I am to you for all your support and kindness."

"No need."

"Yes, there is a need to say it. It's meant a lot to me. But what I also want to say is that Emily is very precious—"

"You don't have to tell me that."

"I know I don't, but I wanted to remind you of it. You're probably going to be busy with your aunt's case in the next while, until this is all cleared up. Try to keep some time for Emily. She needs you. She needs you very much." She looked away. "A little girl without her mother doubly needs her father." Her mouth trembled. "Oh, no. I promised myself I wouldn't do this to you again."

He went to the paper towel dispenser and tore off a couple of sheets and handed them to her. "You'd have to be made of stone not to be emotionally affected by what's happened to you."

"I guess so." She wiped beneath her eyes with her fingers and then blew her nose. "I'm okay now," she said, tossing the paper towel into the trash. "Let's go before they send out a search party."

Rachel was slumped in the wing-backed chair, talking, as they opened the door, but when they entered, she stopped mid—sentence and sat up, head erect. The dark-tinted glasses that hid her eyes were the only sign of what she was going through.

"You shouldn't have been helping in the kitchen," she told Lisa. "You are our guest."

"It's the least I can do under the circumstances," Lisa replied, determined not to join Rachel in this game of *Let's Pretend Nothing's Happening*.

"Thank you," Rachel said, but she didn't sound at all grateful. "Put the tray on the cart, Richard dear, and I'll pour the coffee."

Kate was stretched out on the couch, listening to

268

music on her headphones. Reluctantly, she swung her legs down to make room for Lisa, her leather pants creaking.

"Thanks." Lisa smiled at her. "Was it still as wet out there when you came back?" she asked, trying to make conversation.

Kate slid off the headphones. "Wetter."

Music leached from the headphones. It was very loud and somewhat discordant, but unmistakably twentieth-century classical music. Lisa was surprised. Somehow, she'd expected it to be rock or maybe jazz. "What is it?" She nodded to the headphones.

"Britten," Kate said. "The storm from *Peter Grimes*. Kind of appropriate for now, I thought." She held one of the headphones up to Lisa's ear.

Lisa shivered as she listened. She could hear the wind and driving rain in the music, and the crashing of waves on rocks. She gave Kate a faint smile. Kate didn't respond, but she did switch off the portable CD player.

"Kate took her music degree in composition and the clarinet at the Royal College of Music," Rachel said. There was no mistaking the pride in her voice, but her expression immediately lapsed into one of disappointment.

"Now I work for Tower Records. What a waste!" Kate's words were obviously echoes of ones her mother had frequently spoken.

"It certainly is. All those years of study and hard work thrown away—"

"I don't think Lisa wants to hear our family squabbles, does she, my dear?" Alec's tone was a gentle rebuke.

Rachel flushed, the red seeping through the carefully made-up face. "Of course not. Do you take cream with

269

your coffee, Miss Cooper?"

"Very little. Thanks." Lisa took the coffee from Rachel and set it down on the table before her.

"And what did you do to occupy yourself today?" Rachel asked her when she'd poured for the others.

Lisa felt as if she were trapped in an existentialist play by Beckett. How should she reply? *I was visiting your victim in hospital. She's not likely to live since you ran her down in your car.*

And then should she ask Rachel how her day in court had gone?

"It's such a shame the weather has turned so nasty again," Rachel continued, as if Lisa had replied to her question. "I'd hoped to get out and weed the rose beds today."

"Perhaps tomorrow will be better," Alec said. "Has anyone seen the forecast for tomorrow?"

This family had a serious denial problem. No wonder Kate was such a mess. Lisa's eyes met Richard's, but apart from a tiny flicker at the corners of his mouth, he continued to stare into space. His role as Rachel's solicitor and relative precluded him from discussing any of the subjects with which their minds were occupied.

Lisa set her coffee down on the table, splashing the liquid into the saucer. "I'm sorry. I just can't do this."

They all looked at her with startled expressions. All but Richard, who had risen when she had, and was now leaning on the back of his chair, observing her. Although he looked wary, Lisa felt a sense of approval from him.

"Is something wrong?" Rachel asked.

"I'd better go to bed," Lisa muttered, "before I say something I'll regret."

Kate perked up, suddenly showing some interest in

270

her. "No, stay. It would be a nice change to have someone say something they really mean in this house."

Lisa turned on her. "What's stopping you?" Her eyes flashed a challenge at Kate.

Kate sat up. "Okay. I will. What the hell were you and my father discussing that meant Richard had to get me out of the house?"

Rachel intervened before Lisa could reply. "What on earth do you mean?" she demanded. Kate shrugged, as if she was already regretting what she'd said. Rachel turned to Alec. "What does she mean?"

"I have no idea. Richard merely asked Kate out for a drink, so Miss Cooper and I—"

"Bull!" Kate said. "Don't treat me like an idiot. I can tell a setup when I see one."

"Alec?" Rachel's voice rang out like a pistol shot.

He sat there, frozen at first, and then he bent to stroke Sheba's golden head, avoiding looking at anyone. Lisa thought of the photograph of her father as a youth, the unconsciously arrogant male pose, staring boldly into the camera, and contrasted it with his inability to deal with this situation. Had he always been this way, or had Celia's death sapped the spirit from him?

She spoke for him. "I had to speak to your husband, Mrs. Kingsley. It's a personal matter between us."

Alec stood up. "I think that's enough, don't you?" he said pointedly.

"No, I don't," Lisa said. "I think your wife and daughter deserve better than to be left out of this, but that has to be your decision, not mine."

The charming smile he could switch on at will now appeared. "Why don't I fix you a nice hot toddy as it's such a chilly evening? You must make sure you switch the fire on in your—"

271

"You're his daughter, aren't you?" Rachel's voice cut through Alec's desperate attempt to normalize everything.

Lisa faced her squarely. "Yes, I am, Mrs. Kingsley."

"His daughter?" Kate asked.

Lisa turned to her. "I'm sorry. I thought you knew that your father had a child from his first marriage." She gave Kate a fleeting smile. "Don't worry. I haven't come to usurp your place, or anything like that. I just needed to get some answers to questions I had about my past."

Rachel stood up, steadying herself with one hand on the arm of her chair. "So you wheedled your way into this house without telling us who you were, and then set out to spy on us." Rachel's eyes were hidden by the dark glasses, but Lisa could tell by the tightness around her mouth how furious and shocked she was.

Richard intervened. "I think if you were to listen to Lisa, you'd find out that that was not the case at all."

Rachel swung around, staring at her nephew. "You mean you knew about all this and didn't tell me? How could you, Richard!" She swung back to confront Alec. "And how long have you known? Or was it all a bloody setup from the start?"

"Would you all friggin' shut up and let me get a word in!" Kate's scream of rage cut through the noise.

It was effective in creating a moment of silence.

Kate turned to Lisa. "Now, please, would you tell us why you're here." She fixed both her parents with a baleful look. *"Without* any interruptions."

"I'm your father's daughter by his marriage to his first wife, Celia Templeton. When she died, he gave me up for adoption—"

"I know all that," Kate said, breaking her own com-

272

mand about interruptions. "Why are you here? I thought you were out of his life forever." She glared at her father. "At least, that's what he always told me."

"I thought so, too," Lisa said. "How could I think otherwise when I'd been told both my parents were dead?"

"Who told you that?"

"My mother. The woman who adopted me. I suppose she wanted to make sure I didn't come back here."

"You can see why, can't you?" Kate gave her a wry smile. "Not exactly a cosy little family, are we?"

Lisa said nothing.

"So why did you come back?" Rachel demanded.

"To see where I came from, where my roots were. To get medical records for the future, just in case . . ." Lisa encountered Alec's pale face and anxious eyes. "And,

once I was here, and knew that my birth father was alive," she said, her voice softening, "to find out what happened to my mother."

"You mean you came here thinking your parents were dead," Kate said, "and then discovered that your father—*my* father—was alive, after all?"

"Yes."

"When did you know? As soon as you both met?" Kate seemed genuinely interested, even fascinated.

"No, not right away. I think your father knew immediately, though."

"Because I'd been expecting you." His smile was suddenly warm, affectionate. "Something told me you'd come back, one day."

Kate's eyes narrowed. "How touching. The tale of the prodigal daughter."

"Hardly," Lisa said. "I have my own parents. Or had, until my mother died a few months ago. But my father

273

is still very much alive in Canada." If Alec flinched, she didn't care. He deserved it. Lisa bent to pick up her shoulder bag. "Now, if you don't mind, I think I'd like to go to bed. It's been a long, hard day for all of us." She turned to Rachel. "Would you prefer me to stay somewhere else? I'd understand if you did."

Her face was a taut mask. "You are Alec's daughter. Of course, you must stay here." They were the right words, but spoken without any hint of warmth or welcome.

"Thank you. I'll say good night, then."

Richard was at the door, opening it for her. She stopped to speak to him on her way out. "Thanks for everything," she said in a low voice, so that only he could hear. "I'm sorry for letting it all out, but—"

"I think you did the right thing. There's been too much covering up in this family."

Alec joined them at the door, nodding in the direction of the hall. When they went out, Lisa expected him to admonish her for her outburst, but he surprised her by saying, "Well—done."

"I thought you'd be furious with me for telling them."

"I thought I would be, too." A glimmer of a smile appeared. "But after the initial shock I was glad you had the courage to do it. It had to be done sometime." He gazed down at her. "Are you all right?"

"Yes, I'm fine. Just tired, that's all. You must be, as well. After all, you have all the worry of your wife on top of this." Lisa grimaced. "Rotten timing on my part, I'm afraid. I'm sorry."

"Don't be. I just wish I could have given you a warmer welcome, that's all." Alec glanced at Richard, who was tactfully engaged in picking up some rose petals that had fallen from the vase on the ancient

274

sideboard against the wall. "Whatever the situation here, I am very happy that you're here, and to know that I have such a lovely and spirited daughter." His eyes filled with tears which he blinked away. "Your mother would have been proud of you today. You reminded me so much of her. She would have spoken up, just as you did."

Lisa couldn't find the right response, so said nothing.

Gently, tentatively he put his arms around her. She felt the roughness of his sleeve against her arm, and then his lips against her forehead. "Sleep well, my darling girl," he murmured, then went back into the living room and closed the door.

When she looked around, Richard, too, had gone, and she was alone in the dimly lit hall.

CHAPTER THIRTY

When she reached her room, Lisa was sorry she hadn't taken Alec up on his earlier offer of a hot toddy. It would have relaxed as well as warmed her. The room was cold and the all—pervading dampness from the rain that poured down incessantly seemed to seep into her muscles and bones. She switched on the electric blanket and both bars of the electric fire. Then, having pulled on another sweater, she curled up in the chair by the fire, determined to read a few more chapters of *Lorna Doone* before she went to bed.

But trying to plow through the Somerset dialect, and the seemingly hopeless love of the young farmer John Ridd for his Lorna, kept making Lisa nod off. At one point, she was startled awake by the sound of a car door slamming. She jumped up and, looking out, saw

Richard's Range Rover pulling away.

"He's going home to Emily," she murmured. The thought both pleased and saddened her.

She tried to assure herself that she was in what once had been her home, but that didn't help, either. Too much had happened since that time for it to be any solace. She decided the best thing was to go to bed, and face the next day with the knowledge that she had at least confronted her father and his family. Definitely a major hurdle crossed.

She wasn't sure what wakened her. A creaking floorboard or the squeak of hinges on the door, perhaps. She'd left the door open a crack for Nero to come and go as he pleased. Sometime after she'd gone to bed, he had jumped up on the bed and curled against her legs. She'd fallen asleep to the rhythmic rumble of his purring.

Another creak. This time definitely a floorboard.

Although she was now fully awake, she lay absolutely still, determined to catch whoever it was before he or she fled. It was pitch—dark. Her half—waking eyes had not yet adapted to the lack of light. She could see nothing, but she knew that someone was tiptoeing across the room.

Now the figure was standing over her bed. Lisa breathed in that sweet herbal aroma she'd smelled before in the room. She kept her eyes closed, pretending to be asleep. The figure bent over her. She could hear breathing. The aroma became stronger, emanating from the person. She tensed, expecting a pillow on her face, hands around her neck. Her fingers were curled into claws, ready to grab.

She heard a strange metallic sound, like a hinge on a metal box opening. What followed was so sudden, so unexpected that for a moment she froze, unable to move. She felt small furry bodies on her face, squeaking, scrabbling, and smelled the disgusting smell of mice. Several of them.

Screaming, she flung herself from the bed, her arms flailing. She felt the mice in her long loose hair, on her eyes, running all over her body. In a frenzy, she ran shrieking round and round the room, crashing into furniture, beating herself with her hands, trying to brush the vileness from her body.

After what seemed a like a lifetime of horror, the light snapped on. "What in God's name has happened?" demanded Alec's voice.

"Mice! Mice!" Lisa screamed.

"Mice?" He came to her and tried to put his arms around her, but she hit out at him, still trying to rid herself of the furry bodies, the rank smell.

"Get them off me!" She yelled.

He took hold of her arms and forcibly held her. "There are no mice on you, I promise you. None at all. You've had a bad nightmare, that's all."

He smoothed her hair from her face and drew her against him. She pressed her face against his wine—colored dressing gown and felt the fast beat of his heart against her cheek. Slowly, her shaking subsided. She drew away from him.

"Poor darling," Alec said. "You must have been dreaming."

"No, she wasn't," Kate's voice said.

They both turned. "Don't look," Kate said hurriedly. She was staring down at the carpet at the foot of the bed.

Before she had time to look away, Lisa saw that Nero was crouched there, black tail waving furiously,

277

something caught between his paws.

"Let's get the hell out of here," Alec said.

Kate grabbed Lisa's robe and helped her into it, guiding her arms into the sleeves. Lisa was still shaking, and her legs felt as if they were made of straw. "I'm sorry," she whispered. "So stupid to get that upset, but . . ." She shuddered, reliving that initial feeling of disgusting warm bodies and scurrying feet on her skin and closed eyelids.

"Don't think about it," Alec said. "Let's go downstairs."

"I have to wash my face," Lisa said, shuddering.

"You can do that in the downstairs loo."

"Would you give me my washbag?" Lisa asked Kate. "It's on the dressing table."

Kate handed it to her. "You go on down with Dad. I'll clear up in here," she said.

"Good girl," her father said.

Rachel stood in the hallway, her face white and haggard without its usual careful makeup. "What happened?"

Alec gave Lisa's arm a warning squeeze. "A mouse ran over Lisa and woke her up."

"Was that all?" Rachel said in a scathing tone. "Heavens above! All that noise and bother for a mouse."

"Elizabeth was always terrified of mice," he explained.

She made a derisory sound in her throat, turned, and walked away. "I trust you won't be kept up too long, Alec," she said over her shoulder. "You need your sleep."

"Someone was in the room," Lisa told him, as soon as Rachel was out of their hearing.

"Yes, so I gather. I didn't want Rachel to know that."

278

"It happened just minutes ago. I don't know how they got away without you seeing them. Whoever it was had a cage or a metal box. I heard the hinge opening. And then . . ." Lisa covered her face with her hands, still feeling the scrabbling, although sense told her there was nothing there. "Do you believe me?"

"I do."

"Are you sure? You're not just trying to pacify me by saying you do when—"

"I believe you."

Lisa wanted to be sure. "After all, just because Nero had caught one mouse doesn't mean there were more, does it?"

"There were two more dead mice beside him." Alec's face was grim.

Lisa shuddered again. "Oh!"

"Let's go downstairs. I'll put a match to the fire and we'll all have a cognac."

"We have to talk about this. Not just for my sake. Someone managed to get into the house and—"

"I know that. Cognac first. Then we'll talk. I promise you," he said, when she opened her mouth to protest. "We need to be calm to be able to think clearly."

When they went downstairs, he opened a door in a side passage. "This is our cloakroom. It's a bit cluttered, I'm afraid, but you can find the washbasin, et cetera."

Cluttered was right. Old raincoats and waterproof jackets hung on the hooks around the walls, and there were several pairs of rubber boots and sturdy walking shoes lined up at one end. The smell of old rubber pervaded the room.

Any smell was better than that in the green room. She didn't think she'd ever get the mixture of that sweet—herbal aroma and the sickly stench of mice out of her

279

nostrils.

There was a transparent brown oval of soap on the washbasin. It had a medicinal, wholesome smell. Lisa used it and her face cloth to scrub her face and neck and hands. Then she decided to wash all over. Standing there, shivering, her feet on the small hand towel, she washed herself from head to toe.

Kate knocked on the door. "Would you like fresh pajamas? I brought some down from your drawer."

"Thanks." Lisa put on her robe again and opened the door. "That was thoughtful of you." She grimaced. "I just washed all over."

"You should have had a shower."

"I know. I wasn't thinking."

"Daddy tends to bulldoze people. Don't let him."

Lisa smiled. "I think he wanted to get me out of there as fast as possible. And that's what I wanted, as well. Thanks, Kate."

"Okay. I'm going to put Nero down in the cellar. He's a bit agitated."

"No wonder. Thank God for Nero. I don't think you'd have believed me if he hadn't—"

"Don't think about it. Dad's in the library."

Lisa went into the library just as Alec was getting the fire going. She was greeted by orange flames and crackling logs, a welcome antidote to the sick shuddering that still ran over her.

Alec came to her and put an arm around her to guide her to the fire. "Come and sit down." He put her in Rachel's chair and wrapped a knitted afghan around her. "Here, drink this down. It'll make you feel better." He handed her a brandy snifter with a large measure of cognac in it.

"Thank you," Lisa murmured. She cupped her hands

around the delicate glass and gave Alec a shaky smile. "I'm sorry I screamed so loud and woke everyone up."

"Nonsense." He didn't attempt to discuss it further. Lisa was glad. For the moment this was what she needed: warmth and comfort.

Kate came in. "All done," she said briskly. Clad in her one—piece sleep suit, and minus her owlish makeup, Kate looked about ten, but her eyes were bright in the leaping firelight, and she was obviously alert and brimming with questions.

"I'm sorry, but I can't sleep in that room again tonight," Lisa told her.

" 'Course you can't." Kate said, accepting a glass of cognac from her father. "My room's got two beds in it, if you don't mind sharing. Okay?"

Lisa nodded. "Thanks."

"Don't worry. We've all got our hangups. Mine's snakes. I can't bear even to see pictures of them. And Daddy faints at the sight of a needle. You know, injections . . . that sort of thing."

"Yes, but both are more lethal, potentially, aren't they? Mice . . ." Lisa couldn't bear even to talk about them now. She took a gulp of her cognac and felt its fiery warmth slide down her throat. "Where did your father go?" she asked, suddenly realizing that he'd left the room.

"Probably to make sandwiches. Daddy's panacea for everything is drink and food. The one great source of disappointment in his life is that he can't make roast beef sandwiches for me. Now his other daughter turns up and he can't make them for her, either, poor man."

They both laughed. The warmth that stole over Lisa came not only from the cognac, but also from Kate's casual mention of the "other daughter."

"Does he need any help?"

"Oh no. That would spoil it. This is his way of going out hunting, feeding his brood."

Kate was right. A short while later, Alec brought in a tray laden with two plates heaped with sandwiches, with some mugs of steaming coffee, and the remains of the gingerbread.

"Oh, goody! A midnight feast," Kate said.

Alec glanced at his watch. "A two o'clock feast."

"Whoever came into my room wanted to make sure we were all well asleep," Lisa said, no longer able to put the dark thoughts from of her mind.

"Eat first," Alec said. "Then we'll talk. Pink roast beef for me and—"

"Yuck! What did I tell you?" Kate said to Lisa.

Alec ignored their smiles. "And salmon and cucumber for Lisa, cucumber and cream cheese for Kate."

Although Lisa wasn't at all hungry, she ate two sandwiches to please him. But nothing would persuade her to eat a piece of gingerbread.

"Mmm, smells good, tastes even better," Kate said. "Talking of smells . . . Excuse me for bringing up the subject, Lisa, but there was a strong smell of aniseed in your room, as if you'd been sucking aniseed balls."

"Aniseed!" Lisa exclaimed. *That's* what that smell is. I just couldn't place it. I thought it was some sort of licorice—type smell, but—"

They were interrupted by Alec's sudden fit of coughing.

"Are you okay, Daddy?" Kate hovered over him, ready to help him in case he was choking.

"I'm fine."

"That's what happens when you eat the flesh of

282

animals, even when it's semicooked."

But Lisa, meeting Alec's eyes before he glanced away, was sure that it wasn't the food he'd choked on. "I smelled that same smell in the room when I woke up this morning," she said. "I thought it was from the flowers on the table. *And* I think I smelled it in the nursery on Saturday. But that might have been my imagination. I don't know."

"The nursery?" Alec repeated incredulously.

"Yes, when I went through the house on the tour with Maud Birkett." As soon as she said the name, she wished she hadn't. His face took on that iceberg look she'd seen before. "I'm sorry. I shouldn't have reminded you."

"Perfectly all right." He made an attempt at a smile, which faded almost immediately. "You know she's had a heart attack and is not likely to live, poor woman?"

"Yes, the police told me. I am sorry." Lisa felt her face flush. "Sorry for you, I mean, and also for Maud. I hate to think of her being all alone. I had thought of going back to the hospital yesterday evening, but I didn't think I'd be able to find my way back across Exmoor in the dark."

"I should think not."

"I'd have taken you on the Harley, if you'd asked," Kate said.

Alec stirred uneasily. "In the circumstances, it might be better that you not visit Maud."

"Why not?" Lisa demanded.

"Because now that the police know who you are—I mean your connection with us—if anything were to happen to Maud when you were with her . . ."

Lisa was about to deny this possibility hotly, but then subsided, realizing that, like it or not, she was now undeniably attached to the Kingsley family. Maud had known it. The police knew it.

And someone who had access to Charnwood Court knew it. Someone who knew about her horror of mice.

Lisa put down her glass and leaned forward. "Please don't get mad at me, either of you, but while I was washing I was racking my brain, trying to think of some reasonable explanation for all of this." She hesitated for a moment and then, realizing there was no way of being subtle, jumped in. "Knowing how upset Rachel must be, is it possible she might have overheard our conversation about cats and mice, do you think?" To Lisa, it was the only solution to the mystery that made any sense.

"You mean that my wife went totally berserk and somehow rounded up a cageful of mice while I was lying beside her, and then went to your room and released them?" Alec's voice was cold. "Or maybe Kate did it? She had opportunity *and* the advantage of being alone." He glanced up at Kate, who sat perched on the arm of his chair.

"Don't be ridiculous." Kate was obviously unsure if she should take her father seriously, or not. She swung around to confront Lisa with narrowed eyes. "What was our motive?" she demanded.

Lisa swallowed. "You wanted to get rid of your father's lost child. You wanted her to go back to Canada and never come here again."

"You mean I was jealous of you?" Kate said belligerently. "Or my mother was?"

Lisa looked down at her hands. "Something like that."

"What a load of horse manure!"

Lisa rallied. "Maybe so, but tell me who else it could have been? It has to be someone who knows about my

284

fear of mice."

"How would I know about that?" Kate asked.

"Maybe your father mentioned it sometime."

"My father didn't talk to me about you."

"No, I don't suppose he did," Lisa said with under-standing. "It also has to be someone with access to the interior of the house. I take it the doors were locked," she said to Alec.

"Of course."

"And you have an alarm system?"

"Yes."

"Then you can see what I mean. It had to be someone inside the house. How else could anyone get in without setting off the alarm?"

"Through a window, perhaps," Alec said. "We switch off the sensors at night; otherwise, the dogs and cat would set them off all the time. Only the three exterior doors are monitored."

Lisa could tell that he was holding something back. Although she hated to do it, only by goading him would she get it out of him. "Then it must be one of you," she said, "mustn't it?"

Kate spoke. "I think we're going to have to tell her, Daddy."

"Tell me what?" Lisa asked.

"There's a secret staircase," Alec said slowly. "It was part of the original house. Probably used to hide Royalists from the Roundheads during the Civil War. It connects with the little folly beyond the rose garden."

"A secret staircase. How very Gothic!" Lisa's voice was heavy with sarcasm. "Why didn't you mention it before?"

"It's hardly something we want to broadcast."

"Where does it come out," Lisa asked, "in the house,

285

I mean?"

"In a small room on the top floor. We use it for storage nowadays. Very few people, other than family members, know about it."

Family members.

"Perhaps it is none of my business, but has this staircase been used during these episodes of poison—pen letters?"

Alec gave her a twisted smile. "Whether it's your business or not, you seem to have been dragged into it. The answer is, yes. At least, we believe so. Sometimes the letters came through the post. Other times they just appeared. One was found on the hall table . . . another in the kitchen . . . . The terrorist seems to gain particular pleasure in proving that he or she can get inside the house."

"So the police know about this staircase."

"Yes. In fact, they recommended that we close it up."

"I'm not surprised. Why didn't you?"

"Daddy thought we'd be more likely to catch whoever it was who was persecuting us if we left it open," Kate said.

"But the wretch is devious," Alec said. "Leaves us alone for as much as several months at a time, so that we think whoever it is has gone away, and then just when we think it's all over, and we can get on with living a normal life, at last—the letters start coming again." His face bore a haunted expression.

"That's awful," Lisa whispered.

"It's diabolical. As I told you before, we were sure it was Maud Birkett. She knew about the hidden passage, of course. She had always hated me for marrying so soon after Celia's death. And, as I told you yesterday, she resented Rachel. Not only for taking Celia's place,

286

but also because Maud knew that she was no longer welcome to call Charnwood Court her home."

Lisa thought of the lonely woman lying in the narrow hospital bed. She recalled the loving look in her mother's eyes in the photograph of Celia and Maud on the beach. Alec would never understand what his wife's death had meant to Maud.

"But now," Alec continued, "with Maud lying incapacitated in hospital, we know she couldn't have been here tonight, so we're back to square one. Either she was working with someone else, or it wasn't her, after all."

"Maud warned me of danger."

Alec's head shot up. "When?"

"When I visited her in the hospital."

"I hadn't realized that she was actually able to speak to you. I knew she was capable of understanding and responding to questions; otherwise poor Rachel might be in a prison cell tonight." He reached blindly for Kate's hand and squeezed it.

"She couldn't say much. It was more my anticipating what she meant and having her confirm it. But she actually spoke the word *danger*."

"Danger to you, personally?"

"That's what I understood her to mean. Then she said, *Jennifer*."

There was a long pause. "You didn't tell me that before, did you?" Alec said. His olive-brown skin seemed to blanch beneath the tan.

"No, I didn't. I keep going over it in my mind." Lisa frowned. "The two words weren't said at the same time, you see. She said *danger* and then, later on, *Jennifer*. I asked Maud if she was saying that I was in danger from Jennifer, whoever she was, and she seemed to indicate I

287

was. The policewoman who was with her said she'd been trying to say *Jennifer* before I came into the room."

"Who's Jennifer?" Kate asked.

Alec's eyes clashed with Lisa's. "We don't know if it's the same Jennifer," he said slowly, "but Celia had a sister of that name."

"What happened to her?" Kate asked.

"She went to Australia when Celia died. As far as I know, she's still there."

"Maud doesn't seem to think so," Kate said, succinctly putting into words the thought that neither Lisa nor Alec wanted to verbalize.

CHAPTER THIRTY-ONE

LISA LOOKED DIRECTLY AT ALEC. "KATE'S RIGHT. IT looks as if Jennifer might be nearer Charnwood than you think. It's time you told me more about my mother's sister."

"I've told you all I know, and that's precious little. Jennifer lived with us here after we were married."

"What did she do?" Lisa asked.

"Do?"

"I mean, what was her profession, her job?"

"She didn't really have one then. She helped Celia run this house. It's a business in itself, as I've found, to my cost. Jennifer had a good head for business. I imagine she made quite a success of her sheep farm in Australia."

"She wasn't artistic, then. I wondered if my artistic genes had come from her."

Alec's smile was wistful. "You inherited those from

your mother. Celia painted lovely watercolors."

"Have you any of her work?" Lisa asked eagerly.

His face reddened. "I'm afraid I gave them all away to her friends. Maud took most of them."

"You mean my mother painted those delicate watercolors in Maud's house?"

"I imagine so. I haven't been into Maud's house since Celia died."

"Do you remember if Jennifer took any of her sister's paintings?" Lisa asked him.

"No, she didn't."

"You seem very certain about that."

"I .. am."

"Why?"

Alec's mouth tightened. "Is this an interrogation?"

"Sorry. I'm really trying to find out what my aunt was like."

"Let's just say she was shattered by Celia's death. As I told you, she left suddenly after her funeral and the reading of the will. As far as I know, she took nothing of Celia's with her."

"But you said Celia left her money."

"That's right."

"So you knew where Jennifer went."

"We corresponded solely through her solicitor in London. It was he who told me she had gone to Australia."

"And you haven't heard a word from her since?" Kate asked her father.

"No."

"Yet Maud seems to think Jennifer could be hanging around Charnwood," Kate said.

"That's not what Maud said," Lisa reminded her.

Kate ignored her. "Or maybe Maud's actually been

working for Jennifer. You know, Jennifer sends her ideas, gives her orders by phone or fax, or something. They were probably friends, so they could have been working together to persecute you, Daddy. God knows why."

"Although Maud and Jennifer were part of the same group," Lisa said slowly, deep in thought, "I don't think you could call them friends."

Alec looked surprised. "How did you know that?"

"From Maud's photographs. It was clear that Jennifer was jealous of Maud."

"Jealous?" Kate looked puzzled.

"Jealous of the affection between the two girls, Celia and Maud. I'm right, aren't I?" Lisa demanded of Alec.

He rubbed his fingers across his forehead and sighed. "Yes, you're right."

"In fact, you're holding something back about Celia's sister."

Alec and reached for his brandy glass. "It's all so far in the past. Who wants to dredge up old memories?"

"I do. And you should, too, because they may be crucial to the present. I promised Maud that I would never forget Celia, but how can I remember her when you tell me next to nothing about her and her family?"

"It's better that way," Alec murmured, staring into the fire.

"I know it must hurt to talk about her," Lisa said softly, "but if we're going to work out what's happening here and now, it might be necessary to go back to the past and find out the truth."

"I've told you the truth about Celia's death."

"I know you have. But—"

Alec stood up. "I'm sorry. It's been a long day. I'm exhausted." He looked it, the lines about his eyes etched deep. "I'll be happy to answer more of your questions tomorrow, but I must go to bed now."

"But shouldn't we call the police in?" Lisa asked. "After all, there has been a break-in, hasn't there?"

"They won't be particularly sympathetic. They warned me to close off the entrance to the hidden stairway."

"They're right."

"Don't worry. I'll get it bricked up tomorrow and put an end to these terror tactics. Now I really must go to bed. Rachel and I have to leave for Taunton first thing in the morning. We've got an important meeting with Richard and his associate at his office. I've engaged a barrister in London, and we're having a telephone conference at ten o'clock."

"I'm glad about that," Kate said, "but what about tonight? Whoever got in could still be wandering around the house, couldn't they?"

Lisa's spine tensed. "That's right."

"We'll move that large oak chest across the entrance to the stairway," Alec said. "But, in case this person is still at large, make sure you lock your bedroom door, Kate."

His reluctance to report the break—in to the police made Lisa feel even more sure that Rachel must have run Maud down. She was also certain now that it had been no accident. Rachel and Alec blamed Maud for all the misery that had blighted their lives. Rachel had means, opportunity, and motive.

The entrance to the stairway was in a small oak—paneled room above the nursery. When Alec pressed one of the carved rose bosses on the wood—paneled wall, Lisa was astonished to see a section of paneling swing outward to form a door. Behind it was another door, built of solid unvarnished oak, with a heavy brass lock.

"I should have changed this lock a long time ago," Alec muttered, as he fitted in the key and checked the door. When it swung open, a gust of chill air and the smell of mildew assailed them. The walls of the narrow, spiral stairway beyond the door were of rough—hewn stone.

"It's like a tomb," Kate whispered.

Lisa shivered. Kate was right.

And there was that smell again. "He or she was definitely here," Lisa said. "I can smell the aniseed." She looked at Alec's curiously blank expression. "Or am I getting paranoid and imagining it?"

"No, you're right," Kate said. Now she, too, was shivering visibly. "Let's get this place blocked up and then get the hell out of here. It's giving me the bloody creeps."

Once Alec had closed and locked the inner door and then shut the paneled door, they heaved and pushed the old wooden chest up against the paneling. Then, for good measure, Alec locked the door to the room.

It was a relief to get down to the next floor and settle into Kate's refreshingly ordinary bedroom. Lisa surveyed the posters of U2 and Michael Jackson on the walls.

Kate grimaced. "A bit infantile, aren't they? Shades of my youth that I've never got around to taking down. I was trying to obliterate the fact that I live in a frigging museum."

"Have you ever thought of getting away?" Lisa tried not to make it sound too critical. "I mean, really away. London, perhaps. Or even some other country."

Kate turned away and stood over her bed, small

shoulders hunched. "I'm afraid that if I leave permanently, my parents will fall apart. You may not believe this, but they truly do need me."

"I do believe it. Now, I do. I mean, I don't really know them very well." Lisa made a face. "But it's as if all this . . . this stuff that's going on seems to be eating away at them."

Kate turned around again. Moisture glistened in her eyes. "It's evil, that's what it is. It's changed my mother's personality completely. She used to be vibrant, full of energy and ideas, never still for a moment. And my father loved this place and his work, but all this antagonism from the village, and then giving up his seat before the last election . . . it's all beaten him down. Having to sell this house was the last straw. He seems . . . sort of haunted all the time nowadays, if you know what I mean."

Lisa nodded. "Yes, I do."

"When you talk to him you get the feeling his mind is on something else. My mother thinks it's because he's still obsessed with Celia. I think that's bullshit. It's all these letters and the vicious gossip in the village. Maybe I'm as paranoid as my parents." Kate shrugged. "I don't know. But I do think there's a definite campaign to break them down. The frustrating thing is neither we nor the police can trace the source. Until this accident, I think they were all sure it was Maud."

"Yet they kept her on as a tour guide," Lisa said, still puzzled by this.

"It's the same thing as not blocking up the stairway," Kate explained. "More than once, Dad's sat up all night in that little room upstairs, with his shotgun, waiting for someone to come through the door in the wall. He's convinced that the only way to discover the culprit is to catch her—or him—red—handed. And that's why he kept Maud on as a guide."

"But now we know that it isn't Maud. Or, if she was involved, that she wasn't working alone. Someone struck again tonight."

"Yeah. This time at you. You know what that means?"

"It could mean that I'm being attacked because I'm now considered part of this family."

"That's true, or that they want you gone, out of here, and they're trying to scare you off."

Next morning, when Richard came to collect Alec and Rachel, he didn't employ any subtle tactics to give Lisa the same message. "I think you should go home right away," he said as soon as Lisa had finished telling him what had happened, while he waited for Rachel and Alec in the hall.

His bluntness surprised her. "I thought you might laugh at my being scared by a few mice," she said, with a wry smile.

His expression was solemn. "I think it was a vicious attack, designed to demoralize and terrify you. I also think it was a warning from someone who knew about your fear of mice. I don't think you should ignore that warning."

Lisa lifted her chin. "I object to being driven away from Charnwood before I want to leave."

"I understand that, but something really nasty is going on here at present, and your connection with the family—"

Lisa drew him nearer the front door, to avoid anyone hearing. "Forgive the suggestion, but what if Rachel overheard my discussion with Alec last night? She could have, you know. She might have tiptoed down and listened at the door. I know she's your aunt, but she's going through a traumatic time. What if she resented my turning up out of the blue? Isn't it possible she'd want to drive me away?"

"Alec told me you'd suggested that last night. He also told me what his response had been."

"I know it sounds far-fetched, but so does everything else. I wonder what Paula Willand was doing late last night."

"Paula? Why?"

"Because I don't trust her, that's why."

Richard took her by the elbows. "Go home to Canada, Lisa. Leave today."

"I can't. Haven't you heard?" Lisa raised her eyebows at him. "I've been told to stay here. Officially."

"By whom?"

"The police. I'm not to leave without their permission."

"Damn. We must get this sorted out. I'll be sure to speak to a colleague about representing you when I'm in Taunton today."

"Could you also find out how Maud is? I take it that there's no change?"

"Not as far as I know. She's still alive, but still in critical condition."

"Poor Maud. I knew you'd have told me right away if there'd been any change."

"Of course." He glanced up at the staircase to make sure they were still alone. "We're all hoping that Maud survives. I can check with the police right away, if you like."

"No." Lisa sighed. "We'll know soon enough, either way. I keep thinking I should be there with her."

"Absolutely no visitors allowed, so you can stop

worrying about that."

"Thanks, anyway."

"Maybe you can see her later in the week."

"My flight back to Canada is booked for Friday. It's the kind you can't change. I don't know what's going to happen if the police won't let me leave here on Thursday."

"For your sake, I wish you were going back today, but . . . I'll speak to a lawyer and make arrangements for you to meet her tomorrow."

"Her?"

"Yes. Any objections to a female lawyer?"

"None at all."

"Good. Helen Bristow's got a first—class mind and a good grasp of the law." Richard eyed the streaming rain through the open front door. "Mind you, if the rain keeps on this way, none of us might be going anywhere tomorrow."

"Is it that bad?" Lisa moved over to the door and looked out. Her throat tightened. The front driveway was almost submerged in water.

" 'Fraid so. The river's rising fast. If it floods, the road out of here could be cut off. They're already moving into an emergency standby position, getting ready to evacuate those with homes in the lower part of the valley."

Lisa's eyes widened. "I'm afraid of water and floods," she whispered.

"I'm not surprised," Richard said, sympathy in his voice. "Alec gave me some more details of your mother's death this morning. It must have been terrible for you."

Lisa clasped the doorframe to steady herself. "I don't remember any of it. Only the fear remains. Nothing else."

The sound of Alec's voice stopped her from saying more. He was helping Rachel down the stairs. Despite her obvious frailty, she was dressed in high-heeled black shoes and a chic black suit that hung loosely on her slender figure. The harsh effect of the black was relieved only by a single strand of pearls about her thin neck.

"Right, Richard, we're all ready to go." Alec spoke in a hearty tone, as if they were off for a day at the races or a picnic, not preparing for a possible charge of man-slaughter. "Kate's coming, too. She said she wanted to be with us for the meeting. Is that all right?"

"Absolutely."

"Good. She's taken the dogs for a walk, and should be shutting them in the stable now. She's bringing the car around to the front."

Richard turned to Lisa. "You'll be all right on your own?"

"Of course."

"Betty's in the kitchen," Alec said. "She should be here all morning, cleaning the place." His smile was heavy with weariness. "Getting rid of all our two—pounders' muddy footprints." He gave a mirthless laugh when he caught Lisa's questioning look. "Our visitors who pay two pounds each to see our palatial, happy home," he explained.

Lisa felt Richard's hand press her arm, then they were all gone, leaving her standing alone in the flagstoned hall, by the open doorway. As Richard's Range Rover disappeared into the pall of gray mist, the only sounds to be heard were rain gushing down the spouts and the constant drip—drip of water from the porch over the door onto the broad front steps.

CHAPTER THIRTY-TWO

LISA MADE IMMEDIATELY FOR THE KITCHEN, determined not to be alone in this uneasy house. Although she'd slept remarkably well, until Alec had woken her and Kate at six-thirty with cups of tea and ginger biscuits, she was still edgy from last night. As soon as she'd spoken to Betty, she meant to get as far away as possible from the toxic atmosphere of Charnwood Court.

Betty was emptying the dishwasher, piling the dishes on the kitchen table.

" 'Morning, Betty. Can I help?"

"Not at all, miss. I'll be through with this in a minute." Betty lifted the basket of cutlery out. "Can I help you with something?" She seemed restrained, not as chatty and friendly as before.

"Did Mr. Kingsley tell you?"

"Tell me what?" Betty asked, with a wary expression.

"Who I am."

Betty hesitated, then said, "Yes, miss. He did. I s'pose I should say welcome back to Charnwood Court, shouldn't I?" There was a cool formality about her that chilled Lisa.

"Thank you, Betty. You probably think I deceived you when we spoke on Sunday afternoon."

Betty's hands were busy putting away knives, forks, and spoons into the cutlery drawer. Her face was turned from Lisa.

"At that time, I didn't even know that Celia and Alec Kingsley were my parents," Lisa said. "What you told me literally changed my life."

Once Betty had finished the cutlery, she had to go

back to the dishwasher for the glasses. Lisa went to the dishwasher and confronted her.

"Please stop for a minute and listen to what I have to say."

" 'scuse me, miss, but I'm very busy."

"I know you are. I'll be happy to help you, but I want you to hear me out. Why don't we have a cup of tea together?"

"I don't want a cup of tea, thank you. My tea break is at nine."

"Well, I'd like one." Lisa knew that Betty couldn't ignore her request.

"I'll make a fresh pot."

"No, don't worry. Just drop a bag in a mug and add hot water."

Betty looked shocked. "We don't make tea that way here, miss."

Lisa grimaced. "Sorry." She sat down on the pine bench. "Could you stop calling me 'miss'? My name's Lisa."

"I don't think—"

"You knew my mother. I call you Betty. You certainly have every right to call me Lisa."

Betty's stern expression softened. She poured boiling water into the glazed brown pot and brought it—and not one but two cups and saucers, Lisa noticed—over to the table, and sat down across from her.

"Why are you mad at me?" Lisa asked her. "I promise you I never told Mr. Kingsley about our conversation on Sunday."

Betty took a gulp of hot tea. "You might've told me who you were, instead of pretending you were some stranger. I'd known you since you were born."

"So that's why! Okay, now I understand. I thought

maybe Alec had got angry with you for telling me about my parents."

"I never knew we were talking about them as *your* parents, miss," Betty said, her face flushing crimson. "Then when Mr. Alec told me who you were, I thought you'd come here, knowing Mr. Alec was your father."

"I didn't. My mother—the woman who adopted me—"

"Your nanny."

"That's right. My nanny, Miss Haines. She never told me anything about my parents, except that both of them had been killed in a car crash in Europe."

"That wasn't so," Betty said flatly.

"I know that now. For some reason, she didn't want me to come here and find my family. If it hadn't been for my chance meeting with Emily and Richard, I might never have met the Kingsleys."

Betty gazed down at her cup. "You could say it was meant to be."

"I think you're right. But still, if it hadn't been for you, I might never have found out the truth."

Betty looked up and smiled for the first time. "Mr. Alec's pleased as Punch that you've come back."

Lisa smiled back at her. "Is he, really? I wasn't sure." Her smile faded. "It's not easy for either of us. I can't understand anyone giving up their child, and he's obviously feeling guilty and embarrassed."

"So he bloody should be." Lisa was surprised by Betty's vehemence. "His dear wife must've turned in her grave to see him send you away."

"Yes." An awkward silence followed. What more could she say? "We may never get it settled between us, but at least he knows I'm okay."

"That's what he said to me this morning. Just knowing she's alive and well means so much to me,

Betty,' he said."

Lisa nodded, not trusting herself to speak. She took a drink of the strong tea, then said, slowly, "Did you hear about what happened here last night?"

Betty's face paled. "I did. I weren't sure I should mention it to you. Kate told me how upset you were. You always did hate mice, from a small girl."

"Betty, I need your help, answers to a few questions."

Betty recoiled, her face anxious. "I won't give away anything Mr. Alec or Mrs. Kingsley—"

"Don't tell me anything you don't want to. I won't mind." Lisa was tempted to ask Betty if she'd like a sherry. It had been pretty useful on Sunday. But even Betty might balk at sherry at eight o'clock in the morning. Lisa leaned across the table, and said in a low voice, "Not only did I discover that my birth father was still alive, I also found out that I have an aunt: Celia's sister, Jennifer."

She waited for Betty to respond, but she merely sat there, looking down at her cup, stirring another spoonful of sugar into her second cup of tea.

"I saw pictures of her at Maud's house," Lisa told her. "That's how I knew."

"She's like to die, Maud Birkett is. It's all round the village."

"I know."

"Poor soul." Betty shook her head slowly.

"What was she like, Betty?"

"Maud?"

"No. Jennifer. You knew my mother. So you must have known her sister. What was Jennifer like?"

The spoon kept stirring. "I don't like speaking ill of anyone. 'specially when she's your auntie."

Lisa's heartbeat started racing. "That's okay," she

said in a light tone. "We all have strange relatives, don't we? I guess Jennifer was ours."

"You can say that again." Lisa held her breath for a moment, as Betty paused. Then she was off. "She never fitted in with the family, really. Skinny and awkward as a moorland pony with three legs, she was, whereas your mother was a beauty from the time she was born. They both had the same blue eyes, but where Celia had golden hair, Jennifer's hair was dark. My own mother it was told me that Mr. Templeton, your granddad, doted on his Celia, but he had no time at all for Jennifer, when she was born. Her mother, Mrs. Templeton, had a bad time giving birth to her, and she was never the same after it. A puny, puky baby Jennifer was, Mum said. Later, she became the kind of child that manipulates you to get her way. Deceitful, she was. A tattletale. But she could be nice as pie if she wanted something from you."

Lisa felt a pang of pity for this family misfit. "Didn't anyone like her?"

"Her mother tried to, but most times it didn't work. Jennifer was dead jealous of Celia, of course. She'd make up lies about her sister and carry them to her dad, and then get smacked for it. But that wouldn't stop her. When the girls were older, Jennifer hated Maud with a passion, because Celia and Maud were thick as thieves."

"I thought so," Lisa broke in. "You could tell that from the photographs."

"That's right. Maud was nothing to look at, shy and gangly, but Celia saw something in her others didn't, and she loved her." Betty smiled. "And anybody your mother loved was blessed, 'cause she had a great loving heart and made you feel extra special."

"But she couldn't love her own sister?"

"She tried. God knows she tried. She'd say to me,

302

'She's my sister, Betty. I *should* love my sister, but I can't. She's too mean.' And, of course, when Alec Kingsley came into her life, Jennifer was even more eaten up with jealousy, 'cause she fancied him, as well. And then they were married, and you came along . . . that made it even worse. We all doted on little Elizabeth; she was everybody's pet."

Lisa found it impossible to respond. To have been so loved and then, suddenly, banished from her home . . . It didn't bear thinking about.

"But the thing that caused more trouble than anything," Betty continued, "was this house. You see, when he died, their dad left the house and estate to Celia, with no share of it to her sister. Jennifer got a large sum of money, 'cause he had to be fair, but he didn't want her getting a share of the house."

"Why?"

"They say he was worried she'd find some way to deprive Celia of her share. Well, when she heard about her father's will, Jennifer went haywire, making all sorts of threats, until Celia had to promise that she'd let her live there with her and Alec for as long as she wanted."

"That couldn't have been easy for them."

"It wasn't, poor souls. A young married couple to have such a difficult sister living right in the house with them—and her behaving like it was her house, not theirs—but they did their best. Jennifer always thought the place would go to her, if anything happened to Celia, that it would stay in the Templeton family, but Celia willed it to Mr. Alec."

"This house, you mean?"

"The entire house and estate. It all went to Mr. Alec. None of it for Jennifer. Well! You can imagine the fuss there was when Jennifer heard about it. She was upset enough about her sister's death, screaming and crying and accusing Alec of drowning her, 'cause he—"

"Hold on a minute. How could Alec have drowned my mother when he wasn't even there? At least, that's what I understood."

"Who knows who was there? It was all such an upset, with the river flooding and people driven from their homes, and the electric all out, so that we were trying to do everything with paraffin lamps and torches and candles. Nobody knew who was where that night."

Lisa stored this information away in her mind, not wanting to stop Betty mid—flow.

"Anyway, they had to get Dr. Trewen in to give Jennifer an injection to calm her down after the will was read."

"Celia's will."

"That's right, Celia's will," Betty said impatiently. "She'd left the entire house and the estate to her husband. 'She can't do that,' yells Jennifer. 'It can only go to a Templeton.' But when they looked into it, they found Celia could do it, so Alec got it all, and Jennifer got nothing."

"I thought she was left a lot of money."

"Oh, she was, but money wasn't what Jennifer wanted. 'Twas the Court she were after. The pair of them had a powerful row—"

"Alec and—"

"Mr. Alec and Jennifer, that's right. Mr. Alec tried to calm her down, but you were there, and you were crying fit to bust. Miss Haines and I were trying to get you upstairs, so you couldn't hear what was going on. I heard him saying, Elizabeth will inherit Charnwood Court, Jennifer. She's a Templeton, leastways, half of one.' But there was no pleasing Jennifer Templeton. She

304

was that upset about her sister's death and then the will, and everything. That very evening, she stormed out of the house, and she's never been seen since."

"You're sure about that, Betty. No one's spotted her in the village?"

"Not her. Mind you, not many would know her now. We're talking twenty—six, twenty—seven year ago."

"What about Marion Heasley? She'd know her, surely? Or Paula Willand?"

"Paula is Ron Willand's second wife. She's been here little more than seven or so years."

"I hadn't realized that. What about old Tom? He might know Jennifer, if he saw her. He seems to know everyone in the entire area," Lisa added, recalling her first meeting with Tom at the clinic.

"That thieving old rascal! Grease his palm with silver, and he'll do anything for anybody."

"You can see what I'm getting at, can't you?" Lisa met the older's women eyes.

"You think that Jennifer's at the bottom of all this nasty stuff that's been going on, the letters and that."

"I don't mean that she's actually here, in the village, but she's maybe paying people to do it."

Betty stiffened, and her head went up. "I hope you're not meaning me, miss."

"No, of course not. I don't know who's doing it. I hate to think that my aunt might be behind it, but from what you've told me, it's a distinct possibility, isn't it?"

"We all thought it was Maud. She hated the new Mrs. Kingsley and didn't try to hide it."

Lisa thought, not for the first time, about the seething passions that lurked behind the seemingly tranquil and pastoral village she had come upon just three days ago, bathed in sunshine. Now the gloom of lowering clouds and menacing water seemed better to reflect the malevolence that lay at the heart of Charnwood.

"Are you feeling cold?" Betty asked.

"No, why?"

"I thought you were shivering."

"Just the dampness, that's all." Lisa swung her legs over the bench. "I think I need to get out and blow the cobwebs away."

Betty smiled, displaying pink gums above her dentures. "No cobwebs here, miss. I make sure of that."

"Bet you do. Don't you have any help? Surely you can't manage this big house all by yourself."

"Hilda Martin, the policeman's wife, comes up on a Friday to give it a good going over with me, but it's not enough, really. I'm not getting any younger. They need somebody full—time, but they don't have the money for it." She shrugged. "This place is falling down, 'specially outside."

"Yes, I noticed." Lisa sighed.

"Your mother would have a fit if she saw it now. For that matter," Betty added with a grim smile, "so would your Auntie Jennifer. She made sure this place was kept up, inside and out, when she lived here. She'd hate to see it like it is now."

Lisa didn't want to think about her aunt anymore. She stood up. "Thanks for the tea."

"Pleasure, miss."

"Please don't call me miss," Lisa reminded her.

"It's hard. How about Miss Lisa?"

"That sounds better."

"Like you're one of the family," Betty said, "which you are: After all, I've known you since you were born. For that matter, since before you were born."

A slow smile spread across Lisa's face. Impulsively,

she went to Betty and leaned down to hug her from behind. "I must get some fresh air," she said, and left the kitchen, before Betty could see the tears that were threatening to fill her eyes.

She had intended to walk down to the village, but when she stepped outside, the rain was cascading down. She dashed back inside to get an umbrella from the stand, and put her head in at the kitchen door. Betty was busy mopping the slate—tiled floor. "I'm taking the car. It's too wet to walk. Anything you need from the village?"

"No, thanks. Not much open yet. Only Fowler's, the newsagent. If the road's still clear, I'm driving to the Minehead Safeway store for the groceries."

"I could do that for you, if you gave me the list."

"Thanks, I prefer to do it myself." A sly smile slid across Betty's face. "Mondays, I always treat myself to a curry for lunch at the Indian restaurant in Minehead."

"Mmm, I love curry." Lisa was tempted to ask if she could come along. A curry in a busy seaside town, even in the pouring rain, sounded pretty good to her, but she had the feeling that Betty wouldn't be too keen on the idea of sharing her weekly treat with her boss's daughter.

Besides, it meant having to drive beside the rising river for several miles. She wasn't sure she could face that, not after the strain of last night's visitation. "Okay, I'm going. See you later."

Betty looked up from her mopping, her face red with exertion. "I'll be gone before eleven. You've got a key, haven't you?"

Lisa nodded.

"I should be back with the groceries about three-thirty."

"We'll have another cup of tea together then."

"If I have time. I have to go and make tea for Charlie, my husband. He doesn't like to eat on his own, so I always try to be finished here in time for his tea."

"Of course. I'll see you when you get back from Minehead, anyway."

Lisa shut the kitchen door behind her and went out to the car. Although she had gained some relatives, she'd never felt quite so alone. It seemed as if nearly everyone else, even unfriendly people like Paula Willand or Rachel Kingsley, had someone to share their lives with. She had no one. She had a sudden desire to call Jerry or her father, but it was still nighttime in Winnipeg.

As she sat in the car, waiting for the windows to demist, she thought of Jane's warm kitchen and the welcome she'd received there yesterday morning. But she doubted she'd be welcomed there today, not after she'd deceived Jane by going to visit Maud in the hospital.

Once again, she experienced that feeling of being hemmed in, trapped, with no place of refuge in the village. And no escape to the main road that led to the outside world, unless she wanted to confront the river.

To hell with it, she thought, as she eased down the sodden driveway to the rhythmic tick—tuck of the windshield wipers, *I'm going to get breakfast at the Stag*. The thought of sitting in the dining room, with its log fire and wine—red carpets, eating a hearty breakfast lifted her spirits.

Even if it did mean being frozen by Paula Willand's icy hostility.

CHAPTER THIRTY-THREE

As it happened, Paula was nowhere to be seen, but Jane Tallis was. As soon as Lisa was shown into the half—empty dining room, her gaze raked the room and clashed with Jane's. She was sitting with a copy of *The Guardian* at a small table by a window. Lisa hesitated, then decided it was up to Jane. She followed the young woman dressed in a tight black skirt and black stockings, weaving her way between the tables, and gave Jane a slight smile as she passed her.

"Want to join me?"

Lisa turned and went back to her table. "I wasn't sure you'd want me to."

"Don't be stupid. Sit down. She'll sit here," Jane told the waitress. "And bring me some more toast and coffee, would you?"

Lisa pulled out the chair and sat down opposite Jane.

"So, Miss Cooper. Or should I say, Miss Kingsley?"

Lisa started. She felt her cheeks glowing beneath Jane's piercing scrutiny. "So you know."

"Everyone knows. It's the talk of the village. Sam Martin's wife, Hilda, has got the biggest mouth in town."

"When did you hear?"

"Last night. In the bar here."

Lisa looked down at the menu, but the print blurred before her eyes. "I'm sorry I didn't tell you who I was."

Jane shrugged. "Why should you? It's your business."

"I came to Charnwood to find out what had happened to my mother, thinking both parents had been killed—"

"Look. You don't need to tell me anything. As I said,

309

it's your business."

"I'd like you to know, now that I can talk about it. You've been very kind to me. I hated not telling you." She told Jane about her search based on her adoptive mother's meager information, and how Betty had inadvertently given her the news that her father was Alec Kingsley. "It was quite a shock, considering I thought my birth father was dead."

"It must have been."

Their conversation was interrupted by the waitress taking Lisa's order.

"How did Alec Kingsley take it?" Jane asked, when they were alone again. "I don't know the man at all. I wondered, with all the gossip I've heard about him, how he'd react to meeting his grown-up daughter again."

"It isn't easy for him."

"It can't have been easy for you, either. If what I've heard is true, the man chucked you out of his life when your mother died."

Lisa dug into her half grapefruit. "Something like that," she murmured, not wanting to discuss a subject that was still like salt on a raw wound for her.

"Enough of that." Jane stuffed the pages of her newspaper down at the side of her chair. "What are your plans now? Are you going to stay on at Charnwood Court for a while, or go back to Canada?"

"My flight's booked for Friday."

"That's good. Hasn't been much of a trip for you, has it? You're better out of it, with all this turmoil going on."

"I intend to drive back to London on Thursday, if the police will let me go."

"What have the police got to do with it?"

"It's because of Maud," Lisa said reluctantly.

310

"Of course. Poor Maud. Apparently, she's still in serious condition. Doesn't look good for your stepmama, does it?"

For a second, Lisa didn't know who she was talking about. "No," she said, not wanting to discuss Rachel with anyone outside the family.

"I'm surprised you're not eating breakfast up at the house this morning. Betty usually cooks up a pretty good breakfast for the household and any guests, so I've heard."

"The family's gone to Taunton. They left early with Richard Barton for a legal conference. They'll probably be away most of the day. I was still asleep when they would have eaten breakfast, if they had any. None of us slept very well last night."

"Oh, why was that?"

Lisa was evasive. "Oh, we just sat up talking half the night."

"I should think you've a lot to talk about." Jane sat back in her chair. "So the house is empty, apart from Betty."

"Right. That's why I came here for breakfast. To be honest, I needed some company. The house is so large and empty, with nearly everyone gone. And Betty will have left by the time I get back, so it'll be even more empty."

Jane glanced out the window. "I'd suggest going somewhere, if the weather weren't so bloody awful. But you wouldn't be able to see much of the scenery with this rain and mist."

"I know. I suppose I'll just have to spend the day indoors, read some more *Lorna Doone*."

"How's it going? Not that easy to read, is it? All that dialect."

"But the description of Exmoor and the countryside

311

around here is wonderful. It hasn't changed that much, really, has it?"

"I suppose not. It's years since I read the book." Jane pushed back her chair and got up. "Well, I must be going. Time to open up the shop. Waste of time, though. Not many people are going to drive in, with this foul weather."

"And the threat of the river flooding," Lisa said, voicing the thought that lurked constantly in her mind.

"That, too." Jane changed the subject abruptly. "Tell you what, why don't you drop in at the shop and stay for a while this morning? Then maybe I could come up and have lunch at the house with you, to keep you company."

"That's a great idea. I'd forgotten you'd said you've never been inside Charnwood Court. I could take you over it, while it's quiet."

"If you want to. I warn you, I'm not that keen on historical stuff and stately homes."

"I don't know much about it myself, so let's say it'll be an unguided tour."

"Great. See you later, then. I'll leave the newspaper for you."

As she watched Jane heave her stout leather shoulder bag onto her shoulder and stride from the dining room, Lisa felt much better. Apart from Richard, Jane was the one person in the village she could call a friend.

CHAPTER THIRTY-FOUR

LISA SPENT A PLEASANT HOUR OR SO IN JANE'S SHOP, happily sorting out a large box of tubes of oil and acrylic paints, while Jane unpacked a couple of small crates of needlework canvases and labeled them.

"That's enough, I think," Jane said after a while, groaning as she straightened up. "My back can't take any more bending. And my eyes are stinging from all this dust. Damned contact lenses!" She set the canvases in an open box on a table by the window. "What are we going to eat up at this mansion of yours?"

"It's not mine," Lisa protested.

"You never know."

"We do know. You yourself told me Alec Kingsley was selling it to a hotel chain."

"So I did. You returned to Charnwood a few years too late to get your inheritance."

Lisa merely smiled.

"What about it? Lunch, I mean. Shall we pick up something at the shop to nuke?"

Lisa suddenly remembered Betty and her curry. "Do you like curry? When Betty said she was going for one in Minehead my mouth started watering."

"Sounds good to me. Nuked curry."

They bought their frozen curries and a French loaf at the local food store, plus a bottle of Burgundy Jane insisted on buying, and then drove up to Charnwood Court in Lisa's car. The road was almost impassable in places, the gravel and dirt churned to wet mud by the torrential rain.

From the left, beyond the woodland, came the muffled roar of the river's rushing waters.

Lisa gripped the steering wheel, her knuckles white beneath the brown skin. Her heart was thumping so hard, she was sure Jane could hear it above the noise of the water. She had the feeling that Jane was watching her with open curiosity, but she kept her eyes fixed on the road ahead.

Then the road took the turn that led up the steep rise

away from the river and she could see Charnwood Court's wrought—iron gates looming ahead of her through the thick curtain of rain. Her hands relaxed on the steering wheel and she felt, for the first time, as if she were coming home.

She slowed the car to a halt a little way from the house, to give Jane a chance to view the entire prospect from a distance.

"It's a lovely house in the sunshine," she said, Jane's silence prompting her to say something in the house's defense.

"Why don't they rip that bloody ivy off the walls? It'll rot the stonework."

Again, Lisa wanted to defend the house—and its owners, despite the fact that she'd thought the very same thing the first time she'd seen the house. "I suppose they think it looks romantic that way. Maybe the tourists prefer it."

"Ivy on the walls?" Jane rolled her eyes. "That's not the sort of thing tourists want nowadays. Theme parks and children's zoos, that's what brings 'em in."

Lisa had to smile. "You're probably right." She drove the car around to the back entrance and used her key to open the back door. It seemed strange to be coming in without a member of the household—or Richard—with her. As she stepped into the narrow hallway, she hesitated, feeling as if she were trespassing.

Jane closed the door behind her and stood there, rainwater dripping from her slick yellow jacket. Lisa switched on the light, stuck her umbrella in the tall vase that was used as an umbrella stand, and hung up their jackets.

Jane eyed the cracked vase. "Ming?" she asked with a wry smile.

Lisa grinned back. "I doubt it very much. Come on in." She led the way to the kitchen.

"Now *that's* what I call a kitchen," Jane said, when they went in. "Better than the hole in the wall I've got."

"Would you like something to drink?" Lisa asked her, once she'd put the curries in the freezer compartment. "Tea, coffee?"

"Not yet, thanks. Let's get on with looking at the house." Jane's eyes gleamed.

Lisa was surprised. "I thought you didn't like stately homes."

"I want to get it over with before the Kingsleys come back. They might not be too keen on your taking someone around the house without them."

"I was born here," Lisa said very quietly.

"So you were." Jane looked uncomfortable. "Sorry. Didn't mean to imply—"

"That's okay."

"Just . . . it might be awkward if they arrived back. For me, I mean. Not you."

"Of course. I promise they won't be home for a long time."

"Good."

"But we'll do the tour first and then relax and have lunch."

"And wine."

"Right."

"Bloody dark in here," Jane muttered, as she followed Lisa along the passageway to the main hall.

"I'll switch on the lights." Lisa looked around for the light switches, but Jane had already found them and clicked them on. The lovely old hall sprang to life: the long oak table shining from Betty's diligent waxing, the marble fireplace and carved coat of arms gleaming

315

white, the mellow oak—paneled walls adding warmth.

"Beautiful, isn't it? You can just imagine how it would look in candlelight."

"Even darker than it does now, I expect," Jane said gruffly. She crossed the hall and started up the wide oak staircase.

"Don't you want to see the rooms down here?" Lisa asked, surprised that Jane was forging ahead of her.

Jane turned. "Oh, sorry."

"That's okay. We can do them after we've been upstairs." Lisa followed Jane.

When they reached the top, Jane paused, breathing heavily. "Time I lost some weight." She gazed around. "Where to now?"

"I think the tour started on the right. Yes, it did, because I remember finishing up with the nursery." Lisa pointed to the end of the carpeted hallway. "That's the room at the end, near the entrance to the private section."

"What's that?"

"The part of the house where the family lives."

"And where do you sleep?"

"In the room next to the nursery."

"The green room."

"That's right." Lisa frowned. "How did you know?"

Jane laughed. "Because you told me, remember?"

"Oh, right." Lisa opened the door. "This is the main bedroom. The blue room."

Jane gazed at the oak—paneled walls, the four—poster bed hung with faded blue silk damask and the collection of blue porcelain. "Not very original with their names, are they?"

"Maybe not, but it is beautiful, isn't it?"

Jane glanced at her. "You falling in love with your

old home, or what?" she drawled.

Lisa's face flushed. "Something like that." She looked around. "What I love most is the size of the house. It's not like some of the stately homes I've seen in this country, which are more like palaces. This one feels like a home."

"A bloody damp and drafty home."

Lisa turned on her heel and left the room. Jane's sarcasm was getting to her, making her feel uneasy. She began to wish she'd never agreed to show her over the house.

"Hey, don't get mad at me," Jane called after her. "I warned you I wasn't into stately homes, didn't I?"

"I guess so."

When they went into the gold sitting room, which led into another large bedroom, with walls hung with vast tapestries of woodland scenes, Jane said nothing, merely surveying the rooms, grunting or nodding in response to Lisa's remarks.

Lisa crossed the upper hall. "This is my room." She hesitated, her hand on the doorknob. She hadn't been inside the room since she'd left Kate cleaning it up last night. Kate had fetched all her stuff for her, clothes and makeup and her bag . . .

"Aren't you going to show it to me?" Jane asked.

Lisa swallowed hard. "Of course." She had to go into it sometime, she supposed. She turned the knob and pushed open the door.

"Very pretty," Jane said.

"Yes, it is." Was it her imagination or could she still smell mice? Surely not, considering Kate had left the window by the bed open and the curtain was billowing in the wind.

"That should be shut," Jane said. "If that old fabric

317

gets wet, it'll fall apart."

"You're right." Lisa went to lower the sashed window, but it was too heavy for her to manage by herself. Jane came to help her.

"Stupid windows. The old casement ones are so much better."

"Casement?"

"The kind you push open. They still have them in the blue room. Didn't you notice?"

"I probably did, but I wouldn't know what to call them."

"See, I was right. There's water on the window seat, and the cushion is soaking wet."

"I'll see to it later." Lisa couldn't bear to stay in the room a moment longer. She was sure she could smell aniseed again, if not mice. As she went around the foot of the bed, she held her breath, not wanting to inhale until she'd left the room. Once they were both outside, she slammed the door shut, and took a deep breath.

Jane stared at her. "You okay?"

Lisa nodded. "Let's go see the nursery. I think that's my favorite room of all."

Jane just smiled and shook her head. "You're like a kid showing off her toys."

Lisa bit back a retort. "Here it is. I'll switch on the lights."

The light was, as before, not sufficient to illuminate the doll's house, but Jane immediately strode down to the end of the room and stood before it. She seemed oddly excited.

"There's another switch by the fireplace, for the spotlights," Lisa said. "I'll put them on, then you'll be able—"

"No!" Jane's response startled Lisa. "Sorry," she

added quickly, when she saw Lisa's surprise. "But I can see the doll's house has electric lighting. Makes the little house look more . . . real if it's not too bright in the room." Jane reached behind and light flooded through the windows of the closed doll's house. She moved her hand toward the latch, then stopped. "Do you know how to open it?"

Lisa stood there, frowning, feeling as if something weird was happening, but she wasn't sure what.

"How do you open it?" Jane asked impatiently.

"Oh, sorry. You open these two latches at the side." Carefully, Lisa swung the front open, as she'd seen Maud do only three days ago.

She heard Jane's stifled gasp as the entire house in its miniature magnificence was revealed. Jane reached out one hand to the tiny glasses on the oak dining—room table. Lisa could see that her hand trembled, yet the plump fingers touched the glass with infinite care and delicacy.

"It's lovely, isn't it?" she said as Jane gazed at the perfect little rooms. "Look at this," she reached for a cushioned chair. "Even the cushion is—"

"Watch it!" Jane barked.

Lisa almost dropped the chair. "What?"

"They—they look so old, so fragile. I'd be afraid something might break." Jane grinned at her. "Then you'd be in big trouble with the Kingsleys. I've heard this doll's house is worth a mint."

"Yikes, you're right." Lisa hurriedly replaced the chair. As she stood there, beside Jane, admiring the house, slowly, insidiously, that same clammy coldness she'd felt on Saturday crept over her. She tried to fight down panic, to breathe slowly to calm her racing heartbeat, but nothing worked. Abruptly, she left the room, steeling herself not to run from it, as she had done three days before. She still didn't quite understand why she felt this way.

"What's wrong?" Jane called after her.

"I thought I heard a car," Lisa lied, heart pumping hard as she leaned over the banister rail.

"Shit!" she heard Jane say. "Want me to close the house up?"

"Please. I'll wait out here in case anyone comes in."

It was so quiet she could hear Jane's movements in the nursery: the hinges on the doll's house as she swung the front section shut, the click of the light switches as she turned off the lights.

"Shall I shut this door?" Jane asked in a loud whisper from the doorway.

"Please." Lisa straightened up. "I can't hear anything else. It must have been the mail van or something."

Jane glanced at her watch. "They couldn't possibly be back from Taunton yet. But, just in case, why don't we have lunch and finish the tour after we've eaten?"

"Good idea." Lisa said, but she would have been happier if Jane had decided to leave right then.

They were halfway through their curries, which Jane had insisted on eating in the kitchen, when Lisa really did hear the noise of a car engine.

Jane scrambled up from the pine bench. "Now that is definitely someone coming." The engine stopped. They heard the crunch of footsteps and then someone hammered on the back door. Jane's dark eyes widened. "I'm getting out of here."

"It's not the Kingsleys. Wait here. I'll go see who it is." Why was Jane so worried about meeting the Kingsleys? Even if it were the Kingsleys she couldn't see why Jane would worry so much about being taken

320

around the house. Her constant anxiety about them was making Lisa edgy.

When she opened the door, she found Sam Martin standing there, filling the doorway. He touched his cap. "Hi, Miss Cooper."

"Hi, Sam."

His round face looked very solemn. Lisa's hand went to her throat. "Is it Maud Birkett?"

"No, she's still struggling along."

Lisa sighed with relief. "Thank God for that. Come in."

"Haven't time to. 'Fraid I've got bad news 'bout the river. Looks like it's going over its banks. There's been several breaks. We're evacuating the people in the lower valley right now. If it gets any worse, we'll have to start moving out the village, as well."

Lisa stared at him, struck dumb.

"You all right, miss?" he asked.

She nodded.

"I'm here for two reasons. One, I understand Mr. Barton's in Taunton with Mr. and Mrs. Kingsley."

"That's right."

"Mrs. Clayton, the lady that cares for Emily, is one of them as has to be evacuated. She's moving in with her daughter in Minehead. She was wondering if we could bring Emily up here to wait for her dad?"

"Of course you can. I'll be here all day."

"And secondly, last time there was a flood, Charnwood Court was used as a refuge. We were wondering if—"

"I'll call Mr. Kingsley at Mr. Barton's office right away. He left a number with me, just in case of any emergencies."

"Well, miss, this is definitely an emergency," Sam

321

said, his face grim.

Jane came to join them at the door. "Hi, Sam. Thought I heard your voice."

"So this is where you are. I was trying to get you at the shop. We may have to move you out. River's broken its banks in several places."

"Shit! I'd better get the hell down there and try to save some of my stock." Jane dragged her rain jacket off the rack.

"I'd drive you back," Lisa said, "but Emily's coming here. Do I need to fetch her?" she asked Sam. Her heart pounded in her throat, threatening to choke her, at the thought of having to drive by the flooding river.

"No, Ernie's gone to fetch her and anyone else as needs help. You can come with me, Jane, if you're coming right now," Sam said. "I'll just wait for Miss Cooper to call the Kingsleys."

"Sorry to abandon you," Jane said to Lisa, "but . . ." She shrugged.

"I'm sorry not to come and help you, but I need to stay here and wait for Emily."

"Not only that," Sam said. "We may have people needing to come up here as early as this afternoon, if the riverbank breaks any more."

"Hang on. I'll go call Richard's office." Lisa ran to fetch the number and Alec's portable telephone, carrying it back to the kitchen.

She got Richard's secretary, cutting her off when she started in with her spiel about Richard being in the middle of an important conference. "I know that. Please tell him it's an emergency concerning his daughter, but tell him she's fine, before he starts panicking about her."

The sound of Richard's voice at the end of the line

made her feel much better. As soon as she'd explained the situation, he told her he'd be there as soon as possible. "I'll hand you over to Constable Martin," she told him. "And then he can speak to Alec, as well."

When Sam had finished, he handed the telephone back to Lisa. "Mr. Kingsley for you," he said.

Lisa put the receiver to her ear. "Are you okay?" Alec asked.

She wanted to say, "No, I'm not," but there was no point. "I'm fine."

"We'll be there as soon as possible. But we'll have to take the longer route across the moor, to avoid the river road. What a hell of a thing to happen on top of everything else." Alec's voice broke as if he were close to collapsing.

"I know. I'm so sorry."

"Can you manage there on your own?"

"Of course I can. I must go. Sam and—" She stopped abruptly, aware of Jane's hand gripping her arm tightly to cut her off. "Sam's anxious to leave," Lisa told Alec.

"Right. We'll get a quick bite to eat and then we'll start back. We should be there in a couple of hours. Three at the most."

When she put down the phone, Sam had gone, and Jane was hovering by the open door. "I've got to go. You okay on your own?"

"I won't be on my own for long. Emily will be coming soon and they're driving back from Taunton right away." It seemed important that she let Jane know she wouldn't be alone.

Jane smiled. "Good. You won't be alone for long, anyway, not if the entire village lands up here." She turned and hurried down the two steps to the waiting police car. As she went, she muttered something. The

323

engine was running, making it hard for Lisa to catch the words. She got into the car before Lisa had time to ask her exactly what she'd said.

Frowning, she shut the door. She could have sworn Jane had said something about history repeating itself, but that wouldn't make any sense, would it? Because Jane hadn't been in Charnwood for the 1970 flood . . . had she?

CHAPTER THIRTY-FIVE

JANE'S MIND WAS RACING AS SAM DROVE HER DOWN to the village. She'd made a couple of bad mistakes. Her niece was no fool. She'd soon realize.

She should never have gone up to the house, but she just couldn't resist the only opportunity she'd had since Celia's death to walk through it in daylight, instead of slinking around in the darkness of night.

She wished Sam would stop his yapping and let her think. She'd hoped she could get Lisa to leave Charnwood before she began to suspect, but it hadn't worked. It was Lisa's own bloody fault. If she'd stayed away from the Court, she might have gone back to Canada none the wiser. Trouble was, as before, she hadn't wanted to hurt her niece. A few mice might have scared the wits out of her, but she wasn't hurt physically.

She'd let her niece live when she was a four—year—old kid. That had been her big mistake. She should have eliminated both of them that night, not just Celia. Now, when her goal was almost within her grasp, Lisa had turned up on her doorstep, capable of destroying everything she'd been painstakingly planning for half a lifetime.

Damn her to hell!

Sam drew the car up in front of the shop. "We'll let you know if the village has to be evacuated. Be ready."

Oh, she'd be ready, all right.

"Thanks, Sam." Jane hauled herself out of the police car and strode to the front door of the shop. As she fumbled to get the key into the lock, rainwater spilled onto her from the gutter above, running down her face and neck. The chime tinkled as she pushed open the door. She felt like fetching a hammer and smashing it into a thousand tiny pieces.

Once inside, she closed the door and stood with her back pressed against it, wanting to scream, to yell the bloody place down. What a bloody cock—up! She should have stayed in Australia, kept piling the money into the bank, and been content. But how could she possibly be content, knowing that Alec Kingsley and that bitch Rachel were living it up in *her* home?

She went straight to the rolltop desk in her tiny sitting room and sat down on the wooden office chair. It was too early to write in her diary. She usually did that in the evening, after she'd been for a drink at the Stag.

She took the key she kept on a chain around her neck, beneath her shirt, unlocked the little drawer, and took out both her current diary and the large leather—bound diary that held all the secrets of her earlier life. This original diary had been a gift from her father for her sixteenth birthday. Although its pages had been filled a long time ago, she still loved to run her fingers over its roughened cover with her name in gilded lettering—Jennifer Templeton, the J and T almost worn away—and to inhale the dusty, dried-ink smell of its pages.

Maybe she should write her diary entry for today

right now, just in case. After all, it must be kept up-to-date, whatever happened.

Although she knew she shouldn't waste time, she couldn't resist opening the old diary and glancing through its pages. Some of her writing, where she'd used a fountain pen, had faded so much that it was barely legible. The earliest pages bore splotches that erased whole lines.

She looked at those pages with a grim smile. She'd soon learned that crying into her diary didn't achieve anything. "You need a stiff backbone to get on in this life," her father had frequently told her, and she'd learned that lesson well. Celia, of course, was told that her beauty and sweet personality would open all doors for her. No stiff backbone needed for dear Celia.

Jane leafed through the diary, a letter falling out from between the pages. It was Marion's Christmas letter from six years ago, the one that had changed everything for her. The one telling her that Charnwood Court was starting to fall apart. She couldn't bear the thought of her home disintegrating. In that same letter, Marion had also happened to mention that there was a shop for sale in the high street.

Jennifer had never sent a photograph to Marion. No one in Charnwood would recognize her. Especially when she'd gained sixty pounds. Twenty—seven years ago, when she'd left Charnwood, she'd been as thin as a rail. The hard life of sheep farming in Australia had developed muscles she'd never known she had. And sweets had always been a weakness. When she stopped doing most of the hard labor herself, and could afford to hire lots of help, the muscle turned to fat. Life had grown bloody boring. Once money begat money, there was no challenge.

She reached for a dark red aniseed ball from the jar she hid in her desk. They had always been her favorite sweets. She loved the way the hard, innocuous-tasting ball suddenly exploded with flavor when you sucked it. But she'd had to be careful once Elizabeth came back. Right giveaway aniseed balls were, with their distinctive smell.

Not even Marion had suspected her true identity, and she'd made sure she kept sending her an annual Christmas letter, arranging for her station manager to send it from Australia.

So Jennifer Templeton had become Jane Tallis. The irony of using the same initials always made her smile. Her father had given her a silver pen with JT on it for her seventeenth birthday. She'd cherished that pen. It—and the diary—had prompted her to retain her initials when she changed her name and identity.

The contact lenses changing her eyes from blue to brown had also been an inspired idea, except that they still irritated her eyes after more than five years of wearing the damned things.

The hardest part had been changing her personality. Turning a hard—driving, tough—skinned sheep farmer into an easygoing shopkeeper. But all she had to do was seek out that other half of herself, the one that she knew could have been her, if anyone had cared enough to look for it. But no one had. Not her mother, nor her father, and certainly not sweet, beautiful, vapid Celia. Everyone found it so easy to love Celia, why bother to make the effort to love Jennifer?

Everyone except little Elizabeth. She'd tried so hard to like her Auntie Jennifer, even when that auntie was deliberately cruel to her, to test her loyalty. Smacking her hard enough to leave a red mark on her hand when she touched the doll's house. Telling her she was bad and would go to hell if she took a book from the shelves in the nursery.

Little Elizabeth's persistence in trying to like her Auntie Jennifer had saved her life. It had also been that auntie's downfall, thought Jennifer. Now she was faced with the choice of getting rid of her niece or losing Charnwood Court.

She gathered up the diaries, intending to hide them in the attic, safe from the flood, if there was one. Then she looked around the tiny room, feeling no desire at all to save any of the ratty little bits and pieces that had been her companions for more than five years. For all she cared, her good friend the river could wash them all away. As it had washed Celia away. The shop had never been anything more to her than the means to an end. A way to inveigle herself into the inner workings of an innocuous English village and poison the minds of its inhabitants against Mr. and Mrs. Bigwig Kingsley living up there on the hill above them.

Despite her despair, she chuckled to herself. What fun she'd had! How patient she had been! And how well it had worked. Because she was an outsider and seemed to stand apart from it all, no one had suspected her of being the source, the spider at the center of the web of lies she'd disseminated.

As Alec had sensed the discontent of the villagers, spreading like a cancer throughout his constituency, he'd abandoned all hope of winning the next election and eventually given up the seat, rather than face the ignominy of losing it.

And Rachel, poor pathetic Rachel, had been affected so badly—first by Alec's depression, then by the vicious gossip and the shunning—that she'd started drinking far more heavily than she'd ever done before.

Their disintegration had been a bonus to Jennifer's main goal of getting her home back. But then, just when the contracts for the house were about to be signed—having hidden her identity behind a hotel company—in walks Elizabeth, her knowledge of what really happened the night of the 1970 flood locked away in her mind, just waiting for something or someone to trigger her memory.

"And then you, you stupid cow," she said aloud, berating herself. "You just had to go and see the house, didn't you? You'd waited all these years, but you couldn't wait just a few more months until it was yours."

She crashed the chair back, hitting the table behind it. That little excursion of hers was going to cost Elizabeth her life. Now she had to work out the best way of doing it so that not a speck of suspicion would fall upon her.

She stood by the desk, thinking back to that special day in 1970. For a moment, she closed her eyes, seeing again the rushing water, the terrified child, Celia's horror when she realized what was happening.

Suddenly, it came to her. The solution had been right there in front of her all this time. Now she might be too late. Heart racing, she glanced at her watch. If she called Sam Martin, she might still catch him.

She picked up the receiver and dialed the number at the police station. It rang several times. Then, as she was about to hang up, someone answered.

"Charnwood Police Station." It was Sam's voice.

"Sam? Jane Tallis here."

"Hi, Jane. You just caught me. I was locking up. What can I do for you?"

"Has Ernie got Emily Barton yet? I thought I could

help out by taking her up to Charnwood Court for you."

"You must be a mind reader. I was about to take her there myself. Ernie's had to go to Combe Farm. Thanks, Jane, that'd a real help. I'll bring Emily over right away."

"Perfect!" she murmured, as she put down the telephone. A slow smile spread across her face. As she'd said earlier—stupid git!—when she was leaving the Court, *History repeats itself.*

But this time she'd make absolutely sure there were no witnesses left to come back and haunt her.

CHAPTER THIRTY-SIX

FOR A LONG TIME AFTER JANE LEFT, LISA WAS overcome by a strange lethargy, a numbing of her senses. All she wanted to do was to hide away somewhere warm and shut out the world that raged outside.

She put a match to the fire that Betty had set in the library, curling up in Alec's chair, with the soft wool afghan wrapped around her. Outside, the sky darkened to pewter and thunder rumbled in the distance, but here, at least, she felt cocooned against all storms, external and internal. Her mind seemed to have shut down, crashed like a computer, wiping out all memory, present as well as past, leaving a blank screen.

After staring into the fire in a state of suspended animation, feeling began to creep back. The tingling of nerve ends was like the pain of renewed life in a frost—bitten limb. Her brain clicked on and whirred into action, stimulated by her attempt to marshal facts as well as suspicions about the character and identity of

Jane Tallis.

As she sat there, striving to make sense of it all, Lisa's heart began to speed up. She felt the heightened pulse throughout her body, beating so hard her throat began to tighten, until she was sure she would choke. A clammy sweat broke out all over her. Trembling, she jumped up from her chair, eyes wide, seeking escape.

The telephone began to ring. She grabbed it, but her hand was so damp she almost dropped it. She drew in a long, ragged breath, striving to calm herself. "Hello?"

"Miss Cooper—I mean, Miss Lisa? It's Betty. I wanted to let you know I can't get back. They've closed off the road into Charnwood. I've brung Mrs. Kingsley's groceries to my daughter in Selworthy. I'll be staying here until I can get back to the village. My husband's here, too. The police drove him over. He was that upset, he forgot to bring the cat with him. Lord knows what will happen to her. I left enough food and water for today, but—"

Lisa at last got a word in. "I'll make sure someone takes care of your cat. Have you left a key with anyone?"

"Sam Martin's wife has one, but I can't get hold of her or Sam."

"Don't worry, I'll speak to Sam for you."

"Thanks. Tell Mrs. Kingsley her groceries will be fine. My daughter's got a big freezer. It's all put away. Sorry about this, my lovey."

"It's not your fault. I'm sure it won't be long before everything's back to normal."

Betty rang off. Oddly enough, instead of causing her to worry more, the call had calmed her down, forcing her to focus on the reality of Jane's visit.

Slowly, inevitably, everything fell into place, but she

331

felt the need to set it down, to have some tangible proof that what she now suspected was true. She went to Alec's desk and found a pad of paper. Then she began to list all the things that had troubled her about Jane's visit to Charnwood.

There was Jane's knowledge that the bedroom she was in was called the green room. A guess? Perhaps. But, contrary to what Jane had said, Lisa was pretty certain she hadn't told Jane the name of her room.

The fact that Jane knew exactly where to find the switch for the lights in the hall and the doll's house, yet she was supposed never to have set foot in the house before.

The casement window. A small thing, but how many people would have noticed that one room had a casement window; another a sash window? Especially someone who kept saying she had no interest in old houses.

None of these small things, however, added up to much without the fact that, despite her cynicism and seeming lack of interest, Jane's excitement as they'd walked through the house had been tangible. Lisa saw it clearly now. Jane's hands had been shaking, her eyes glittering with repressed excitement. However hard she'd tried, she just couldn't hide it.

She was also the right age. Jennifer would be in her early fifties now, about Jane's age.

And, lastly, there was the smell of aniseed. Lisa had been prepared to accept that her imagination was in overdrive after last night's episode, but it was more than that. The smell was still there, despite the fact that Kate had left the window open for hours. It wasn't too difficult to conjecture that the smell was coming from Jane, not from the room.

Lisa wrote everything down, item by item, numbering them. Then she sat looking at the list, setting it into the overall picture. When had Jane come to Charnwood? She'd have to find out, but she was sure that she'd said it was about five years ago. It could be that someone, perhaps Paula or Marion, had been working for her even before she arrived. Perhaps not. Lisa had seen the photographs of the scrawny teenager who'd been such a contrast to her beautiful sister Celia. It wasn't too hard to accept the premise that anyone who'd known her then wouldn't necessarily recognize her now.

But Maud *had* recognized her—or at least she had guessed that Jennifer Templeton was behind all the bizarre things that had been happening in Charnwood— and that was why she was lying in a hospital bed, unconscious. Lisa started, so that the pen skidded across the page.

Jane had been in the hospital on Monday, the day Maud had suffered a heart attack. They said no one had been allowed in to see Maud once Lisa had left, but . . .

She thought of how devious the person who'd persecuted Alec and Rachel had been, never getting caught. Even entering this house at night. She flung a glance over her shoulder, her eyes widening. Although she'd locked all the doors, back and front, locks had never stopped Jennifer getting into the house before.

Lisa shoved back the desk chair and rushed out of the library, down the corridor to the main hall. She stood in the center of the hall, gazing around, slowly realizing how impossible it would be to check every door, every window, every inch of the vast house.

If Jennifer Templeton wanted to revisit the house that was her home, there was no way she could keep her out.

As she stood there, Betty's words filtered into her

333

mind. *The thing that caused more friction than anything else was this house.*

Twice, Jennifer Templeton had been shut out of the house. The first time, by her father's will. The second, by her sister's. *It can only go to a Templeton,* Jennifer had shouted, when Celia's will was read.

If this house was so important to her, might not a devious, strong—willed woman like Jennifer have schemed to get it back? Could Jennifer possibly be behind the hotel corporation that was buying Charnwood Court?

Lisa's mind was spinning. She wasn't sure she was capable of rational thought. Not only did she now suspect Jane Tallis of being the aunt who'd probably drowned her mother, but now there was also the imminent threat of yet another flood invading her life. She could imagine towering waves of water gushing in the tall windows in the hall, crashing through the ancient glass, engulfing the entire house—and her with it.

She rushed back to the library and checked the door. "Thank God," she whispered, when she saw the lock on the inside. She slammed the door and locked it. Locks couldn't shut out a flood, but they could stop her aunt from getting in. Or could they? She swiveled to gaze wide-eyed at, the paneled walls. It wasn't too hard to imagine that there might be another secret passage into this room as well.

She picked up the portable telephone from the table beside Alec's chair. Richard probably had a cell phone. She could get the number from his secretary. But he'd said he'd be driving straight back, hadn't he? What was the point of worrying them all when there was absolutely nothing they could do to help her?

She looked up the number of the police station and

then punched it in. Even if it might sound crazy, she could at least alert the police to her suspicions. She got an answering machine, with Sam Martin's rural accent drawling more quickly than usual the message that, "Because of the flood emergency, the police are working to evacuate those in low—lying areas to safer venues." He ended by advising callers to leave a message on the machine and someone would get back to them as soon as possible. Meanwhile, they should stay tuned to the local radio station for further information.

Lisa stared at the telephone. What was the point of leaving a message? What would she say? "Jane Tallis is Jennifer Templeton. Arrest her." The police were busy enough as it was, and it was highly unlikely they'd stop in the middle of an emergency to listen to Lisa's paranoid accusations.

She would have to deal with this herself. Surely nothing was going to happen in the next hour or so. After that, Richard and Alec would be back and she'd be safe.

But she needed advice, fast.

She pressed in the number she knew by heart. Jerry's voice answered, but not Jerry himself. He'd changed his message on his machine at home. "I'm unavailable for a few days. Leave a message, and I'll get back to you as soon as possible."

Lisa crashed the phone down. "Damn you, Jerry!" she yelled. "Where the hell are you when I need you? That means no one's in the gallery. Great for business!"

She felt cut off from everyone she cared about. Jerry had abandoned her. Richard was en route, but still at least an hour away. She wasn't about to call her father in Winnipeg and worry the life out of him. The one person in this blighted village she'd thought was her friend was probably her mortal enemy.

There was a set of stereo components on a stand in a corner of the room. She went to it and turned on the radio, searching for the local station Sam had mentioned in his message, but the reception was broken up with static from the storm. All she could get was music on the stereo band. She tuned into rock that blasted suddenly from the speakers, making her jump.

She quickly turned it off. Music would drown any sounds in the house, and she needed to be able to hear.

She glanced at her watch. More than an hour had passed since Sam and Jane had left. Then, remembering why Sam had come to the Court, her spirits soared.

Emily! Ernie would be bringing Emily here. In fact, they should have been here by now, but Ernie probably had a lot to do on his way up.

Once Ernie arrived, she'd be fine. The traffic warden might be officious, but Lisa knew he was reliable. She released some of the unbearable tension in a long sigh.

She'd make sure Ernie stayed with them or insist on going with him and Emily to some safe refuge until Richard arrived.

Courage renewed, she switched on as many lights as she could find and made her way to the kitchen. As she ran water into the kettle, she peered through the rainspattered window. Outside, the sky had turned black, and the rain seemed even heavier, if that was possible. She could hear it pelting down on the tiled roof. She thought of the river furiously pounding against its fragile banks. A shiver ran across her shoulders and down her spine.

The telephone rent the silence, jangling her nerves, so that she almost dropped the cup she was getting down from the cupboard. She picked up the receiver. There was so much static on the line she could barely hear.

"Sorry," she yelled. "The line's really bad. You'll have to shout."

This time the voice came through clearly. "It's Jane."

Lisa's breath caught in her throat. She said nothing. She knew now that her safety, her very life, might depend on not letting Jane know she suspected her of being Jennifer. She released her breath slowly.

"They made me leave the shop. They think the village is going to be flooded. I was on my way up to you, but my car's bogged down in the damned mud." The voice was unmistakably Jane Tallis's. It had the slightly nasal quality that Lisa had taken for a London accent, but she realized now, with hindsight, that it could be Australian. "I have Emily with me," she added.

The words were like a hammerblow over Lisa's heart. "I thought Ernie was bringing Emily here," she said, striving to keep her voice light, easy.

Calm now, keep calm. Don't panic. Emily could be in danger.

"I offered to take her to help the police out. Good Samaritan Jane, they call me." Jane's voice sounded so natural, so commonplace, that Lisa wondered for a brief moment if her suspicions were nothing but paranoia on her part.

"Where are you?"

"I'm stuck on that narrow stretch, just before the turn up the hill."

Lisa slid her tongue over her parched lips. "The one near the river?"

"That's right. The bend by the river."

"Is Emily okay?"

"Emily's fine. I've got a rope. I just need something to haul me out. Can you bring your car?"

Lisa closed her eyes for a moment. "I'll be right there."

CHAPTER THIRTY-SEVEN

THERE WAS NO TIME FOR THOUGHT, NO TIME FOR PHONE calls. All that filled Lisa's mind was that Jane had taken Emily.

As Jennifer had taken Elizabeth.

This was what Jennifer must have done that night twenty—seven years ago. Stolen away Celia's child. Lured her from the busy house by some devious means.

That time, everyone had been involved in the frantic search. This time, only she could rescue Emily. There was no one else available to help. As she ran to the car, Lisa fought down the panic that leapt in her throat, ignoring her fluttering heart, her shaking legs. She must stay calm. Everything depended on her. Emily was all Richard had. If something happened to Emily, it would destroy him.

Tears sprang to her eyes, but she dashed them away. There was water enough without her adding to it. Water everywhere, in the air, on the ground. As she reversed the car out of the covered parking area, tires squealing, then spun into the driveway, she felt as if she were submerged beneath the sea, water hammering on the roof, streaming down the windows. She set the windshield wipers at the fastest speed, but still they couldn't clear the deluge. It was like trying to drive through an endless car wash.

She'd turned on the lights, but she was driving blind, the blurred outline of trees and bushes her only guide to where the edge of the driveway was.

She leaned over the steering wheel, peering out at a watery hell, praying to God and all his angels and saints to protect Emily. Did Celia Kingsley know that night

338

what she was going to face? Did she have time to pray?

Drive faster! Lisa's brain shrieked at her, but she knew that she must be cautious, that if she were to crash the car it could be disastrous for Emily—and Richard.

When she reached the bend at the foot of the hill, she peered out the windshield, searching for Jane's car, but there was no sign of it. She inched the car along. A hundred yards or so down the road, she came to the turning, and the lane not much wider than a pathway, marked with a wooden signpost. She couldn't read it. She didn't need to. She knew where it led.

To the river.

As she turned the car, she was drawn inexorably, by instinct, to the roar of the water. This was her destiny. She was a robot programmed to return to this place, the scene of her mother's death.

She saw Jane's car at the end of the short lane, blocking it, so that there was no way out, other than reversing the way she had come. Time only to say one last prayer for strength in the coming confrontation. Then, her heart pounding, she pulled up behind Jane's car and got out.

An ice-cold deluge of rain and spray swamped her. Gasping for breath, she peered into Jane's car, but there was no sign of Jane or Emily. No point in shouting for them. The river had become a torrent, its roar filling her ears, deafening her. She walked toward it, the muddy ground a morass sucking at her feet so that each step was in slow motion.

Then she saw them, standing on the edge of the river bank. The woman and the child. They were watching her as she drew nearer, the woman holding back the child, who was straining to run to Lisa.

Lisa forced herself not to dash forward, to keep to this

slow pace across the patch of land that separated them.

Then she was there, facing them. Facing the raging river that looked as if it might rear up at any minute and engulf them all.

"Hi, Emily." She shouted to be heard above the incessant roar.

She reached out to her, but Jane's arm clamped Emily to her side. The little girl was shivering violently. Her terrified gaze went from Lisa to Jane, and back again.

"Please let her go," Lisa said. The words were swept away on the wind as soon as they issued from her mouth, but she knew that Jane had heard her. "She looks so cold. That jacket's not warm enough for her."

"She's fine," Jane shouted. "Aren't you, Emily?" She smiled at Lisa. "You came."

"Yes, of course I did." Keep things normal. "Where's the rope?"

"In the car." Jane made no move.

"Then let's get going. I'm soaking wet already. So are you and Emily."

"I want to go home." Emily's lips quivered. "Please take me home, Lisa." She struggled to get away from Jane's grip, but Jane jerked her back.

Emily started to wail.

Jane cuffed her across the head. "Shut up, kid."

Lisa's eyes narrowed. Hatred seethed in her, giving her a much—needed shot of adrenaline. She took a step forward. Jane smiled again at her . . . and took a step backward, a little way down the riverbank's muddy slope, dragging the struggling Emily with her.

Lisa took a deep breath. "I'm going to get these cars tied up," she shouted. Slowly, deliberately, she turned her back on them and began to walk away in the direction of the two cars. She could hear Emily crying,

340

the sound tearing at her heart, but she steeled herself and kept walking.

"Emily feels like a swim, don't you, Emily?"

Lisa spun around. Her ruse hadn't worked. Jane stood at the very edge of the sloping bank now. As the waves of cold water swept over her feet, Emily began to scream, her shrieks of terror slicing through the roaring wind and water.

Lisa didn't hesitate. She charged to the riverbank and down the slope. For one terrifying moment she felt her feet slipping from beneath her. She was sure she was about to be precipitated into the river, but somehow she managed to retain her footing.

Taken by surprise, Jane loosened her grip on Emily. Lisa grabbed the child from her and swung her onto the top of the bank. "Run, Emily, run!" she yelled. "Lock yourself in my car. All the locks. You know how."

Emily hesitated, her mouth open in distress. Lisa felt Jane's arms grab her around her shoulders. As she crashed to the muddy ground, the weight of Jane's body on top of her, she managed to yell, "Run, Emily, run! My car—"

Jane's fist slammed into her mouth, stunning her. *Please, dear God, keep Emily safe. Please, God, please!* Blinded by wet mud, she struggled against the weight of Jane's body.

"You stupid bitch," Jane's voice yelled in her ear. "Do you really think I'd let that child get away to rat on me? I learned from my mistake last time. I should never have allowed you to live. I'll make up for it this time."

Lisa found herself hauled up on her feet, being dragged closer, closer to the river. Its icy spray slapped against her face. "Come along, Elizabeth," Jane yelled. "I'm going to show you the exact spot where your

341

mother died."

Lisa didn't waste any more energy on words. Hampered by mud and water, she fought against the weight and size of this woman who was her own flesh and blood. There was muscle, not just fat, in the arms and shoulders that held her in a wrestler's grip. She tried to shout again to Emily, but Jane's hand clamped down on her mouth. Opening it, Lisa bared her teeth and bit down, hard, tasting the metallic flavor of blood in her mouth.

Jane yelled and punched her again, this time hard in the breast. The sickening pain sent Lisa's head whirling. It spun faster, faster . . . and all at once she remembered. She saw everything that had happened that night twenty-seven years ago as clearly as if it were in Technicolor. And with remembrance came added vigor. She was both child and woman, fighting, screaming, biting, kicking at this woman who was dragging her, dragging her down the muddy slope to the river. She was Lisa and Celia and Elizabeth, and she fought for the three of them, summoning up all her strength, lashing out, fighting savagely, striving with all her strength to save both the child and the woman, to exonerate herself for her part in her mother's death, to save her child.

She felt, as Emily had—as Elizabeth and Celia had—the water swamping her feet. For a moment she broke away, sliding from her aunt's grip. She was reliving her dreams, her nightmares. Her paintings had come to life. She was her anguished mother, her arm upraised as she was washed away by the raging waters. She was the terrified child on the riverbank, screaming for her mother.

A primeval snarl came from her mouth and nostrils, and she launched herself on the other woman. "You killed my mother!" she screamed. Her feet sliding on the mud, she struggled with Jane on the riverbank, both of them grunting like animals, both striving to keep from falling into the raging torrent.

Then, for one horrible suspended moment, Lisa felt her feet slip from under her . . . and the next moment she was in the river. The bitter coldness of it shocked her, cutting off her breath. Spluttering, gasping, she fought the pressure of water against her. Then she felt the grasp of Jane's hands again, forcing her head below the water.

Lisa fought to break the other woman's hold on her, their bodies locked together in a mortal embrace. Choking, she reached out and grasped a handful of Jane's hair that had come loose from its pins. She yanked hard on it and the hands loosened their grip on her head. She pulled even harder, viciously tearing and twisting the hair, knowing that she would soon black out if she didn't get air.

She felt a wrench . . . and she was suddenly free. Their bodies had been parted by a massive eddying of water, which surrounded only the other woman, not Lisa. Kicking out, Lisa fought her way to the surface for air . . . and watched with horrible fascination as the vortex spun faster and faster, with Jennifer Templeton, shrieking, at its center. Then, the whirlpool sucked, dragging her down . . . and carried her away. Gasping and retching, coughing up water, Lisa dragged herself, hampered by her waterlogged clothes, out of the water. When she reached the bank she hauled herself up to safety and stared down river, but all she could see in the eerie darkness was the incessant, teeming rain and, through it, the blurred outline of trees on the opposite bank.

And—all she could hear, apart from the massive and incessant roar of water, was her own painful breathing as she sucked in air. She lay there, gasping like a landed fish, for what seemed like several minutes.

Despite the deadly chill, all she really wanted to do was sleep.

Emily! She lifted her head. She must get to Emily to make sure she was all right. Dragging herself to her feet, she half ran, half scrambled to the two cars parked behind each other. She went directly to her car and pounded on the window. No response. Then she tried the car door. It was locked.

She peered in and was able to make out the small hunched figure of Emily, crouched down on the floor in front of the backseat.

"It's me, Emily. Lisa," she shouted. "It's Lisa, sweetie. Let me in."

She must be a terrifying sight to poor little Emily. Water streaming from her, mud all over. Like some swamp creature from a horror movie. She tried to clear some of the mud from her face so that Emily would recognize her, but managed only to spread it further.

Her teeth chattered together. She was shaking so hard she could barely stand. Dear God in heaven, if she didn't get warm very soon she was afraid she'd collapse. She hammered on the window. "Emily, it's Lisa," she yelled. "Please let me in. I'm all wet and cold."

She ran to Jane's car and tried the doors. No luck. Jane had made sure no one could escape in her car.

Lisa ran back to her car again. This time she could just make out in the shadowy light that Emily was standing, watching her with round, terrified eyes. "It's me, Emily. It's Lisa. The other lady's gone away. Just open the window a bit and you can hear my voice. Then you'll know it's me."

Lisa made the motions of turning down the window. To her utter joy, Emily slowly wound it down about an inch. Lisa put her mouth to the narrow opening.

"Hi, Emily. It's me, Lisa, darling. I'm all cold and wet. Can you let me in? Then we'll drive home to Daddy."

The mention of her daddy made Emily's mouth quiver. She began to cry. "I want my daddy."

"Of course you do, sweetheart. I'll take you to him right away. Open the door for me."

Emily fumbled at the door. Lisa tried it again. This time it opened. She went to hug Emily, but the child shrank away from her. *No wonder*, Lisa thought.

She got into the driver's seat. "Sit on the seat and buckle up," she told Emily, trying to keep her voice as normal as possible.

Emily did as she was told.

"I think there's a sweater on the backseat beside you. Can you pull it around you to keep you warm?"

Emily nodded.

"Good girl. We'll be back at your Auntie Rachel's house in no time." She started the car, thanking God she'd left the keys in the ignition. If she'd put them in her pocket when she went to the riverbank they'd have been in a watery grave by now.

"Mustn't think of that now," she muttered through chattering teeth. She began to reverse the car very slowly back down the lane. She wasn't really in a fit state to drive, but she must get Emily back into the warmth of the house.

She was backing the car out into the road when a car tore down the hill and came to a screeching halt. A man jumped out and ran toward them.

"Daddy!" Emily shrieked.

It was Richard. Emily was safe. Nothing else mattered. Lisa heard the rear door open. Weak with relief, she turned off the car, leaned her arms on the steering wheel, and put her head down.

The next thing she knew was the sound of Richard's voice in her ear, asking urgent questions, but she was too exhausted to reply.

"Lisa! Lisa! What in God's name has happened here? Did Emily fall in the river? Lisa! Are you okay? Are you hurt?"

She shook her head.

She felt his hands on her. "My God, you're frozen and soaking wet."

"Where's Emily?" she whispered.

"In my car." He bent and lifted her from the car. She felt rain on her cheeks and forehead yet again, and turned her face against his chest to escape it. "We'll fetch your car later," Richard said. "Mine's warmer than yours."

Warmer. She doubted she'd ever be warm again. But Emily was safe. Emily was safe with her father. Her father would look after her. She had no mummy, but her daddy would protect her. Daddy would treasure her and keep her safe from harm, always.

Tears filled her eyes and streamed down her muddy cheeks. Then her senses came stealing back. She grasped at Richard. "Jane! I have to tell you—"

"It can wait until we get you back to the house."

"No. You don't understand—"

He was breathing heavily as he carried her to his car. "I understand that we have to get you and Emily warm and dry before anything else, okay?"

He bent again and slid her onto the backseat beside Emily.

"Lisa's very cold and wet," he said in a matter-of-fact tone.

Emily shrank from her. Lisa summoned up the energy to turn and smile at her. "And very muddy," she said.

A brief spell of hesitation, and then Emily's small hand reached out to touch hers.

"Soon be home," Richard said.

Chapter Thirty-eight

At the house: bright lights, a clamor of voices asking questions, a sea of faces. One predominated: Alec, his lean face haggard. "Thank God you're safe." His arms tight around her, despite her warning that she was wet and muddy. The warmth of his tears on her face. "I thought I'd lost you again."

"Jane was Jennifer."

"We know."

"How?"

"Maud is well enough to speak now. She told the police."

The Lord gives and the Lord takes away. A silent prayer of thanks to God.

Kate pushing people aside. "I'm taking Lisa upstairs. She has to get these wet clothes off. Then a lovely hot shower, right, Lisa?"

Tears filling her eyes. "Sounds wonderful."

"I have questions to ask Miss Cooper." Bill Brewster's voice.

"They can wait until she's recovered." Richard said. "She's not going anywhere."

347

She *must* tell them. "Jane. She's in the river. Swept away." Shaking her head to rid herself of the image of that whirling vortex of water, Jane at its center.

"Thanks, Miss Cooper." Sergeant Brewster again. "Don't you worry now. We'll look after it."

Later, after she'd had a hot shower, Kate wrapped her in an oversized, fluffy bathrobe. Lisa curled up on the bed in Kate's room and tried to get some sleep, but her mind was so overwrought that it jigged and darted, conjuring up nightmarish images of upraised arms and dark branches and swirling water.

"I just can't sleep," she told Kate, who'd stayed with her. "My mind's spinning like a top."

"I'm not surprised."

"I think I'd rather stay awake as long as I can. I'm going to get dressed."

"I'll help. What do you need?"

"Just my jeans and the big red sweater. They should be on the same hanger in the wardrobe."

Kate went out and brought them back a few minutes later. "Want me to go while you dress?"

"Of course not." As Lisa pulled on her bra and fastened it, she winced with pain.

"You should have those bruises checked," Kate said, compassion in her voice.

"That's all they are, just bruises. Has Emily gone home?" Lisa asked, quickly changing the subject.

"No, she and Richard are staying here tonight."

"I'm worried about her, Kate." She looked up at Kate. "I'm worried that she'll end up with some sort of phobia, like I did."

"She's got Richard. And it's not really the same as what happened to you. After all, it was your mother who drowned. Do you remember what happened? I mean . . . with—with your mother." Kate's face flushed almost as red as her hair.

"Yes. I do now." Lisa shuddered. "I don't think Emily could see much of what was going on from the car. I hope not, anyway. But I'm going to stick around to answer all her questions, once she starts asking them."

"Tell her you were having a mud fight," Kate said.

Lisa had to smile. "She'd believe that, the way I looked." Her smile faded. "Poor little girl. She must have been terrified." She looked away from Kate, eyes blurring. Tears were perilously close to the surface.

"Don't think about it now. Time enough later."

"How's your mother?" Lisa asked as she pulled the sweater over her head. It felt warm and comforting around her bruised chest.

"Looking after Emily has done her a power of good. She's putting her to bed now. She said she'd stay with her until she falls asleep."

"I'd like to see her."

"Emily? Right, let's go."

Lisa's legs felt weightless, as if she were gliding an inch from the ground. Kate guided her down the corridor to the green room. "We've put Emily and Richard in here. Hope you don't mind."

"I'm glad. I couldn't sleep in it. Not tonight, anyway. Too many bad memories."

"Don't blame you."

Rachel broke off from reading and looked up as they came in, her eyes luminous in her white face. "Feeling better?"

"Thank you, yes." It was going to take a while to ease the awkwardness between them. "How about you?"

349

"Much better, thank you."

Emily was watching Lisa with round eyes. "You look like Lisa again."

"Good." She smiled. "That's because I *am* Lisa. I've always been Lisa, even with all that mud on me."

"What happened to the—the other lady?"

"She went far away."

"Will she come back?"

"No, she will never come back."

"Did she die?"

Lisa hesitated. She felt Kate and Rachel watching her. "Yes, she died. She won't be coming back, ever."

"Why was she so cross with me?"

"Enough questions," Rachel said. "Time to sleep."

"I'll answer this one," Lisa said. "The lady wasn't cross with you, Emily, she was cross with me. That's why we had a mud fight." She flicked a smile at Kate.

"Did you push her in the river?" Emily asked.

"No, she fell in. If she hadn't been fighting, she wouldn't have fallen in, would she?"

"I'm glad she fell in. I didn't like her."

A fitting epitaph for Jennifer Templeton, thought Lisa. But somewhere in a small place in her heart, she knew she would mourn the person she had liked, and the aunt she had never really known.

"I'm going to say good night now, but I'll be here to answer all your questions tomorrow." Lisa went to the bed she'd slept in last night, when Jane had made her visitation. She bent to kiss Emily's cheek. "God bless." Emily's arms went around her neck, and her small lips clamped a kiss on Lisa's cheek.

Lisa turned away quickly so that Emily wouldn't see the tears filling her eyes.

"She'll be fine," Rachel said softly. "I'll stay with her

until she's asleep."

Lisa nodded and hurriedly left the room. She turned as Kate followed her down the corridor. "I wish I could stop this stupid weeping all the time," she said, wiping her eyes.

"It's natural. You must be suffering from shock."

"Relief, as well. I'm lucky to be alive."

"Don't talk about it unless you want to."

"I have to sometime, but not yet. Not all of it, any-way." She stood at the head of the stairs, her hand on the railing. "She drowned my mother, you know. I saw her do it."

"God! When you were a kid, you mean?"

Lisa nodded. "I'd blotted it from my mind."

"Then my wonderful father sent you away and there was no chance of your recovering those memories." Kate's voice rasped with bitterness.

"Maybe that was a good thing, in a way," Lisa said lightly.

"Do you really think so?" Kate's eyes searched Lisa's. "How could he have done that to his daughter?"

"Let's not think about that now. I'm here. It's over. Now I can get on with my life."

There was a commotion down in the hall. A voice Lisa recognized as belonging to Ernie, the traffic cop, was shouting at someone, "You'd no right to force your way through the barrier. You could see clear as day that the road was closed."

Then a voice that was dearly familiar to her, yet couldn't possibly be here, said, "I don't give a damn about your barrier. I want to see Lisa Cooper."

"Jerry!" Lisa shrieked. "What the heck are you doing here?" She saw Richard and Alec's surprised faces looking up at her. Laughing, she ran down the stairs, energy flowing through her. Then Jerry was lifting her from her feet, hugging her close, and she was breathing in the familiar aroma of his cologne.

"Darling, darling Lees. You're okay. They said you'd fallen into the river and all my premonitions came horribly true. I saw you drowning, just like those hellish paintings of yours. I just knew you were in *big* trouble and got on a plane as fast as I could." He hugged her tight in a bear hug, and then held her at arm's length. "Are you really okay?"

"Yes. Really. I'm fine."

"You look *ghastly.*"

She punched him hard on the arm. "Thanks a lot." She was suddenly aware of everyone staring at them. Richard, in particular, was giving her one of his frowning assessment looks. She took Jerry's hand. "I'd like you all to meet Jerry, my partner."

"Why don't we all go into the library?" Alec said. "I see no point in standing out here in the drafty hall. We don't want Lisa getting a chill." He led the way into the library and immediately became the perfect host, offering drinks to everyone, telling the police officers and Ernie that they must be starving after all the good work they'd done. "Go into the kitchen. You know the way. There's cans of ale and lager on the counter, Bill. I'll be right there to make up some sandwiches for you."

Lisa had to smile. He managed to get rid of them without hurting their feelings. But she knew they'd soon be back, asking all their questions. As she sat on the couch with Jerry's hand clasping hers, she looked up to find Richard's eyes fixed on her intently.

She smiled back at him, but he glanced away. Leaning on the arm of the couch, she stood up, swaying a little. She was still woozy. Jerry put his arm around her. "I want you to meet these three people," she told him. She looked at the three people who, a few days ago, had been utter strangers to her. "Very important people," she added, her face warm.

"If they're important to you, they're important to me," Jerry said.

"This is Kate, my half sister."

Jerry beamed. "Hi, Kate."

Kate grinned. "Hi, Jerry. Do we kiss, or what?"

"Course we kiss." Jerry gave her a hug.

"And Richard." Lisa's face grew even warmer.

"Ah, so *this* is Richard." The men shook hands, Jerry heartily, Richard warily.

"Richard has been a rock for me these past few days."

"Not much help today," he said, his face grim. He blinked, and looked down at his feet.

"I'm going to be fine, Richard," she said softly. "Really, I am. And so is Emily."

She turned to Alec, who stood across the room, in the shadows. "Now you must meet Alec Kingsley." She lifted her chin. "My father."

Alec came forward to take Jerry's hand. "I know Lisa's father already," Jerry said, belligerence in his voice.

Lisa put a hand on his arm. "Down, boy. I have two fathers now."

Jerry raised blond eyebrows at her. "You okay with that?"

"Yes."

Jerry shrugged. He shook Alec's proffered hand. "Great to meet you all."

"I must explain that I've been keeping in touch with Jerry by phone, so this isn't all new to him. I tried to call him when I knew that—" She halted, finding it hard to say the name, and felt Jerry's hand squeeze hers. "—that Jane was Jennifer, my aunt." She turned to him. "I was mad as hell with you when your message said you were away. Apart from needing to speak to you, I wondered what the heck you were doing abandoning the gallery."

"Why on earth didn't you call my cell phone number?" Richard asked her. "You could have got me in the car."

"I was going to, but I didn't want to worry you. Once I knew Jane had Emily I knew I had to deal with it myself, as it was still going to be a while before you got here."

She frowned. "Come to think of it, how *did* you get here so fast?"

"The police allowed us to come by the upper road. Although they'd closed it, they'd built a detour for police access and it was still clear enough for us to get through. Once Maud started communicating, we wanted to get here as soon as possible."

"Is Maud going to be okay? That really is a miracle, isn't it?"

"More than you realize," Alec said, his lips compressed. "She told us that Jane Tallis had come to her door at the hospital and made some sort of secret sign at her, behind the policewoman's back. A sign from their childhood, which made Maud realize she was Jennifer Templeton."

Lisa's legs suddenly buckled beneath her. She slumped down onto the couch. "Oh, my God! So that was why—"

"She had a heart attack? Looks like it. Anyway, we tried to get you on the phone, but the line was busy."

"That must have been when I was calling Jerry—or

speaking to Betty. She was on for several minutes. That reminds me, I have to speak to Sam Martin about Betty's cat."

"Her cat!" Richard exploded. "You mean she was bothering you about her bloody cat when your life and Emily's were at stake!"

Lisa had never seen Richard quite so heated before. He stood there, unable to speak, his lips clamped together. She stood up and went to put her arms around him, not caring that everyone in the room was watching. "Emily's going to be okay. I promise you, she is." She looked up into his face. "She's already asking questions—and getting the right answers."

His eyes were fixed on hers, oblivious to the others. "You think so? I don't want her to suffer for this, like you did."

"She won't." She broke away from him. There was so much she wanted to say to him, but not now, not with everyone listening in. "What bothers me is that we'll never know the reasons behind what Jennifer did. There are so many unanswered questions." She turned to Alec. "Like, for instance, was anyone else working with her against you and Rachel? Or how did she manage to take Rachel's car on Sunday, knock Maud down, and then get the car back to the pub without being seen?"

"That's not difficult to answer," Kate said. "It was such a rotten day, hardly anyone was out."

"True, but it would have been better to know exactly what happened—and why. Now we shall never know."

CHAPTER THIRTY-NINE

THAT EVENING, THE POLICE FOUND JANE'S DIARIES IN A plastic bag in the attic above her shop. They were a record of her life, first as Jennifer Templeton, then as Jane Tallis.

Although the diaries would be used as evidence in the inquest, once the body was recovered, and in the reopening of the file on the death of Celia Kingsley, Sergeant Brewster was authorized by his superiors to allow Lisa to look through them.

"You being her next of kin, Miss Cooper," he explained, when he'd finished interviewing her that evening.

Lisa looked down at the stack of books, topped by the old leather-bound diary with its faded gilt lettering on the cover. "I don't want them," she whispered. She couldn't bear even to touch them.

Richard came to her side. "One day you may want to find some answers."

She shook her head.

"They'll be yours, anyway, once we've finished with them," Bill Brewster said.

"Are you—" Lisa drew in a deep breath and slowly exhaled. "Are you going to look for her tonight?"

"No point. Not in this weather, and it being pitch-dark. Tomorrow we'll be searching. Won't take us long."

"You think you'll find her, then?"

"Surely, we will. Her body'll be caught up in some rushes or branches somewhere downstream."

Lisa shuddered, but his assurance relieved her. The

356

thought of never knowing for sure that Jennifer Templeton was well and truly dead was a particularly terrifying one.

"There was a letter addressed to you in her current diary," Brewster said.

"To me?"

"You can read it, but I must warn you I'll have to take it away with the diaries. For evidence, you know."

Reluctantly, she took the envelope from him. *To be given to Elizabeth in the event of my death,* she read. "Should I read it now, do you think?" she asked the room in general. "I don't really want to."

"Why not get it over with?" Richard suggested. "Otherwise, you'll be lying awake tonight wondering what was in it."

"Good thinking," Jerry said.

Lisa stifled a smile. Jerry and Richard had established a sort of guarded rapport during the time they'd all eaten a meal together and shared a couple of bottles of Alec's best Burgundy.

Alec himself had been very quiet all evening. He'd made sure that Rachel was settled for the night and brought back her apologies for not coming down again. Then he'd sat in a chair, his gaze fixed on Lisa as if he couldn't bear to have her out of his sight, but refusing to be drawn into the conversation.

"Okay," Lisa said. She took the letter opener Alec handed to her and slit open the envelope. "Excuse me." She went to the window to set some distance between herself and the others and opened the letter.

Dear niece, she read.
If you're reading this, I must be dead I suppose that's for the best, really. I never

357

wanted to harm you, but your return threatened my plans to get Charnwood Court from the Kingsleys and restore it to its rightful family. Which means me—and you. Only we two have the blood of Templetons in our veins. How dare Alec Kingsley reign up at the Court like a king in his castle, when he has no right to it whatsoever!

My stupid sister was so besotted with Alec that she took my home from me and gave it to him. Well, he's not going to keep it. I'm sorry, but I've worked for too long to regain Charnwood Court to have you come back and ruin my plans.

But, of course, if you're reading this, it means I won't be getting the Court, after all. It's in your hands now. You'll soon discover that I've amassed a great deal of money over the years. Twice, I was betrayed by my own kin but given money as compensation. Then, I was very successful in Australia. As you'll find out, once the will is produced, I've left everything to you with the proviso that you carry out my plans to buy Charnwood Court from the Kingsleys and restore it to its former glory. My last request is that you arrange for it to go to the National Trust upon your death, so that no other individual can own it. It's all explained in my will. I just want you to know now, as it may take a while to get all the papers in order.

I didn't want to kill you that night years ago. You were the only one who'd tried to love me, but your affection came too late for me. I liked you, Lisa. I like to think we could have been

good mates in another life.
    Your Aunt Jennifer.

"Oh God!" Lisa groaned. She put her head in her hands, dropping the letter on the floor. Alec came to her and bent to pick it up, but she snatched it from him. "No! You mustn't read it." Then, seeing the hurt in his eyes, she touched his hand. "I'm sorry," she said softly. "It would only cause you more pain. I'd like Richard to read it, for legal reasons. Then Sergeant Brewster can have it."

Alec shrugged. When Lisa went to give the letter to Richard, Alec remained by the window, pulling the velvet curtain back to gaze out at the rain, his shoulders hunched.

Richard read the letter, then gave it to Brewster without comment. His eyes met Lisa's. The understanding and sympathy she read in his expression warmed her.

"I think it's time I went to bed," she said. "I don't think I can stay awake much longer."

Kate jumped up. "Can I help?"

"Thanks, Kate. But before I go, I'd like to speak to each of you, just to explain some things." She looked at the three men. "Sort of separately, if you don't mind. I know it sounds a bit weird, but . . ." She lifted her shoulders in an eloquent shrug. "Then I'll go to bed. Oh, can we find a bed for Jerry?"

"Of course," Alec said, moving to the door. "Don't worry your head about it. Can I bring you up a mug of hot chocolate to help you sleep?"

"That would be great," she said quietly. "I'll see you up in Kate's room."

Alec's face brightened. "Fine."

359

"I'll come and help you," Kate said to her father. They both left the room.

Richard gathered up a few glasses. "I'll go and make myself useful in the kitchen," he said, glancing from Lisa to Jerry.

"I'll be sending Jerry to the kitchen in a minute." Lisa grinned. "He's good at washing dishes, and he always has to have his bowl of cereal before he goes to bed."

"I have no intention of going to bed yet," Jerry protested. "You forget, it's still the middle of the afternoon by my time clock."

"I must go and check on Emily, too," Richard said.

Lisa gave him a warm smile. "Give her a kiss from me."

"I will." He went out, pulling the door shut behind him.

Lisa turned to Jerry. "Stop looking so miserable. I said I'm going to be okay, and I am."

"You had me worried sick."

"That wasn't me, that was your ESP thing."

"Whatever it was, it was hell. I had to take the most convoluted flight with stops at Ottawa and Montreal to get to London. Then I hire a car and drive on the wrong side of the road, with my heart in my mouth the whole time I'm driving, wondering if I'm going to make it in time. And then when I'm almost here, they tell me the road's closed because of a flood. Imagine how I felt, knowing you and floods!"

"Well, you came, and I'm okay, that's all that matters." She hugged him tight. "You're the best friend in the world. Did you tell Dad you were coming?"

"No, I thought it best not to worry him. I said I had urgent business in Toronto. Felt bad lying to him, but there it is."

"Is he okay?"

"He's fine." Jerry gave her one of his comical looks. "I like your Richard, by the way."

Lisa felt her cheeks grow warm. "He's not *my* Richard."

"Whatever he is, I like him. He's not sure what to make of me, though, is he?"

They both giggled.

"Shall I play him along, make him jealous? I could, you know."

"I know you could, but you're not going to. He's special, Jerry. Not just him, but his precious daughter, too." Lisa closed her eyes for a moment, reliving her terror when she first saw Jane with Emily. "I was afraid Jane would—" She shook her head.

"Well, she didn't, thanks to you, so stop thinking about it." He pushed back a strand of hair from her cheek. "So, what's the plan? Are you staying on here or what?"

She'd hoped he'd leave this discussion until tomorrow, at least. "I honestly don't know, Jer. First thing tomorrow I must call Air Canada and cancel my flight home. I'll probably have to buy a new ticket, but I want to stay for a while for Emily's sake and to get to know this other family of mine."

"You mean the father who abandoned you?"

"I know you don't like him, but there's more to him than you think. Now that I'm here, I'd also like to find out more about my mother, and the family background. And I want to go and see Maud Birkett. If she does get better, she'll be able to tell me about my mother when she was young. I've a feeling she'd enjoy that. I'd also like to start painting again. Real painting, I mean."

Jerry looked stricken. "That's quite an agenda you've

361

got there."

"I don't mean I'm not coming back to Winnipeg," she said hastily. "I've got the gallery and you and Dad . . ." Her voice faltered as she met Jerry's eyes.

"But you won't be coming back permanently, right?"

"I don't know, Jer. Time will tell. Besides, you've got Daniel now. I think you two work very well together. With his business ability, Daniel would be a great partner for the gallery."

Jerry launched into all kinds of reasons why she shouldn't make any hasty decisions. She was rescued by a knock on the door and Richard peering around it. "Am I back too soon?"

"Not at all," Jerry said. "I've been ordered to the kitchen for my midafternoon cereal." He leaned down to hug Lisa. "We'll talk about all this tomorrow. Don't worry, I'm sure it'll work out okay. Sleep well, my lovely. No dreams tonight."

"I hope not. Love you, Jerry."

"Love you, too. She's all yours," he said to Richard on his way out. The door closed, leaving Lisa and Richard alone together.

"We've been friends since university days," Lisa said. "Just friends," she added, wanting to make the relationship clear.

Richard smiled, unable to hide his relief. He sat down beside her. "He must be a very special friend to come all this way on a hunch."

"Not a hunch. Jerry has ESP where I'm concerned. I have it, too, about him. It's genuine. Spooky, eh?" She tried to laugh, but it turned into a little choking sound. "I'm so sorry, Richard."

Blindly, she put a hand out to him, and he grasped it firmly in his. "What do you have to be sorry for?"

"For putting Emily in danger."

"You weren't responsible for—"

"Yes, I was," she said vehemently. "All of this would never have happened if I hadn't come to Charnwood."

"I'm glad you did," Richard said softly. His smile lifted the corners of his mouth, and then he was too close for her to see anything but his eyes and the intense expression in them. He pressed his palm to her cheek, his fingers lifting her hair.

Lisa's eyes closed as she raised her face to his. Their lips met in a kiss of infinite tenderness, a kiss filled with solace and promise and hope for the future for both of them.

Richard drew away from her. She could see a pulse beating hard in his throat. "I hope that wasn't inappropriate."

She brushed away healing tears. "I think it was singularly appropriate." She reached for a tissue from the box by the fireplace and blew her nose. "It's difficult to believe I arrived only a few days ago, isn't it?"

"It hardly seems possible. You've become such an important part of our lives, Emily's and mine."

The mention of Emily brought reality crashing in again. "Is Emily okay?" Lisa asked. "I don't want her obsessing about what happened, like I did when I was a child."

"She was awake when I went up."

"She can't sleep? Oh God, I knew that would happen."

"Now who's obsessing? I woke her up by going into the room. She said you'd told her the lady was dead and wouldn't come back."

"I wasn't sure what to tell her when she asked."

"What you told her was good."

363

"If Jane really is dead." Lisa's eyes widened. "What if she isn't?" she whispered. "What if her body's washed out to sea, and we never know?"

"The police will be here first thing tomorrow morning to tell us they've found her body," he said firmly.

Another knock. This time it was Alec, to tell Lisa that he was taking her hot chocolate and biscuits up to Kate's room.

"I'll be up in a couple of minutes, okay?" Lisa said.

The door closed.

She exchanged smiles with Richard. There was so much she wanted to say, but her mind wouldn't function.

"Are you staying?" he asked carefully.

"For a while. It depends on Alec. If I do, Jerry can look after the gallery until I decide what I'm going to do."

"He's your partner there, in the gallery?"

"Yes." A pause. "Only in the gallery."

"So you mentioned," he said with a faint smile.

"I want to spend a little time with Alec and Kate, get to know them better."

"Only Alec and Kate?"

She hesitated before answering. She felt the need to slow down, to start over again now that they had more time, but she also wanted to let Richard know that what there was between them was special for her, as well. "I'd like to get to know you better, too," she said softly. "And Emily."

"I'm glad to hear it." Richard's slow smile warmed Lisa's heart. Then his smile faded. "Now that I've found you, I don't want to lose you."

"You're not likely to," she assured him. "I won't run out on you." Then, wanting to ease the emotional

364

intensity between them, she added, "I'd like to be here to make sure Emily is okay. Answer any questions she has. Help erase today's bad memories."

"Thank you"

"I'd better go," Lisa said. "Alec's waiting." But she didn't move.

Richard took her hands in his. "I know you'll have to go back to Canada soon to make arrangements, but I'm glad you're staying for a while."

"So am I"

"I mustn't keep you, but I don't want to let you go." He pressed her hands, then released them.

"I know what you mean, but I'll be here in the morning." She went to the door, which he opened for her. "Thanks for everything, Richard."

"I haven't done anything."

"Yes, you have. You could have hated me for involving Emily."

"I could never hate you. We're both going to make sure Emily is fine. Now, go to bed and sleep well. I'll see you in the morning. Good night, Lisa."

"Good night."

Her step was buoyant as she went up the stairs . . . until she remembered that she still had Alec to face. Then, thank heaven, she could go to sleep. Or try to.

When she went into Kate's room, Alec was sitting on the small sofa staring into space. He sprang up when she came in.

"Ah, there you are. I hope the hot chocolate isn't cold. If it is, I can make more."

She felt the stoneware mug on the bedside table. "It's fine. Please sit down." She sat on the edge of the bed. "I hope you don't mind, but I'm really tired. We'll have plenty of time to talk tomorrow."

He looked disappointed. "Shall I go now?"

"No, no. I meant I'm too tired to talk for long."

"Are you going back to Canada with your friend?"

"Would you like me to?"

"What do you mean?" His face looked even more haggard than before.

"Would you prefer that I go straight home?"

There was a tiny tremor at the corner of his mouth. "Do I have a choice?"

"Of course. I'd like to stay on here for another week or so, spend some time getting to know Kate and Rachel and you—a little better."

A flicker of a smile. "That was what I was hoping. . ." His voice died away. "Thank you."

"So I can stay here?"

"This is your home," he said.

Yikes, thought Lisa, *little does he know.* She was glad he hadn't read that letter. Mind you, he'd have to know soon enough that Jane—she'd never be able to think of her as Jennifer—had been Charnwood Court's secret buyer.

She leaned forward. "Tell me something."

"Yes?"

"Did you know that Jennifer had killed Celia?"

He sagged as if she'd punched him, a stunned expression on his face.

"You did, didn't you?" she said slowly.

He moistened his lips. "There was absolutely no proof."

"Apart from me, apart from what I'd seen that terrible night?"

His eyelids fluttered.

"But you suspected that it might have been Jennifer, didn't you?"

"God help me, I did."

Like the blinding light of a huge flashbulb, it came to Lisa, the truth she'd been searching for ever since she'd known he was her father. "That's why you sent me away."

He stared at her blindly, and then there were tears in his eyes. "Jennifer was dangerous, unhinged. Even when she left Charnwood, I was afraid of what she might do to you," he said, his voice almost inaudible. "She wa .insane with rage that day the will was read. I'd promised Celia that I would never turn her sister away from her home. It was the one thing we fought about, constantly."

A shiver of horror ran across Lisa's shoulders. "You sent me away because you thought even then that I was in danger from Jennifer?"

"I had never liked Jennifer, never trusted her. She'd always been jealous of Celia. I had no proof, but I saw Jennifer watching you like a hawk during those few days after Celia died. You didn't remember anything, thank God. I realized that your losing your memory might save you, but I couldn't be sure. Miss Haines was the one person I could trust. Celia had chosen her to be your nanny, and they'd grown close. Miss Haines agreed with me about Jennifer. She, too, feared that she might harm you. When Jennifer stormed from the house, she told me she'd make me and my family suffer for what Celia and I had done. Miss Haines and I devised this plan to spirit you away from Charnwood, so that Jennifer would never be able to find you."

"And that was why my mother—Miss Haines——concocted this story about both my parents having been killed, so that I'd never try to find them?"

"Exactly. We thought it was for the best. Later on, I

367

knew I had made a terrible mistake. But I was so numb with grief at the time, I hadn't realized how much I would miss you when you'd gone. Many times, I came very close to putting an end to it all. Then Rachel dragged me back to life again. I found I could cope if I made a constant effort to forget. I never really managed to do so, of course. It was always there, beneath the surface—"

"Like my memories of the drowning."

"Yes, but we get on with living, don't we? Never realizing that the hidden memories are there all the time, ruining our lives."

"Not anymore."

He put his head in his hands. "God, I hope not." He looked up to stare at her. "What I cannot understand is how Jennifer lived for . . . what, five, six years in Charnwood and no one knew who she was. I'd met Jane Tallis several times. At the Stag or in the high street. She bore no resemblance whatsoever to Jennifer."

"I think it was a game to her, deceiving everyone who'd known Jennifer. She got a kick out of it. The horrible thing is that I liked Jane." Lisa turned her face away. She glanced down at her hands, clasping them tightly to still their shaking. "I'm sorry. I'm feeling terribly tired."

"No wonder." He got up. "No more talking. I'll send Kate up, so you're not alone."

"No rush. I'll be fine." She looked about the room and laughed. "Nothing scary about this place, unless you're afraid of fluorescent colors and posters of rock stars."

He hesitated, hovering near the door. "May I kiss you good night?" he asked.

"Of course you may." She went to him.

His arms folded around her, holding her tightly against him, as if he would never let her go again. "Good night, my darling Elizabeth. Sleep well."

"Good night, Daddy. See you in the morning."

Later, when she was lying in bed, Lisa felt more at peace than she had ever felt before. Apart from worrying about one person, her father in Winnipeg, she could look to the future with optimism and a sense that were was an excellent chance of healing herself—and others.

Then she remembered the letter and her heartbeat became ragged again. Jennifer Templeton might be dead, but she'd left her with a terrible burden. Of course, she could walk away, go back to Canada, forget all this ever happened, but somehow she knew that was not how it was going to be.

I wonder if Dad would like to come back to England, she suddenly thought. He'd love the lawn bowling club and darts matches in the pubs, and being able to watch Coronation Street regularly on television. She could even imagine him and Sam Martin enjoying a pint together.

This brought another picture into her mind: her dad and Alec Kingsley together . . .

Smiling, she turned over, burying her head in the soft feather pillow, and switched off her mind.

EPILOGUE

LATER THAT NIGHT, THE WIND DIED DOWN. THE RAIN eased, and by dawn it had stopped. Several miles away, the excess waters poured into the boisterous sea. In its upper reaches, near Charnwood, the river grew calmer.

The woman's body was found early the following morning, caught up in the twisted branches of a willow that had been ripped apart by the torrential waters.

Gradually, the River Charn became a gentle stream once more, flowing sedately within its banks of rust—red soil, its mission accomplished.

Dear Reader:

I hope you enjoyed reading this Large Print book. If you are interested in reading other Beeler Large Print titles, ask your librarian or write to me at

Thomas T. Beeler, *Publisher*
Post Office Box 659
Hampton Falls, New Hampshire 03844

You can also call me at 1-800-251-8726 and I will send you my latest catalogue.

Audrey Lesko and I choose the titles I publish in Large Print. Our aim is to provide good books by outstanding authors—books we both enjoyed reading and liked well enough to want to share. We warmly welcome any suggestions for new titles and authors.

Sincerely,